A DESERT
TORN
ASUNDER

Also by Bradley Beaulieu from Gollancz:

THE SONG OF THE SHATTERED SANDS

Twelve Kings
Blood Upon the Sand
A Veil of Spears
Beneath the Twisted Trees
When Jackals Storm the Walls
Of Sand and Malice Made (novella)

A DESERT
TORN
ASUNDER

BRADLEY BEAULIEU

Book Six of
The Song of the Shattered Sands

First published in Great Britain in 2021 by Gollancz
an imprint of The Orion Publishing Group Ltd
Carmelite House, 50 Victoria Embankment
London EC4Y 0DZ

An Hachette UK Company

1 3 5 7 9 10 8 6 4 2

Copyright © Bradley P. Beaulieu 2021

Maps by Maxime Plasse

A CIP catalogue record for this book is
available from the British Library.

ISBN (Trade Paperback) 978 1 473 23346 1
ISBN (eBook) 978 1 473 23348 5
ISBN (Audio Download) 978 1 473 23349 2

Printed in Great Britain by Clays Ltd, Elcograf S.p.A.

MIX
Paper from
responsible sources
FSC® C104740

www.quillings.com
www.gollancz.co.uk

The Story so Far

The Song of the Shattered Sands is a vast and complex tale. I consider that a good thing, and if you're reading this, you likely do too, but it can present a problem. It's easy to forget what happened in the earlier volumes. I do my best to catch readers up with little reminders along the way, but even so, I recognize the need for a refresher.

It is with this in mind that I provide the following synopses.

As always, thank you for joining me in this grand tale. I hope you enjoy your return to the Great Shangazi.

—Bradley P. Beaulieu

* * *

The Song of the Shattered Sands

The Song of the Shattered Sands is an epic fantasy series in the vein of *One Thousand and One Nights*. The story centers on Çeda, a young woman who lives in the slums of the great desert city of Sharakhai and fights in the pits for money. In the eyes of the city's wealthy, she is nothing. She is one step above slavery, a fate that constantly nips at her heels. Through clues in a book left to her by her mother, Çeda realizes she is one of the thirteenth tribe, a legendary group of nomads who were nearly eradicated by the Twelve Kings of Sharakhai four hundred years before. In the decades that followed those dark days, Sharakhai became the single, unquestioned power in the desert. In more recent years, however, the city's iron grip has weakened.

The asirim, strange and powerful creatures of the desert, once members of the thirteenth tribe, have always protected Sharakhai, but they have become fewer, their power enfeebled. Sensing weakness, the kingdoms bordering the Great Shangazi close in like jackals, hoping to snatch Sharakhai, a jewel they've long coveted. But it may be the wandering people of the desert, insulted by the very presence of Sharakhai, who prove more of a threat.

After a grand bargain with the gods of the desert, the thirteenth tribe were betrayed by the Twelve Kings of Sharakhai and transformed into the cursed creatures they are now. Fearing retribution, the Kings sent the asirim to hunt their own kinsmen, to kill every man, woman, and child who had blood of the thirteenth tribe running through their veins. The asirim wept, but they had no choice. They were bound as surely as the sun shines on the desert. Çeda's book is one of the last remaining clues to their secret history.

Twelve Kings in Sharakhai

Çeda uncovers secret poems hidden in a book left to her by her mother. Through clues in the poems, she learns more about Beht Ihman, the fateful night when the people of the thirteenth tribe were enslaved and turned into the asirim. She also learns that she, herself, is a descendant of the thirteenth tribe, which gives her a clue to why her mother was in Sharakhai. She later discovers, to her shock and revulsion, that she may be the daughter of one of the Kings, and that this too was part of her mother's plan.

Refusing to let the mystery go unresolved, Çeda goes into the desert to the blooming fields, where the adichara trees shelter the asirim when they sleep. The Kings are immune to the adichara's poison, and their children are resistant. To all others the poison is deadly. To prove to herself once and for all that she is the daughter of one of the Kings, Çeda poisons herself and is later brought to the house of the Blade Maidens, where the warrior-daughters of the Kings live and train. There, with the help of an ally to the thirteenth tribe, Çeda survives and is allowed to train as a Blade Maiden.

As she recuperates, Çeda investigates the clues left in her mother's book. Her mother died trying to unlock the secrets of a fabled poem that promises to show Çeda the keys to the Kings' power and the ways they can be defeated.

Meanwhile, the Moonless Host, a resistance group made up of *scarabs* who hope to end the reign of the Twelve Kings, hatch a plan to break into the palace of King Külaşan, the Wandering King. Hidden in its depths is his son Hamzakiir, a blood mage and a man the Moonless Host hopes to use for their own purposes. It won't be so simple, however. The Kings stand ready to stop them, and their resources are vast.

There are also Ramahd Amansir, a lord from the neighboring kingdom of Qaimir, and Princess Meryam, who travels with him. They have different plans for Hamzakiir. Ramahd came to Sharakhai in hopes of gaining revenge for the loss of his wife and child at the hands of Macide, the leader of the Moonless Host. He stumbles across Çeda in the fighting pits, and the two of them come to know one another.

They might even have become involved romantically, but Çeda has more to worry about than love, and Meryam has other plans for Ramahd. Meryam knows that allowing Hamzakiir to fall into the hands of the Moonless Host would be terrible for her cause, so she makes plans to steal Hamzakiir from under their very noses.

At the end of the book, Çeda manages to unlock the first of the poem's riddles. Along with her best friend, Emre—who against Çeda's wishes has joined the ranks of the Moonless Host—she infiltrates King Külaşan's desert palace and kills him. Emre and the Moonless Host manage to raise Hamzakiir from his near-dead state and steal him away from the palace. Before they can reach safety, however, Meryam and Ramahd intercept them and take Hamzakiir.

Of Sand and Malice Made

Roughly five years before the events depicted in *Twelve Kings in Sharakhai*, Çeda is the youngest pit fighter in the history of Sharakhai. She's made her name in the arena as the fearsome White Wolf. None but her closest friends and allies know her true identity, but that changes when she crosses the path of Hidi and Makuo, twin demigods who were summoned by a vengeful woman named Kesaea.

Kesaea wishes to bring about the downfall of her own sister, who has taken Kesaea's place as the favored plaything of Rümayesh, one of the ehrekh, sadistic creatures forged aeons ago by Goezhen, the god of chaos. The ehrekh are desert dwellers, often hiding from the view of man, but Rümayesh lurks in the dark corners of Sharakhai, toying with and preying on humans. For centuries, Rümayesh has combed the populace of Sharakhai, looking for baubles among them, bright jewels that might interest her for a time. She chooses some few to stand by her side until she tires of them. Others she abducts to examine more closely, leaving them ruined, worn-out husks.

At Kesaea's bidding, the twins manipulate Çeda into meeting Rümayesh in hopes that the ehrekh would become entranced with her and toss Ashwandi aside. To Çeda's horror, it works.

Çeda tries to hide, but Rümayesh is not so easily deterred; the chase makes her covet the vibrant young pit fighter all the more. She uses her many resources to discover Çeda's secret identity. She learns who Çeda holds dearest. And the more restless Rümayesh is, the more violent she becomes. But the danger grows infinitely worse when Rümayesh turns her attention to Çeda's friends. Çeda is horrified that the people she loves have been placed in harm's way. She's seen firsthand the blood and suffering left in Rümayesh's wake.

Çeda is captured but manages to escape, and in so doing delivers Rümayesh into the hands of Hidi and Makuo, who torture her endlessly. But the ehrekh is still able to reach out to Çeda, forcing her to experience the torture as well. Knowing that she can never be free unless she liberates Rümayesh from the godling twins, Çeda recruits one of her childhood friends, a gifted young thief named Brama, to aid her in her quest. With Brama's help, Çeda steals into Rümayesh's hidden desert fortress in hopes of freeing her through the use of a sacred ritual.

Çeda succeeds, but at the cost of Brama becoming enslaved instead of her. Knowing she can't leave Brama to the cruelties of an ehrekh, Çeda searches for and finds a different, more ancient ritual that prepares a magical gemstone, a sapphire, to capture Rümayesh. In a climactic battle, Çeda manages to trap Rümayesh within the stone and free Brama. In the end, Çeda knows that Brama is perhaps the one person who would be most careful with the sapphire, and so leaves it with him.

With Blood Upon the Sand

Months after the events depicted in *Twelve Kings in Sharakhai*, Çeda has become a Blade Maiden, an elite warrior in service to the Kings of Sharakhai. She's learning their secrets even as they send her on covert missions to further their rule. She's already uncovered the dark history of the asirim, but it's only when she bonds with them that she feels their pain as her own. They hunger for release, they demand it, but their chains were forged by the gods themselves and are proving unbreakable.

Çeda could become the champion the enslaved asirim have been waiting for, but the need to tread carefully has never been greater. The Kings, eager to avenge the death of King Külaşan, scour the city for members of the Moonless Host. Emre and his new allies in the Host, meanwhile, lay plans to take advantage of the unrest caused by Yusam's death. They hope to strike a major blow against the Kings and their gods-given powers.

Hamzakiir escaped Queen Meryam and Ramahd and insinuated himself into the ranks of the Moonless Host. Through manipulation and sometimes force, he is slowly taking the reins of power from Macide, leader of the Moonless Host, and Macide's father, Ishaq. Hamzakiir's plan for Sharakhai is bold. The many scarabs of the Moonless Host, who itch for progress, buy into Hamzakiir's plans, which are nearly upended when Davud, a young collegia scholar, is captured along with many others from his graduating class. Hamzakiir's spells trigger Davud's awakening as a blood mage, nearly stopping Hamzakiir and his dark agenda. Davud fails, however, and burns his fellow classmate, Anila, in a cold fire, almost killing her.

The Moonless Host fractures in two, many following Hamzakiir, others following Macide, who is revealed to be Çeda's uncle. In a devastating betrayal, Hamzakiir kills many of the old guard in the Moonless Host, giving him near-complete control of the group. With them at his beck and call, he attacks Sharakhai, planning to take for himself the fabled elixirs that grant the Kings long life.

Emre and Macide, however, want the elixirs destroyed so that neither Hamzakiir nor the Kings can have them. Meryam, recognizing that depriving Hamzakiir and the Kings of their ability to heal themselves will only help her cause, commands Ramahd to help Emre.

An attack on Sharakhai unfolds, where the abducted collegia students, now grotesque monsters, are used to clear the way to King's Harbor. As the battle rages, both Hamzakiir and his faction, and Macide and his, infiltrate the palaces in search of the caches where the fabled elixirs are stored. Two of the three primary caches are destroyed. The third falls into Hamzakiir's hands.

Çeda, meanwhile, caught up in the battle in the harbor, tries to kill Cahil the Confessor King and King Mesut. The Kings are not so easily destroyed, however. They discover Çeda's purpose and turn the tables, nearly killing her. Sehid-Alaz, the King of the Thirteenth Tribe, is so fearful Çeda will be killed that he manages to throw off the shackles of his curse and protects her long enough for her to free the wights, the trapped souls of the asirim, from King Mesut's legendary bracelet. Once free, the wights come for their revenge and kill King Mesut.

Çeda, having been revealed as a traitor to the Kings' cause, flees into the desert.

A Veil of Spears

The Night of Endless Swords was a bloody battle that nearly saw Sharakhai's destruction. The Kings know they won a narrow victory that night, and since then, their elite Blade

Maidens and the soldiers of the Silver Spears have been pressing relentlessly on the Moonless Host. Hundreds have been murdered or given to Cahil the Confessor King for questioning. Knowing that to stay would be to risk destruction at the hands of the Kings, the scarabs of the Moonless Host flee the city.

Çeda is captured by Onur, the King of Sloth. Onur has returned to the desert and is raising an army of his own to challenge the other Kings' right to rule. After escaping Onur, Çeda finds the scattered remnants of the Moonless Host, who are now calling themselves the thirteenth tribe. Her people are gathering once more, but the nascent tribe is caught in a struggle between Onur's growing influence and the considerable might of the Kings who, with Sharakhai now firmly back under their rule, are turning their attention to the desert once more.

In Sharakhai, meanwhile, a deadly game is being played. Davud and Anila are being kept by Sukru the Reaping King. They're being groomed for their powers, Davud as a budding blood mage, Anila as a rare necromancer. A mysterious mage known as the Sparrow, however, is trying to lure Davud away from King Sukru for his own dark purposes. As Davud and Anila both grow in power, they fight for their very lives against the machinations of the Sparrow.

In the desert, Emre comes into his own as a prominent member of the thirteenth tribe. More are looking to him as a leader, including Macide. Emre helps to navigate the tribe toward safety, but the threat of King Onur grows by the day. Even with Emre's help in securing allies among the other tribes, it may not be enough. Things grow worse when the Kings of Sharakhai sail to the desert to confront Onur. They hatch a deal with him: crush the thirteenth tribe first, and they can deal with one another later.

Çeda knows that the thirteenth tribe will be destroyed unless she can free the powerful asirim from their bondage. She vows to lift the curse the gods placed on them, and soon returns to Sharakhai and its deadly blooming fields to do just that.

The Kings have not been idle, however. Nor are they fools. They know the asirim are the key to maintaining power. Making matters worse, their greatest tactician, the King of Swords himself, has made it his personal mission to bring Çeda to justice for her many crimes. Queen Meryam has also decided to throw in her lot with the Kings. She's even managed to steal away the sapphire that contains the soul of the ehrekh, Rümayesh.

The night before the final confrontation, Çeda manages to liberate the wights still trapped inside Mesut's bracelet. The tribes and the Kings clash, and as the battle unfolds, Ramahd, Emre, and the young thief, Brama, stage an ingenious attack on Queen Meryam's ship. There, they free Rümayesh, adding a powerful ally to their fight.

Near the end of the battle, it is revealed that Queen Meryam has long been dominating the mind of the blood mage, Hamzakiir. She has designs on more than just Macide or the Moonless Host. She wants the city for herself. In order to secure it, she forces Hamzakiir to take on the guise of Kiral the King of Kings. Kiral himself, meanwhile, is sent into the battle and is killed.

In the battle's closing moments, Çeda is nearly killed by the fearsome ehrekh, Guhldrathen. Guhldrathen, however, is swept up by Rümayesh and destroyed. This frees the path for Çeda to kill King Onur, which she does in single combat.

Beneath the Twisted Trees

Sharakhai was sorely weakened after the Battle of Blackspear, the intense conflict that saw King Onur die and the thirteenth tribe narrowly escape the royal navy and the Sharakhani Kings. Sensing that Sharakhai is ripe for conquest, the kingdoms of Malasan and Mirea sail hard across the Shangazi Desert, each planning to take the city for their own.

Unbeknownst to all, Queen Meryam sent Kiral, King of Kings, to die in the Battle of Blackspear, while putting Hamzakiir, disguised with her blood magic, in his place. To further secure her power, she forces Hamzakiir, in his guise as Kiral, to marry her, thus cementing her place as a queen of Sharakhai. Their nuptials are interrupted by the goddess, Yerinde, who demands that the Kings kill Nalamae, her sister goddess, who has remained in the shadows for centuries but who Yerinde fears may interfere with her plans. Knowing Yerinde could undo all they've worked for, the Kings agree and a hunt for Nalamae begins.

Çeda, meanwhile, searches for a way to liberate the asirim from the curse placed on them by the desert gods. She frees a family of asirim that, against all odds, has remained together since Beht Ihman four centuries earlier. Çeda discovers a way for the asirim to bond with her handpicked warriors, the Shieldwives, which helps them to resist their compulsion to obey the Kings.

Using a legendary bird known as a sickletail, the Kings find Çeda in the desert and attack, but she and those with her are saved when Nalamae suddenly returns. While escaping, they take a lone prisoner, none other than Husamettín, King of Swords. Nalamae was wounded in the battle, however, and is in desperate need of a safe haven, so Çeda sends her to a valley where the bulk of the thirteenth tribe hides.

Çeda, meanwhile, along with Sümeya, Melis, and the asirim, sneak into Sharakhai and corner her former sister in the Blade Maidens, the famed Kameyl. Çeda explains to Kameyl the Kings' betrayal of the thirteenth tribe on Beht Ihman, the enslavement of the asirim, their deceptions to hide their crimes. Kameyl is unconvinced until Çeda tricks Husamettín into revealing many of his long-held secrets. Realizing it's all true, Kameyl helps Çeda, Sümeya, and Melis to steal into Sharakhai's uppermost palace, Eventide, and free Sehid-Alaz, King of the thirteenth tribe, from imprisonment.

In the process, they're nearly captured, but King Ihsan has been working behind the scenes to forestall the gods' plans. After reading a prophetic entry in the Blue Journals—of Çeda's freeing Sehid-Alaz—Ihsan helps her and the others to escape but is captured by King Emir of Malasan, who has begun his invasion of Sharakhai. King Emir's father, Surrahdi the Mad King, was long thought dead but is revealed when Ihsan arrives in the Malasani war camp. Surrahdi created hundreds of golems for the assault on Sharakhai but was driven mad in the process. On seeing Ihsan, Surrahdi cuts out Ihsan's tongue, robbing him of his magical voice and its power to command others.

Emre has been traveling to the southern tribes on a mission for Macide. He hopes to form an alliance among all thirteen tribes to act as a unified force not only against Sharakhai, but Mirea and Malasan as well. Emre hopes to secure peace with the Malasani King, but when King Emir makes it clear that any accord will entail the desert tribes' bowing to the will of Malasan, Emre is certain he's failed.

Queen Meryam, forced to deal directly with the looming threat of Mirea, goes with Sharakhai's navy and confronts them on the sand. The Mireans have managed to entice an ehrekh, Rümayesh, to work with them. Rümayesh has a servant, Brama, who eventually sympathizes with the Mireans when a plague is introduced into their ranks. The plague is voracious, but Brama finds a way to nullify it with the help of Rümayesh, thus saving a good portion of the Mirean fleet.

After her near capture in Eventide, Çeda returns to the desert and works to free King Sehid-Alaz, finally succeeding when she realizes that Husamettín's own sword, Night's Kiss, can be used to kill and rejuvenate. Sehid-Alaz, his chains broken at last, frees the rest of the asirim. This momentous event occurs just as Meryam is throwing the might of Sharakhai's royal navy against the weakened Mirean fleet. Things look to be going Meryam's way, but when the asirim all flee at Sehid-Alaz's bidding, the tide turns and the royal navy is forced to retreat toward Sharakhai. The Mirean fleet, badly weakened, remains to lick its wounds in the desert.

During the battle, Brama learns that Rümayesh has been trying to steal his soul. He stops her using a powerful artifact, the bone of Raamajit the Exalted, but Rümayesh manages to save herself by fusing her soul to Brama's. Brama and Rümayesh are now inextricably linked, their souls sharing the same scarred body.

King Emir, meanwhile, renews his assault on Sharakhai using the Malasani golems, an unstoppable force. But Ihsan, even though imprisoned and mute, is not powerless. He's learned the reason for Surrahdi's madness: the golems themselves, each of which required a splinter of Surrahdi's soul, weigh on him, putting him on the very brink of insanity. Ihsan, using his gift of manipulation, convinces Haddad, a woman Surrahdi loves and respects, to force Surrahdi to face his misdeeds. Surrahdi becomes distraught and slips entirely into madness. The golems do too, and the entire Malasani assault is thrown into chaos.

Davud the blood mage, Anila the necromancer, and Lord Ramahd Amansir of Qaimir are in similar circumstances: they're on the run from the powers of the city. They join forces for mutual protection but are split up when King Sukru captures Anila and takes her back to his palace in the House of Kings. King Sukru wants the return of his brother, the blood magi known as the Sparrow, and he hopes Anila can help him using her power over the dead and the wondrous crystal beneath the city, which acts as a gateway to the farther fields. When her family is threatened, Anila agrees to help, but tricks Sukru in the end and then kills him when her brother is summoned from the dead.

As the battle for Sharakhai reaches a fever pitch, Davud and Ramahd work to free Hamzakiir from Meryam's imprisonment. They manage to do so in grand fashion, breaking the chains Meryam has placed on him and, in the process, revealing Meryam as a traitor to her own throne and to Sharakhai. Meryam, however, has allied with the children of the Sharakhani Kings to start a new order. With them, she overthrows the old power structure and takes a position of leadership among the new.

Never abandoning the quest for Nalamae, King Beşir goes with a sizable force to conquer the thirteenth tribe in their mountain fastness. Çeda kills King Beşir and returns to the fort where she finds Yerinde standing over her wounded sister goddess, Nalamae. Çeda sneaks up on Yerinde and slays her with Night's Kiss, a sword forged by the dark god, Goezhen. Nalamae, having been given a mortal wound by Yerinde, dies moments later.

As the story closes, Emre frees King Ihsan in repayment for his help in saving the city. When Emre returns to the tribe, however, he's intercepted by Hamid, a childhood friend of Emre's and once a rising star in the Moonless Host. Hamid, both jealous of Emre and incensed by his actions, attacks Emre and buries him alive in the sand.

King Ihsan, meanwhile, gets the Blue Journals from Queen Nayyan, planning to read them all to find a path to save Sharakhai.

And in the valley, Çeda plants the acacia seed her mother left for her. The acacia tree begins to grow at an incredible rate. Knowing Nalamae would have been reborn, Çeda vows to find her in her new incarnation—Çeda is determined to learn the plans of the gods and stop them once and for all.

When Jackals Storm the Walls

Çeda's quest to find Nalamae in her new incarnation leads her to the dusty streets of Sharakhai. After working with Queen Nayyan to secure access to King Yusam's fabled mere, Çeda finds signs that the goddess will be found in King's Harbor. Along with two former Blade Maidens, Sümeya and Kameyl, and the Shieldwife Jenise, Çeda finds and captures a shipwright named Varal, who doesn't yet realize she is the goddess reborn.

In the desert, King Ihsan has been reading the Blue Journals, which contain prophecies penned by the deceased seer, King Yusam. The entries lead Ihsan to reconcile with Kings Husamettín and Cahil, who both fled Sharakhai after nearly being killed by Queen Meryam. Ihsan convinces them to kidnap King Zeheb, who is still mad from Ihsan's command to listen to the whispers around him. He further convinces them that, for Zeheb to regain his sanity (and therefore his god-given abilities) Ihsan must be healed of his own affliction: his missing tongue. The restoration of Ihsan's tongue does indeed allow him to lift Zeheb's spell of insanity, but it comes at a cost. Zeheb escapes and returns to Sharakhai.

When Ihsan, Husamettín, and Cahil return to Sharakhai, Zeheb himself finds *them* and leads them to their true quarry: Nalamae, who Ihsan is convinced is key to saving the city. In following her trail, they stumble across Çeda, who has secreted Nalamae away on the estate of Osman, the owner of the gladiatorial pits Çeda once fight in. In liberating Nalamae from Çeda and her friends, Osman is killed by King Cahil.

Vowing revenge, Çeda goes to save Nalamae, only to find that Goezhen, god of chaos, is hunting for her as well. A hasty, unwilling alliance is formed between the Kings, Çeda, and her allies. They fight the dark god together, their combined might not inconsiderable. Even so, the god nearly destroys them. They're saved when Nalamae awakens for the first time and Goezhen is forced to retreat under her surprisingly potent assault.

Emre, meanwhile, has narrowly escaped death at the hands of his childhood friend, Hamid. He finds Hamid in the desert and challenges him to a duel to the death. With Frail Lemi's unexpected help, Emre defeats Hamid, and Hamid flees into the desert. After securing an agreement from the three final tribes to join the tribal alliance, Emre sets sail for the valley to speak to Macide, Çeda's uncle and shaikh of the thirteenth tribe.

In the valley, Çeda and Emre are finally reunited, but their joy is short-lived. Nalamae, on seeing a prophetic vision from the magical acacia tree that Çeda herself planted, departs the valley, saying she must stop her brother and sister gods alone. Shortly after, the thirteenth tribe sets sail for Mazandir to broker peace with Queen Meryam, that their individual forces might concentrate on the desert's invaders, the kingdoms of Mirea and Malasan.

The tribe doesn't realize that a dark plot is unfolding. Hamid has long coveted the role of shaikh, and Meryam has long sought revenge for Macide's slaying of her sister, Yasmine. The two work together to betray Macide and set *Hamid* up as shaikh. Hamid, knowing that Sehid-Alaz, the ancient king of the asirim, could put a stop his plans, convinces him that Çeda has betrayed the tribe by allying with the Kings of Sharakhai. Though Sehid-Alaz loves Çeda like a granddaughter, his hatred of the ancient Kings is so great he reluctantly agrees to allow Hamid's plans to unfold.

So it is that a climactic battle takes place in Mazandir that sees Çeda and Macide taken by Queen Meryam, the thirteenth tribe torn in two, and Ramahd Amansir failing in his quest to capture Meryam and bring her to justice.

In Sharakhai, Queen Meryam has been preparing a terrible ritual she hopes will rid the desert of the thirteenth tribe altogether. The ritual begins in the cavern below the Sun Palace, where a crystal fed by the adichara trees has slowly been growing in power over the last four centuries. Macide's own blood is used to trigger the ritual, and it works, compelling those with blood of the thirteenth tribe to journey to the blooming fields and throw themselves to the twisted trees.

What Meryam doesn't realize is that the gods have been manipulating her. As the victims of the ritual die, their blood feeds the twisted trees, which in turn feeds the crystal. The crystal, unable to contain so much power, begins to crack. Soon it will shatter, creating a gateway to the farther fields, the very thing the young gods have been hoping for since making their dark bargain with the twelve Kings on the night of Beht Ihman four hundred years ago.

Knowing the worst is about to happen, the necromancer, Anila, and the thief, Brama, use the fabled artifact, the bone of Raamajit the Exalted, to step through to the farther fields and hold the doorway closed. Nalamae, meanwhile, performs a ritual to prevent her brother and sister gods from approaching the city and interfering. She does so by using the heart of Goezhen, whom she slew on the edges of Mazandir.

In the end, the crystal shatters, but the gateway formed isn't wide enough for the young gods to step through. Ramahd captures Meryam and strips her magic from her in a ritual known as burning. The resulting chaos allows Queen Alansal of Mirea to sweep into Sharakhai and take it as her own, forcing the heroes to flee into the desert.

As the story closes, the young gods, knowing they still have a chance gain the farther fields, find Meryam in Mazandir and free her from imprisonment. They give her Goezhen's corpse and bid her to find the fallen elder god, Ashael, that she might regain the power she lost in Sharakhai. Seeing a glimmer of hope that the desert might still be hers, Meryam agrees.

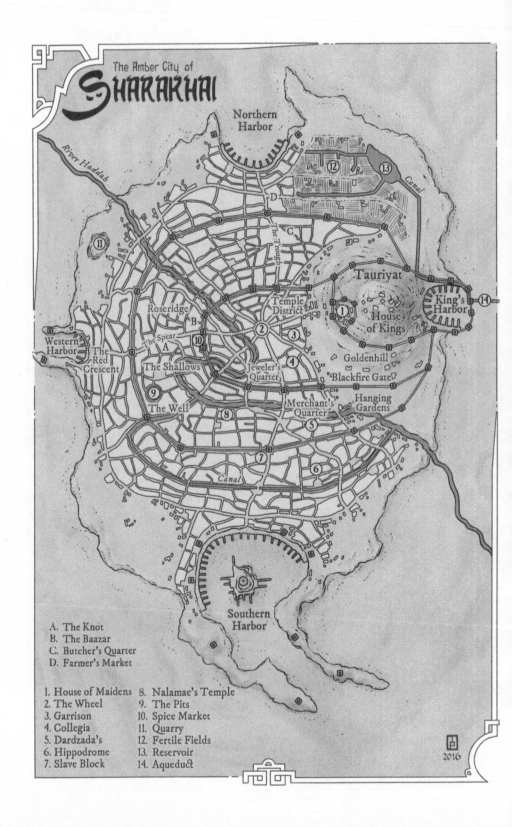

The Amber City of

Sharakhai

Northern
Harbor

River Haddah

Tauriyat

King's
Harbor

12

13

Canal

D

The Trough

C

House
of Kings

14

11

Temple
District

1

Roseridge

B

2

3

Goldenhill

The Spear

10

4

Blackfire Gate

Western
Harbor

The
Red
Crescent

A

The Shallows

Jeweler's
Quarter

Hanging
Gardens

9

The Well

8

Merchant's
Quarter

5

7

Canal

6

Southern
Harbor

A. The Knot
B. The Baazar
C. Butcher's Quarter
D. Farmer's Market

1. House of Maidens
2. The Wheel
3. Garrison
4. Collegia
5. Dardzada's
6. Hippodrome
7. Slave Block

8. Nalamae's Temple
9. The Pits
10. Spice Market
11. Quarry
12. Fertile Fields
13. Reservoir
14. Aqueduct

2016

Chapter 1

AN AGE HAD passed since the elder gods left the world. In the time since, the goddess Tulathan had felt anger and resentment over her abandonment. She'd grieved, knowing she'd never again feel the touch of the first gods. Sometimes she'd lashed out, destroying that which the elders had wrought. Rarely had she felt anxious—for so long there had been nothing to be anxious *about.* As she floated through the air toward a misshapen hill of red sandstone, however, she found her chest tightening, her heart pounding.

And why shouldn't my soul be stirred? The decision I make this day will decide my fate.

She alighted on a rock. As the sunbaked stone warmed her feet, a hot wind blew. It toyed with her long, silvery hair, throwing it about like gossamer. The wind's scent, redolent of sandalwood and myrrh, was peculiar to this part of the desert and yet another reminder of the long-lost elders. The unique scent had been Raamajit's doing. Tulathan had loved it once. Now she loathed it.

Sailing in this part of the Great Shangazi was particularly dangerous. Stones plagued the sand. Many stood out starkly like foreboding sentinels and were easily avoided. But more lay just below the sand's surface. Stones that could ruin a ship's skis, or worse, shatter its struts. They were the very reason most ships avoided sailing in this part of the desert and, in a round-about way, the reason King Ihsan, one of the Sharakhani Kings, was sailing these treacherous sands.

In the distance, his ships, a trio of royal galleons, snaked their way through the towering stones, moving ever closer to their destination: one particular cove. Tulathan swung her gaze to her right to look upon it, a patch of hidden sand all but indistinguishable from thousands of others sprinkled throughout the desert—except this one had secrets buried within it, secrets the King had come to collect.

What King Ihsan didn't know was that a fleet of junks lay hidden beyond the cove's craggy arms. The junks were owned and crewed by a Kundhuni warlord, and bore fierce grassland warriors. There were more besides—three full companies of Mirean infantry plus several qirin warriors—an indicator that Sharakhai's conqueror, Queen Alansal, had a special interest in this particular mission.

At a disturbance beside her, Tulathan turned to find her sister, Rhia, suddenly standing on the same sun-baked stone. Her flaxen hair was plaited. Her golden skin glittered beneath the sun. Her eyes were dreamy, half-lidded, an indication she was sifting through the sands of fate, searching for the bright grains that would reveal the path to the treasure they all sought.

"Return to me, sister," Tulathan said in the desert's most ancient tongue. "I have need of you *here*. We all do."

Rhia blinked, then regarded Tulathan with a wounded expression. "I have much to attend to, even now." Her eyes shifted to the royal galleons wending their way among the rocks, then the bay with the Kundhuni junks. Moments later, her gaze drifted beyond the horizon once more.

Deciding to let her be for the time being, Tulathan turned toward a colorful thread of light hovering in the air nearby as her brother, Bakhi, stepped through it. He wore high leather sandals, a belted chiton, and a laurel wreath. His beard was trim, his brown hair tousled. Of them all, he'd always been the most sanguine, but just then he looked as troubled as Tulathan felt.

After a nod to Tulathan, Bakhi strode past dream-eyed Rhia and re-garded the galleons. "So the Honey-tongued King has come at last."

There was a crunch of footsteps below. Rounding an outcropping of rock farther down the tilted landscape was the fourth of their number: Thaash, god of war. He had a bright shield strapped to his back. The golden sword given to him by Iri hung at his side. One could hardly look upon Thaash without thinking of war, an effect that was only enhanced by his bronze skin and coppery hair. He marched up the incline and came to stand beside them, silent and brooding as a golden roc.

Despite Tulathan's vow not to dwell on the past, their somber gathering was made all the more subdued by the absence of two. Four centuries earlier, when they'd begun their quest to reach the farther fields, none of them had been confident they would succeed, but each had been willing to gamble on it, thinking the worst that happened would be simple failure. None feared death, yet two of them *had* died. Yerinde had been slain by the mortal, Çedamihn, in the stronghold of the thirteenth tribe, using a sword forged by Goezhen. Goezhen had followed his sister into death mere months later. Fixated on the struggle between the Sharakhani Kings and Queen Meryam in Mazandir, Goezhen hadn't sensed Nalamae's approach. She had trapped Goezhen in a pool of water and used Yerinde's adamantine spear to pierce his heart. The twist in fate had created a sort of ruinous chiaroscuro, the weapon of each being used to kill the other.

"Have you managed to catch Nalamae's scent?" Bakhi asked, echoing Tulathan's own thoughts.

"Alas," Rhia replied, "our sister remains elusive."

Rhia's gifts had led their grand plan to the very brink of fruition, but even foresight had its limits, and Nalamae had learned how to foil Rhia's visions. She'd learned the trick of rebirth as well. Time and again, just when they thought they were rid of her, she would return in a new form. And while the rest of them had to take the utmost care when meddling in the affairs of mortals, Nalamae, who'd resigned herself to remaining in this world, never to see the elders again, had no such limitations and was using that to her advantage.

The end game had come. Nalamae was no longer content to hide. She had become the hunter, *they* the hunted. If they grew careless now, all would be for naught.

"She will not have remained idle," Thaash said in his throaty voice. "We need to know what she's discovered, what she has planned."

Rhia turned toward him, her eyes regaining their focus. "Nalamae is but part of the challenge that faces us."

"Perhaps," Thaash replied, "but she's the most dangerous part."

Rhia gave a knowing smile, the sort that infuriated Thaash, who too often found solutions to his problems on the edge of a blade. "Danger comes in many forms, brother. Would you have me find her, only to lose our path to the farther fields?"

Thaash's expression turned stormy, but he said no more. He wanted revenge for the deaths of Yerinde and Goezhen, but he wouldn't trade that for his place in the next world. If any of them meddled too much in the affairs of mortals, it would bind them to this world and prevent their passage to the farther fields. But Rhia was special among them, her gift of foresight crucial to their plans—if she used that gift too heavily, or too often, she might lose the objectivity she needed to see clearly. It could leave all four of them stranded in the world of mortals forever.

"We're here for King Ihsan," reminded Rhia.

Tulathan waved to the nearby bay. "The Mirean queen, Alansal, has learned of his destination. Her water dancers saw it. She knows he's on a journey to reclaim the Blue Journals, and she wants the prize for herself." The journals King Ihsan meant to retrieve were filled with prophetic visions penned by King Yusam before his death. "The question before us now is, do we allow it?"

After four hundred years, they'd reached uncharted territory. The asirim had culled tributes from Sharakhai. Those tributes had been given to the adichara trees, which had fed on their blood. In turn, the trees had slowly fed the crystal in the cavern below Sharakhai. They'd been certain that when the crystal shattered, a rift between worlds would be created, allowing them to step through to the farther fields. And their plan had nearly worked. The crystal *had* shattered, and a gateway *had* opened, but not far enough. They couldn't step through. Not yet.

Everything now rode on the move they'd come together to discuss: allow Ihsan to take the journals and it may lead to all they hoped for. But the danger was just as great that, if they let him live, he would find a way to close the gateway for good.

They turned to Rhia. Worry creases marked her brow; her lips were pinched into a stark line. Though she'd guided them unerringly thus far, of late she'd been plagued by indecision, making it clear her prescience was uncertain at best, the way ahead filled with fog.

Thaash snapped his fingers before her eyes.

When Rhia blinked, the confidence she'd displayed moments ago was gone, making clear it had been vain optimism all along.

"Do we allow King Ihsan to continue?" Tulathan repeated.

"I cannot say," Rhia said in a tremulous voice.

Thaash's look darkened further. "Has your power been stripped from you, then? Has the loss of your brother and sister undone you?"

Rhia looked suddenly vulnerable and mortal, a being who sensed her end was near. "I . . . I don't know."

"I consider it a *good* sign, not ill," Bakhi said.

All turned to him, disbelieving.

"Our fate now intertwines with Ashael's," Bakhi went on. "The very fact that our sister can no longer see our future is an indication that we're following the right path"—he waved to the desert, to the trio of sandships—"that what we do here today will lead us to the farther shore."

They all knew their decision to put Queen Meryam on the hunt for Ashael, the fallen elder, was a dangerous one, but there had been no choice. Had they done nothing, Nalamae would have succeeded—the gateway would have closed and they would be forced to begin anew, or resign themselves to this world until the end of days. But give Queen Meryam Ashael's scent and they might yet make it. Ashael might be vile-hearted, but he wanted the same thing they did: a path to the farther fields, the consequences to the world they left behind be damned.

"Let Ihsan have the journals," Rhia said into the still, hot air. Her tone was buoyant—overly so, it seemed to Tulathan, as if she were trying to convince herself.

"We must be certain, sister," Tulathan said.

Rhia said nothing. What *could* she say? They all knew it was a calculated guess.

"Who will do it?" Bakhi asked.

"I've meddled enough," Tulathan said immediately.

"As have I," Bakhi added.

When they looked to Rhia, she blanched. "I must remain on the outside of events, to better view the threads of fate."

And so they turned to Thaash, who, of them all, had taken the lightest hand in the manipulation of mortals. Leaving everything he could to the others was a gambit, a way to ensure his place in the farther fields. His silence spoke of guilt over his own inaction, as did his siblings' flat stares.

He turned and looked at the bay where the Kundhuni fleet was anchored. His severe expression turned grim. "So be it," he said, and headed down the slope toward the bay, unslinging his shield from his back as he went.

Bakhi, clearly pleased, re-formed his wavering thread and stepped through it.

Rhia dissolved to dust.

Tulathan regarded the Sharakhani galleons, then disappeared in a twinkling of sunlight.

Chapter 2

ON THE DECK of the royal galleon, the oddly named *Miscreant*, King Ihsan held a spyglass to one eye and scanned the line of jagged hills in the distance. "There!" he called to the captain. "The one shaped like a chipped falcon's beak."

"Aye!" Nearby, the ship's captain, Inevra, a cantankerous woman with decades of experience sailing the sandy seas, was sighting through a spyglass of her own. "Two points larboard!" she bellowed.

"Two points larboard!" came the helmsman's reply.

As the *Miscreant* adjusted course, Ihsan turned and swung the spyglass along the horizon behind them. Ten days ago, mere hours after leaving Sharakhai, they'd been ambushed by a small fleet of Kundhuni junks. They'd managed a narrow escape, but the incident served as a reminder of how dangerous Sharakhai and the desert around it had become. The Kundhuni warlords had once fought on Sharakhai's side, but Queen Alansal had gained their loyalty through simple bribery—not only were they given a share of the stolen riches from the House of Kings after Alansal's swift, decisive invasion, the warlords had been allowed to ransack whole sections of the city's west end for days to take what they wanted in coin, valuables, and lives.

With King Hektor of Qaimir preparing to retreat to his homeland, Sharakhai's royal navy had been forced to fight alone against the combined might of Mirea, Malasan, and Kundhun. They had strength yet, but their numbers were slowly being gnawed away. It was only a matter of time before Sharakhai's enemies caught the royal fleet and destroyed it once and for all. When that day came, the city would truly be lost.

For several days after their initial attack, the Kundhuni junks had given chase. Ihsan had been forced to order his ships to sail in random directions to hide their true destination; the detour had lengthened their journey, but he couldn't afford for the Kundhuni to guess where they were going.

Then, three days ago, their pursuers had disappeared.

"They've returned to Sharakhai," growled Captain Inevra the following morning.

Ihsan had shrugged. Perhaps they had. Or perhaps the junks were still in the desert, biding their time until Ihsan returned to the city. Either way, it made him nervous. The danger increased by the day. It felt as if any small mistake would doom not only him and Nayyan, but Sharakhai and the desert as well.

"Please tell me we're close," called a husky, feminine voice.

He turned to find Nayyan, a Queen of Sharakhai and Ihsan's lover these past many years. She strode across the foredeck toward him, cradling their baby girl, Ransaneh, in her arms. The bolt of blue linen wrapped around their child was stained with spit-up. The image clashed mightily with the ebon blade hanging from Nayyan's belt, a sword she'd once wielded as a Blade Maiden.

Nayyan still had cuts along her hands and a bandage along her wrist and forearm, evidence of the battle against a fierce qirin warrior who'd fought with the Kundhuni. The famed qirin warriors were the elite of the Mirean forces, akin to the Blade Maidens of Sharakhai in both stature and renown. That several had been assigned to the Kundhuni ships made it clear their mission was of the utmost importance to Queen Alansal.

Ihsan took Ransaneh from Nayyan. "We're nearly there." He smiled at Ransaneh's bright eyes, one of which was hazel, the other brown. "We'll reach the place where I buried the Blue Journals before sundown."

Nayyan, one hand held up against the lowering sun, peered beyond the haze of dust blowing across the dunes. "I hope this is worth it."

Ihsan said nothing. They both knew the chances of this gambit paying off were slim. After the terrible battle in the cavern below the Sun Palace, the crystal that had been fed by the adichara roots for centuries had been shattered, creating a gateway between worlds. The gateway was the prize the desert gods had schemed for hundreds of years to attain. It was meant to allow the desert gods to pass to the farther fields, but it hadn't worked. Or not completely. Through the valiant efforts of Anila and Brama, coupled with the bone of Raamajit the Exalted, the gateway's opening had been stalled, preventing the gods from passing through. The race was now on. Ihsan, Nayyan, and their not-inconsiderable sum of allies needed to find a way to close the gateway before the desert gods found a way to open it wide.

Ihsan had read the Blue Journals from cover to cover dozens of times and recalled nothing that mentioned a gateway, nor did he recall a vision or a note from King Yusam, their former seer, that might help them decide what to do about it. But that didn't mean there wasn't *something* there.

Please let there be, Ihsan prayed as he gazed at the distant hill. *Everything depends on it.*

"I still think we should have tried Yusam's mere first," Nayyan said.

"It was too risky." Ihsan shifted Ransaneh onto his hip. "It still is. With Alansal in Eventide, and her army occupying the other palaces, how long could we have remained to use it? One night? Perhaps two? We'd likely gain nothing in that time, and put ourselves"—he tugged on Ransaneh's tiny ear—"and our daughter at risk."

It was at times like these, while holding the babe, that Ihsan felt their peril most keenly. Sharakhai, indeed the desert itself, was living on the razor's edge. Many said there was no telling what would happen were the gateway to fully open, but Ihsan knew better. The very journals they were sailing to retrieve detailed that event clearly: Sharakhai destroyed, the desert around it laid to waste.

"Let's just get in and out," Nayyan said while scanning the hills ahead. "I don't like the looks of this place."

Ihsan rocked Ransaneh gently. She burped and smiled while blinking her mismatched eyes. "We will."

It was nearing nightfall by the time they reached the right place and Ihsan bid three Silver Spears to dig with shovels. After the recent autumn rains, the nearby mountain laurel, the tree Ihsan had chosen as a marker, was blooming. Its clusters of bell-shaped flowers filled the air with a scent like violets laced with anise.

As the sun kissed the hills to the west, the Silver Spears suddenly stopped.

"Here, my Lord King," Captain Inevra called.

They had the two small chests up a moment later. Ihsan, inexplicably nervous, fearful that he'd find them empty, opened the first. The Blue Journals were inside, wrapped in oiled canvas, just as he'd left them before going to find Husamettín and Cahil in Çalabin, a caravanserai only a few days' ride away. He opened the second chest and found the others, safe and sound.

"Have them brought to the ships," he said to Inevra.

"Right away, Your Excellence."

Four Silver Spears had just begun hauling them away when Yndris, daughter of Cahil the Confessor and a warden of the Blade Maidens, called worriedly from a nearby rise, "My Lord King?" She had a spyglass held to one eye and was using it to peer at something beyond the ridge.

"Yes?"

"You should see this."

Ihsan climbed the hill with Nayyan at his side. When he reached Yndris, he saw a sandy bay at the base of the slope. It was accessible from the desert via a narrow channel that wormed its way between two lumpy hills. Within the bay was a fleet of ten Kundhuni junks.

Nayyan's footsteps crunched as she came to stand beside him. "They're the same ships?"

"Yes," Ihsan said.

"Look closely." Yndris handed the spyglass to Ihsan.

As he used it, his skin began to prickle. Lying on the ships' decks and over the sand were dozens of warriors. None moved. Blood stained the sand around them.

He handed the spyglass to Nayyan.

"They're all dead," she said after a moment.

A terrible feeling bloomed in the pit of Ihsan's stomach. His instinct was to leave, to take the ships and return to the sand immediately. Instead, he headed down the slope toward the bay. He had to know what had happened.

"If it please my Lord King," Yndris called, "I'll take my sister Maidens and scout the area."

Ihsan denied her with a wave of his hand. After handing Ransaneh over to her wet nurse, they headed down to the ships and found dozens of Kundhuni warriors, ships' crews, and Mirean soldiers, all dead. The powerful qirin lay slain within the ships' holds. The place felt like a boneyard, a place that should be left untouched lest they anger Bakhi, the god of death.

Except Bakhi is now my enemy. I have no choice but to anger him should we hope to save Sharakhai.

"Here," Nayyan called from beyond one of the nearby junks. He saw her pointing to a patch of sand. A sign was drawn there: circle with a line running vertically through it. It was a shield and sword, the sign of Thaash, god of war and vengeance.

"A warning?" Yndris asked.

"Perhaps," Ihsan replied, not wanting to reveal his suspicions yet. "Come," he said. "It's time we sail."

They set the junks ablaze, then returned to their galleons. As they set sail, the smoke column rose, looking rather like a line cut through the circle of the sun's final fading.

When Nayyan was alone with Ihsan in their cabin, she said, "It wasn't a warning, was it?"

"No." They lay in the bunk with Ransaneh between them. Ihsan paged through a journal, the very first journal King Yusam had penned, but he was hardly able to pay attention to what he was reading. He was too troubled by the implications of what he'd just witnessed.

"The gods *wanted* us to retrieve the journals," Nayyan went on. "Thaash slew the Kundhuni to ensure we did."

"Yes."

"So what do we do?"

"What is there *to* do? We go on. We remain wary." He lifted the blue, cloth-bound journal. "We read."

"But what if we're doing exactly what they want us to do?"

Ihsan wished he had an answer, but he didn't, so he kept reading. Beside him, Nayyan took up another journal.

Chapter 3

ÇEDA GRIPPED THE *Red Bride*'s forestay to steady herself on deck. Her other hand rested on the pommel of River's Daughter, a shamshir forged of ebon steel. The stiff wind tugged at her turban, made the skirt of her wheat-colored battle dress flap. The yacht's lateen sails were full and rounded. The day was bright and beautiful, the wind pleasantly warm.

It reminded Çeda of a similar day, what felt like a lifetime ago. She'd been sailing with her mother, Ahya, toward a salt flat, a pilgrimage to witness the great flocks of Blazing Blues that congregated there in spring. Back then, the skis of their skiff had hissed over the sand, just as the *Red Bride*'s were now.

"It's a good day to be alive," Ahya had said in a rare moment of bliss.

Çeda had been confused at first, even wary—her mother simply didn't share those sorts of emotions. Eventually, though, she'd relaxed and shared in her mother's joy. She'd stood on the thwart and gripped the mast, reveling in the wind as it flowed through her unbound hair.

Her mother had actually laughed.

Çeda smiled wistfully at the memory but sobered as she cast her gaze over the amber dunes. Sailing the Great Shangazi had become dangerous, now more than ever. She and the others aboard her two ships had to remain wary of white sails, of dark hulls, along the horizon.

Sailing in the *Red Bride*'s wake was *Storm's Eye*, a schooner that carried the bulk of warriors accompanying Çeda toward the mountains. All told they were a respectable force—eighty swords and shields in all, including the Shieldwives, the fierce desert swordswomen Çeda had trained herself. Even so, Çeda worried they wouldn't be enough. The task she'd set for herself and the others was formidable. They sailed east to bring the traitorous Hamid, their childhood friend, to justice and regain control of the thirteenth tribe. The number of warriors at Hamid's command would dwarf their own, but it couldn't be helped. They had to try.

To the ship's port side lay easy, rolling dunes with patches of perfectly flat sand. Along the starboard side were dunes the size of caravanserais. Known as the mounds, the dunes lounged like lizards, content in the knowledge that no ship could navigate their steep slopes. The formation was a strange phenomenon that occurred near summer's end, a time when fitful sandstorms plagued the open sands. In a few more weeks, the winds would pass, the shift toward winter complete, and the dunes would slowly disappear.

The mounds represented a strange combination of danger and safety. Pirates or enemy ships sometimes lay in wait along their gutters, which was why Çeda had ordered three lookouts to watch them, but sailing on open sand had its dangers, too. Çeda and her allies had no shortage of enemies, after all. Sailing close to the mounds allowed her the option of sailing into them to lose their pursuers, be they desert tribespeople, Sharakhani, Mirean, or Malasani.

Hearing the scrape of footsteps, Çeda turned to see Emre climbing up from belowdecks. A smile tugged the corner of her mouth on seeing Emre work his way past Frail Lemi, who had strung a hammock between the foremast and a cleat on the cabin's roof.

Emre gave him a shove as he sidled past. "Who let this bloody ox on our ship?"

His eyes still closed, his fingers laced behind his head, Lemi grinned his handsome grin as he rocked back and forth. "The gods gave me much, it's true. No need to be jealous."

"Why don't you string your hammock at the *top* of the masts? At least then you'd be out of the way."

"No!" Kameyl, a brawny ex-Blade Maiden Çeda had fought alongside countless times, called from the ship's wheel. "He'd tip the damned ship over."

Lemi's grin only broadened.

Emre rolled his eyes, then gave Çeda a wink as he came to stand beside her. He wore sirwal trousers, sandals, and a loose shirt that revealed the dark hair along the top of his chest. His broad, boiled leather belt and bracers were new, but they reminded Çeda of the ones he'd worn years ago when they had lived together in Roseridge.

Emre scanned the desert, his eyes a bit bleary. He'd just woken, having taken night watch. Çeda ran her fingers through his hair, feeling the scar from his surgery. To relieve the pressure from a terrible, lingering head wound delivered by Hamid's lover, Darius, Dardzada had cut through Emre's skin and used a carpenter's drill to pierce his skull. She missed his long hair, but she had to admit the shorter hair, along with his pointed beard and mustache, gave him a roguish look she rather liked.

A sharp whistle cut through the hiss of the skis.

Çeda turned to see Shal'alara of the Three Blades, an elder of the thirteenth tribe, waving from the foredeck of the much larger *Storm's Eye* sailing in their wake. She wore a battle dress similar to Çeda's but, in her customary style, had dyed it a bright orange and embellished it with beaten coins, bracelets, and necklaces. The ruby brooch on her cream-colored head scarf glinted brightly in the sun.

"There's an oasis to the north," she bellowed across the distance.

There was no doubt everyone deserved a rest, but Sharakhai and the desert itself were still in deep danger. Making Hamid pay was only one of the reasons they needed to return to the valley below Mount Arasal. Çeda also needed access to the acacia tree, which granted prophetic visions. Çeda hoped to use them to learn how to close the unearthly gateway beneath Sharakhai.

"We sail on!" Çeda called back. "We have enough water to reach the next."

Shal'alara nodded and began relaying the orders to Jenise, a fierce swordswoman and the leader of Çeda's Shieldwives. Çeda was grateful to have them both. Shal'alara had rallied dozens to their cause, and Jenise had

trained them, drilling them relentlessly with her Shieldwives. If Çeda succeeded in her quest, it would be thanks to their efforts as much as anyone
else's.

Sümeya, the former First Warden of the Blade Maidens, came up from
belowdecks wearing her black battle dress, her Maiden's black. With five clay
mugs of water gripped tightly in her hands, which she proceeded to pass
around, she looked more than a little like a west end barmaid.

Frail Lemi was just tipping the largest of the mugs back and swallowing
noisily when Çeda felt something peculiar. It started as a tingling in the meat
of her right thumb, where the adichara thorn had pricked her skin. It flowed
through her fingers and up along her arm. It suffused her chest and for some
peculiar reason made her keenly aware of the tattoos inked across her arms,
chest and back. The sensation felt achingly familiar, though she couldn't
place it.

As they came abreast of a colossal sand dune, the feeling became so
strong Çeda's ribs and chest tickled from it. It was enough to jog a memory
loose.

"Stop the ship," she called immediately.

Kameyl followed Çeda's gaze to the crest of the massive dune, but made
no move to obey. "Why?"

"Just stop the ship!"

Kameyl shared a look with Sümeya, then shrugged. "As you say."

They pulled in the sails and let the *Bride* glide to a halt. Behind them,
Storm's Eye did the same. All the while, Çeda faced the dune.

"What is it?" Emre asked in a soft voice.

Before Çeda could answer, an animal with cup-shaped ears, a long,
pointed snout, and a ruff of red fur lifted its head over the top of the dune.

"Breath of the desert," Çeda breathed.

It was a maned wolf, one of the long-legged creatures that roamed the
desert in packs, often competing with black laughers for dominance over a
territory.

Frail Lemi set his mug down, grabbed his greatspear, and stared at the
wolf as if fearful that hundreds more would come storming down the dune.
"What's happening?"

But his words hardly registered. Another wolf was lifting its head along the dune's crest. A third came immediately after, then a fourth. Soon more than twenty were staring down at the ships.

Çeda held her breath, waiting, hoping.

"Çeda?" Emre called.

She raised one hand, and he fell silent. Several long breaths passed. The wind kicked up, causing spindrift to lift in curls and whorls. The sun beat down, warming Çeda's cheeks, her neck, the backs of her hands.

"Çeda—"

"Shhh!"

She took a deep breath. Released it slowly, praying.

She was ready to give up hope when another wolf, a female with a white coat, lifted her head.

For long moments, Çeda could only stare. She knew this wolf. Çeda herself had named her Mist. She'd been the inspiration for Çeda's guise of the White Wolf in Sharakhai's fighting pits. Gods, how powerful she looked now. How regal. On Çeda's very first foray to the blooming fields with Emre, she had seen Mist as a pup. Years later she'd come to Çeda on the Night of Endless Swords, shortly after Çeda had killed King Mesut, and the two of them had traveled with the asir, Kerim, far into the desert. They'd stayed together for weeks until Çeda was discovered by scouts from Tribe Salmük.

It seemed a lifetime ago. So much had changed since then, both in Çeda's life and Mist's. Thorn, the largest and fiercest of the pack, was nowhere to be seen. Mist seemed to be their leader now. The rest waited as she padded forward. At first Çeda thought Mist was going to come down to meet the ship, but she didn't. She halted less than halfway down, as if waiting for Çeda to come to her.

Çeda leapt over the gunwales, landing on the amber sand with a crunch. The sand sighed as she attacked the slope. Emre joined her, as did Sümeya.

"Play with a pack of mangy wolves all you wish," Kameyl called from deck. "I'm staying here with the olives and the araq."

A broad smile lit Frail Lemi's face. "Olives and araq!" he roared, and fell back into his hammock. "I like the way you think!"

When Çeda reached Mist, she hugged the rangy wolf around the neck and scratched her fur. Her musky smell whisked Çeda back to their days hiding with Kerim in their desert cave.

Mist was a lithe beast, and taller than Çeda. While she wasn't the biggest wolf in the pack, she had a confident air. The others were attentive, subservient, courtiers awaiting their queen's next pronouncement. For a while, she seemed content to revel in Çeda's scratches, then she nipped at Çeda's wrist, something she used to do when she wanted Çeda to follow.

"Go on, then," Çeda said with a smile, curious.

Mist yipped, then howled, as if trying to speak. Then she turned and padded up to the crest, and the pack parted for her, creating a lane. One growled, but fell silent when Mist barked loudly.

At the crest, Mist stopped and looked back, as if ensuring Çeda was following, then stared at something hidden behind the slope.

Çeda's breath was on her by the time she reached Mist's side. Below them, half buried at the base of the dune, was a sandship. Its skis had long been swallowed by the sand, and the hull was almost wholly submerged, a thing that happened to unattended ships in the deeper parts of the desert. The bow had been lost to the sloping edge of the dune's windward side, but the stern and the quarterdeck were still visible.

"That's a royal clipper," Sümeya said.

Çeda suddenly recognized it. "It's one of the ships that attacked us."

Along the leeward side of the next dune, she saw signs of a second clipper, that one broken beyond repair, a victim of the goddess Nalamae's power when she'd come to save Çeda and the others from the Kings.

Mist headed down the slope. Çeda, Emre, and Sümeya followed. The other wolves paced alongside them in two broad wings—an honor guard of sorts.

"Are you sure they're not taking us somewhere to eat us?" Emre asked.

"Be quiet," Çeda said, "or I'll offer you up as a snack."

Mist led them to the half-buried clipper and onto the main deck. From there she took the stairs down into the ship.

"What—?" Emre began. He stared at Çeda with a confused expression but soon fell silent.

They took the stairs down, where Mist led them to the captain's cabin. The door was open, hanging from one hinge. Inside, a sifting of dust covered everything. Bottles and glasses and books had fallen from the shelves built into the hull. Broken glass lay everywhere, glinting. The shutters were closed, but light filtered in at an angle, segmenting the chaos into ordered ranks.

The feeling that had blossomed inside of Çeda on recognizing the clipper grew stronger by the moment. There were wolf prints on the dusty floor. Retracing them, Mist wove beyond the desk to a locked chest in the far corner of the cabin, the sort the captain would use for valuables, the ship's treasury, and more. Mist sniffed at the lid, yipped and whined, then tugged at Çeda's sleeve.

The air within the cabin felt suddenly oppressive. It was getting harder and harder to breathe.

Above the shutters, mounted to the hull, was a ceremonial spear. Çeda took it down and wedged it beneath the lid. With Emre and Sümeya helping, they pushed and pried, and eventually the lid gave way.

Çeda knelt before the chest. She balled her hands into fists. After taking one deep breath, she threw the lid back.

"By the gods . . ." Emre said. "How?"

Words failing her, Çeda could only stare in wonder. Her heart pounded as she reached in and took the object on top, a helm, the sort gladiators wore in the fighting pits. It had a wolf pelt along the top. The face guard, made of highly polished steel, was a mask molded into the likeness of a goddess: Nalamae. Beneath the helm was a set of boiled leather armor: a breastplate, a battle skirt, greaves, bracers, and gloves, all of which had been dyed white.

It was her old armor, the set she'd used when she'd fought in Osman's pits for money.

Utterly confused, Çeda looked up to Sümeya, still holding the mask.

"The armor was meant for the sickletail," Sümeya said. "Nayyan told me they'd needed something of yours in order for the bird to find you."

"But how could they have found her armor?" Emre asked.

"Osman," Çeda said. "They had him in their prison camp. He must have told Cahil where it was. Or Ihsan might have commanded him to give up its location."

Çeda hardly knew what to feel. So much was rushing back to her. Her time in Roseridge with Emre. Her days learning the ways of pit fighting from her mentor, Djaga. Her many bouts in the pits. Her brief affair with Osman, owner of the pits. The journey she'd undertaken with Emre, which had led her to her uncle, Macide, and eventually to the King of the asirim, Sehid-Alaz—the start of her long and winding journey.

Mist panted beside her, her tongue hanging out. Her ivory eyes were alive, her gaze flicking from the armor to Çeda and back. She knew she'd done good. Çeda hugged her tight, ruffling the fur of her mane and the spot between her ears she liked so much to have scratched.

Mist leaned into it. Her tail wagged. For long moments she reveled in the attention, then suddenly broke away and faced the hull as if looking *through* the wood and sand to the *Red Bride* beyond. She hopped in the way she did when she wanted to run free.

A moment later an attenuated whistle reached them. Çeda and Sümeya knew what it was immediately. Emre, however, didn't know how to decipher the Blade Maidens' whistles.

"What?" he asked, staring at them.

"It's Kameyl," Çeda said as she gathered up the armor. "She's spotted ships."

They left the ship and took the slope up toward the crest of the massive dune. When they reached it, four ships could be seen sailing in from the north. Emre and Sümeya immediately began their slip-slide descent, but Çeda stayed behind. Shifting the armor's bulk under one arm, she crouched and hugged Mist close.

"Thank you," she whispered.

Mist's gaze flicked from Çeda to the distant ships. Several of the other wolves growled. One whined. Ignoring them, Mist butted her head against Çeda's hand. After Çeda gave her one more scratch, she barked, then padded down the slope, away from the ships. Her pack followed in her wake.

Çeda watched them go until Kameyl whistled again, then she turned and rushed down the slope toward the *Bride*.

Chapter 4

THE SUN WAS high when the former queen of Qaimir, Meryam, and her most faithful servant, Amaryllis, reached Sharakhai's western harbor. There was a time when Meryam could have walked anywhere in the city, including the western harbor, without fear, not because she'd once been a queen of Sharakhai as well—though she had been—but because then she'd had *power*. *Real* power, not the ephemeral sort that comes from wearing a crown. Meryam had been a blood mage then, one of the most fearsome her homeland or the desert had ever seen.

Those days were long gone. Meryam no longer had any power to speak of. Her throne had been taken by her cousin, King Hektor. Worse, Lord Ramahd Amansir, the husband of Meryam's dead sister, Yasmine, had ordered the very ability to use the blood of others to be *burned* from her. In the short time the ritual had taken to complete, Meryam's world had been reduced to one of craven fear and endless regret, a thing the sheer press of humanity only intensified.

She found herself watching everyone—from the work crew resurfacing a yacht's skimwood skis, to the line of women bearing baskets away from a docked ketch, to the gutter wrens who sized Meryam and Amaryllis up, judging their worthiness as marks. She spotted no less than twelve Mirean patrols during their short walk, the result of a display of force from the city's new monarch, Queen Alansal of Mirea. Hundreds more moved along the piers and the crescent-shaped quay: men wearing thawbs and turbans, women wearing abayas and chadors. Ship's crews laded and unladed ships. An auctioneer cried out bids at the auction block while caravan ships traded wares over the gunwales. Meryam watched them all, wondering which of them was planning to inform her enemies of her whereabouts.

That very morning, she'd sat at the edge of her bed, telling herself to get dressed. She knew in her bones how important their mission to the harbor was, and yet she'd been unable to do more than hold herself tight, rock back and forth, and stare at the clothing Amaryllis had laid out on the nearby rocking chair.

On seeing Meryam's state, Amaryllis had prepared a tincture. "Take this."

The cup she held out contained a purple liquid, and its depth of color made clear how much Amaryllis had upped the dose of calming medicine that had become part of Meryam's daily routine.

It probably would have been wise to take it, but the medicine muddied her thoughts. She couldn't afford to fail in the coming negotiation. Too much depended on it. So she'd waved it away and got dressed.

Her nerves steadied as she and Amaryllis neared the end of the quay. They returned, however, as the old sloop, *The Gray Gull*, came into view. *The Gray Gull* had been taken by the Moonless Host when the last of their high-ranking members, including Macide Ishaq'ava, had fled from Shara-khai. Adzin and most of the crew had been killed at the end of that wild escape. The ship itself, abandoned by the Moonless Host, had eventually fallen into the hands of Adzin's closest relative, Yosef.

Meryam stopped at the head of the pier and stared at it. By the blood of the one true god, it looked like a ship of the dead. Tatty sails, threadbare rigging, hull half-eaten by dry rot. It wasn't so much the ship's ghulish air, nor the meeting that was about to take place within it, that made Meryam's footsteps falter and then stop; it was the weight of all that would follow. In Mazandir, the goddess Tulathan had given Meryam the body of the desert god, Goezhen, who'd been slain by his sister, Nalamae. She'd bid Meryam to take Goezhen's corpse and use it to raise Ashael, the lone elder left behind when the other elder gods had departed this world for the next—except she hadn't told Meryam where Ashael was, nor *how* to raise him. The search for Ashael had only just begun in earnest and Meryam had already lost count of the number of times she'd nearly given up. It all felt too big for her. Unattainable.

"We don't need to do this today," Amaryllis said.

Meryam shook her head. "To wait another day would be to tempt the fates, and those old hags probably think they've allowed us too much time already."

She headed down the pier with Amaryllis following. The ship's captain, Yosef, stood at the gunwales. He had the bronzed skin of a Malasani. His baggy trousers, tall red fez, and bejeweled vest, which appeared to be waging a valiant but losing war against his ample potbelly, gave him a look that bordered on the foolish. But everyone Amaryllis had spoken to said it was an act, a way to put one off-guard. All said he was as shrewd as any captain in the western harbor, a place famous for chewing up and spitting out the unwary.

Yosef waved her aboard with a grin. "Tulathan shines on our meeting."

"Yes"—Meryam did her best to ignore the way he was staring at her ivory eyes, a byproduct of her magic having been burned away—"we'll see about that."

The crew traded nervous glances as Yosef led Meryam down the nearby ladder and into the ship's bowels. As strange as the ship looked from the outside, it was even stranger within. Hundreds of oddities hung from rusty hooks along the passageway. There were bloodstained carvings of animals in tortured poses, tufts of hair with bits of skin still attached, strings of what looked to be fingernails, and rag dolls whose eyes had been eerily painted in kohl.

Disturbing as they were, seeing them was a relief. When she'd learned about the man who'd once owned this sloop, and the sort of scryings he'd once performed, she'd thought surely whoever had taken ownership after his death would have taken everything down. That Yosef *hadn't* gave her hope that he would have more of the soothsayer, Adzin's things, things she desperately needed.

"You're the cousin of the previous owner, are you not?" Meryam asked as they entered a cabin with a low table and large, overstuffed pillows around it.

Yosef's wide smile revealed yellow, tabbaq-stained teeth. "You've heard of his miracles, then."

Meryam waggled her head. "Recently, yes."

Yosef waved his hands broadly. "You're interested in the ship, then!"

"Not exactly, no."

His smile faltered. "What, then?"

"I'm interested in Adzin's maps, his writings."

Yosef was the sort of horse trader who treated people nicely until he knew he no longer had a sale, at which point they meant less to him than a pile of mule dung. Meryam could tell he was already precariously close to dismissing her. "I'm not selling maps," he said, "nor writings. I'm selling a ship."

"I have no use for a ship. What I want are Adzin's notes on his forays into the desert."

The collapse of Yosef's smile was like a wall succumbing to a battering ram. Giving up the pretense of pleasantries altogether, he licked his teeth. "I have no such things."

"Are we speaking about the same man? Your cousin was Adzin the soothsayer, was he not?"

"Most certainly."

"What do you know about his trips to the desert?"

Yosef looked more confused. "As much as anyone."

"Then you'll know that on occasion he visited peculiar places. Places filled with ancient power."

A hint of a smile returned. "Yes, which is precisely why this ship is so valuable."

"He would have had maps that marked those locations. He would have notes about the sort of power conferred by each."

"There are several maps and a ship's log, all of which you can have if—"

"Fetch them."

Yosef's face turned hard, giving him an ugly, bulldog look. "They aren't for sale."

The words were hardly out of his mouth when Amaryllis sent a golden rahl flying through the air. It landed on the table with a sound that, for a man like Yosef, would speak of fragrant tabbaq and the rarest of liquors. The rahl circled noisily for a moment, then fell with a clatter.

Yosef stared at the coin. His eyes lifted, judging both Meryam and Ama-ryllis anew, then he scooped up the coin, stood, and left the cabin. He re-turned shortly with four maps and an old, leatherbound log. Meryam looked through all of them, but they were run-of-the-mill documents. The maps showed no signs of special markings, the routes Adzin might have traveled out to the desert, nor did the log show anything out of the ordinary, only trips to and from various caravanserais and notes of mundane cargo bought and sold.

Meryam realized her fingers were shaking. "There must be more."

"There isn't."

"Did Adzin ever mention the Hollow?"

Yosef shook his head. "Should he have?"

The very name, the Hollow, was known to only a few. No one Meryam had spoken to, nor any of the many ancient texts she'd read, had been able to give her its exact location. She'd hoped that Adzin's notes would hold the answers she sought.

Meryam turned toward Amaryllis. "Give us a moment, won't you?"

Amaryllis nodded and left, sliding the cabin door shut behind her.

When her footsteps had faded, Meryam regarded Yosef with a cool ex-pression. "I understand what Adzin did. He could peer into the future." She waved to the doorway, beyond which lay the passageway with the grisly oddments hanging from hooks. "For the right price, he used all manner of techniques and tokens to separate the threads of fate, then helped his patrons choose one. I understand that he may have had discerning clients who wouldn't have wanted their fates revealed. I assure you, I'm not interested in any of that. What I want is knowledge about his techniques, the resources he used here in Sharakhai and in the desert."

Meryam had heard of Adzin only by chance. After escaping from Ramahd in Mazandir, the goddess Tulathan had come to Meryam and offered her a way to rule the desert alone. She'd given Meryam only two things to help: the body of the fallen god, Goezhen, and the name of an elder god, Ashael.

Much of what Meryam had since learned about Ashael terrified her. He'd been abandoned by Iri, Annam, Raamajit, and the other elder gods when they'd left this world for the next, which naturally made one wonder: *Why* had Ashael been left behind? Her research made the answer clear. Every text spoke of terror, of destruction, of a god who reviled the creations of others.

If that was true, why *wouldn't* the gods leave him behind? Who would want such a cancer despoiling the new world they were about to create?

Meryam knew she was playing with fire, but the knowledge she'd gained gave her hope she could have everything Tulathan had promised. Goezhen was part of the puzzle—Tulathan meant for her to use his body in some way, perhaps as an offering, to control Ashael—but she needed to find him first.

She'd searched through hundreds of texts Amaryllis had procured for her using their quickly dwindling fortune. Adzin had been mentioned in an obscure text written by an amateur soothsayer, a woman who'd heard of Adzin's fame and had managed to apprentice herself to him. She'd had eager eyes at first, a lust for hidden knowledge, but everything had changed after a voyage she and Adzin took to a place of raw, malevolent power.

It's a place that feeds many of Adzin's wondrous abilities, she'd written. *A depthless pit in the desert where many demons dwell.*

Meryam had thought little of it at first, until she'd read one of the woman's final entries.

I asked Adzin of the pit today, after plying him with the best araq my meager silver could buy. I had hoped to learn how to control the creatures that come from it, as he does. In a drunken slur he admitted that it isn't necessary to control the creatures. It's necessary to control their master.

And who is their master? I asked.

Ashael, said he.

A chill ran through me at the very name. I've learned enough about Ashael to know one does not toy with elder gods. One leaves them where they lie, sleeping.

She'd abandoned her apprenticeship the next morning, making excuses that her father was sick, that she needed a job with better pay. When Adzin had offered her more, she'd declined and had never spoken to him again.

In the cabin of *The Gray Gull*, Yosef waved vaguely to the ship again, this time with much less enthusiasm. "I daresay with a ship like this, a smart woman like you could suss out Adzin's methods given time."

"Let me make myself perfectly clear. I don't want the *ingredients*. I want the *recipe*."

"You're asking me for something I don't have."

"Let me search the ship then," Meryam said, hating the pleading sound in her voice. "I'll make it worth your while to let me have a look about."

"So you can take what you want while no one watches?"

"Watch me if you wish. I only need access to the ship for a day or two."

Yosef stood, a dour look on his face. "This meeting is over."

"No, please."

But Meryam could tell she was losing the battle. She was trying to find the right words to convince Yosef to help her when Amaryllis called from the passageway.

"My lady?"

Meryam opened the door to find Amaryllis holding one of the oddities from the wall, a raven's skull. "Look," she said, holding it out to Meryam.

Meryam accepted it, but could find nothing strange about it.

"Look through the eye."

Meryam did, and saw at last what Amaryllis had spotted. Within the skull, in the smallest script Meryam had ever seen, words were written. It was a note, penned, no doubt, by Adzin himself. *Only when Tulathan is in her first quarter, Rhia in her third, can one find the path to solace in the desert.*

Her curiosity piqued, Meryam took up a painted carving of a doe, slain by an arrow. No message was apparent until Meryam held it up against the light filtering down from the hatchway above. There were small cuts in the red paint, made by a scalpel, perhaps, all over the doe's skin. More words, Meryam realized.

When the summer doldrums are strongest, go to the plain of glittering stone. There can the efrit be found, dancing beneath the stars. Promise them fresh silver and they will reach to the heavens. Diamonds will they place in your palms before they vanish in a glimmer of stardust.

The grisly oddments, Meryam realized. *Those* were his journal. *Those* were his notes. Find the right ones and she would have Ashael's location. Find the right ones and the desert would be hers.

When she turned toward Yosef, she discovered the fear that had been so oppressive only moments ago had vanished. She was filled with purpose now. She'd found the head of the path that would lead her to everything she'd ever wanted.

"How much for the ship?" she asked.

Chapter 5

IN THE DESERT, two leagues east of Sharakhai, the blood mage Davud rode a tall akhala mare with a glimmering pewter coat. Beside him, Esmeray, a one-time blood mage whose abilities had been burned from her, rode a brass gelding with pearlescent white patches. Both horses had bulging leather bags laid across their rumps.

Davud unslung a water skin from around the horn of his saddle. The cork squeaked as he pulled it free. He tipped the skin back and took a long pull of warm water. When he was done, he passed the skin to Esmeray, who accepted it with hardly a glance at him and drank.

The path they took skirted a grove of adichara trees, one of hundreds that made up the blooming fields encircling Sharakhai. For four hundred years, the blooming fields had stood as a testament to the power of the Sharakhani Kings. The mere mention of the fields struck fear and wonder into every man, woman, and child in Sharakhai. They'd once been lush with life. No longer. Now the trees were ashy white, their branches devoid of both leaves and moon-fed blossoms. It made the grove look like a vast pile of bones.

Esmeray downed one last swig from the water skin, then handed it back. Her long hair was done up in braids. A purple head scarf wrangled them into an unruly mop atop her head. The tattoos adorning her cheeks and forehead gave her a wild look. It was partly why Davud was so attracted to her. She was everything he wasn't: bold, decisive, someone who fought ferociously for everything she believed in.

Like the trees, Esmeray's eyes were bone white. They had been since the Enclave burned away her magic. Though she'd come to accept the loss, there were times when it was clear it was weighing on her. Lately, it was during these forays, when Davud was casting spells all day long.

The sun shone off her trove of bracelets as she pointed to a grove a quarter-league ahead. "There."

Davud spotted it a moment later, a hint of green among the white, a lone tree still clinging to life. He kicked his horse into a trot. "Let's hurry. Willem gave me several new drafts of our proposal. I need to read them tonight."

Esmeray took the statement in her stride, but the very fact that she was ignoring it made it clear how opposed she was to the project Davud had begun with Willem, the brilliant young man from the Collegia who for years had been enslaved to the blood mage, Nebahat.

"You still think it's a pipe dream?" he asked.

She shrugged. "No King or Queen of Sharakhai, be they elder, son, or daughter, is going to cede power willingly."

"In the end, you may be proven right"—he jutted his chin to shimmering light along the horizon, the vault that hung over the House of Kings in Sharakhai—"but I have to try. We have to be ready when the gateway is finally closed."

She stared at him with an expression that might, just might, have contained a glimmer of hope. The look vanished as she kicked her horse into a gallop. "Let's just get this over with."

Davud hid a smile as he snapped his akhala's reins. Esmeray was like a force of nature—mercurial and stormy one minute, calm and caring the next. She might be short with him from time to time, but it came from a place of love. She was a grounding force for him, a woman unafraid to tell him when he'd erred, a thing he admitted needing more of since becoming a blood mage. By the same token, when the time came to celebrate his victories, she was more vocal than anyone.

"You two are like the golem and the efrit," Frail Lemi had once told Davud.

It was a reference to the old children's tale, and Davud couldn't deny it. In many ways he and Esmeray were opposites, but that was precisely why he'd fallen in love with her.

He urged his horse to catch up, and soon they reached the grove and slipped down from their saddles. From the saddlebags, Davud retrieved a different sort of water skin—unlike the one he and Esmeray had drunk from earlier, this one was filled with blood.

Slinging the skin over one shoulder, they headed into the grove. The passage they took wound like an errant stream. Around them, the trees wavered in the wind. The sharp thorns along the branches clicked and clacked, the sound like a rain of pebbles. They arrived at a clearing, at the far end of which stood the lone survivor: an adichara with green leaves and branches that swayed with an animus the breeze couldn't fully account for.

The death of the adicharas was yet another byproduct of the sweeping ritual that had ended with the shattering of the crystal. While alive, the adicharas had fed the crystal with their essence—an essence distilled from the blood of the tributes culled from Sharakhai by the asirim. The process had fed the crystal for centuries. At some point the trees had begun to die, a process hastened by Queen Meryam's ritual in the cavern beneath the Sun Palace—a ritual that had seen hundreds with blood of the thirteenth tribe running through their veins giving themselves to the twisted trees. The ritual had caused the crystal itself to shatter, which had, for whatever reason, led to the deaths of nearly all of the adichara.

Only a bare few had been saved by the asirim. Those very same asirim now safeguarded the remaining trees, feeding them, supporting them lest they perish and the gateway beneath the city be opened wide.

As they neared the tree, Davud pulled the stopper from the skin and upended it near the adichara's base. The blood pooled on the dusty earth, mirrorlike, and began seeping into the arid ground.

The blood had been donated by many—those Davud, Esmeray, and Meiying had rallied to their cause. The grisly enterprise, meant to brace the adichara that still lived, had been taken up by the Enclave at Davud's bidding. It seemed to be working. The asirim had all said it seemed easier for them to sustain the trees, and the knowledge that the blood had been given willingly buoyed their spirits.

It was a vast relief to Davud. Were the trees to die, the glittering vault that hung over the city would, presumably, expand farther. It would swallow all of Sharakhai, and who knew what would happen then?

When at last the fields do wither,
When the stricken fade;
The gods shall pass beyond the veil,
And land shall be remade.

That was the final verse of the poem, as recited by the gods themselves on the night of Beht Ihman four centuries earlier. *The gods shall pass beyond the veil.* That had been their plan all along. The verse as a whole had been a monumental discovery, but it was the last line in particular that sent chills along Davud's spine. *Land shall be remade.* When coupled with the visions of Sharakhai's destruction that King Yusam had seen, it struck fear in his heart. The gods had to be stopped.

"Sand and stone," Esmeray breathed.

Lost in his thoughts, he hadn't noticed her scraping at the adichara's bark. Some of it had fallen away to reveal a dark splotch beneath. Now that he'd seen it, he saw other places where the bark, normally a mottled brown, was darker. Like a melon going bad from within, the tree would soon blacken entirely. Its leaves would fall off. The bark would turn gray and finally an ashy white. It was dying, which implied that the asir that had been lending it strength was dying as well.

Esmeray held out her wrist to Davud. "Hurry."

Nodding, Davud pierced her wrist with his blooding ring and sucked from the wound. The coppery taste of her blood filled his mouth. Power suffused him, enough that he was able to close off the wound with a sizzling swipe of his thumb.

He knelt beside the tree and drew a sigil in the sand, one that combined *summon* with *soul*. The casting allowed him to feel Talib, the asir who lay buried among the adichara's roots. The spell normally allowed Davud to call up the asir hidden beneath the sand that he might speak with them.

He could feel Talib trying, but his reserves were almost spent.

Esmeray hugged herself around her waist. "He doesn't have the strength, does he?"

Davud shook his head.

Hoping to preserve whatever remained of Talib's energy, Davud banished the spell and wiped away the sigil in the sand. Even so, the adichara's roots began to writhe. A mound formed at Davud's feet, the asir lifting up. Davud felt Talib's desperation, his desire to stand beneath the desert sun one last time.

Davud knelt and bent close to the earth. "Don't," he said, hoping his words could be heard below the roots. "Please, just rest."

When the earth stilled a moment later, Davud thought it was because the asir had heard. But that wasn't it at all. The glow of the asir's soul was fading until it finally winked out altogether.

Davud looked up at Esmeray and shook his head.

Esmeray stared at the mound, the dying tree, then took in the dead grove around them with a forlorn expression. "How long can the others last?"

Davud shrugged. "I've no idea."

It felt as if the sands of the desert were opening up, ready to swallow not only him and Esmeray, but the grove, the entire blooming fields. Soon Sharakhai and everything he'd ever known would be swallowed as well, never to be seen again.

Esmeray crouched and took up a fistful of sand. "May you find what you're looking for in the land beyond," she said as it sifted through her fingers.

Davud repeated the gesture. "May you find peace."

The ritual complete, he took a small journal from a pouch at his belt and turned to the page for this particular tree, this particular asir. At the top of the page was written *Talib Zandali'ala*, followed by the tree's precise location. Below were various dates and notes from the times either he or Esmeray had come to feed blood to the adichara and speak with Talib. The notes chronicled a slow accumulation of fatigue and exhaustion.

He felt insensitive for chronicling Talib's final moments, but Talib had believed in their mission as much as any of the asirim, so Davud swallowed his discomfort and described the circumstances of Talib's death in as much detail as he could.

Then they were back in their saddles and riding to their last stop of the day, the tree where Sehid-Alaz, the legendary King of the thirteenth tribe, lay hidden. Like the previous grove, Sehid-Alaz's adichara was the lone green island in a sea of bleached bones.

After taking time to pour blood at the foot of his tree, Davud thought twice about summoning the ancient King. Lifting from their sandy graves was a draining experience, but he needed the King's thoughts on what had just happened. So he took Esmeray's blood and cast the spell. The earth mounded at his feet. Roots pressed upward and delivered Sehid-Alaz to the surface. Their work done, the roots spilled from his frame and splayed out over the dry earth, an alabaster blossom on a sea of amber stone.

Sehid-Alaz stood crookedly. His hair hung in long, lank strands. His skin was blackened and shriveled. The crown he'd worn for so long no longer adorned his head. *"I am a King no longer,"* he'd said to Davud on one of his first visits.

Like all the asirim, he'd been given new clothes when he'd been freed from his curse, but they were of an older style and sand-ridden, making him look ancient as the desert itself.

"I know what you wish to ask, Davud Mahzun'ava," he said in his hoary voice, *"but I cannot answer. I do not know how long we will last, only that we grow weaker by the day."*

"Is the blood no longer helping?"

Sehid-Alaz seemed saddened by the question. *"We fight a disease that rots from within. In the end, no amount of sustenance will cure it."*

"But there must be *something* we can do."

"There is." The glint in Sehid-Alaz's eyes intensified. *"Close the gate."*

That had been the goal all along, of course. The trouble was, none of Davud's and Esmeray's endless hours of research had led to a solution. They were no closer to sealing the gateway than they'd been the day of the terrible battle in the cavern beneath the Sun Palace, when Brama and Anila had stepped through to the land beyond.

"Move quickly, Davud Mahzun-ava." The roots lifted around Sehid-Alaz's

feet, his ankles. Soon they were wrapped around his legs and waist. *"Talib may have been the first, but more will follow, and soon."*

"How much time do we have?" Davud asked.

"I cannot say for certain." He descended slowly into the earth. *"Ask the queen about it when you speak to her."*

"The queen?"

Before the ancient King could reply, he was lost, drawn back below the tree.

"Davud . . ." Esmeray's voice was tinged with worry.

A moment later, Davud heard the jingle of tack and the rhythmic thump of horses' hooves coming through the trees. From the sound of it, there was a whole bloody regiment headed toward them.

They wound their way back to open sand and found twenty Mirean soldiers approaching on horseback. The one in the lead, their commander, wore a bright steel helm with a nose guard and a white horsetail sticking out from the top. Riding beside him was a man in light blue clothes cut in the square style favored in Mirea. He had bone-white skin. His ivory hair was pulled into a tail that flowed down along his back. On his head was a conical reed farmer's hat. After slipping easily from his saddle and down to the sand, he removed the hat and bowed respectfully. "Good day to you," he said with a barely noticeable Mirean accent. "My name is Juvaan Xin-Lei, and I come with fair tidings. Her Royal Highness, Queen Alansal, has requested your presence in Eventide."

Davud bowed his head politely. "Thank you, but . . . How did you find us?"

"Our queen is well aware of your efforts here," Juvaan replied easily. The implication, of course, was that Davud and Esmeray's movements were being watched, and had been for some time.

Davud waved to the mounted men. "Is it common for her to send a full company of soldiers to make an invitation?" He was well aware their numbers were to do with his nature as a blood mage, but he wanted to gauge the Mirean ambassador he'd heard so much about.

"My queen thought it prudent," Juvaan waved to the dunes around them. "One never knows what dangers one might find in the desert."

Hiding a smile, Davud tipped his head to Juvaan. "I suppose one can't be too careful."

"I'm glad you understand."

Beside Davud, Esmeray sat taller in her saddle. "Is this a request or a command?"

"I would rather we consider it the former," Juvaan said with an easy smile.

Esmeray stabbed a finger at the mounted soldiers. "Then you shouldn't have brought—" she began, but fell silent when Davud raised a hand.

"We'll come," he said.

Juvaan's smile broadened incrementally. "Forgive me, Master Davud, but the queen requires your presence alone."

An uncomfortable silence passed between Davud and Esmeray. He was tempted to insist she be allowed to accompany him, but this was an opportunity he couldn't let pass him by. Esmeray, every bit as aware of it as he was, shrugged noncommittally, effectively granting her permission.

"I accept," Davud said to Juvaan, "but I have to ask, is the queen aware that I've been requesting an audience for weeks now?"

"She is."

"Then why the sudden interest in a humble bread-baker's son?"

The expression on Juvaan's pale, handsome face gave nothing away. "We both know you are vastly more than that. As to your question, let us say there's a dance Queen Alansal wishes you to see."

"A dance?"

"A very intricate one, yes, which I'm sure you'll find most interesting."

Chapter 6

B Y THE TIME Çeda had made her way down the sand dune and reached the *Red Bride*, it was easy to spot the four ketches headed their way.

Kameyl stared at the ships while leaning against the transom and cutting slices from a shriveled pear. "Tulogal from the look of them," she said around a mouthful.

Çeda set down her helm and gladiator armor, then took up the spyglass and saw Kameyl was right. The pennants flapping from the top of the mainmasts showed a shooting star against a field of sable, the sign of Tribe Tulogal.

"Do we outrun them?" Kameyl asked.

"No," Çeda said, "but let's get underway. We'll speak to them under sail."

As Kameyl relayed the orders to *Storm's Eye,* Çeda, Emre, and Frail Lemi began making the ship ready.

"It's a dangerous decision," Sümeya said. "We could still outrun them."

Çeda headed toward the mainmast. "Tribe Tulogal are sailing east for a reason. I want to know what it is. Besides"—from a small wooden chest at the mast's base, she took out a white pennant, clipped it to a rope, and ran it to the top of the mainmast: a request for parley—"all the moves left to us are dangerous."

Sümeya frowned. "At least prepare the ships for a fight."

Çeda considered, then nodded. "And keep us close to the dunes," she said to Emre at the ship's wheel. "Be ready to sail into them at a moment's notice."

"Aye," Emre called.

As the *Red Bride* and *Storm's Eye* pulled anchors and gained speed, the Tulogal ships closed the distance aggressively, adding to the tenseness of the moment. Soon, the ketches were a mere stone's throw away and it was impossible not to notice their catapults and ballistae were loaded and pointed toward the *Red Bride*. None of the crew were currently manning them, but it would take only seconds for them to do so.

She was just about to call out a warning when Kameyl leapt onto the gunwales. "Disarm those weapons!" she bellowed across the distance.

A pregnant pause followed. When a stately old man in a green thawb and striped turban waved his hand, the crew unloaded the ballistae and catapults, then disengaged the tension on their arms and strings.

"That's Shaikh Zaghran," Sümeya said. "He's belligerent, but he pales in comparison to the woman standing next to him, his wife, Tanzi."

Çeda cupped her hands to her mouth and shouted across the distance, "Do you come in friendship or with hands upon your blades?"

The gap closed even more, enough that she could see Shaikh Zaghran more clearly. He had a round face with a graying beard that traveled halfway down his chest. "Who are you that sails these sands?"

"You're far from Tulogal lands," Çeda replied, "and have no right to ask who sails the stretch now claimed by the thirteenth tribe."

Tanzi wore a flowing jalabiya dyed the same green color as her husband's thawb. Covering much of her face was a red burqa with a cascade of bright silver coins that arced from the bridge of her nose, past her jawline and ears, to a strap that wrapped around the back of her neck. The way the burqa laid across her nose, combined with the disdain in her eyes, gave her the look of a carrion feeder. She leaned in and said something to her husband.

"We go to a council of the thirteen tribes," Zaghran called when she'd finished. "We were invited by their shaikh, Hamid, and are welcome in his lands." He paused, letting the words settle. "Are you similarly welcome, Çedamihn Ahyanesh'ala?"

Çeda was only mildly surprised Zaghran knew who she was—the *Red*

Bride had a unique shape, and seeing two women dressed in their Maiden's black was a not-so-subtle clue as to her identity. What concerned her more was that Shaikh Zaghran had been invited by Hamid for a council in which all thirteen tribes would be in attendance. "Hamid has no right to invite anyone to anything. He is a usurper. A murderer."

"A *murderer*, is it?"

"A murderer," Çeda repeated, louder this time. "Dozens died at his hands in Mazandir when he betrayed Shaikh Macide, our rightful ruler."

Zaghran's wife leaned in again, and then Zaghran shouted across the distance, "Macide was not all-powerful. No man, even a shaikh, can give solace to his enemies and expect no consequences."

Word had spread quickly. For the good of Sharakhai, Çeda had swallowed her hatred and allied herself with four of the remaining Kings—Ihsan, Zeheb, Cahil, and Husamettín. That alliance and the thirteenth tribe's hatred of the Kings had proved to be all the leverage Hamid needed to gain enough support, including from Sehid-Alaz, the King of the asirim, to overthrow Macide. Now Hamid was using it to gain support from the tribes harmed most by the Kings.

Çeda's own actions were going to make it all the more difficult to convince the thirteenth tribe that Hamid was a cancer, but there was nothing for it. She'd done what she'd done for the good of the desert. Even if she could go back in time and change it, she wouldn't.

No, Çeda thought, *I'd change one thing.*

Her decision to keep her alliance with the Kings hidden from Macide had been a terrible mistake. She should have confessed it to him. She should have given him the chance to agree with her plan. Failing to do so had set him up for a fall at Hamid's hands and led to his eventual death. She'd just been so desperate to get the reborn Nalamae to the valley, to have her visit the acacia so she might remember who she was and help them defeat the gods' plans.

"As you say," Çeda said to Zaghran, "shaikhs are not all-powerful, nor are they all-seeing. Hamid has blinded himself to the dangers in Sharakhai."

"Sharakhai will fall," Zaghran replied, "as has been foreseen for centuries. The old war is about to resume."

The words struck like a hammer. The implications were vast. Hamid couldn't hope to stand against Sharakhai—or Malasan or Mirea, for that matter—on his own, nor could he do so with a handful of tribes banding with him. It could only happen if all of the desert tribes banded together.

"He's calling on the Alliance," Çeda said.

She'd said it to Zaghran, but it was Tanzi who answered. "Just so," she said in a loud, shrill voice, "and it's long past due. It's time Sharakhai pays for its countless crimes, its generations of slaughter, its centuries of raping the people of the desert."

"The *Kings* should pay for those crimes," Çeda called, "not the people of Sharakhai."

It looked like Zaghran wanted to say something, but Tanzi went on. "Who do you think *supported* the Kings all these years? Sharakhai's people ignored their cruelties, so long as they kept getting rich. They enabled and upheld the Kings' cruel decisions at every step!"

"Some did," Çeda allowed. "Those in the House of Kings. Those in Goldenhill. But not the people in the streets."

Tanzi stabbed a crooked finger at Çeda. "They benefited from the rule of the Kings as much as those who walked the golden halls of Tauriyat. They must pay as well."

Breath of the desert, this is the cost of letting someone like Hamid spout his poison. How many tribes are now of a like mind? How many are ready to take up their banners once more and sail on Sharakhai? "We must look past that for now," Çeda said, "There is something terrible unfolding, which could mean the destruction of not only Sharakhai, but the desert itself."

Tanzi laughed. "Don't think to sway me with tales of fancy. We've heard of the vault, the strange light over Tauriyat and the House of Kings. We've heard how it draws the living toward death and how the dead come back to life. We in the desert can see, even if you can't, that it is the will of the gods. Let the House of Kings be eaten by this malignancy. Let Goldenhill and Hanging Gardens and Blackfire Gate be devoured. Let the entire city be consumed if that is the will of the gods! Whatever's left, be they Sharakhani, Mirean, or Malasani, will fall to our blades. The city will burn, and the desert will return to the old ways, as it was always meant to be."

What a fool I've been. Çeda thought she'd be able to expose Hamid's lies and treachery and win back the hearts and minds of the thirteenth tribe. She thought she'd find many who wished to forge peace in the desert. Now she saw the truth. She had a war on her hands. How many shaikhs agreed with him? Not all, certainly, but of those who sought peace, how bold would they be? Too often the sensible voice was timid, easily drowned by those spewing hatred and nonsense.

"Çeda."

The worry in Emre's voice made her take in the scene anew. Several Tulogal crew members were inching toward the catapults and ballistae. Zaghran himself seemed tense, and Tanzi looked like a condor ready to descend upon her prey.

Çeda made a show of taking the weapons in. "You may have convinced yourself that you want this battle," she said over the sounds of the rushing skis, "but believe me, you don't."

"This doesn't need to end in bloodshed," Zaghran said. "Surrender to us. Submit to the judgment of your shaikh. That's all we're asking."

"That would be a death sentence for us all." Çeda tightened her right hand into a fist and felt the old, familiar pain in her thumb. She pumped her hand, felt the pain heighten as she drew the desert near. "I cannot allow it."

Through her gathered power, Çeda sensed the heartbeats of those who stood behind her. She heard them readying their weapons. A glance back showed Emre with his bow. Kameyl and Sümeya had their ebon blades and shields in hand. Shal'alara, Jenise, and the others aboard *Storm's Eye* had readied themselves as well.

On the Tulogal ships, the crew reached the catapults, the ballistae. As they began loading them, Zaghran spread his arms wide, an expression of peace. "I say to you one last time, stand down. Submit."

But the words were hardly out of his mouth when Tanzi flung her arms to the sky and cried, "Let loose!"

On Çeda's left, she heard the thrum of Emre's bowstring. An arrow streaked through the air and was buried in the chest of the Tulogal crewman aiming their forward ballista. Another arrow flew, blindingly quick, and sunk into a crewman about to reach a catapult at the ship's stern. More arrows were launched from *Storm's Eye*. In a blink, a half-dozen Tulogal crew were downed.

Zaghran and Tanzi retreated behind the skiff lashed to the side of the

ship. Other Tulogal warriors, men and women, released war cries, high ululations, and returned fire. Catapults flew. Iron cat's claws soared through the
air, snaking and twisting toward the *Red Bride*'s skis. The farther ships
launched clay fire pots. They arced high, trailing smoke.

By then Çeda had a tight hold on the desert's power. She called upon it,
sending a gust of wind and sand that threw off the trajectory of claws and
fire pots enough that none of the claws struck their ships' struts, and only
one of the fire pots hit the deck of *Storm's Eye*. Jenise had the Shieldwives
ready with blue dousing agent, and they quickly put the fire out.

Arrows streaked through the air. The wind Çeda had drawn upon fouled
many launched from both sides, although some made it through. Warriors
fell. One man, launching arrow after arrow from the vulture's nest of Zaghran's
ship, was caught in the throat by an arrow from Emre. He fell, spun along the
far shroud, and was lost behind the ship as he plummeted to the sand.

Sümeya and Kameyl were whirlwinds. They blocked arrow after arrow
with their shields, one of which, despite the high winds, had been headed for
Çeda's belly.

A ballista bolt tied to a hawser sped toward the *Red Bride*. Çeda tried to
direct the wind against it, but all it did was alter the bolt's course so that
it fell across the deck instead of the foremast's rigging. The Tulogal crew
cranked the windlass that would reel the hawser in and draw the ships toward one another. They were hoping to board, to overwhelm the *Bride* with
superior numbers. But Kameyl was already on the move. As the *Bride* was
pulled ever closer to the Tulogal ketch, she ran along the gunwales and with
a roar sliced her curved black shamshir across the hawser, freeing the ships.

Çeda, meanwhile, took a deep breath and spread her arms wide. She
reached toward the sand in front of the Tulogal ships. The desert's heat was
now her anger. The very dunes bowed to her will.

She forced the sand ahead of the Tulogal ships to soften, to *welcome*
rather than support. In moments, the flat stretch of amber ahead of the four
ketches turned to slipsand. Instead of gliding over it, the ships' skis sunk
beneath the surface, ploughing great furrows. The ships slowed precipitously,
then came to a lurching halt as the skis sunk so deep they were lost beneath
the surface.

The crew were thrown forward. They slid over the decks. Many near the fore, unable to halt their momentum, were thrown over the bow. Falls like that could cause serious injuries, but the sand below was soft as flour. Those who fell were all but swallowed by it, the sand exploding in golden fans around them.

As the swaying of the masts and rigging quelled, Zaghran and Tanzi rose. Çeda headed to the *Bride's* stern, where she cupped her hands to her mouth. "Think on my words," she shouted. "We are all of us in grave danger from the desert gods. *That* is what we must unite to fight against, not one another."

The shaikh and his wife said nothing in reply, and soon they were dwindling into the distance as the *Red Bride* and *Storm's Eye* sailed on.

Chapter 7

RAMAHD AMANSIR LEANED against the rough, mudbrick wall of a saddlery in Mazandir. Beside him was Cicio, his stalwart companion. The two men were similarly dressed. Both wore trousers, shirts made of light, breathable cloth, and black leather boots, the style common in their homeland, the southern kingdom of Qaimir. Ramahd had his long brown hair pulled back into a tail, while Cicio wore a brimmed leather hat with a black plume, the sort that had become more popular among the sandsmen of their country.

Across the dusty street, a boy guided a colt in circles with light flicks from a training whip. Cicio had caught wind of a stablehand, the boy's sister, who'd been telling everyone a wild tale about the goddess, Tulathan, visiting a woman along Mazandir's northern edge. At the time, when they'd found her, she'd refused to say anything. But then, a day ago, a note had arrived, an offer to meet, assuming the reward was still good.

"She should be here by now," Cicio said in Qaimiran.

"With the coin we're offering," Ramahd said, "she'll come. Have a little patience."

"Patience, he says . . ." Cicio spat onto the street. "This fucking desert stole all I had."

Ramahd chuckled. "Your coffers weren't exactly overflowing when we arrived."

"Maybe not, but I swear to you, if we don't make some progress, I'm likely to find an oud parlor and start drinking until someone starts a fight."

"Until *you* start a fight you mean."

Cicio shrugged. "I don't care who starts it."

Ramahd didn't reply. It would only rile Cicio up. The tolling of a bell drew his gaze to a series of blocky stone buildings, the remains of Mazandir's original caravanserai. Around the buildings, dozens of ship's masts jutted upward like the spears of an approaching army. He and Cicio had passed them on their way to the saddlery. The majority of the ships moored there were owned by the desert tribes. Others hailed from Sharakhai and Qaimir. There were even a few flying the pennants of Kundhun. For the first time in a long while they were largely trading ships, not ships of war. Life in Mazandir was returning to normal, due in large part to King Hektor's decision to withdraw from the caravanserai.

The Qaimiri fleet was still nearby. King Hektor, long worried that Malasan or even Sharakhai's royal navy might attack, had insisted the bulk of the fleet wait until all Qaimiri warships had gathered. Only then would the fleet set sail, assured all would survive the journey back home.

After the wild events in Sharakhai, Hektor had given Ramahd a ship and a crew to command so that he could hunt for Meryam. But forty ships were already anchored to the south of Mazandir. When the stragglers arrived, King Hektor would order them south, Ramahd included, abandoning his vow that he would do everything in his power to see Meryam brought to justice.

How much time did that leave? A few days, perhaps. A week at the most. "It feels like we're giving up," Ramahd said absently.

Cicio followed Ramahd's line of gaze. "Can you blame him?" Cicio waved to the stables. "Maybe he'd have given us more time if we'd found anything beyond the word of a fucking horse hand."

As if summoned by his words, a girl of sixteen came jogging out of the stables. She had a dimpled chin and wild hair. She was tall for her age, taller than Cicio. Her trousers, baggy shirt, and straw hat were common in Mazandir, but her dark skin, more than anything, marked her as a child of the desert.

"Took you long enough, ah?" Cicio said, switching to Sharakhan.

"I told you to wait by the apothecary," she said with a surly expression. "The master caught sight of you yesterday. Made me slop the stalls and brush all the horses *again* before he'd let me leave." Without waiting for a reply, she walked briskly down the street.

Cicio laughed as he launched himself after her. "You can buy a—what you call it? When you sew designs in cloth?"

"Embroidered," groused the stablehand.

Cicio snapped his fingers. "Embroidered. You can buy embroidered kerchief with the reward, ah? Sop up all your tears."

She glowered while heading toward the edges of the caravanserai.

"Why did you decide to come forward now?" Ramahd asked her.

"What?" The girl seemed distracted.

"For the reward. We offered you money weeks ago."

"Give me the money and I'll tell you," she said.

"Story first," Ramahd replied.

She came to a stop and stared at him, perhaps debating whether or not to press. Then she shrugged, pointed to the way ahead, and resumed her brisk pace.

They passed through a cluster of squat, mudbrick homes and arrived at a stretch of terrain dominated by ironweed, scrub trees, and pools of water. In the distance lay the desert's endless, rolling dunes.

The girl pointed to one of the nearest pools. "I saw the woman walking from the trees to the edge of the black pool, there."

The pools were verged with green grasses and cattails, all save the one the stablehand was pointing to. That one was barren. The grass around it had died, and the muddy earth along its edges was black. It was the pool that held Goezhen's body before it had miraculously gone missing.

"The surface was still like glass then, yes?" Ramahd asked.

The girl nodded, then stepped closer and pointed to the pool's center. "She walked onto the water and stared down at the dead god." She touched her fingers to her forehead, a sign of blessing. "She spoke to him for a time."

"What did she say?"

"I wasn't close enough to hear."

The water's surface, no longer solid, rippled in the warm wind. Goezhen's body was gone, but it still stank of rot and brimstone. It was why, even though the other pools were untainted, the people of Mazandir avoided them. No one swam in them any longer. No one took water from them to cook or to feed their livestock. They wouldn't even use it to irrigate crops.

Ramahd stepped into the dead grass along the pool's verge and stared into the depths of the water. "What happened next?"

"I saw the goddess walk down from the heavens along a shaft of moonlight."

"Describe her," Ramahd said.

"She was taller than any woman or man I've ever seen. She had straight silver hair that glowed. It ached to look upon her for too long. She spoke with your queen—"

"She is no our queen—" Cicio broke in, but stopped when Ramahd raised a hand.

"She spoke with your lady," the stablehand revised. "Or I think she did. I heard only soft sounds, like chimes, but your lady would answer as if she'd understood. She said her throne was gone, her magic taken from her. I don't know what the goddess said next, but your lady seemed to take heart from it."

"What makes you say that?"

"She looked angry when the goddess arrived, but by the end there was a brightness in her eyes. Like when you find a copper khet lying in the street."

"You said she fell in the water?"

The girl nodded. "She took off a necklace she'd been wearing and clutched it to her breast. She didn't seem to want to give it up, but when Tulathan turned and began walking away, she said she could do it. She could leave the past behind. Then she threw the necklace onto the pool. I swear by the gods it shattered at that very moment. Lady Meryam fell right in."

"And Tulathan?"

She pointed toward open sand. "She walked away, lost like moonlight to passing clouds."

"And then?"

She shrugged. "I left."

"You didn't see where Meryam went?"

"No."

"You weren't curious?"

"Curious?" She laughed. "I would have left earlier if I hadn't feared the goddess would see me. With her gone, it was time for me to go. I came back the next day, though. And the next. Just checking up, you understand. One night, when the moons were dark, I spotted men with lanterns. They had horses and a sleigh." She motioned to the fetid pool, then pressed her fingers to her forehead again. "I saw them drag Goezhen's body out and haul it away."

"Where?"

She pointed to the open desert. "That way. To a ship, I reckon."

"That's the last you saw of Meryam or her people?"

"Yes, I swear." She glanced back the way they'd come. "I really should be getting back."

Judging they'd get no more out of her, Ramahd nodded to Cicio, who sent a small leather bag jingling through the air. The stablehand caught it with ease.

"So why now?" Ramahd jutted his chin toward the purse. "You promised to tell."

The stablehand shrugged. "Your fleet's leaving. Everyone says so. Why not get paid twice before you've all left?"

"Twice?"

She skipped backward, then raised the hand holding the bag of coins and pointed to the far side of the pool. "Ask *him*."

With that she spun on her heels and jogged away.

More than a little confused, Ramahd peered beyond the tall grasses on the far side of the pool and saw a man wearing a long black coat and a white shirt with frills at the neck and wrists. There was a leatherbound book in his right hand. He looked familiar, but the almost ludicrously wide brim of his hat was shading his face, making it all but impossible to make out his features.

As he began walking around the pool toward him, recognition finally dawned. *"Fezek?"* Ramahd said in disbelief.

"We are one and the same!" Fezek smiled broadly. It was not a pleasant look. His pale skin was putrid. One eye had clouded over. One leg ended in a wooden prosthetic. It was a step up from the peg leg he'd once worn. Nevertheless, it lent his gait a boneyard shamble, which was rather fitting for a ghul.

Ramahd looked him over, unsure where to begin. He decided to start with the most superficial question running through his head. "What in the great wide desert are you *wearing?*"

Fezek stopped dead in his tracks and looked himself over. "Why, do you like it?" The clothes were decidedly Qaimiri but from an era of fashion that had come and gone decades ago. As the seconds passed, Fezek's hopeful expression faded. "I'd hoped it would put you at ease."

In truth, the clothes looked rather ridiculous, but it was an endearing effort just the same. "They certainly make a statement," Ramahd said, then took a deep breath, wondering how to broach the subject without causing offense. "Fezek, I thought you were lost to us in the cavern. When Anila left—"

"Oh, I know! So did I! I thought my time on this earth would be cut short. *Again.* But the fates saw fit to leave me here. They kept me alive for a purpose, I believe. Or Anila did. It amounts to the same thing, either way." He held up the book in his right hand, as if that explained everything. When Ramahd said nothing, he shook it. "I've been chronicling the entire, grand tale!"

In Sharakhai, Fezek had been composing a sweeping poem in hopes of chronicling his journey with Anila, Davud, and many others as they fought to understand the purposes behind the desert gods' plans. "Mark my words," he'd once told Ramahd, "it will become the desert's greatest epic. It will dwarf even the tales of Bahri Al'sir!"

"And your research"—Ramahd jutted his chin toward the book—"led you here?"

"Yes! Well, sort of. I remained in Sharakhai for a time. I got word of a Malasani captain who trades out of the city's western harbor. I went to him, and I think he was scared of me at first, but once we got to talking, and I told him about a man I once knew"—Fezek leaned in conspiratorially—"a rather close friend, if you get my meaning. But I didn't tell the captain that. He didn't seem like a man—"

"Fezek."

Fezek blinked. "Yes. So. Meryam." He cleared his throat, a thoroughly gruesome sound. "Yosef told me Meryam was looking for a place known as the Hollow."

"What's the Hollow?"

"A great pit in the desert. Apparently Meryam hoped to buy a set of journals to learn its location, but then her assistant, a comely young woman—"

"Amaryllis," Ramahd said.

"Amaryllis, yes . . . She found something in the odd little items Adzin kept around the ship, and Meryam offered to buy the whole thing! I thought you'd like to know where she was going."

Ramahd paused, confused. "Are you saying you know where the Hollow is?"

Fezek's smile was a ruin of rotted teeth. "I've a *vague* idea, yes." He paused again, and pasted on the sort of face stage actors use to draw out tension.

"This fucking ghul," Cicio said under his breath.

Ignoring him, Ramahd focused on Fezek. "*How* vague?"

"Since the vault's formation, calling on the departed to have a bit of a chat has become a relatively simple thing. I scoured five boneyards and spoke to a hundred lost souls before I found a cooper who used to crew on a small pirate fleet. He was a pleasant man. He told me a tale of dousing one of King Külaşan's granddaughters in mulled wine, purely by accident, of course—"

"Fezek."

Another clearing of the throat. "Yes. My apologies. He told me about the Hollow. It lies west of Sharakhai, a day's sail away, maybe less."

Ramahd stood there for a moment, stunned. Meryam would have found the Hollow's location as well. It was where he had to go. That's where he would find her.

It left a burning question in Ramahd's mind. "So you came to Mazandir and arranged this meeting," he said. "Why the cloak and dagger? Why not come directly to me?"

"Well"—Fezek shrugged while avoiding Ramahd's gaze—"this old playwright wasn't sure, on the occasion of our long-anticipated reunion, whether you'd . . ."

Fezek stopped, and Ramahd prompted, "Whether I'd what?"

"Send me away," Fezek blurted. "But then I heard the girl telling her tale, and I thought you'd want to hear it. I gave her a goodly sum and bid her find you, hoping it might ease the blow of seeing me again."

"Fezek, why would you say that? Why would you *think* that? You were a great help to us."

"That may be, but—" Fezek's cloudy eyes took in the pool, the ragged trees. "We both know you only tolerated my presence because of Anila."

For a moment, Ramahd was taken aback. While it was true he hadn't exactly *enjoyed* Fezek's presence at first, he'd taken a shine to the old playwright after a time. "You helped us immensely," he repeated. "And you saved us more than once. Don't think I've forgotten that."

Fezek's smile slowly returned, then brightened. It was difficult to imagine a more stomach-churning sight. "And now here we are, together again at the end of things."

Ramahd paused. "Then end of what, Fezek?"

Fezek struck a theatrical pose. "Why, it *all*, of course. I hope to capture it. Give it just the right notes."

Ramahd stared at the book in Fezek's hand, suddenly optimistic. "Everything you've told me, did you write it all down?"

"Of course!"

"Would you be willing to share it with my king?"

Fezek seemed suddenly self-conscious. "I don't know that it's ready for wide consumption, but . . . I suppose I can share it."

Ramahd made for the streets he and Cicio had left earlier, but Fezek paused. His gaze swung to the pool, at which point his eyes lit up, as if he'd just remembered something. "Wait, there's one more thing!" Handing his journal to Cicio, he began walking into the stinking pool with no preamble whatsoever—ridiculous hat, frilly clothes, and all. He was soon lost, fully submerged. His hat floated on the water's surface, twirling in circles like a foundering ship.

Ramahd looked to Cicio, who made a disgusted face and shrugged, as if there were no accounting for the addled decisions of a half-dead ghul.

A short while later, the surface of the black water parted and up rose Fezek again. Bits of black detritus covered his skin and clothes. And by the gods, how he *stank*. Yet he was smiling, for he'd returned with a prize. In his hands he held a red beaded necklace, which he held out to Ramahd. "For you."

It was Meryam's necklace, the one she'd been given by her sister, Yasmine, when they were young. It had great significance to Meryam. That she'd sacrificed it at the pool, and that it had somehow broken the pool's glasslike surface, was significant, which made the necklace itself important.

Ramahd hardly knew what to say. "Thank you," he finally managed.

Fezek's smile was the sort of thing that made children cry. "Is it time to see the King now?"

Ramahd motioned to Fezek's state. "Not like this it isn't."

Fezek stared down at himself. "Oh my."

"Come on, Fezek." Ramahd led him toward Mazandir. "It's time for a bath. Several, perhaps. We'll find you new clothes after burning these, and *then* we'll go and speak to King Hektor."

Fezek smiled as he took his journal back from Cicio. "It really is going to be a grand tale, isn't it?"

"I certainly hope so," Ramahd said.

Chapter 8

ON REACHING SHARAKHAI, still on horseback, Esmeray squeezed Davud's hand, sent a withering glance toward Juvaan, then guided her akhala away, west along the Corona. Davud continued with Juvaan and his contingent of mounted soldiers south along the Trough.

The traffic along Sharakhai's busiest thoroughfare grew congested as they passed through the old walls. Their progress had soon slowed to a crawl, forcing the soldiers at the front to spur their horses on to forge a path through the crowd. The streets in this part of the city were a hive of activity, even more so than in years past. Queen Alansal, fearing the people might be turned into wights and attack her soldiers, had ordered the land that fell within the boundaries of the vault to be cleared. Her soldiers had emptied every building, block by block, and set up a cordon outside the vault to prevent reentry.

Ahead, the vault itself loomed. The massive, glittering dome enveloped not only Tauriyat but a swath of land beyond it besides. The neighborhoods it encompassed were some of the oldest and most densely populated in Sharakhai. The displacement of tens of thousands had placed no small amount of strain on the rest of the city.

The air cooled as they approached the shimmering curtain. Juvaan's soldiers drew coats from their saddlebags and pulled them on. Juvaan did the same, then handed a flame-orange khalat to Davud, who had worn only a loose thawb on his journey to the blooming fields.

Davud accepted it gratefully and pulled it on. "Thank you."

As they passed into the vault proper, Davud's stomach lurched. He felt as if he were suddenly falling, and grabbed the saddle horn to steady himself. The feeling settled into an undeniable *pull* toward the gateway itself, which was hidden away in a cavern beneath the mountain.

The cold grew steadily as they passed through the temple district. The temples themselves had long lines of people waiting before the entrances. Knowing there would be riots if people weren't allowed to pray, Queen Alansal had authorized a controlled flow of people to visit the temples each day.

By the time they'd entered the House of Kings, ridden up the winding King's Road, and reached Eventide's courtyard, Davud was chilled to the bone.

"How can the queen maintain a residence here?" he asked Juvaan as the horses came to a halt.

"We have a custom in Mirea. You may be unfamiliar with it, coming from the desert. It's called *building a fire*." He winked at Davud. "Mulled wine helps too."

"I know, but this is a cold that seeps to the bone."

"True." He waved Davud toward the stairs. "But we're used to the cold in Tsitsian."

"She could live outside the vault," Davud countered as they took to the stairs and entered the palace.

"And leave Eventide unoccupied? No. Cold or not, all must recognize that the House of Kings and the city beyond are now Mirea's."

Davud held his tongue. Taking a massive city like Sharakhai and keeping it were two vastly different things. He hoped to have no small say in the matter before all was said and done, but that was a battle for another day.

Strangely, as they headed deeper into the palace, a sound like pattering rain filled the air and as they reached the large hall that had once served as King Kiral's audience chamber, Davud stared in wonder. He remembered the vaulted ceiling, the walls of stout granite, and the floor of veined marble.

More curiously, a large bamboo pipe issued forth from a hole in the far wall. The lone pipe had been split, then split again, forming a bamboo grid that hung from the ceiling by twine and covered all but the dais and throne to Davud's left. Holes had been drilled in the pipes so that the water being fed through the main pipe could rain down. The runoff collected in a channel in the floor and drained away through a small service door.

The falling water was strange enough. Stranger still were the women dancing beneath it. There were eleven of them, all dressed in green silk with teal accents, a cobalt scarf wrapped around the arms of each. The women were drenched, but they hardly seemed to notice. Indeed, they seemed to revel in it. As they spun like dervishes, water flew in hypnotic arcs. The water caught the sunlight slashing down through the windows set high into the far wall, making it look like they were scattering jewels with every turn.

There's a dance Queen Alansal wishes you to see, Juvaan had said.

Davud could hardly take his eyes from it, and only eventually became aware that someone else had entered the room. He turned and saw Queen Alansal herself stepping down the dais stairs. She wore a dress of pearl silk. Patterns of dragonflies and reeds were rendered in fine scarlet thread. A bolt of russet silk wrapped her small waist. Her hair, done up high, was held in place with two steel pins as long as her forearms. She looked no more than fifty, but she had an ancient quality about her.

It's her eyes, Davud decided. *They're hungry and knowing.*

She skirted the edge of the room, avoiding most of the spray. "Welcome," she said to Davud, then waved a dismissal at Juvaan.

Juvaan bowed and left. The sentries closed the doors behind him.

Davud motioned to the dancing women. "I must admit, none of the accounts I've read about your water dancers do them justice."

"Yes, they are a wonder." Her accent was more pronounced than Juvaan's, her pace of speaking slower, but her command of Sharakhan was formidable.

With a polite wave, she guided Davud toward the dais. One of the dancers spun dreamily toward them, close enough that her movements flung cold water over them both. As the dancer spun away they reached the dais, and Alansal sat upon her throne.

"Do you know what my water dancers do?"

"They see the future."

Alansal smiled a humoring smile. "In the end, yes. Glimpses of it, in any case. But the visions the water grants them are complex and difficult to interpret. There are eleven dancers because none alone can interpret them. It takes many working together to understand what the future holds, and even then mistakes are not uncommon."

Frenetic earlier, the dance had eased into a more restrained pace. Each of the women had been moving with her own unique rhythm when Davud had entered. Now they were moving in sync, the water being thrown in consistent, geometric patterns as they wove around one another.

Alansal tipped her head toward them with a satisfied smile. "When they've taken in enough and find they must confer with one another, they move as one."

Indeed, mere moments later the dancers formed a circle and came to a halt. Each held their final pose while staring at a dancer opposite. After a long breath, they relaxed, bowed to one another, and stepped away from the falling water. At the foot of the dais, they knelt before their queen.

"They saw me in their visions, didn't they?" Davud asked.

Alansal nodded. "They did."

"And what did the visions show?"

"You may rise," Alansal said to the dancers.

As one, they did. Servants rushed in with towels and began drying the women's clothes and hair.

"In fact," Alansal said, still staring at her dancers, "there were many visions of you, any one of which might foretell a real event or not. If I told you of them, it could taint the process and the conclusions they draw from it. I'm asking you as your queen to speak to them and answer their questions."

Davud found her presumption annoying. "Toward what end?"

Alansal turned her piercing gaze on him. "To stave off what I'm ever more convinced is going to be a slaughter."

Davud was already cold, but at this a terrible shiver ran up his spine. "A slaughter of whom?"

"I've already said too much." She waved to the dancers who, to Davud's embarrassment, were undressing so the servants could dry their skin. "I leave the rest to them."

Davud chose his next words carefully. "I've made several requests to visit the cavern, to study the gateway. Have you been made aware of them?"

"I have."

"Then I propose we make an agreement, for our mutual benefit. I'll talk to your water dancers if you'll grant me access to the cavern. I'll share all I know, and all I learn, with you. About the vault, the adichara, the asirim."

"I'll consider your request"—Alansal's smile was condescending—"but only *after* a show of good faith."

He considered calling her bluff. He was certain she wanted to know about the gateway as much as he did. But in the end he was simply too curious to learn how he fit into the water dancers' visions.

"Very well," he said.

Alansal nodded. "Very well."

She left the room, and the water dancers surrounded him on the dais. A box inlaid with mother of pearl in the design of a peacock was passed among them. The box contained a white powder, and each dancer took a pinch of it, held it to her nose, and inhaled sharply. Their pupils dilated, and their faces took on dreamy expressions.

"What does it do?" Davud asked.

The young dancer who answered him had eyes so yellow they reminded Davud of dandelions. "It's called *zhenyang*. It means *truth*. It grants"—her eyes roamed the ceiling as she searched for the right word—"*clarity*."

The dancers began peppering him with questions. Most spoke Sharakhan well; those who didn't received help from the others. They wove around each other as they spoke. They traded places, one stepping forward while another stepped back. It was a complex ritual and felt related to what they'd performed beneath the falling water.

They asked him of his upbringing in Roseridge, about his family and his friends. They asked him of the collegia and his travels since. For a long while they focused on his abduction by the blood mage, Hamzakiir, and Davud's subsequent awakening to the red ways. They asked of Çeda and her quest to bring down the Sharakhani Kings. Given their questions, they seemed to know quite a bit of the story already, much more than he would have guessed.

"Did your dance show you all of this?" Davud asked them after a time.

Chow-Shian, with the dandelion eyes, laughed, then continued to rain questions down on him.

They asked if he knew Nalamae. If he'd ever spoken to the other gods. If he'd ever tasted their blood, which seemed a very strange thing to ask. It grew stranger still when they spoke of demons, the warped creations of Goezhen or those left over from the passage of the elder gods. Had he seen any of them? Had he interacted with them? Had any ever preyed on him? Had he killed one?

Then came one of the oddest exchanges. Chow-Shian stood directly in front of him, so close he could feel her body heat. She stared deep into his eyes and said, "Have you ever watched someone die?"

A vision flashed through his mind's eye: Anila standing within a cavern before the blindingly bright crystal, then collapsing against the brittle roots of the adichara as she gave up her life and passed beyond the veil. Brama doing the same a moment later.

"Yes, I've watched someone die."

"Did you let it happen?"

Davud's head jerked back involuntarily. He'd never thought of it that way, but when it was stated so bluntly, he had to consider it. His first instinct was to lie—of course he hadn't let Anila die, nor Brama—but it felt important, somehow, that he not hide the truth. It felt as though to do so would harm not only their interpretation of their visions, but would rob *him* of the truth as well.

"In a way, I did. They sacrificed themselves that the rest of us might live, and I did not stop them."

Chow-Shian's dandelion eyes blinked several times, then the whites of her eyes turned red. Tears gathered, crept down along her round cheeks.

"What is it?" he asked.

But she didn't respond, and another took her place with questions of her own.

He spent well over two hours answering their questions, and when they were done, Juvaan came and escorted him from the room.

Davud thought Juvaan might be leading him to Alansal, but it quickly became clear he was leading him back toward the entrance. "Your queen said we'd speak of the cavern, the gateway." His voice contained a good deal more desperation than he'd meant to convey.

They passed through the arched entry doors, but Juvaan stopped short of the stairs. On the fine gravel circle below, a stable girl dressed in winter clothes stood holding the reins of Davud's akhala. "I'm afraid the queen is indisposed at the moment."

"Queen Alansal and I had an agreement."

"An agreement she hasn't broken. She's only chosen to discuss it at another time."

"This is important, Juvaan, to both our countries."

For the first time since meeting him, Juvaan seemed cross. "Unless I'm very much mistaken"—he spun on his heels and began walking away—"those two are now one in the same."

Chapter 9

DEEP IN THE desert, Çeda, Emre, Sümeya, and Frail Lemi anchored their skiff as Tulathan and Rhia stared down from a sable sky. Far ahead, a massive fleet of ships had gathered below the Taloran Mountains.

"Bloody gods," Çeda said, "the size of it."

"It's as big as the Malasani fleet," Frail Lemi said.

"Bigger," Emre replied. "King Emir's fleet numbered three hundred when they fell on Sharakhai. That"—he pointed to the ships—"is at least four."

"More like five," Sümeya said.

Frail Lemi nodded sagely. "More like five."

As the sound of drums, rebabs, and doudouks drifted to their position, they took in the spectacle. To say it was impressive would be an understatement. All thirteen tribes had gathered. A weeklong celebration had begun to mark the occasion. Pavilions had been pitched. Thousands of men, women, and children milled over the sand, sharing food and drink and conversation. In the coming days, common affairs would be discussed. Plans would be made.

It was hard to overstate how momentous an event it was. That every tribe had agreed to band together represented nothing less than a foundational shift of power in the desert. Çeda was immensely proud, not only of Macide for having started the effort, but of Emre for helping to orchestrate it. He had gained no small amount of respect from several of the shaikhs in the process, which was precisely why he was about to infiltrate the gathering. Someone needed to get a sense of where the shaikhs stood. They also needed to lay the groundwork for Çeda's arrival, which meant garnering support for all that Çeda meant to do in the coming days.

Emre caught Frail Lemi's eye. "Best we get moving."

Frail Lemi fell into step alongside Emre as they headed toward the ships, then turned and began walking backwards. "Don't worry," he said to Çeda. "I'll keep our boy safe."

They were headed to gather news, but also support for a tribunal so Hamid could be tried for his crimes. Of the seven shaikhs that would need to agree, Emre felt certain he could secure four that very night. The rest would prove more difficult, which was why his secondary goal was to enlist the help of Aríz, the charismatic young shaikh Emre and Frail Lemi had grown quite close to. Çeda was worried the effort would fail in the end, but she had to admit, with Aríz on their side they stood a good chance.

As the crunch of their footsteps faded, Çeda and Sümeya sat cross-legged on the sand. There was no real reason for either of them to have come— tonight's mission was Emre's to complete—but Çeda and Sümeya both wanted to witness the gathering for themselves, to gauge what they were up against.

When Emre and Frail Lemi had been reduced to tiny silhouettes in the distance, Sümeya said, "You seem glum."

"I am." Çeda waved to the ships. "This was Macide's greatest wish, to see the tribes banded together for mutual protection and prosperity. He championed the Alliance to all who would listen, and convinced many shaikhs to join on his own, but didn't live to see his plans come to fruition."

Sümeya's history was deeply linked to Sharakhai and its Kings. Her father was Husamettín, the King of Swords himself. Husamettín was Çeda's father, too, though she hadn't discovered that until recently and hadn't known him growing up. In Çeda's eyes, he was a despot and nothing more.

Sümeya, on the other hand, had been a faithful servant to the Kings for most of her life, which made it more than a little surprising when she said, "A pity he didn't live to see this day."

"Perhaps he sees it from the land beyond," Çeda said with a sad smile.

"Perhaps."

Sümeya lapsed into silence. Her hands began to fidget. She seemed to be avoiding Çeda's eye, and she'd been silent and stiff on the sail in. Sümeya was normally so direct. She was starting to make Çeda nervous.

"Care to tell me what's bothering you?" Çeda asked.

Sümeya sighed. "I should have said something sooner."

The nervousness inside of Çeda intensified. "Should have said *what* sooner?"

Finally Sümeya did meet Çeda's gaze. "I think we made a mistake in coming here."

For a moment, Çeda was caught flat-footed—that wasn't at all what she'd thought Sümeya had been about to say. "You agreed this was the right course."

"I know, but seeing it with my own eyes . . . Knowing how much power Hamid has already gathered . . . If he has Zaghran by his side, he'll have more shaikhs besides. He may have everything he needs to declare war before you set foot in their camp."

"You'd have me walk away?"

"Yes."

"I need the acacia, Sümeya. I need its visions."

"You don't even know if you can command it. You said so yourself."

"I said I wasn't sure," Çeda countered, "but I was there when Nalamae used it. I felt her coaxing visions from it so she could learn about her former selves and piece herself back together."

"Feeling *her* use of it and controlling the tree yourself are two different things."

"I can only say it in so many ways." Çeda flexed her right hand. She felt the dull pain there, felt the desert through it. "I feel a part of that tree. It will listen to me. I'm sure of it."

"Wouldn't we be better off searching for Nalamae? She must have learned more by now. She must have a plan. We can *help* her."

"We could if we knew how to find her. But we don't. And the fact that she hasn't found *us* tells me she's not ready for our help. Or that she'd find us a distraction."

No one had seen the goddess since she'd disappeared in the old stone fort below Mount Arasal. Rumors spoke of her sudden appearance in Mazandir and a terrible battle with Goezhen, but beyond that no one knew her current whereabouts—or if she was even alive.

"If she's anywhere"—Sümeya flung a hand east—"she's in Sharakhai. Or near it. She must be."

"You don't know that."

"Even if I'm wrong, we'd do better adding our strength to the Kings'. We need to regain control over the *city*."

Çeda jutted her chin toward the distant ships. "What good would regaining the city do us if we immediately lose it to the tribes?" Before Sümeya could argue the point, Çeda went on. "I *must* go to the acacia."

"If you must," Sümeya said, "then let's steal into the mountains and visit the acacia at night."

"It's too dangerous."

Stunned, Sümeya swung her gaze to the fleet of ships. "No more dangerous than walking into the jaws of a lion."

In the distance, light flared against the hulls of the outer line of ships—probably from someone tossing araq onto a fire. "Leave now, and Hamid's ideology is likely to take hold. I can't let that happen. What the people of the desert need now is truth and hope, and that's precisely what I mean to give them."

Sümeya looked like she wanted to argue further, but she held her silence. After wrestling with her emotions for a time, she seemed to resign herself to the fact that Çeda wasn't going to change her mind. "I had to try."

"I understand," Çeda said, "and I appreciate it. I appreciate *everything*, Sümeya. I've never said so directly, but I know how much you gave up in order to help the thirteenth tribe. Melis and Kameyl as well. I'll never forget it."

"It was the right thing to do." In a rare show of emotion, Sümeya gripped Çeda's hand. "But thank you for saying so."

Time passed. Çeda was content to listen to the music and sounds of revelry. So, apparently, was Sümeya. Çeda was surprised to see how far the moons had traveled across the star-strewn sky before they spotted Emre and Frail Lemi returning.

Çeda didn't mean to, but she sensed Sümeya's heart beat more rapidly. Her sense of it, however, was quickly suppressed. Sümeya was consciously trying to mask it.

"I'm happy for you," Sümeya said.

And suddenly the host of butterflies had returned. Çeda knew precisely what she meant. She was touching on the very subject Çeda *thought* she'd been ready to broach earlier.

"Thank you," Çeda said awkwardly.

"And I'm sorry"—Sümeya breathed deeply—"about what happened between us."

She meant their romantic encounters. The first had been before they knew they were half sisters, the second had been after. For Çeda's part, she'd never seen Sümeya as a sister. She still didn't. Not really. They'd grown up in completely different worlds, neither aware the other even existed until Çeda had arrived at the gates of the House of Maidens, poisoned and near death.

"I regret parts of it as well." Çeda reached out in turn and gripped Sümeya's hand. "But I don't regret meeting you. Your heart is good, Sümeya. You are true child of Sharakhai, one of its brightest jewels."

Sümeya said nothing in reply, but she squeezed Çeda's hand back, and soon Emre and Frail Lemi had arrived and the four of them were sailing back toward the *Red Bride* and *Storm's Eye*.

"So?" Çeda prompted as they sidled over a dune.

Emre, sitting at the tiller, told them how he had gone in to speak to the shaikhs he knew while Frail Lemi waited in the darkness.

"We have five votes," he finished, "and Aríz thinks he can get us a sixth."

"We only need one more," Frail Lemi said proudly, though he hadn't actually done anything to help.

"I couldn't reach Shaikh Neylana, but we'll sail back in tomorrow and . . ." Emre's words trailed away as his gaze shifted from Çeda to Sümeya and back again. "What's going on?"

"What do you mean?"

"You two are acting weird."

"Are we?" Çeda asked.

"I have no idea what you're talking about," Sümeya said with mock sincerity.

When Emre's face turned sour as a Malasani lime, Sümeya smiled then burst into laughter. Çeda laughed too, which only served to make Sümeya laugh harder. Frail Lemi laughed with them, though it was clear he had no idea why. Emre just rolled his eyes and worked the tiller to guide them around a large dune.

All the while, the music of the gathered tribes slowly faded behind them.

Chapter 10

MERYAM HEADED DOWN a ladder into the hold of *The Gray Gull*, the grisly sloop she'd purchased. Amaryllis followed. On Meryam's orders, her crew had remained on the yacht they'd used to ferry Goezhen's body from Mazandir—she needed silence if she was going to make headway with the task she'd set for herself.

Within the hold, the sounds of the harbor were muted. Light canted in through half-open shutters, illuminating the object that dominated the space: Goezhen's body, which they'd transferred to the *Gull* a few days back. The corpse looked horrific, a nightmare come to life. Goezhen's skin was shriveled like a prune and graying. His cheeks were drawn. The pits of his eyes were deep and his cloudy white eyes gave the impression that he was staring at Meryam from beyond death, promising pain and misery for treating his remains like some alchemycal ingredient.

The god had been dead for months, and yet the threat seemed real, which made Meryam feel inadequate to the task she'd set for herself. She quickly smothered the feeling. Goezhen represented a chance to regain her power. He was the key to her taking control over the desert and the lands beyond. All she need do was unlock a few more precious secrets.

Tulathan had made clear that if Meryam hoped to claim the desert as her own, Goezhen's remains were an essential component. Except she hadn't said how. Meryam had puzzled over it for days, becoming angry and frustrated that the goddess hadn't divulged more. In time, her anger faded and the reason for Tulathan's reticence became clear: the gods *couldn't* meddle in the affairs of mortals. Do that and they bound themselves to this world, which would prevent them from crossing over to the farther fields.

Meryam was well aware that if she succeeded in her plans with Goezhen, it would further their goals.

So be it, she thought.

The gods could go to the farther fields if they wished. They would leave behind a desert ripe for the taking. Without their influence, it would be that much easier to secure Sharakhai, retake Qaimir's throne from King Hektor, and move on to the other neighboring kingdoms. It would be the beginning of the greatest empire the world had ever seen.

Amaryllis stepped across the deck, avoiding the piles of Adzin's oddities they'd culled from the sloop's passageways and cabins. Staring at Goezhen with an inscrutable expression, Amaryllis ran a hand over the stubby remains of one horn. It had been shorn free by Nalamae during their battle in Sharakhai's northern harbor. The other was still intact. Bumpy and ridged, it curved up and around Goezhen's great head, one half of a ram's crown.

"What of the fears of the Sharakhani Kings?" Amaryllis asked. "They say the gateway could destroy the city."

"That's the Kings sowing seeds of doubt," Meryam replied as she sat on an overstuffed pillow. "They hope those seeds take root and force Queen Alansal to listen to their demands."

After the city had been taken, Kings Ihsan and Husamettín, the only two remaining of the original twelve, had sent Queen Alansal a message consisting of two parts. The first was an urgent warning that meddling with the glimmering gateway below the Sun Palace could result in the destruction of the city. The second was an offer to cease hostilities that together they might solve the mystery that plagued Sharakhai, namely how to safely close the gate. It was an invitation that, so far, at least, Queen Alansal seemed disinclined to accept.

Amaryllis sat on another pillow and took up a piece of driftwood from one of the nearby piles. "What if they're right?"

"They aren't."

"But what if they are?"

Meryam looked up at her. "They aren't."

Amaryllis forced a smile. "Of course, my queen."

As Amaryllis used a magnifying glass to inspect the driftwood, Meryam couldn't help but think that Amaryllis might one day turn on her, as both Ramahd and Basilio had done, but she refused to dwell on it. If she couldn't trust Amaryllis, she could trust no one. Instead, she focused on the piles of oddments before her. They'd spent days searching through them all, and they were far from done. So far, they'd identified a dozen that were linked to Ashael and to the pit in the desert that Adzin referred to as the Hollow.

A hundred more still needed deciphering and categorizing. They had to take care not to overlook clues. Doing so could lead to failure, either in trying to raise Ashael or in controlling him once raised.

Meryam took up a bent awl with dark stains on it. Using a magnifying glass, she read the words along the rounded end of the wooden handle.

The ifin are attracted to silver, as many demons are, but they are particularly attracted to coins. If one hopes the ifins will do one's bidding, a steeping of the coin in the fate of the supplicant is necessary. There was no explanation of how one might "steep" a coin in the fate of the supplicant.

Setting the awl on the pile of items with no link to Ashael, Meryam took up another, the spiral tip of a narwhal tusk. Along one curving trench was more of Adzin's script: *Ivory is the key to the wakeful mind.*

It was part of a longer passage from the Al'Ambra. *Ivory is the key to the wakeful mind, horn the key to dreaming.* It referenced the way the elder gods first entered the world. Some stepped through gates of ivory: the gods of perception, logic, and fact. Others came through gates of horn: the gods of dreaming, creativity, and ambition. *So they came,* read the Al'Ambra, *and so the living were made.*

She set the tusk on the same pile as the awl, then pinched the bridge of her nose. "Mighty Alu, his script is difficult to read."

Amaryllis nodded without looking up from the grisly string of fingernails she was inspecting. "At least he was neat."

They worked for several more hours and were nearing the last of the macabre curiosities when Amaryllis breathed, "By the gods . . ."

With a look of sheer wonder, she handed Meryam a hulking silver ring with a setting of what looked to be children's teeth. It's inner surface held an inscription: *A half day's sail from Sharakhai at twelve knots steady, on a bearing toward the setting sun at the autumnal equinox, will a plateau of rock be found. A short walk in the same direction delivers one to a circle of standing stones. The Hollow lies within.*

Meryam knew she should be pleased but could only stare at the ring with a feeling of numbness.

"I thought you'd be happy," Amaryllis said.

"I am, but . . ." Meryam took up another item from the pile. "Let's just finish."

Amaryllis paused, then took up a compass with what looked to be blood-stains on its glass face. "Very well."

They went through the last of the items, but it went precisely as Meryam feared.

"What's wrong, my queen?" she waved to the silver ring beside Meryam. "It's good news, is it not?"

"The location of the Hollow does us no good if we don't know how to control Ashael."

"We'll find it," she said, but her tone made it clear that she, too, thought it unlikely they could find a way to raise and control an elder god.

They spent hours going through every item again. The sunlight through the shutters shifted from port to starboard. The rays of light crawled up the wall and faded by the time they were done. As Meryam had feared, they discovered nothing new of value.

"Fetch me a lamp," Meryam said to her, "then get some rest."

"*You* should rest as well."

"I will." She waved toward the piles before her. "I only wish to look a few of them over again."

Amaryllis didn't look convinced, but she left anyway and returned with a lantern, a cup and ewer of water, a bowl of nuts and dried fruit to see Meryam through the night, and a shawl, which she lay around Meryam's shoulders. "May Alu shine his light on you."

She headed up the stairs, leaving Meryam alone with the two piles of curiosities: one pitifully small, with writings that shed light on where Ashael's body could be found and how Adzin had profited from it; the second stag-geringly large with notes on other magical minutiae, some practically useless, others tantalizingly powerful, all of which had no relevance Meryam could discern to the problem at hand.

After sipping some water and stuffing a handful of the dried fruit and nuts into her mouth, Meryam set to again, going through each item and consider-ing it in a dozen different ways before setting it aside. She tried the pile of relevant objects first, and felt comfortable that not only could she find the Hollow, she could perform many of the rituals Adzin described. None would help her with her true goal, however, so she moved on to the second pile.

The sounds of industry in the harbor faded, replaced by the sounds of revelry and music as sailors and work crews visited the oud parlors, the broth-els, the inns. Eventually that faded too, leaving Meryam feeling cold and alone. *As it should be,* she mused, *for what am I if not cold and alone?*

The sun was just rising as she came to the narwhal tusk once more. *Ivory is the key to the wakeful mind.*

She read it over and over again, considering Ashael, how long he'd been there, the state the elder gods might have left him in.

"He's dreaming," Meryam said to the empty hold.

Outside, the harbor was waking. A mule brayed. Mallets thudded rhyth-mically. A woman yawned, an exaggerated sound that was followed by tired laughter and muted conversation. Meryam, meanwhile, stood. She held the tusk before her, her mind running wild.

"What is it?" Amaryllis stood at the foot of the stairs holding two steam-ing mugs of jasmine tea. Her eyes were dark, her curly hair wild.

Meryam held the tusk toward her. "Ashael is dreaming."

Amaryllis blinked. "And?"

"And we have to wake him." She went up the stairs, and fetched both hers and Amaryllis's chadors. After wrapping hers around her head, she handed the other to Amaryllis, who accepted it with a confused look.

"Where are we going?" she asked.

Meryam was already rushing along the passageway, then heading up to deck. "To the bazaar."

"For what?" Amaryllis called behind her.

"Ivory, Amaryllis, from the eldest creatures we can find."

Chapter 11

IN A SUBTERRANEAN room deep below the collegia, Davud sat before a table. He was reading a book on the parliamentary system of Quang-Li, a country far to the east of the Shangazi Desert.

Quang-Li was little more than a few interconnected valleys but was famous for its long and unusually stable history. For well over half a millennium, Quang-Li had remained untouched by foreign invaders, hidden away as it was by a range of unassailable mountains. But its stability was attributable to much more than a mere lack of foreign invasion. Quang-Li was ruled by demarchy, a system in which citizens were given seats in the ruling government through sortition, or random selection. It had proven remarkably durable.

"Interesting," Davud said to Willem, who sat on the opposite side of the table.

Willem had a curly mop of brown hair and striking brown eyes. His nose was buried in a philosophy tome. He lifted his head and gave Davud a circumspect look. "Interesting," he said with exaggerated slowness, "and . . . ?"

Willem was only a few years older than Davud, but he always seemed much older. At a young age, Willem had been enslaved to a blood mage, an evil man who'd handed him over to Nebahat, another mage who'd been just as cruel. Both men had taken advantage of Willem's ability to read quickly and to recall what he read almost perfectly.

Nebahat was dead, slain in a terrible battle between several blood magi. It felt strange to be using his hidden lair, but Willem grew anxious anywhere outside the collegia grounds. And while Davud could have arranged for rooms in the teachers' dormitories, doing so would expose them to too many people. Plus, Nebahat's lair was conveniently filled with hundreds of rare books, books that had been helping Davud in his many pursuits since the Mireans had swept into the city two months earlier.

It also had easy access to the rest of the collegia's libraries. All Davud had to do was mention a subject, no matter how obscure, and Willem would rattle off a series of titles, a summary of the books' contents, and would even fetch them if Davud wanted. It made Davud uncomfortable to use Willem in the exact same manner as the men who'd enslaved him, but Willem believed wholeheartedly in their quest to find a new path forward for Sharakhai, for the desert—indeed, for *all* the Five Kingdoms. He was free to go but had *chosen* to stay.

Davud waved to the book on Quang-Li. "Demarchy seems to work for them, but I don't know that a lottery could ever work here."

"Oh, I don't know," Willem countered. "I think you'd be surprised what people could get used to."

He was alluding to his own enslavement—Willem had endured much and managed to come through it with a kind heart—but that hardly meant the people of Sharakhai were ready for such a seismic change in the way their world worked. Davud was about tell him as much when Esmeray and Meiying swept into the room.

"We've got trouble." Esmeray, her hair bound in a rust-colored scarf, looked more worried than Davud had seen her in a while.

Meiying, a young but unusually powerful blood mage, approached the table. She wore a bright yellow silk dress cut in the Mirean style. Her long straight hair fell down along her back. "You're aware I've been following the Kestrels' movements?"

The Kestrels were elite swordswomen, highly trained in the arts of war, spycraft, subterfuge, and assassination. They were led by the Crone, a woman who'd once reported to Zeheb the Whisper King, but since his death in Mazandir had taken orders from King Husamettín. "I seem to recall you saying that, yes," Davud said.

"Well, Husamettín just ordered them to assassinate Queen Alansal's water dancers."

"He *what*?"

Meiying nodded. "He hopes to rob Alansal of her ability to predict his movements. The mission is to be carried out tonight. The new Crone, Shohreh, has decided to see to it personally."

After the crystal shattered, Davud had formally joined the Enclave, the fellowship of blood magi who had operated from the shadows for centuries. He'd effectively become part of their inner circle as well. While no formal vote had been taken, Meiying had vouched for him. She was the only member left alive after the intense battle below the Sun Palace that had led to the crystal's shattering. With so few magi who could command the sort of power Davud or Meiying could, they'd ceded authority to the two of them, at least until the question of Sharakhai's survival had been answered.

"You're certain about this?" Davud asked.

"Have you ever known me to share knowledge when I'm not entirely sure?"

"No," Davud admitted. "It's just, there's a lot riding on it."

"I understand," Meiying said. "We all want something from Queen Alansal. But this leaves us with a choice. We could warn her about the threat to her water dancers, use it to get into her good graces."

"Or we could let them die," Esmeray said, "and remove her ability to predict what we, the Kings, or anyone might do."

Meiying and Esmeray were both realists and knew the price of war was dear. Willem, on the other hand, looked as if he were about to cry. His mouth opened and closed several times before he finally said, "You can't let them *die*."

Esmeray scoffed. "Do you know how many have died in *our* city because of the visions those dancers fed to their queen?" She turned to Davud. "Let her greatest weapon be taken from her. The last thing she'll worry about afterward is the cavern below the Sun Palace. We can use the chaos to find whatever we need."

Davud turned to Meiying. "And your advice?"

"It could work to our benefit either way"—she shrugged, seeming un-comfortable, a rarity for Meiying—"but I think Esmeray's right."

Davud was momentarily taken aback—Meiying was siding *against* the country of her birth. But her parents had emigrated from Mirea when she was only a babe. Sharakhai had long been her home.

He would normally begin weighing the possibilities, the repercussions he and others could expect from Queen Alansal, but just then all Davud could think about was the intense way Chow-Shian had stared at him as she asked whether he'd ever seen someone die.

Did you let it happen? she'd asked.

He'd answered that he had, thinking of Brama and Anila, thinking she was asking about the past. But now he wondered. Had she asked the question to gauge what he was going to do in the future? Had she seen her own death in the patterns formed by the falling water?

He realized he wasn't ready to make a decision. Not yet. He had to speak to Chow-Shian first.

"I'm going to Eventide," he said to the others.

"To do what?" Willem asked.

With gut-wrenching uncertainty, Davud replied, "I wish I knew."

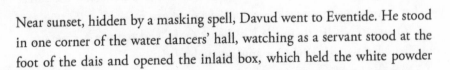

Near sunset, hidden by a masking spell, Davud went to Eventide. He stood in one corner of the water dancers' hall, watching as a servant stood at the foot of the dais and opened the inlaid box, which held the white powder know as zhenyang.

Braziers were spaced along the walls, warming the air and suffusing the space in an orange glow. All eleven water dancers lined up before the servant. Each took a pinch of zhenyang between thumb and forefinger and snorted it. When they'd all partaken, the servant left and the dancers proceeded to whirl and spin beneath the bamboo pipes. Water flew in dizzying patterns, thrown by the dancers. The water and the dancers combined into a single entity, a lively gyre of stretched limbs and water droplets that shone like carnelian under the braziers' low-burning light. It made Davud dreamy just to watch.

As arresting as it was, his attention often shifted to the dancers' eyes. They were intense. Far-seeing. He was particularly enchanted by Chow-Shian, with the dandelion eyes. He could be wrong, but she always seemed to be the first to change her step or pace, a lead the others soon followed.

At times one, two, even three at a time would stare into Davud's corner as if they'd pierced his spell of concealment. But never once did they stop, or slow their motions, or alert the guards to his presence.

An hour into the dance, a bell rang and the dancers came to a slow halt. After undressing near the braziers and drying themselves off, they donned fresh attire handed to them by waiting servants and retired to a small feasting hall. Food was laid out on a round table with pillows spaced around it. There were fried dumplings, pork buns, steamed vegetables, and noodles doused in a thin red sauce flecked with dark spices. Davud's mouth watered from the savory smells. The dancers sat and ate. They snorted more zhenyang, a ritual their lives apparently revolved around. They spoke in rapid Mirean while soldiers watched from the corners of the room.

Davud stood beside the fire, basking in the warmth as he tried and failed to understand what they were talking about. He knew the language, but they were speaking so quickly it was difficult to follow. Over time, he came to understand that they were talking about the visions the dance had granted them—trading their impressions as they digested it all.

Though there were many conversations taking place at once, they were more like a unified whole than a group of individuals. Several times, one dancer would make a comment that made the entire group stop and laugh. There were other times when they all stopped speaking at once. One would continue, the others listening, rapt, as if they'd set their own stories aside for what was clearly a dominant concern for them all. Then, as abruptly as the conversation had ceased, it would resume.

It was a whirlwind of sights and sounds, a scattering of tesserae which these women were somehow, improbably, trying to piece together.

Throughout the meal, Davud was on the lookout for signs of an infiltrator. The Kestrels' leader, Shohreh, was supposed to come tonight. Had her mission been delayed? Had she failed to reach Eventide? Had she been caught? It was certainly possible—Davud knew from experience that Alansal's defenses in and around Eventide were robust—but the Kestrels were legendary for good reason. If even a fraction of the stories told about them were true, they'd done many things that seemed impossible.

Then something strange happened. It started with a pause in the conversation. The water dancers froze, several with dumplings or noodles halfway to their mouths. Their arms lowered. Their gazes went distant. They were no longer staring *at* one another but *through* one another. A single word was spoken by Chow-Shian.

"Demon," she said in Mirean.

"Demon," echoed the others.

And then a name.

"Ashael."

"Ashael," repeated another.

"Ashael," they intoned in unison.

For nearly a minute they sat in silence, backs stiff, eyes wide, as if the tesserae they'd considered unrelated earlier were coming together, forming the mosaic of a grim, horrifying future.

They returned to their meal in silence, and when they were done they were led away to a large hall that had been converted into a communal residence. A great hearth held a blazing fire that pressed back the vault's ever-present cold. Men and women were brought in. Prostitutes, Davud quickly realized—some Mirean, others Sharakhani, Kundhuni, Malasani, or Qaimiri.

The water dancers stripped and lay with them, sometimes three, four, five at a time, moans of pleasure, of ecstasy, rising then falling then rising again. Davud was uncomfortable at first . . . but the longer it went on the more he wished he could join in.

All changed when an old Mirean woman entered with a tray of eleven glasses filled with mijiu, a potent alcohol distilled from rice.

By then the orgy had wound down. Their partners and the servants left. Alone now, the water dancers donned robes, sat on pillows around a circular table, and handed the glasses of mijiu out until each of them held one.

It was in that moment—as it dawned on Davud how serious they were, how fey—that understanding came like a bright bolt of lightning. They *knew* the fate that awaited them. The mijiu was poisoned. *That* was how Shohreh planned to kill them, and this evening's feasting and pleasures had been their final goodbye.

But why? If they knew about the poison, why would they drink the wine? What vision of the future would convince them to take their own lives? And why had they spoken so strangely of demons and the elder god, Ashael? It must be related to the earth-shaking events of the recent past or those about to unfold, but that hardly explained such an irrevocable decision.

Davud had come to Eventide ready to decide their fate, but now it felt as if *his* fate were in *their* hands. It felt as if letting them die would doom Sharakhai itself. Even so, he felt frozen. The moment felt too big for him, as if any move he made would be the wrong one.

Chow-Shian slowly turned toward him and stared for so long it felt as if she were giving him permission to reveal himself. As he let the spell fall, her expression didn't change in the least.

"What did you see?" he asked her.

"An endless tunnel," she said dreamily. "I saw you leading me along it, our hands clasped." Chow-Shian touched her heart. Her eyes went distant. "It was the most beautiful thing."

"Chow-Shian, I don't understand."

With no small amount of effort, it seemed, she drew her attention back to him. "Once I'd passed through the tunnel, I saw you leading the snow queen through the gates of ivory, that together you may light the darkest day."

"The snow queen?" Davud asked. "Alansal?"

"Yes." Chow-Shian frowned. "Perhaps."

"What are the gates of ivory?"

"Zhenyang." She touched one finger to her nose. "Zhenyang is the key."

Before Davud could say more, the door opened and a guard peeked in.

His eyes went wide as he spied Davud. "Intruder!" he shouted in Mirean, then charged forward, drawing his sword as he came.

He managed no more than two long strides before the water dancers tipped their glasses back and drank their mijiu.

"No!" Davud cried, and lunged for Chow-Shian.

She'd downed half of hers before Davud managed to slap the glass away and spill the wine down the front of her silk robe. She reached for the glass as it rolled against the table and tried to drink more, but there *was* no more. On realizing it, she reached for another's glass, which still had a measure of liquid within it.

Davud snatched her wrists and held her tight. "Tell me what you saw!"

But she would say no more, and soon the guards had reached Davud. He'd just begun casting a spell when Queen Alansal herself swept into the room and threw something at him. It exploded in the air around him, a scintillant rain of light that confused him, made him dizzy. The spell he'd just begun to gather, to make himself invisible once more, was interrupted, but the power had to go somewhere. He barely managed to release it, which threw everything and everyone around him outward, away from him, the heart of the spell.

Davud grunted from the pain of the aborted spell. He was no newcomer to the casting of magic. He might still have managed to cast another spell and escape, but by then Alansal was there, one hand held high like vengeful goddess ready to strike him down. As her hand blurred toward his forehead, he noticed a flat jade stone, roughly the size of a grape, cupped within her palm . . .

The pain of it was chaotic and intense. It felt as if his skull had been pierced.

A moment later, the wild sight of Alansal's burning anger, the water dancers writhing on the floor, the opulent pillows and the round table topped by empty glasses, all went dark.

Chapter 12

IN DARKNESS, EMRE and Frail Lemi crouched near the edge of the tribes' vast fleet. In a clearing at the fleet's very heart, a great bonfire raged. Hundreds danced around it, driven by a rolling beat played by tanburs, rebabs, doudouks, and skin drums of every imaginable size.

Unlike his voyage the previous night with Çeda and Sümeya, Emre and Frail Lemi had sailed to the fleet alone. Emre had already managed to secure five votes from the shaikhs most closely allied with the thirteenth tribe. Aríz had agreed to get another from a shaikh who owed Tribe Kadri several favors. Emre needed only one more.

Though he knew the shaikh in question, he suspected she might be the most difficult of them all. "Everything rests on a knife's edge," he said absently.

Beside him, Frail Lemi drew his gaze from the revelry and stared at Emre soberly. "Time to go nudge it in the right direction, then."

Emre stood and brushed sand from the knees of his trousers. "May the fates will it."

"Sometimes we make our own fate, Emre." The surprisingly lucid comment was spoiled, somewhat, by the drinking motion Frail Lemi mimed immediately afterwards. "Don't forget the araq, okay?"

They'd run out days ago. Frail Lemi had made Emre promise to pinch a bottle of it on his way out. "I said I'd *try*."

"Well, try *hard*!"

Stifling a smile, Emre trudged across the sand, heading toward the ships marked with the sign of the Rushing Waters, Tribe Kenan's ships. As was true the night before, with so many wandering about, it wasn't difficult to fit in. He made sure to skirt the light of the fires, though. If he was seen and word of it reached Hamid, his mission would be over before it began.

Soon he reached a clearing where a group of Kenan elders sat on over-stuffed pillows around a low fire. The air was thick with the smell of tabbaq: old leather, moist earth, roasted almonds. A few of the elders were deep in conversation, but most seemed spellbound by the tale spinner, a handsome young man who was waxing on about Fatima the Untouchable. Shaikh Ney-lana lounged on a pile of pillows, watching the tale spinner with languid eyes while taking a long pull on a shisha pipe. The tale spinner had just reached the part where Fatima used an amethyst, one of the pieces of the fabled Sunset Stone, to hide her soul while the efrit she'd stolen it from scoured the desert looking for her.

Neylana blew out a long trail of smoke, then took up the glass of citrine liquor beside her, downed it, and held out the empty glass. As a woman with gold chains running from her left ear to a piercing in her nostril knelt and refilled Neylana's glass, Emre stepped close enough to be seen.

Neylana's eyes passed over him, then snapped back. The wrinkles around her mouth and eyes deepened as she frowned. Emre tilted his head toward the nearby pavilion, a request to speak. The nod she gave in return was ag-grieved, as if his very presence was a curse laid on her by a vengeful desert spirit. As he backed away from the fire, she stood unsteadily and smoothed the skirt of her crimson jalabiya. "Keep the fire warm for me."

Raised glasses all around. A bow from the handsome tale spinner.

She tottered toward Emre, her movements loosening up the longer she walked. "Around the back," she said without so much as looking at him. She continued toward the pavilion's entrance, where two sentries with spears pulled the flaps wide. "Out!" she called as she headed inside. The sound of people rushing from the tent followed.

By the time Emre reached the rear of the pavilion, the ties to one of the support poles were being undone and the canvas wall was lifting up. After a glance to make sure no one was watching, Emre dropped to the sand and rolled through the gap.

"You're a bloody fool for coming here," Neylana said in a soft voice.

Emre stood and brushed the sand from his clothes. "Tell me something I don't know."

The pavilion's interior was lit by several oil lamps made of colorful blown glass. Neylana motioned to a circle of carpets, and they sat.

"I know why you've come," Neylana began. Her eyelids were heavy from the tabbaq, but the set of her jaw and lips made it clear how wary she was, how defensive. "The thirteenth tribe is young, and already it's been turned upside down. I've no doubt you're here to drum up support for Çedamihn, but things have changed since you and I last spoke."

"Have they, really?" As he spoke, he ticked things off on his fingers. "Sharakhai is still threatened by her neighbors. The desert tribes have now allied, as we knew they would. Hamid remains a threat to both."

"It's revenge you've come for, then?"

"Justice, not revenge. But I come for deeper reasons besides."

"Oh?" Neylana's eyes blinked slowly. "Enlighten me."

"We're fighting for something that goes beyond tribes. Beyond cities in the desert." He motioned to the pavilion walls, toward the sounds of revelry. "Everything we know is threatened."

"You're being dramatic."

"You think so? I could tell you tales about the vault in Sharakhai. I could tell you about the crystal that shattered, having been fed the blood of the thirteenth tribe for centuries. I could tell you about the pair of brave souls who stepped through and even now prevent the gods from completing the plan they formed long before Beht Ihman. Hamid must pay for his crimes, but we look beyond that. We need access to the valley so Çeda can use the acacia. We need to inform the shaikhs about the *real* threats to the desert so that we can stop the plans of the gods."

"Are Malasan and Mirea not real threats?"

"They are. And both must be shown that the desert is not theirs to take. But what Hamid wants is slaughter. He'll kill us all if he gets the chance. He'll do the same to Sharakhai."

"The Kings had too much power."

"I don't disagree. The Kings wielded their power ruthlessly. But that doesn't mean I want to see Sharakhai burn. It doesn't mean I want to see her people starved and dying of thirst."

A strange transition overcame Neylana in the moments that followed. She'd always struck Emre as a rock, a woman who stuck to her convictions. He'd never thought he'd see her look ashamed. "Sharakhai has earned its fate," she said after a time.

"Those are Hamid's words."

"So what if they are?"

Emre took a deep breath. He was worried about pushing Neylana too hard. She might react badly, but he judged she *needed* pushing. She had to be shown the consequences of what she was considering. "I know what Hamid told you and the other shaikhs during your first council."

Neylana's jaw jutted. "Been speaking to Aríz, I see."

"Hamid plans to destroy the aqueduct," he continued, neither acknowledging nor denying the accusation. "He wants to tear down the reservoir walls and poison the wells that remain. He plans to harry Mirea and Malasan's supply lines and force them to retreat. He'll starve the city. With a dry winter coming, every man, woman, and child would be dead before spring."

Aríz had told Emre more. He'd said the hardline shaikhs stood beside Hamid. The others had been given two days to consider their decision, which gave Emre and Çeda only a very short time in which to turn things around.

"Aríz plans to deny Hamid's request," Emre explained. "Shaikh Dayan is inclined to do the same, but the others are pressuring him, saying they'll be considered the enemy should they withhold support for the coming assault. They were promised a thirteenth of the plunder if they agree: the riches of Sharakhai will be spread among the tribes while the city itself turns to dust."

The words lingered in the air between them. Outside the pavilion there were whistles as the storyteller finished his tale.

"I assume you were given the same ultimatum," Emre prodded.

"What if I was?"

"Countless thousands would perish. Beyond its base cruelty, you'd be succumbing to the gods' plan. You *can't* give in to Hamid's demands."

Neylana's crow's feet deepened as she frowned. "You don't understand how dire things have grown in the south. Our caravans are plundered by the Malasani and Kundhuni raiders. Our young have been taken by a disease we don't know how to fight. My physic tells me it passed through Malasan decades ago, and that the Malasani invasion has delivered it to *us*. I resisted the Alliance for a time, as you know, but that was before our mountain resting lands were struck by drought." The sheer desperation in her voice was palpable. "I need this. My *people* need this."

"No," Emre said flatly. "What Hamid is talking about is genocide. It will stain the honor of Tribe Kenan for a thousand generations."

"You would have us stand aside?"

"I would have you help us to save Sharakhai before it's too late!" Neylana opened her mouth to speak, but Emre talked over her. "I've seen the gateway with my own eyes, Shaikh Neylana. I've seen the dead come back to life. I've seen the souls depart the living. If you wish for a future for your people, for *all* the people of the desert, we must find another way."

"And how do I feed my people in the meantime?"

"Together," Emre said. "We do it together."

"What do you want from me, Emre Aykan'ava? State it plainly."

"I'm heading back into the desert tonight. Tomorrow, I will return with Çeda. She's going to demand a tribunal for Hamid to answer for his crimes. We need seven shaikhs to vote to authorize it."

Neylana nodded. "And how do you think you're to prove his crimes to the satisfaction of the tribunal?"

"Let *us* worry about that. What I need is your assurance that you'll vote for the tribunal to be convened."

Outside, music played. Just beyond the pavilion doors, a boy laughed, then screamed gleefully as he was chased over the sand.

"You have six votes," Neylana realized. "I'm the seventh."

"Yes."

She waved one arm, encompassing the empty pavilion. "I don't see Aríz beside you. I don't see Dayan. What makes you think you can convince me alone?"

"Because I've seen your heart." He rose from the pillows and stepped away, toward the gap where he'd snuck in. "I knew you would do the right thing in the end." He crouched down, ready to leave, but paused. "We're going to see this through. You, me, and all the rest. The desert will live to see a brighter day."

"I hope you're right, Emre Aykan'ava."

"You'll agree then? We have your vote?"

"I'll agree to the tribunal. The rest is up to you."

Emre smiled. "Be ready for us tomorrow."

With that he slipped back under the canvas and into the night. He didn't feel optimistic, precisely, but he no longer felt *pessimistic*. It was with that lighter mood that he headed toward a nearby schooner, ready to return to Frail Lemi. All thoughts of Neylana and the tribunal vanished, however, when he caught a glimpse of the bonfire. On the far side, sitting cross-legged on the sand, was Darius, Hamid's companion, his lover. Surely Hamid wouldn't be far.

Another heartbeat passed before Emre saw him. Hamid's husky frame loomed over Aríz as the two of them spoke. Aríz looked like he was trying his best to control his emotions. Hamid, on the other hand, was red-faced, angry. Likely he was trying to browbeat Aríz into agreeing to his demands. Emre could hardly think about the council, though, or Sharakhai's fate. Visions of Hamid throwing sand over him suddenly loomed within his mind. He heard the shovel's rhythmic crunch. The thump as the sand was thrown on top of him. He felt the terror of realizing he was being buried alive.

His heart pumped madly. His hands shook. He balled them into fists, trying and failing to calm himself. Nearby stood a weapons rack holding spears, shields, and unstrung bows. Quivers of arrows hung from hooks. He could take up one of the bows, put an arrow through Hamid's heart and slip into the night with no one the wiser.

Except he'd promised Çeda he wouldn't.

"Kill him," she'd said to Emre, "and he'll become a martyr."

Emre had been in a vengeful mood, fueled by too much araq. "Kill him," he'd replied, "and his allies will lose heart."

"No," Çeda said flatly. "This is a war of *ideas*. Those ideas will not be snuffed out by the edge of a blade or on the point of an arrow. Hamid's allies must led to see *reason*, not blind hatred."

A deep voice called out behind Emre. "Who are you, friend?"

Emre turned to find a tribesman with a long beard and a plethora of blue face tattoos standing near the pavilion he'd just left. Emre recognized him. He was one of the sentries who'd opened the pavilion flaps for Neylana.

"I asked you a question." The sentry stepped closer, his face hardening. "I heard you scurrying about like a dune mouse. Are you a spy, come to listen in on our shaikh?"

It was a relief he hadn't seen Emre sneaking out from the pavilion—the fewer who knew his purpose, the better—but the sentry was clearly not going to let this go.

"I'm no spy," Emre said while stepping back.

The sentry mirrored his movements. "Then why are you sneaking around Neylana's tent?"

With the danger of being recognized growing by the moment, Emre turned and walked faster toward open sand. "I'm no spy."

As the sentry's footsteps quickened, Emre ran. He was just passing the ship's stern, ready to sprint for the darkness, when a large figure rushed in from his left. He was certain it was the second sentry, but it wasn't. It was Frail Lemi.

In a blur of movement, Frail Lemi crashed his fist into the sentry's face. The man dropped like a tree and lay there unmoving. For a moment, Emre feared he was dead, but then, thank the gods for small favors, he saw the man's chest rising and falling with breath.

"I told you to wait," Emre hissed.

"I did." Frail Lemi shrugged. "Then I started to get worried."

That was when Emre saw what he was holding in his left hand. A bottle of araq. "Worried you weren't going to get any bloody araq, you mean."

With a wide grin that looked ghastly by the dim light of the bonfire, Frail Lemi held the bottle up. "Sometimes we make our own fate."

"Lemi . . ."

Frail Lemi popped the cork and took a swig. "Try it." He held the bottle out to Emre. "It's not half bad."

But Emre ignored the bottle. He turned instead and stalked toward the darkness. When Frail Lemi caught up to him and held the bottle out again, however, he realized the memories of being buried beneath the sand were still haunting him. He swiped the bottle and downed a healthy swallow.

Frail Lemi was right. It wasn't half bad. He took another swallow then handed the bottle back.

Lemi took it with a chuckle, and the two of them walked into the night.

Chapter 13

IN THE CAPTAIN's cabin of his king's capital ship, Ramahd sat beside the ghul, Fezek. King Hektor sat in a large, throne-like chair. Basilio Baijani, the pompous Qaimiri lord who'd once served as an advisor to Meryam but who now gave counsel to King Hektor, stood behind him, listening with only half an ear. Fezek was just finishing his tale of seeing Meryam's crew hauling Goezhen's rotting corpse onto a yacht before sailing away from Mazandir.

If Hektor seemed concerned by Fezek's story, Basilio seemed bored. He held an orange-scented kerchief to his nose, some small defense against the scent of Fezek's decay. Pulling the kerchief away momentarily, he asked, "How can our king be sure any of this is true?"

"Because I will vouch for Fezek," Ramahd replied. In truth, he wasn't all that surprised at Basilio's reaction. The courage he'd shown in betraying Meryam for the greater good of their country had long since vanished. "You know Meryam as well as any of us. Do you think it beyond her?"

"The question isn't whether Meryam would do it," Basilio countered, "but whether Tulathan truly came down and spoke to her. If all you and your"—the kerchief came and went like a startled firefinch—"*friend* have told us is true, she has no more ability to command magic than I do."

What could Ramahd say? "The fates work in strange ways."

"An elder god, though?" Hektor waved toward the desert. "Assuming Ashael remained in our world, and I'm not convinced he did, how could a woman like Meryam, powerless as you freely admit, hope to raise him?"

"I don't know, but you saw what happened with the crystal. You witnessed the vault's creation."

"What does that have to do with Ashael?"

"If everything Çeda and King Ihsan said is true—"

"*If,*" Basilio interjected.

Ramahd took a deep breath. "*If* it's true, and the gods must take care to meddle as little as possible in the affairs of mortals, then what better way to keep their distance than to manipulate a woman with a *deep* knowledge of the arcane?"

Basilio looked contemplative. "Let's allow the scenario to play out, shall we? Assuming the elder gods left Ashael behind, they did so for a reason. They didn't want an evil like that tainting their new world. The young gods must know this."

King Hektor, still holding Ramahd's gaze, tipped his head toward Basilio. "It does seem a rather foolhardy gambit, Ramahd. Why would they be so desperate?"

"Perhaps they fear the gateway will soon close. Perhaps they're convinced they *can't* pass to the land beyond on their own. Whatever the reason, the fact that they would use a long-buried evil, a being that stained the earth with every step he took—"

"Oh, that's a nice turn of phrase." A quill and ink at hand, Fezek began writing in his book.

Stifling his annoyance, Ramahd went on. "That they would use even Ashael proves they'll resort to anything to get their way."

"I say we let them!" Basilio said. "Who cares if the desert gods leave? What does it matter to Qaimir if they rouse an elder to do it? When it's done, the world will be rid of a being that, in your own words, stained the earth with every step he took."

"What Çeda and her friends uncovered—"

Basilio rolled his eyes. "My King, the trust he places in a traitor to her own land . . ."

Ramahd focused on King Hektor, if only to avoid wrapping his hands around Basilio's neck. "What Çeda and her friends uncovered was that the gods' passage would wreak untold devastation."

"Excellence," Basilio said, "these are presumptions from a poem that is four hundred years old."

Ramahd couldn't take it anymore. He stared straight into Basilio's round, red-cheeked face. "A poem that has provided untold insights into the Shara-khani Kings. A poem that led to their downfall. A poem that allowed the asirim to be freed. Its verses have yielded truth after truth."

"Granted, and yet, as you've admitted in the past, the Kings not only suppressed it, they planted *false* verses. How do we know this isn't another?"

"Because it feels true."

Basilio's condescending laugh filled the cabin. "It *feels* true. My King, are we to remain in this accursed land because Lord Amansir has had a *feeling*?"

Ramahd sat back down so that he was once again eye-to-eye with Hektor. "Your Excellence, Meryam is our responsibility. She has yet to pay for what she's done, both to our country and the desert. Let us go to the Hollow. Let us stop her. Let us bring her home to face justice. Meryam is a stain on our country's history. It's time we turn the page on it."

Fezek's cloudy eyes brightened. "Oh, that's good as well!"

"Fezek—" Ramahd snapped, then took a deep, calming breath. "Please, my King."

"Our soldiers, our *people*, are waiting to go home, Ramahd."

Ramahd sat there, stunned. Hektor was still a young man. Together they'd taken great risks to stop Meryam in Sharakhai. Since becoming king, however, he'd lost his sense of daring, always preferring the safer path. It was due in large part to Basilio, who for some reason Hektor had allowed to counsel him. Even so, Ramahd still hadn't expected words like these from Hektor's mouth.

"There is a *war* on, my King," Ramahd said.

"A war in which Qaimir no longer has a part."

"But it *does*. It must! The people of Sharakhai depend on it."

Basilio sniffed. "Let them take care of themselves."

"They can't. Not with Mirea occupying their city. Not with the Malasani hounding their royal navy across the desert."

Hektor licked his lips, clearly conflicted. When he glanced up at Basilio, however, his eyes hardened, which made Ramahd's gut sink like a stone. "I'm sorry, Ramahd. We're leaving. Our fleet is going home."

"Let me take my ship, at least. Let me see what Meryam is about and—"

"But it *isn't* your ship," Hektor said, his voice harder now. "It's mine, and I forbid you to use it. We will remain here until the last of our ships arrive, and then we'll set sail. All of us, including you. Do you understand, Lord Amansir?"

Ramahd steeled himself. "You are talking about genocide. About letting it happen."

"Don't you think you're being a bit dramatic?" Basilio asked.

Ramahd stared at him in disgust. "Did you learn nothing from your time as Meryam's advisor?"

It was Hektor, red in the face, who answered. "And what is *that* supposed to mean?"

"It means he's never been able to see beyond his own nose." He swung his gaze to Hektor, who straightened in his chair as if he felt threatened. "I'm going to my ship, my King. If you won't believe me, I'll go. I'll find the proof you need and bring it back to you."

He turned and left the cabin. After a pause, Fezek's heavy footsteps followed.

"Lord Amansir!" King Hektor called.

Ramahd kept walking.

"Lord Amansir!" He sounded angry now. Ramahd was taking the stairs up to the main deck by the time Hektor reached the cabin door. "Ramahd!"

Ramahd turned. Hektor's cheeks and forehead were red with anger, embarrassment, or both. Ramahd was certain he was about to be thrown in the brig. The longer the silence went on, however, the clearer it was that Hektor wasn't ready to take that step. Not yet.

"You're willing to go this far?" Hektor asked. "You're willing to risk your own lordship over this? Your land? Your own country?"

"I am."

"Your life?"

"Yes."

Behind Hektor, Basilio had puffed himself up like a pheasant preparing to take flight. "My King, you cannot—"

He fell silent when Hektor raised a hand. The flush faded from Hektor's cheeks as he sized Ramahd up. There was something in his eyes—respect, maybe even admiration—that revealed his answer before he opened his mouth.

"Take your ship, then, Lord Amansir. See what you can learn about our former queen."

"Your Excellence!" Basilio gasped.

But Hektor waved his concerns away. "Go," he said to Ramahd, "before I change my mind."

"Thank you," Ramahd said to him.

"I owed you a debt, Lord Amansir. It is now repaid." With that he closed the cabin door, leaving Ramahd feeling exposed and alone.

So be it, Ramahd thought, and left the king's ship with Fezek in tow.

Chapter 14

AVUD STOOD IN the room with bamboo pipes hanging from a vaulted ceiling. Around him, standing in a circle, were Queen Alansal's water dancers. Water fell from the pipes, the sound of it like the rattle of wind-blown leaves. The air was cool but not cold, which in the desert was a rare and wonderful thing. The water dancers smiled, telling him without words that he was loved.

Then everything changed.

The falling water gained a violet tinge. The smell turned acrid. It was poison, Davud knew, yet instead of running from it, the dancers spread their arms wide, threw their heads back, and opened their mouths wide.

The tainted water fell on their upturned faces, pattered against their tongues and into their open mouths. They screamed as the poison worked its way through their systems. They had just begun to crumple to their knees when Queen Alansal swept into the room, a demon in a red dress. One hand held high, she stormed toward Davud so swiftly he had no chance to stop her.

The palm of her hand came down and struck his forehead. A scream unfurled as the burning pain sunk deep beneath his skull. He tore at the flat, oval stone she'd held, only to find it sunken beneath his skin.

He tore his skin bloody trying to remove it, but the more flesh he cut, the deeper the stone went. The pain intensified, until it consumed him entirely.

Davud woke in a great lurch, gulping for air, his breath fogging in front of him. He was curled on his side, his hands clutched over his forehead. He was cold. Very cold. Fortunately he still had on the thick clothes he'd been wearing when he'd entered Eventide, or he might have frozen in his sleep. He rolled over on the tiny cot, and saw the sunlight filtering into the cell through the tiny hole cut high into one wall. His head ached, particularly his forehead, but thankfully it was nothing like the dream. Only a dull headache, the sort that came from too much drink and too little water.

When he touched his forehead, however, pain flared. He snatched his fingers away, remembering only then that Alansal really had slapped a stone against his forehead. Gods, it felt like he'd taken a flaming brand to the head. And the jade stone was still there, too, grafted to his skin.

With ever-so-gentle movements, he probed the stone and the surrounding flesh. The stone had a smooth surface with subtle ridges. Any pressure sparked an intense pain that was slow in fading. Even so, he tried to remove it with a sharp tug.

When he returned to consciousness some minutes later, the pain was spectacular. He didn't so much as consider touching the stone again. Part of him feared he'd never wake up if he did. Instead, he lay still and let the pain fade.

Eventually he was able to sit up. His head throbbed. It felt like one of the burly workmen in the rock quarry was taking a sledge hammer to it, and there was something more, he realized. He couldn't touch his magic. He had no sense of it at all. It had likely been hours since he'd fallen to Queen Alansal's assault. That was enough time for the blood he'd consumed to have faded beyond his being able to use it, but his sense of it shouldn't have faded altogether.

His ability to sense magic had been taken from him, he understood, by the strange stone in his forehead.

He sat on the edge of the cot a long while. The cold seeped into his skin. There came faint sounds from outside his cell, a ticking sound, perhaps from the gaoler's room. Moments later, his cell door clicked loudly and the door swung open.

By the gods. It was no gaoler who stood in the doorway, but Willem, holding a set of lock picks. For several heartbeats, Davud could only gape like a fish.

"How did you get in here?" he finally managed.

"Never mind," Willem whispered as he slipped into the room and closed the door. "I've come to—" The words died as Willem took in Davud's forehead. "Breath of the desert."

Worry marred Willem's pale features as he reached for the stone. Davud recoiled, fearing the pain it would bring on, and Willem snatched his hand back and stepped away. He became smaller, as he often did when he feared he'd erred. He seemed to be having a hard time even looking at Davud. Eventually, he said, "What has she *done* to you?"

"It's an artifact that prevents me from walking the red ways."

"Then let me remove it."

Willem had amazing abilities. He wasn't a mage, but when he concentrated, he could force spells to *slip* from him like water over oiled canvas. He could alter spells, too, by unraveling parts of them or reweaving them altogether. He was asking permission to remove the spell worked into the jade stone so that he could separate it from Davud's skin.

When Davud nodded, Willem held his hands near the stone. Davud felt a prickling sensation. It quickly grew into a pain that pierced through his skull.

"Stop!" he cried when the pain became too much.

Willem snatched his hands back and held them to his breast. "I'm sorry," he whispered. "I'm sorry, I'm sorry . . ."

"It's all right. It's just . . ." Davud's ears rang with the pain emanating from his forehead. "It hurts."

"I'll go slower." Willem's Adam's apple bobbed several times. "I'll find a way. I promise."

The ringing subsided. So, thank the fates, did the pain. Still, Davud waited several breaths before nodding for Willem to try again.

No sooner had Willem raised his hands than the clank of a door being opened reached his cell. It was probably the gaoler. He must have heard their conversation and was coming to investigate. He'd find Willem. They'd both be punished.

"Hurry," Davud said, "hide down the hall."

A heartbeat passed, then two, but Willem remained, terrified of leaving Davud alone.

Davud stabbed a finger at the open door. "Go!" he hissed.

Willem cringed, then burst into motion. Like a mudskipper heading toward deeper water, he flew from the room and retreated into the darkness.

As the footsteps grew louder, Davud closed the door as silently as he could manage. He placed one foot against it as a Mirean soldier with a scar across one eye came and unlocked the door. Had the man been the regular gaoler, he would likely have known how the locks felt when opening and closing them. He would have realized it was already open. As it was, he had no clue. He seemed more concerned about Davud.

"Back," he said in Sharakhan.

Davud stepped away. Only then did the soldier swing the door wide. He didn't enter, though. Instead, he stepped aside and bowed.

Behind him came Queen Alansal. "Leave us," she said as she swept into the cell.

The guard gave another bow, sent a wary look Davud's way, and retreated. As his footsteps faded, Davud noted that Queen Alansal held a jade stone in her right hand, apparently the twin to the one on Davud's forehead.

Alansal took a sharp breath. "My advisors say you deserve to lose your head over what happened."

Coupled with the intensity of her anger, the statement made it clear that many of the water dancers, perhaps all of them, had died from the poison they'd swallowed. "Did Chow-Shian survive?"

Alansal squeezed the stone in her hand, and the ache in Davud's head turned to agony. Pain spread outward from the gemstone until it felt as if a pickaxe had pierced his skull. His knees buckled from it, and his screams reverberated through the dungeon.

As quickly as the pain had come, it vanished.

"I'll ask the questions," Alansal snapped when Davud's moans had subsided. The skirt of her fur-lined dress flared as she paced his cell floor. "Are you aware that Chow-Shian is my granddaughter?"

"I wasn't, no."

"Before slipping into a coma, she tried to convince me it wasn't you who poisoned them."

"I didn't."

Queen Alansal's expression grew harder by the moment. "Then why you were you there?"

Davud wasn't sure how much to reveal. If he told Alansal the truth, he would also need to confess what he knew about the Kings' involvement.

Alansal suddenly stopped pacing. With an expression of pure fury, she squeezed her right hand again, and the pain returned with a vengeance. Davud fell to one knee with his hands pressed to the sides of his head. The pain subsided a moment later, though it took several long breaths before he could lift his head and regard Queen Alansal.

"Tell me why you were there"—she held up the jade stone for him to see—"or I'll squeeze until your heart stops."

"I'd learned of the Kings plan to poison them, but I didn't know how. I went to find out."

"Why go yourself? Why didn't you warn me instead?"

Long moments passed in which Davud debated on what to say. He could hardly tell her the truth. He might have found some acceptable white lie, but it was so hard to think.

For a moment, Alansal looked angry enough to fulfill her promise, but then an eerie calm settled over her and she lowered the stone. "You came because you hadn't decided whether to let it happen."

"I did by the end, though. I tried to *save* Chow-Shian."

"But not the others."

"They were all so accepting of it. I didn't understand until it was too late."

For a time, Alansal simply breathed, her nostrils flaring as she did so. "And the poisoning itself, who ordered it?"

"The Kings."

"*Which* Kings?"

Davud might have told her Husamettín had ordered it. He might have identified the Kestrel, Shohreh, who'd been tasked with infiltrating Eventide to perform the deed. But the truth was he didn't wish to tell Alansal any more than he had to. "I don't know."

"Then how did you learn of it?"

"An informant," he said simply.

"Did the Enclave play a part in it?"

"No."

She resumed her pacing, reminding Davud of a caged snow leopard he'd once seen in the bazaar. "Tell me what Chow-Shian said to you."

"She said she saw me leading her down an endless tunnel. I think she meant I would help her reach the land beyond. Then she said I would lead you through the gates of ivory."

She stopped and snapped at him, "That's *nonsense!*"

Davud's mind was muddled, but he understood that Alansal had heard those words before. "Chow-Shian told you the same thing, didn't she?"

"You think I would believe that Chow-Shian *saw* the others die and let it happen? Why would she do that? Why would any of them?"

"I don't know, but I think I understand what she meant about using her. If she's in a coma, she stands between life and death. I could use her to examine the gateway. I could—"

"You would *use* her?" Alansal held the jade stone as if she were going to punish him for the very thought, then she slowly lowered it. "I want you to *heal* her."

"I'm no healer," he said.

"Be that as it may, you will try."

In that moment, he realized they were no longer alone. Willem stood in the doorway. His cheeks and nose were red. He was shaking. He looked struck dumb with fear and worry. And there was a knife in his hand.

Queen Alansal hadn't noticed him. If Davud didn't do something, Willem was going to stick the knife in her back. Part of him was willing to let Willem do it, but if Alansal died, Davud would lose any chance he had of studying the gateway. He wanted, he *needed* Alansal's approval. He would only abandon his cause if she gave him no choice.

"Don't," he said, staring straight at Willem.

Such was Alansal's intensity that it took her a long breath before she realized he wasn't talking to her. She spun, saw Willem, and took a step back while reaching for something at her belt.

"No!" Davud cried, but he couldn't reach her in time.

She threw down a small glass sphere, which broke at Willem's feet.

"Willem!"

Willem's slender form was lit in green flame. It didn't appear to be touching his skin, though. Not a single hair on his head was singed. His clothes didn't blacken or burn. He *slid* through the magical flames as if he were made of so much glass. And the look on his face . . . It was murderous.

"Willem, stop!" Davud cried. "Both of you, stop!"

Willem, thank the gods, obeyed. Alansal dropped the jade stone she'd been holding, which fell to the floor and skittered away. She gripped her steel hairpins and held them like a pair of fighting knives, but made no move to use them.

"Chow-Shian spoke of demons," Davud said quickly, before either she or Willem could change their minds. "She and the others spoke of the elder god, Ashael. What they saw and *why* they saw it, I have no idea, but I'm certain it's linked to Sharakhai's fate. I'm certain it's linked to their decision to take the poison."

Alansal pulled her gaze from Willem long enough to stare Davud straight in the eye. "If that were true, Chow-Shian would have told me."

"Not if she feared it would endanger you. Or your people, or Mirea itself. The end of this grand tale is nearing, Your Excellence. Whatever the desert gods had in mind when they bargained with the Kings on Beht Ihman is about to come to fruition. You need look no further than the gate, or the shimmering vault that hangs above us. Both are proof that the gods still don't have what they want."

"Passage to the farther fields," Alansal said.

"Yes," Davud replied. "They see it as a right that was denied to them. But how do they plan to reach it? *That* is the question that plagues us. Grand fleets have amassed in the desert. The Sharakhani Kings have lost their houses and fled, making them all the more desperate to take it back. The gods toy with us, maneuvering the pieces on the board. And if that weren't enough, there is evidence that demons will arise. Ashael may walk the earth once more." He took a step toward her. "We must learn what they mean to do before it's too late."

"A task made all the more difficult without my water dancers."

"Which means the burden falls to *us*." Davud waved to Willem. "Let us help you. Let us help to find the answers to these riddles."

Alansal's gaze flitted from Davud to Willem and back. "You will do as I command." She spat the words, as if she expected Davud to be cowed by them.

Being careful to avoid the jade stone, Davud touched his forehead. "I will do nothing as a slave."

Alansal was not simply powerful, she was someone around whom the gears of the world turned. But just then she looked lost.

"Please," Davud said, "remove the stone. Then you and I can visit Chow-Shian together."

With practiced ease, Alansal wrapped her hair around her wrist, formed a bun, and stuck it through with the two pins. With slow, deliberate movements, she reached down and picked up the fallen jade stone. Holding it to her lips, she breathed a sharp puff of air onto it, and just like that, the larger stone on his head fell away. Davud caught it and stared at it in wonder for a moment, then handed it to Alansal.

"Come. I fear Chow-Shian has little time." She swept from the room. "And the Kings are owed a measure of justice."

Chapter 15

ERYAM STOOD AMIDSHIPS on *The Gray Gull*, staring at the horizon, hoping to spot a particular rise of rock. From the ridges of snaking dunes, the gusting wind threw spindrift skyward in long, swirling plumes. The scene looked like an artist had run out of blues and greens to paint a windswept sea and had decided to render it in amber and ochre instead.

Including the captain, her crew numbered eight. They were patriots, one and all, committed to Meryam's cause. They'd proven so time and time again, protecting her from King Hektor's spies in the city, and yet Meryam found herself relieved that they were out in the desert, alone, where the opportunity to betray her to Queen Alansal or the Sharakhani Kings was nonexistent.

The *Gull* crested the next dune, the bow dipped, and Meryam's stomach lurched—one beat of the miserable rhythm that had plagued them for hours. The ramshackle sloop creaked so badly Meryam wondered if it would hold together long enough to reach their destination. She rued her decision to take the *Gull* and not the yacht they'd procured in Mazandir, but the chances of missing some crucial note from Adzin had been too high. Most of his cryptic notes had been penned on the oddments he'd collected, but she couldn't be sure there was nothing else hidden away on the ship.

"A half-day's sail," Amaryllis said miserably. She was leaning against the gunwales, one hand pressed against her gut. "We've been fucking sailing the whole fucking day already."

Amaryllis looked as miserable as Meryam felt. Even her crew—seasoned sandsmen and sandswomen, all—looked green around the gills.

"The note said twelve knots steady," Meryam said. "We're hardly scratching six."

Amaryllis steadied herself as they took another dune. "I just want it to be over." She retched a moment later.

"Bloody gods"—Meryam waved to the gunwales—"there's no shame in it."

Amaryllis shook her head, the back of one hand to her mouth. "I'll be fine."

Moments later they took one of the worst dips yet, and it became too much for Amaryllis. She turned, leaned over the gunwales, and loosed the contents of her stomach over the ship's side. Seeing it brought on a wave of nausea so strong Meryam nearly told the captain to slow their pace. But that risked their coming to a complete halt as the ship failed to crest the high dunes. They'd need to sail the gutters then, and who knew how far that would take them from their path?

Perhaps sensing her thoughts, the captain, a barrel-chested man with surprisingly spindly legs, said, "The wind should calm soon, my queen." He lifted one knobby finger and pointed off the port bow. "See there? It's looking clearer already."

One hand pressed to her stomach, Meryam nodded, and allowed the ship to sail on. Despite the captain's prediction, the wind didn't ease. She was about to call for a halt, delays be damned, when the watchman called, "Reef ahead!"

"Mighty Alu be praised," Amaryllis breathed.

Meryam saw it a moment later: a spill of ink along the horizon. Blessedly, the wind *did* lessen and the dunes smoothed out. As they sailed closer, the dark ink transformed into a collection of rocky fingers and rounded knuckles jutting up from the sand. They lowered their speed and navigated the sandy reef for another hour before the watchman called again.

"Land, ho!"

The relief was palpable as they dropped anchor near an impassable plateau of rock. In the distance stood a circle of standing stones.

"Remain here," Meryam said to the captain, then turned to Amaryllis. "Bring the chest."

"We don't even know if this is the right place yet."

"The standing stones, Amaryllis. The smell of brimstone. They tell you everything you need to know."

"Very well," Amaryllis said, clearly disappointed, "but we've only just arrived."

"I've waited a lifetime for this." Meryam headed down the gangplank. "Bring the chest."

Upon reaching the hot sand, Meryam headed onto the rocky plateau. Amaryllis joined her, bearing a small wooden chest.

"Can you feel it, Amaryllis?"

"Feel what?"

Meryam waved to the tall stones, the source of her unease. It felt like they were being watched—as if creatures, dark spies, watched over Ashael's resting place, peering from behind the stones. The feeling became so strong Meryam's mouth went dry. Years ago, she would have had little fear of such things. She would have called upon her own power. No longer.

"We could call the men," Amaryllis said.

Meryam steeled herself and stepped forward. "We have no need of *men*, dear Amaryllis."

For a moment Amaryllis looked as if she wanted to argue, but she held her tongue and followed Meryam toward the tall stones. The scent of brimstone and rot grew stronger. They passed through the circle of stones, where a deep pit was revealed.

Amaryllis set the chest down beside it and held the back of one hand to her nose. "Mighty Alu but the smell is foul."

Meryam crouched and threw the lid of the chest back to reveal eight leather bags. Each was filled with a powder ground from some form of ivory, everything she'd been able to find in the bazaar: mammoth tusks from the frozen wastes beyond Mirea, warthogs from the hills of Malasan, walruses from the southern shores of Qaimir, elephants and hippopotamuses from the distant plains of Kundhun. She'd even found a pair of elk molars, their provenance unknown, and killer whale teeth, delivered from the Austral Sea. The prize, however, was the complete narwhal tusk she'd found, late in their search, in a small shop just off the Trough. There was a certain poetry in stumbling across it, having found Adzin's script on a similar tusk.

Meryam took up the bag with the narwhal ivory powder first. For some reason it felt heavier than it should. Her hands were shaking so badly she gripped them tight lest Amaryllis notice.

Amaryllis noticed anyway. "We can take our time, my queen. We have weeks of provisions aboard."

"Fear not." Holding the bag, Meryam took more, tentative, steps toward the pit's edge. "Today is only a small test."

They'd agreed on the way that they would use the powder to awaken Ashael. When he'd gained consciousness, she would give him her offering: Goezhen. For surely that was the reason Tulathan had given Meryam her brother god's corpse. Ashael would need to be given a sense of Meryam's desires, a thing that would, she dearly hoped, give *him* purpose.

Meryam tugged the mouth of the bag open and took a pinch of the powder from within. Holding it to her nose, she drew in a sharp breath. The desert wind blew. Amaryllis waited, wary of any small change in perception.

Little happened at first, but then the world seemed to sharpen. The outlines of the stones grew radiant, chromatic, an effect made intense, even dizzying, as Meryam moved her head from side to side. Amaryllis became so bright, so disorienting, it forced Meryam to shut her eyes.

Meryam felt herself tipping. "Mighty Alu," she breathed.

"My queen!" Amaryllis was suddenly there, gripping her arm and leading her away from the pit's edge.

It took long moments for Meryam's dizziness to pass. When it did, she opened her eyes. The bizarre effect was still present, but manageable now.

She patted Amaryllis's hand. "Thank you. I am well."

Amaryllis released her arm, but stood ready to act again. Meryam, meanwhile, took a healthy pinch of the powder and tossed it into the pit. It shimmered white in the afternoon sunlight, a drape of bright silk over the onyx rock before her. The wind carried some away but most drifted down, swallowed moments later by the pit's great, open maw.

Moments passed. Then minutes. And there was nothing. Nothing whatsoever.

"Another form of ivory, perhaps," Amaryllis said.

"Be quiet."

The pit's mouth rippled with vibrant colors. *Come, Ashael. Awaken. Open your eyes and witness the world you helped to forge.*

The incessant wind began to die, the sun lowered in the sky, and still Meryam watched.

"My queen—"

"I said be *quiet!*"

Meryam had seen something below. A swirl of color in the gloom. It came again a moment later. She heard the sound of wings flapping. It was faint at first but grew ever stronger. The smear of color reappeared and resolved into a winged figure. Then came another, and another. Soon there were a dozen, a score, a hundred. They lifted up from the darkness, lit by the setting sun. They were small, black creatures. Each was the size of a falcon, but they were featherless, with leathery skin and two sets of bat-like wings.

They were ifin. Meryam recognized their description from Adzin's curiosities. More than a dozen of his messages had mentioned the creatures—how to find them, how to attract them, how to control them. *Give an ifin a scent,* Adzin had written, *and it will follow it to its source, be it a thing lost, a person gone missing, or even a destiny.*

They flew up and around Meryam. They circled her like buzzards. What their presence might mean she had no idea. Perhaps they'd been affected by the ivory dust and had come to investigate. Perhaps Meryam's presence at the pit's mouth had made them curious. Or perhaps they rose from the pit every sunset. Whatever the case, she pondered how she might make use of them. She might have them search for Ashael below. She might have *them* wake him.

She'd just begun to ponder that when Amaryllis's voice broke through her haze.

"My queen?"

Meryam glanced over and saw her staring down into the pit. Another winged creature, large as a man, was flying up from the depths. A pair of broad wings bore it into the sky. It had dark skin like the ifin, but was more humanoid, with two arms and two legs. Where its eyes should have been was a ridged hollow in its skull. Its nose was two slits. Its thin lips pulled back, revealing rows of long, razor sharp teeth.

In one hand it bore a trident of dark iron. Pointing the weapon at Meryam, it opened its jaws wide and shrieked. The shriek became a maddening caterwaul that went on and on. It was like a nest of rattlewings, a cacophony of mismatched doudouks playing all at once. It made Meryam's skin itch. Made her vision swim.

"My queen, step back from the edge!"

But Meryam was rooted to the spot, beholden to the circling ifin and the demon hovering in the air before her.

As the demon's smile widened, the drone rose in pitch and Meryam's eyelids fluttered closed. She felt herself being swept away. She saw herself standing in the desert. She was surrounded by stone and a sea of endless dunes. On the stone around her were hundreds upon hundreds of bodies, all dead, all bloody. They were arrayed in formation—a sigil, she realized, formed by the one whose dream Meryam was now being shown.

It's Ashael's. I'm seeing his dream.

The sigil seemed familiar. She searched her memories for its meaning, but was startled by the appearance of a goddess floating in the air before her. Her name was Annam, and she was tall and beautiful. Another appeared beside her: Iri, he of lissome form and skin of midnight sky. Golden Bellu came next, then scintillant Treü and quizzical Raamajit. One after another they came to the plain of stone and stared at the sigil of dead bodies.

Their disturbed looks turned to disapproval. One lifted an accusatory finger. A second followed. Soon all were pointing at Ashael, all save Iri, who held a misshapen spike of ebon steel in one hand, a blindingly white bandage in the other. In silent concert, Annam and Treü held his arms, and Bellu and Raamajit gripped his sweeping horns, the four of them holding him in place. Iri stepped forth and wrapped the bandage around Ashael's head, covering his eyes, then drove the spike into Ashael's chest, piercing his heart. As his screams shook the heavens, they forced him down, through the stone and earth they had all, including Ashael, made together. Ashael fought them, but he was blinded, the cloth fixed to his skin, and the steel spike crippled him.

How his rage burned. He vowed that he would one day break from his prison. He would return to the surface, and then they would pay. *All* the elders would all pay.

Then Ashael felt their smugness and understood their intent. They were leaving. As they had for millennia beyond count, they were preparing to depart this world for the next, but this time, they would leave *him* behind.

He railed against them. He tore at the earth. He tried to bring the heavens down on them. But they were too strong, and he was soon lost to the darkness.

Meryam was suddenly returned to the desert. She felt wings beating against her arms, her sides. Felt them fluttering against her bound hair. She was staring down into the pit. The large, eyeless demon, only a few paces away, beat its wings while smiling perversely.

She heard Amaryllis scream, but the sound was faint, dreamlike. "Help!" she shouted. "We're attacked!"

From the corner of her eye, Meryam saw the ifin swarming Amaryllis. Gods, there were so many of them. And Meryam was doing nothing to help her because, in that moment, she didn't care what became of Amaryllis. She wanted to descend. She wanted to meet Ashael. She would witness his greatness before she died.

Suddenly there were more figures around her, roaring, fighting, using clubs and swords to swing at the ifin—her crew, coming to save their queen.

"My queen, you must wake!"

Amaryllis was suddenly there. She had Meryam by the arms and was shaking her roughly. The look on her face was one of abject fear.

In the end, it wasn't Amaryllis who woke Meryam, but the demon. It swooped onto Ernesto, a kind, paunchy fellow with red hair and sad eyes. Ernesto swung his sword, to no effect, then shouted in surprise as the demon used its trident to stab the next closest crewman through the leg.

Meryam rushed toward Ernesto, hoping to fend the demon off, but the demon had already wrapped its wiry limbs around the flame-haired crewman. The demon beat its wings, lifting Ernesto and carrying him over the pit's mouth.

It sunk its teeth onto Ernesto's neck as it flew, and he screamed, the sound crazed, manic. The sounds of his pain faded as the demon stopped flapping and the two dropped like a pair of commingled stones. As their outline shrank, then faded altogether, the cloud of ifin burst outward. They followed the larger demon down, their screeches fading until it was gone and they too were lost from sight.

In the silence that followed, everyone stared at Meryam. All wore the same expression, one that asked a very simple question: If they'd already lost one of their number, and Ashael hadn't even awoken yet, what would become of them once he did?

Chapter 16

QUEEN ALANSAL LED Davud and Willem up from Eventide's dungeon. When they reached the palace proper, Davud sent Willem to tell Esmeray everything that had happened.

Davud continued with Alansal to the infirmary, where the lone surviving water dancer, Chow-Shian, Alansal's own granddaughter, lay unconscious. Her black hair was messy as an old broom. Her bedding was rumpled. Leather straps held her wrists and ankles in place. Combined with the ashen hue of her skin, it painted a dire picture.

An old woman with pepper gray hair wrapped into a tight bun was sitting by Chow-Shian's bedside. Chow-Shian's thick woolen shirt was open. The woman, a physic, surely, rubbed scented oil over her chest. On seeing her queen's approach, she quickly finished her work and tugged Chow-Shian's shirt back into place.

"Why is she restrained?" Davud asked as he reached the foot of Chow-Shian's bed.

"She thrashes," Alansal replied, "violently, sometimes. Lost in her visions, we think."

As if she'd heard, Chow-Shian's eyes suddenly shot open. Her golden eyes took in her queen with a crazed expression. "He stirs!" she screamed while railing against her bonds. "Ashael awakens!"

Davud knelt by her bedside and tried to take her hand, but it only made her thrash harder.

"Please," Davud said in Mirean, "tell me what you saw."

Her eyes locked on Davud's. "Flee! You must flee the desert!"

"Don't you remember? We need to stop Ashael, but we don't know how."

Chow-Shian's expression turned to one of disgust. "He is an *elder*. There *is* no stopping him."

Davud shook his head. "You said I would help you to reach the land beyond. You said we'd walk hand in hand."

"The land beyond . . ." Chow-Shian's eyes went distant, as if the memory were but a spark she hoped to fan into a flame.

"You said I would lead the snow queen through the gates of ivory that together we may light the darkest day."

Chow-Shian blinked. "Zhenyang."

Davud nodded encouragingly. "Yes."

A terrible coughing fit overtook her. She tried to curl up, but the restraints held her in place. After a spoonful of some thick syrup from the physic, Chow-Shian's fit slowly passed. When it was done, she looked spent but seemed calmer. "Use me," she said. Her voice was weak, her eyes heavy. "Use me to reach the land beyond."

With that she collapsed back onto the mattress.

For long moments, Queen Alansal was unreadable. "Can you do it?" she asked Davud. "Can you use her to close the gate?"

"I'll need the help of my friend, Esmeray—"

"Granted."

"—and even then, I don't know if we'll succeed. But I'm willing to try."

For long moments Alansal stared at Chow-Shian, but then she took in a sudden, noisy breath. "Then try we shall, Davud Mahzun'ava."

In less than the turn of an hourglass, Queen Alansal was leading Davud and Esmeray into the cavern below the Sun Palace. Behind them were the old physic and a cohort of soldiers, two of whom were bearing Chow-Shian on a stretcher. The cavern had completely changed from the root-filled space Davud remembered. Only a handful of the roots now remained.

"They shriveled and dried," Alansal told them. "A few days later, the dead ones fell from the walls and ceiling. I had them cleared away."

The few that remained wound their way in from the tunnels, up the walls, and connected with one another until they formed one lone tendril that hung down from the cavern's roof. The crystal was gone, but the tendril remained, a drop of clear liquid falling from it every so often to land with a soft *pat* on the stone below.

From that spot, where the crystal had once stood, a piercing column of light shot upward. It was bright enough that it lit the entire, vast cavern, though not so brightly as the crystal in the moments before its shattering. A fog fell from the column of light and spread outward along the uneven floor, collecting here and there in pools.

Davud stared at the cavern's roof, where the column of light tapered slightly. "Does it emerge above? Can it be seen in the Sun Palace?"

Alansal's brow furrowed. "The cavern doesn't lie directly below the Sun Palace."

"From the slopes of Tauriyat, then?"

She shrugged. "Not that I'm aware."

"Have scouts search the mountain at night for signs of it."

Alansal nodded to a soldier, who bowed his head in turn. "I'll see to it myself, my Queen."

Chow-Shian roused again as she was laid carefully on the cavern floor a few paces from the light. The golden irises of her eyes shone as she stared upward.

Davud knelt beside her. The cold was intense so close to the gateway. His skin prickled from it—or perhaps it was from the gateway's nature, a doorway to another world. Above them, sheets of light broke away from the central column. They would drift like leaves caught in an updraft, then fade away or recombine with the main body.

"Are they souls?" Esmeray asked as she knelt beside him.

"I imagine so," Davud said as he took Chow-Shian's wrist. "Esmeray will ground us," he said to Chow-Shian in Mirean. "You and I will enter the gateway together, but we won't go far. Today we go to *learn*, not to *do*, all right?"

Chow-Shian nodded, and Davud pierced her skin with his blooding ring.

He drank from the wound, quickly closed it off, then repeated the ritual with Esmeray.

Since the crystal's shattering, souls near the gateway could easily separate from their mortal shells, becoming wights. He suspected Chow-Shian was on the verge of doing just that. With his arcane senses, he saw her soul glowing from within, while her physical self seemed more like a chrysalis she might shed at any time.

Esmeray drew a sigil in the air before her, the sign for *anchor*, over which she laid *corpus*. Davud drew a more complex sigil that combined *soul, pursue, gateway*, and *reveal*. Using the energy derived from Chow-Shian's and Esmeray's blood, he allowed both spells to blossom. New senses were opened to him. He became aware of the soldiers, Esmeray, Queen Alansal, and especially Chow-Shian. Her soul was like a skein of wool with one spinning thread being drawn toward the land beyond. Davud followed it and entered a place of deep calm. His breathing, his heartbeat, slowed. He lost feeling in his fingers and toes. Soon he felt as if *he* were the one being drawn to the land beyond.

He blinked, and found himself standing before the souls of three others. One he recognized as Anila, his fellow collegia scholar, who'd gone to the farther fields to keep the gate open. He dearly wished he could speak to her but feared that doing so would take him too far—indeed, it felt as if speaking to *any* of them would risk giving himself over to the farther fields.

As he waited, hoping Anila would speak to him, the other two souls gained clarity. It came as no surprise that one was Brama, the witty and sometimes cruel street thief Davud had grown up with. The other one *did* surprise him. It was Rümayesh, the ehrekh who'd tricked the fates into allowing her entry into a place forbidden to all demonkind. Davud thought Brama would be freed from her after passing to the world beyond, but their souls, as they'd been in the mortal plane, seemed inextricably linked.

"Davud?" he heard a distant voice call.

It was Esmeray. She sounded worried. But somehow that didn't seem to matter. As fearful as he'd been only moments ago, he was becoming more and more convinced that speaking to Anila and Brama, perhaps even Rümayesh, was vitally important, for surely that was what Chow-Shian's visions had intended him to do.

"Davud!" Esmeray's voice sounded not just fearful, but panicked.

He ignored her and stepped closer. She didn't understand how close he was.

He felt himself being shaken a moment later. "Davud, come back! You're dying!"

Only then did it strike him how far he'd gone. He'd told Chow-Shian they were only going to explore, but he hadn't counted on how disorienting the experience would be. He was drifting away—from his own world, from the people he loved, from the problems that plagued his home and the desert beyond. Esmeray was right. If he didn't do something soon, he would die.

He turned away from Anila and the others and tried to use the thread of Chow-Shian's soul to pull himself back, but it was so thin . . . and then it was gone. He despaired. For Chow-Shian. For himself.

Then he felt something tighten. The anchor, the tether to Esmeray. It was holding him. He felt himself being drawn back toward the cavern, but Chow-Shian herself was nearly gone. Her former brightness had dimmed.

As quickly and precisely as he could manage, he combined the sigils of *soul* and *graft* and attached his own soul to Chow-Shian's. As he felt himself being whisked away, he wasn't at all certain the spell had worked. He lost sense of her as the rush of blood filled his ears. He felt his chest broaden with breath. He felt the ache of muscles clenched for too long.

When he opened his eyes, he saw the column of light stabbing upward. He turned his head to find Esmeray, blinking away tears as she held his hand. His fingers felt terribly cold. And his skin was a startling shade of blue.

Next to him, Alansal's old physic was bent over Chow-Shian, listening to her heart.

"Is she alive?" Davud asked weakly.

Long moments passed before a relieved look spread across the old physic's face. "She's returned to us, thank the small gods of Tsitsian."

Chapter 17

S INCE RETRIEVING THE Blue Journals, the *Miscreant* had sailed many days.

"Ships, ho!" Ihsan heard the lookout call from the deck above. "The Royal Fleet approaches!"

He sat at his desk in the captain's cabin, a journal laid open before him. Sunlight knifed through half-open shutters, casting bands of honey-colored light across the pages, while the *Miscreant* swayed rhythmically over a stretch of blessedly light dunes.

Nayyan lay in the nearby bunk, her eyes closed.

Ihsan spoke to her softly. "Did you hear the lookout?"

Nayyan shifted, finding a more comfortable position. "I heard."

Ihsan glanced at Ransaneh, swaddled in blankets beside Nayyan. Their child squirmed and smacked her lips, then fell back to sleep. "Thank the fates for small kindnesses," he mumbled.

Ransaneh had been suffering from colic. She'd hardly slept more than an hour at a time, which broke Ihsan's and Nayyan's sleep into interminable pieces. It grew so bad that Ihsan had offered to watch Ransaneh while Nayyan

slept on another ship, thinking they would take turns. But Nayyan had declined, fearful Ransaneh would pass in the night.

"*I* would be with her," Ihsan replied.

"I know, but"—she blinked languidly, the dark bags beneath her eyes
making Ihsan feel more tired than he already did—"I need to be by her side."

Ihsan didn't fault her for it. Mothers and nagging fears were often stalwart companions, particularly with their firstborns. Thankfully, the *Miscreant*'s rhythm had eased yesterday evening, allowing all three of them a
measure of deep, satisfying sleep.

Even as tired as he'd been, Ihsan's worries had woke him halfway through
the night. Ever since digging up the Blue Journals, he and Nayyan had
combed the entries and compared notes, identifying passages from Yusam's
visions that might shed light on the days ahead. The search hadn't been
fruitless, but it was hardly a treasure trove. Yusam saw far, but it wasn't uncommon for his visions to illuminate some alternate path of fate. It had led
to their setting most entries aside as irrelevant, either because they referred
to events that already happened or because it was clear they would *never*
come to pass.

Ihsan had lain awake for nearly an hour, trying to will himself back to
sleep. But the more he'd stared at the slats along the cabin's ceiling, the more
he felt the need to get back to the journals—a single clue could mean everything.

Giving up on sleep entirely, he returned to the desk and continued reading. In a red, leatherbound journal of his own, he had jotted down passages
that required further reflection. He returned to one of these as the ship's skis
sighed across the sand.

*In the desert shall five falcons meet. Two are real, three are pretenders. As
they sit around a candle flame, a ruby-throated raptor descends upon them. (In
the marginalia was written: a kestrel?) The raptor speaks, sharing a tale of how
it slew a flock of emerald-crested loons. Before the tale is complete, however, a
grinning demon invades, making straight for one of the falcons—the one with
the faltering call, the one who is meant to die. The falcon is saved by the ruby-
throated raptor, after which the falcon flies west over the city, making for a great
gathering of nests among the rocks, where it searches high and low for a heron.*

The passage had drawn Ihsan's interest because of the first of its symbols, the falcon, an ancient symbol for a tribal shaikh. In the early days of Shara-khai, well before Ihsan's time, the symbol was coopted as a sign of the Kings of Sharakhai. *Two are real, three are pretenders.* Ihsan was set to meet with King Husamettín in only a short while. It seemed likely that they were the two falcons. The other three likely alluded to the lesser Kings and Queens. Nayyan, one of the new guard, would be in attendance, which meant there would be two more. What the rest of the entry might mean, he wasn't sure.

On deck, Captain Inevra began calling orders, routing them toward the remains of Sharakhai's once-mighty fleet. Nayyan pushed herself off the bed. She was bleary-eyed, but less haggard than she had been.

Naked, she washed herself from head to toe with a clean cloth and water from a ewer. She looked over his shoulder while toweling her hair dry. "You would call *me* a pretender?"

She was referring to the phrase *two are real, three are pretenders*—not being one of the original Kings, Nayyan naturally fell in to the latter camp.

"Of course not." Ihsan closed his red journal with a thump. "But think of it from Yusam's perspective. Only your father was dead at the time. Yusam still felt, we all felt, that the Kings would rule over Sharakhai forever."

The smile she gave him as she pulled the dress over her head was un-steady. Her comment had been a quip, but behind it lay the nagging doubt that Ihsan didn't consider her a proper queen. "The heron is a sign of Qaimir, you know."

"Of certain houses, Lord Amansir's among them."

"It's a sign of royalty as well. Like the falcon in the desert, the heron was once used by the Kings of Qaimir."

The *Miscreant* began to slow. They could hear the sounds of the larger fleet: soldiers drilling to the sharp calls of officers, hammers pounding and saws rasping as work crews made repairs to ships.

Ihsan, meanwhile, sat before the Blue Journal, stunned. Nayyan was right. How could he have forgotten? The entry was from early in Yusam's reign, nearly four hundred years ago, when the Qaimiri kings used the heron. It made perfect sense that it might refer to the newly crowned King Hektor or, as Ihsan now suspected, the recently deposed Lady Meryam, a woman on the run from her accusers.

The story of her escape from Amansir's custody in Mazandir was most strange. She'd clearly had help, which was not strange in and of itself. A fallen queen would still have plenty of allies. But he was concerned that, shortly after she'd escaped, Goezhen's corpse had gone missing.

The desert gods were to blame, Ihsan was sure. They continued to play their games. They'd likely arranged for Meryam's escape and then for her to take Goezhen's body. The question was why? And what had they asked Meryam to do with it in return for her freedom?

Soon they dropped anchor, and Ihsan and Nayyan received a captain of the Silver Spears who updated them on a few skirmishes with the Malasani fleet, and on general news of Sharakhai. Soon after, as the sun was setting, Ihsan found himself seated across a fire from Husamettín. Like a meeting of two shaikhs a thousand years earlier, they sat in a trough between dunes. Beyond them, barely visible in the light of the fire and the stars above, stood a circle of twelve tall galleons. More were anchored beyond—over a hundred warships, the remains of the royal navy, once the mightiest force in the desert, now considerably weakened by the war with Mirea and Malasan.

In addition to the navy proper, they had re-tooled fifty ships to caravan supplies, to scout, and to raid enemy lines. All were outfitted with battle-hardened soldiers. It was not an overwhelming force, but neither was it one that could be dismissed out of hand.

All is not yet lost in the desert, Ihsan mused—though one would hardly know it from the grim look on Husamettín's face as he poked the fire with an iron. The King of Swords was often the last to arrive at such meetings, not from rudeness, but because he kept himself so busy. The sheer focus he gave to his work often made him seem unapproachable, but just then it seemed as if Husamettín welcomed Ihsan's company.

"I'll admit," he said while shifting one glowing log onto another, "sometimes it feels like the others are still out there in the desert, and that one day they'll come and sit across the fire from me."

Ihsan knew precisely what he meant. He'd felt the very same thing. However difficult it might have been to imagine only a few short years ago, the twelve original Kings were now down to two. "Our road has wound in peculiar ways."

Husamettín seemed to be staring *through* the fire. "We should have foreseen more of it."

"That's one way of looking at it."

Husamettín lifted his head. "You have another way?"

Ihsan shrugged. "Perhaps we should count ourselves lucky that our reign lasted as long as it did."

"Lucky?" He practically spat the word.

"We ruled the desert for centuries, my good King."

"We rule the desert still!"

Ihsan waved to the carpets around the fire, the galleons encircling them. "You call this *ruling*?"

"I call it a temporary withdrawal."

Though he knew how a prideful man like Husamettín would take it, Ihsan couldn't help it. He laughed. "I've never known you to be such an optimist."

"Perhaps you don't know me as well as you thought. I've always been clear-eyed about you, though. I always knew you would betray us."

Ihsan shrugged. "Betrayal is such a harsh word. I was looking out for my best interests, as were we all, in our own ways."

"Yes, well, *my* interests are still with Sharakhai." He stabbed the iron into the fire, sending embers skyward. "Mark my words, Ihsan. The city will be ours again, then you and I will have our reckoning."

Ihsan was saved from responding when Nayyan entered the circle of light. She stopped immediately. "What's wrong?"

Husamettín sat in stony silence.

"Nothing to worry about." Ihsan patted the space on the carpet beside him. "A brief discussion of the straits we're in, which was bound to stir up a raft of emotions."

Nayyan didn't seemed convinced it was as simple as that, but she took her place next to Ihsan just the same. Soon King Alaşan, the son of Külaşan the Wandering King, joined them. Next came Queen Sunay, the daughter of Sukru the Reaping King.

Five falcons, Ihsan mused.

Queen Sunay, who'd inherited her father's vulpine looks, opened with a report of her dealings in Sharakhai. She'd been working with several militant groups, people loyal to the Sharakhani Kings. With their help, she'd orchestrated a series of attacks against Queen Alansal's forces. "We've been thwarted at every turn," Sunay said with disgust. "Alansal's soldiers root us out. She's slain many. More have been taken to the camps inside the House of Kings, *our* camps, for questioning. We've been unable to loosen her grip over Sharakhai. Quite the opposite, in fact. In the weeks since her forces stormed the city, she's managed to cement her command over the House of Kings, the temple district, and the Fertile Fields."

The young, charismatic Alaşan flicked some sand from the carpet before him. "It's her water dancers."

"Well of *course* it is," Sunay shot back. "The question is what we're going to do about it."

Husamettín motioned to a woman in a battle dress standing beyond the light of the fire behind him. "I have some fortunate news to share."

As the woman approached, Ihsan realized she wasn't a Blade Maiden, as he'd first assumed, but a Kestrel in a red dress. Instead of greeting the gathered Kings and Queens, she was staring at Ihsan. She looked familiar, but Ihsan couldn't place her.

"Meet Shohreh, our new Crone," Husamettín said.

With that name, the reason behind the Kestrel's stare became abundantly clear. Shohreh was the very Kestrel who'd subdued him in Zeheb's palace those many months ago, the one who'd chased Çeda and her allies through Eventide and down the mountainside, the one Ihsan had ordered slain by the Silver Spears with the power of his voice.

Ihsan raised his cup in a pale imitation of the salutes and nods the others were giving her. "Pray tell, what happened to your predecessor, Ulaan?"

Shohreh's eyes were locked on his mouth as he spoke. She was deaf, her ears put out so she would be immune to Ihsan's commands. "She was found dead in the Shallows several weeks ago."

Now this is news, Ihsan thought. "A random stabbing?"

Shohreh gave away nothing beyond a clear lack of concern about Ulaan's death. "Apparently."

There was more to the story, Ihsan was sure. He would once have vowed to look into it, to make plans to neutralize the threat Shohreh represented. But there was too much else to worry about. He had more than enough threats to deal with. Shohreh would simply have to wait her turn.

"Tell them," Husamettín said, making sure to face Shohreh as he did so.

"Last night, I infiltrated Eventide's kitchen and poisoned the water dancers' wine. All are dead save one, Alansal's own granddaughter. She stands on the very doorway to the farther fields and likely won't recover, and even if she does, there are no other dancers to perform the ritual with. We have effectively cut Alansal off from her prophecies."

"She'll just summon more from Mirea," Queen Sunay said with a frown.

"Water dancers," Ihsan jumped in, "are a rarer breed than you might imagine. There are some few in Mirea, but none as gifted as those who journeyed to Sharakhai. And without the others to train them, they may *never* become as gifted."

"It presents us with an opportunity." Husamettín waved Shohreh to stand down. As she bowed and stepped away from the fire, Husamettín took them all in anew. "With Alansal blinded, we must press the attack on the Malasani fleet. Once they've been neutered, we can begin the siege on the city."

"Besieging our own city," King Alaşan scoffed. "Who would have thought to see the day?"

"We'll begin with a series of riots," Husamettín said, "to see how prepared they are to handle civil unrest. If they react as I think they will, a second wave will be even larger and bloodier. It will allow us to—"

He was interrupted by a strange trumpeting sound from the edge of the camp. Another followed, louder and closer than the first. A bluish-green light reflected off the hulls of several distant ships. It came again moments later from another location. There were shouts of alarm, crisp orders were given.

Husamettín stood and drew Night's Kiss, his two-handed shamshir. "Everyone, to arms!"

The dark shamshir buzzed as it moved, the sound like a swarm of rattlewings. The blade seemed to devour the firelight. It looked like a piece of the firmament itself, fallen and forged for the King of Swords himself to wield.

As Nayyan drew her own sword, a burst of aquamarine flame washed against the hull of a nearby ship. The crackle and whoosh of the fire were followed by screams of pain, shouts from soldiers for their squads to retreat.

A rhythmic, thumping sound grew. Something was galloping toward them.

"Protect the Kings!" someone bellowed.

A moment later, a mounted soldier in lacquered armor and a grinning demon mask rounded the prow of a galleon. He had bow and arrow at the ready, his fingers already laid across the string, and he rode a qirin, a tall, four-legged creature with two coiled horns jutting back from its forehead. Its head, chest, and clawed forelegs were those of a dragon with red, iridescent scales, while its back end was that of an ivory-colored horse. Its eyes were alight and turquoise flames issued from its nostrils. Burning blue oil dripped between its sharp teeth, painting a bright, dotted line as it pounded over the sand.

Ihsan didn't understand everything that was happening, but he knew this much: Queen Alansal's forces had arrived to avenge the loss of their queen's greatest treasure. "Halt!" he shouted, putting power into that one word.

The qirin's charge continued, and the rider, heedless of Ihsan's command, drew his bow and released. The arrow streaked in toward Ihsan's chest, only to be blocked by the Kestrel, Shohreh, with a swift raise of her buckler.

"Halt!" Ihsan yelled again.

But the warrior kept coming. He loosed three more arrows in quick succession.

Shohreh managed to block the first, which had been flying toward Nayyan. Husamettín, sprinting toward the mounted warrior, ducked the second arrow. The third struck King Alaşan dead in the chest.

Alaşan stumbled backward, one hand gripping the arrow shaft. His breath whooshed from his lungs as he struck the sand, and he lay there, motionless, his breath shallow, eyes staring disbelieving into the star-filled sky.

Husamettín continued his charge.

"Hup hup!" called the qirin warrior, and the qirin released a blast of blue fire toward Husamettín.

But Husamettín was ready. He dodged, then ducked the stream of flames as the qirin adjusted its aim. Then he rolled forward as the warrior with the grinning mask released another arrow.

Husamettín grunted as it clipped his right shoulder.

The warrior reined his qirin over, perhaps hoping to guide it away and regain proper distance. He realized his mistake a moment later. Husamettín was already close, and was swift as a hungry jackal. For a moment Ihsan saw the eyes behind the mask, and they were wide with fear.

In a blinding move, the warrior dropped his bow and drew his straight, double edged dao. But Husamettín was already bringing Night's Kiss down in a powerful blow. Shadows trailing behind it, the sword buzzed mightily and severed the qirin's neck clean from its body.

Oil gushed from the severed ends and lit with a whoosh as it touched the nearby flames. As the qirin collapsed and a cobalt fire lit along its thrashing remains, the warrior leapt free.

The man was clearly well trained. He traded blows with Husamettín for many long seconds. But in the end, he stood no chance. After a wild parry that made a ringing sound the entire camp could hear, he bit on a feint from Husamettín. Night's Kiss fairly growled as it cut deep into the warrior's side.

As he collapsed in a heap, the sounds of the greater battle began to fade, and a Blade Maiden rushed into the clearing. "They're retreating," the Maiden reported. "It began shortly after we engaged."

"It was a diversion," Husamettín said as he regarded the dying qirin warrior. "Chase them. We need one of them alive."

"Yes, Your Excellence."

Husamettín strode to where King Alaşan lay on the sand. Queen Sunay was already there. Nayyan and Ihsan joined them. Alaşan, still breathing, stared up at Husamettín, then Ihsan, with a confused expression. He looked like he wanted to speak but did no more than choke on red froth.

Husamettín, Ihsan, and Nayyan shared looks. The fabled draughts created by the late King Azad, Nayyan's father, were gone. The three of them had some of the new elixirs created by Nayyan, but Ihsan wasn't about to bring that up. Until they could regain control of the city and gather the ingredients and equipment needed to make more, their supply was limited. Husamettín, apparently of a similar mind, remained silent.

Nayyan, meanwhile, stared down at Alaşan with an unreadable expression. There was pity in her eyes, but something more as well, a thing Ihsan could only describe as deep-seated worry.

Alaşan went still and his eyes turned glassy.

Queen Sunay, now glaring at Ihsan, flung a hand toward the dead qirin warrior. "Why didn't your bloody command work?"

Ihsan couldn't admit how unstable his power had become, so he shrugged. "It's going to be difficult to find out now, but if I had to guess I would say that Queen Alansal was well aware I might be here. She likely had the warrior's ears put out"—he waved toward Shohreh—"as our good Kestrel did on Zeheb's orders."

Sunay seemed none too pleased with that answer but spoke no more of it. She spat on the qirin warrior, then turned and stalked toward her ship.

Shohreh, meanwhile, was staring at Alaşan's unmoving form with a haunted, almost angry expression. "His aim was true," she said while turning toward Ihsan. "It's fortunate I was there to save you." With that, she spun on her heels and strode away into the darkness.

As Alaşan was placed on a sleigh and Husamettín went to see about the fleeing qirin warriors, Ihsan and Nayyan retired to the *Miscreant*.

"Would your power have worked if he *could* hear?" Nayyan asked Ihsan when the two of them were alone with Ransaneh.

His first instinct was to lie, to assuage her fears by telling her his power was still intact, but one glance at Ransaneh made Ihsan rethink it. It felt like a betrayal to lie in front of his daughter.

"I don't know," he said truthfully.

Nayyan cradled Ransaneh in her arms, stared into their baby's mismatched eyes. "The dream of us ruling the city together was once so bright." She lay in their bunk and curled around their child. "Now I wonder if we'll live to see our daughter become a woman."

Ihsan disrobed and lay across from her while Ransaneh squirmed between them. He reached out and stroked Nayyan's hair. "Why so grim?"

A tear slipped along one cheek. She quickly wiped it away. "The falcon is saved by the ruby-throated raptor," she said, "after which the falcon flies west over the city, making for a great gathering of nests among the rocks, where it searches high and low for a heron."

She was quoting the journal entry Ihsan had been reading before their arrival. In the excitement, he'd forgotten all about it, but of course it was true: it had all just happened, all but the final part. *He* was the falcon who'd been saved by the kestrel. The vision foretold him going west to search for the heron.

"It's the western harbor," he said in a stunned voice. "That's where we'll find Meryam's trail."

Nayyan nodded and closed her eyes.

Nayyan's bleak state of mind was concerning, but he let her be and closed his eyes as well. They needed rest, that was all. Tomorrow was a new day. If they could make progress on their quest to find and stop Meryam, Nayyan would see that all was not lost.

Chapter 18

ÇEDA, EMRE, AND Shal'alara of the Three Blades stood side by side as Aríz, the handsome young shaikh of Tribe Kadri, stepped down the gangplank of his caravel, *Autumn Rose*. His thawb and turban were dyed the color of autumn leaves. Behind Aríz came Ali-Budrek, his prickly, barrel-chested vizir.

Aríz stopped a few paces short of Çeda and raised his hands, displaying the orange tattoos on his palms, a sign of peace and welcoming. "Well met."

Çeda displayed her palms as well. "Well met."

Aríz turned to Shal'alara. Earnest grins spread across their faces as the two clasped forearms. When Aríz turned to face Emre, his smile broadened. Emre, smiling as well, embraced him. As the two of them thumped one another's backs, Çeda suddenly found herself on the outside looking in. Aríz, Emre, and Shal'alara had been through much together over the past few years. Shal'alara had been a legend in the desert for longer than Çeda had been alive, and Emre might only have been sailing the desert a short while, but he'd blossomed in that time, becoming the man he'd only pretended to be in Sharakhai. And while Çeda had met Aríz only a handful of times, she could see how his confidence had grown since he'd become shaikh. He was *filling out his thawb,* as they said in the desert.

Suddenly Frail Lemi was barreling toward them. "Fancy little shaikh with his fancy little clothes!" He proceeded to pick Aríz up, throw him over one shoulder, and spin him around.

Ali-Budrek waved his hands and shouted for Frail Lemi to put Aríz down, but Aríz only laughed. "How long are you going to keep doing that?"

Frail Lemi dropped him unceremoniously to the sand and steadied him. "Until I grow too old"—he patted Aríz's belly—"or you grow too fat, like your vizir."

Ali-Budrek glowered. "Exaltedness, need I remind you how unbecoming it is for a shaikh to be hoisted like a sack of grain?"

Aríz raised a hand, silencing him, then clapped Frail Lemi's bulging arms. "Been lifting ships again, I see."

Frail Lemi squeezed Aríz's biceps daintily, as if he were afraid of breaking them. "I see you haven't. We'll fix that, though, young falcon. We'll fix it sure."

The two embraced properly, then Aríz turned to Çeda and Emre. "You've caused quite a stir in the desert."

"Well, that's hardly *our* fault," Çeda said.

Aríz feigned surprise. "Are you saying you *didn't* attack Shaikh Zaghran on his way to the valley?"

"*He* attacked *us,*" Çeda replied evenly.

"He knows," Emre said. "I told him."

"That may be true," Aríz said, "but Zaghran, or more accurately his wife, Tanzi, has been telling *their* version of the story to any who'll listen. By now been it's been passed around every campfire."

Çeda had known it would be so the moment they left Zaghran's ships behind, but there'd been no helping it. They'd needed to delay so Emre could gather the support they needed and get a lay of the land. Go any sooner and they risked failure—Hamid had had weeks to prepare for their arrival, after all.

"Please tell me you've come with our seventh vote," Çeda said.

Aríz nodded. "It took three frigates and a pair of our finest akhalas to convince Shaikh Valtim of Tribe Ebros, but yes, you have it."

Çeda didn't know what to say at first. That Aríz would do this for her made her heart swell. "Thank you," she said, holding her arm out.

Aríz accepted it and the two shook much as he and Shal'alara had done a short while ago. Then Çeda pulled him in for a tight hug.

"Thank you," she repeated softly in his ear.

Aríz came away with cheeks blushing. "It was nothing."

They set sail immediately after and arrived at the massive bay below Mount Arasal near midday. As the *Amaranth*, *Red Bride*, and *Storm's Eye* sailed in and dropped anchor, thousands stopped what they were doing and watched. Çeda felt the weight of their stares as she, Aríz, Emre, Shal'alara, and Sümeya headed along the winding path leading up the mountains. Behind them came Jenise and twenty of her Shieldwives, each wearing wheat-colored turbans and battle dresses.

By the time they reached the valley with its old stone fort, the sun was lowering in the west. The scorching heat of the desert was replaced with a pleasantly warm breeze. The surrounding peaks were tall and imposing, the slopes green, a welcome sight after weeks of sailing the endless amber sea.

As in the bay, many in the valley stopped what they were doing and stared. Ignoring them, Aríz led Çeda and the rest to a striped pavilion, where the council of tribes was taking place. As Aríz headed inside to announce their arrival, Çeda tried to calm her nerves. Little helped save the sight of the tall acacia beyond the pavilion. The colored glass hanging from the acacia's branches by thread of gold shimmered in the late afternoon light, dreamlike. It was a soothing reminder of Nalamae.

"More beautiful than ever, is it not?" came a hoary voice.

Çeda turned to see her great-grandmother, Leorah, tottering toward the pavilion with a staff in hand for support. Çeda felt a pang of sympathy on seeing how painful walking seemed to be for her. Then she noticed the staff itself. It was tall and charred, as if someone had tried to burn it. Bits of darkened crystal were worked into the head.

"That's Nalamae's staff," Çeda said.

"*Was* her staff." Leorah's proud smile revealed several missing teeth. "She gave it up. Now it's mine."

Çeda waved to the fort on the slope above them. "But I *saw* it. It was burning in the courtyard."

"A goddess bore this staff for many long years." Leorah patted the staff's gnarled head. The massive amethyst on her right hand glimmered as she did so. "It doesn't burn so easily."

Çeda smiled. She was glad it had been saved. Its burning had seemed a tragedy at the time.

Before she could say more, the pavilion's flaps parted and Aríz stepped outside. "Shall we?"

After a deep breath, Çeda entered with him. Emre gave his arm to Leorah and followed. Shal'alara and Sümeya brought up the rear.

"The sun shines on our meeting," said Shaikh Dayan of Tribe Halarijan, a bejeweled man in a stunning green khalat. He had a curling mustache, a trimmed, pointed beard, and a pleasant smile. "Please," he said, motioning to the gap in the large circle of men and women.

Çeda sat on the pillows. Emre took the space beside her, while Shal'alara, Leorah, and Sümeya sat behind them.

Two dozen others sat on similar pillows. Hamid was directly across from them. Rasime—a lithe woman, especially compared to Hamid's husky frame—sat by his side. Shaikh Zaghran and Tanzi, both with scowls on their faces, sat to Hamid's left. Çeda recognized the others only through descriptions Emre had given her. The style of dress, the colors, the patterns in the cloth, all varied widely. Some had jewelry around their necks and wrists. Others wore pins and brooches on their khalats, dresses, or turbans. Others had no jewelry at all, having chosen more staid garb. Most had tattoos on their faces, and the sheer variety was impressive. Some had simple designs to either side of their eyes or over the bridge of their noses; others had covered nearly every part of their face in blue or orange ink.

Shaikh Dayan spread his arms wide. "We understand you've come to ask for a tribunal to be convened."

"I have."

"To adjudicate a grievance against one of our own."

"Not *a* grievance," Çeda said, "but many."

"Who is the accused?"

"Hamid Malahin'ava." She purposefully left off the name of their tribe, Khiyanat, an indication she considered him an outsider, a pretender. And the jab worked. Hamid's eyes flared with anger.

"Your claim?" Dayan continued.

Çeda stared directly into Hamid's cold, half-lidded eyes. "That he tried to murder one of his own tribesman, Emre Aykana'ava. That he fled justice, leaving a duel to the death unfinished. That he betrayed his tribe, murdering more than a dozen in Mazandir during a parley with Queen Meryam. That he willingly gave our shaikh, Macide Ishaq'ava, to the Qaimiri queen so that she could use him in a ritual do destroy the thirteenth tribe."

Each claim saw the flush in Hamid's face deepen. "Lies!" he shouted. "All lies!"

Dayan raised his hand. "We agreed this was neither the time to argue nor present evidence."

"*You* agreed that," Hamid said. "*I* am the shaikh of Tribe Khiyanat, and I acted to protect the tribe from Macide and Çeda and their betrayal of all we stand for."

Dayan's pleasant face turned severe. "No trial has begun. Are you saying you wish it to begin now?"

"They treated with the Kings!"

"Enough!"

This came from Shaikh Zaghran, whose look was steely. Çeda hardly knew him—they had only spoken once, in the moments before his ships had attacked hers—but he seemed the sort who embraced convention, who would be easily angered at the brashness of a man like Hamid.

Shaikh Dayan settled himself like an amberlark preparing to nest. The entire assemblage seemed to give Zaghran a fair amount of respect, which Çeda noted with interest.

"Proceed, Dayan," Zaghran said at last.

Dayan tipped his head in deference, then regarded Çeda anew. "You are aware that two patrons are required before a vote can be taken."

"I am," she said, hoping she sounded confident.

"Who is your first?"

"I am." This came from Aríz.

Dayan cast an expectant gaze over the gathering. "Do we have a second?"

"Yes."

This came from the alluring Shaikh Elazad, a woman whose people,

Tribe Salmük, had suffered greatly under the rule of King Onur. When Onur fell to Çeda, Elazad herself had expressed her gratitude.

Hamid rolled his eyes, clearly struggling not to speak.

Shaikh Dayan, meanwhile, nodded. "We'll put it to a vote, then. Who wishes for the tribunal to be convened to take up this matter?"

Aríz, Dayan, and Elazad raised their hands immediately.

Çeda held her breath as the shaikh of Tribe Narazid, a portly man who reminded her of the rotund Malasani god, Ranrika, did so as well. Shaikh Neylana of Tribe Kenan raised her hand next, followed by the wrinkled, weatherworn shaikh of Tribe Rafik.

Moments passed in which no others raised their hands. She had six votes so far. The seventh, the man Aríz had promised so much to, was Valtim, the baby-faced shaikh of Tribe Ebros.

Oh gods, Çeda thought, *he's changed his mind.*

Valtim had worn a severe look when Çeda entered. Now he wouldn't even meet her eye.

Dayan frowned. "Are there no more?"

"You've called for a vote"—Hamid, a smug look on his face, spread his arms wide—"and now you have your answer."

It was Hamid, Çeda realized. Somehow he'd learned of their efforts. Through bribery or threats, he'd convinced Valtim to withhold his assent.

"Are there any others?" Dayan repeated, louder. "One more is needed for the tribunal to convene."

A long breath passed in silence. Hamid laughed and waved one hand to the assemblage. "Your answer lies before you."

Before Dayan could say another word, Çeda stood in a rush. "Are there none among you who will fight for justice?" She regarded those who'd abstained, letting her gaze fall on Shaikh Valtim last. He looked defensive, embarrassed. "Are there none among you brave enough to stand up to one of your own?"

"Enough." Hamid stood as well and stabbed a finger at her. "I move that Çeda and those on her ships be given to me for judgment."

"They came under the sign of truce," Aríz said.

"They came to sue for a tribunal and to slander me. It was a sham from the beginning, a gambit that failed miserably. They were granted peace only so long as their claims were upheld, and they haven't been."

Çeda only had seconds in which to act. She was tempted to appeal to Shaikh Valtim, but in the end decided whatever Hamid had promised him would be too much to overcome, especially as he'd already made his intentions clear. She let her gaze fall on Shaikh Zaghran, instead. "Are you afraid of the truth?"

"Sit down, you dog," said his wife, Tanzi.

Hamid took half a step forward, tried to intimidate her with his presence, but she refused to be cowed. She kept her eyes fixed on Zaghran while stabbing a finger at Hamid. "Are you afraid of *him*?"

"I said—" Tanzi began.

But she fell silent when Zaghran raised a wrinkled, sunspot-covered hand. "I'm not afraid of anything," he said evenly.

"Then support the tribunal," Çeda said.

Zaghran weighed her. "Why?"

"Because you're an astute man. Because you sense, as I do, that following Hamid's plans will lead to ruin for the desert tribes. Because if you don't learn the truth of it now, you'll regret it forever."

Tanzi levered herself to a stand and faced Çeda. "You are a traitor to your own people!"

She raised a quavering hand as if preparing to strike Çeda, but Zaghran snatched her opposite wrist and tugged her arm until she'd retaken her pillow. Only when Tanzi had settled herself, red-faced, did Zaghran speak.

"How can you convince us," he said evenly, "when it's your word against his?"

Çeda pointed to the canvas wall. She hadn't wanted to go down this road because the outcome was so uncertain, but there was no choice now. "Through the acacia."

The gathering seemed rattled by this.

"The acacia?" Zaghran repeated.

"Just so," Çeda said. "The tree grants visions. They're often visions of the future, but sometimes they're visions of the past."

Zaghran's bushy eyebrows pinched. His eyes grew dark. "What are you saying?"

"I'm saying the acacia can *show* you the truth of my words. All of you can see it for yourself."

Hamid's gaze swept over the entire assemblage. For one brief moment he seemed afraid. Then the look was gone, replaced by one of righteous indignation. "This is ridiculous. You can't let her—"

His words trailed off as Zaghran raised a hand to him. "The acacia can show us this?" he asked, focusing his attention on Çeda once more.

"Yes."

"Then prove it." He stood and took a step forward so that he and Çeda were face to face. "Prove it, and you have my vote."

"Very well—"

"But should you fail," he went on, "we will grant Hamid's request." He waved to Çeda, Emre, Shal'alara, and Sümeya. "You and your people will surrender to him for judgment, as is the right of any shaikh with the people of his own tribe."

"I will not bargain with the lives of others, but I willingly offer my own."

"It's all four or I withhold my consent."

Hamid looked smug. Çeda felt caught in a trap. They couldn't afford any delays—Sharakhai's fate depended on what happened in the valley—but she meant what she'd said. She wouldn't gamble with Emre's life, nor Shal'alara's nor Sümeya's.

Emre was suddenly by her side, his warm hand on her elbow. She turned to him, certain he was going to say it was time to leave, to find another way, but he didn't. He merely nodded, giving her his permission to accept. Behind him, Shala'ara did the same. Sümeya paused. In a way, this wasn't her fight, but then she nodded as well.

The very thought that they might pay for her failure with their lives was nearly enough to make Çeda decline. But they couldn't walk away now. She couldn't allow the Alliance to be subverted by Hamid. She had to trust in the powers of the tree, a thing created by the hand of Nalamae herself.

"Very well," she said to Zaghran. "Come with me."

Zaghran looked anxious, but he followed Çeda from the pavilion, as the others rose to trail after them. Soon the entire assemblage was headed over the grass toward the acacia.

Once they were gathered, Çeda motioned to the tree. "The tree grants visions—"

"To Nalamae," Zaghran said.

"To anyone who asks for them." Çeda recalled one of her first visits to Nalamae, who'd gone by the name of Saliah then. At the time, Çeda had thought her a desert witch, not a goddess in disguise. She'd been only a child, but Nalamae had bid her to summon a vision from the tree. "Come," Çeda said to Zaghran, using the same words Nalamae has used with her, "see if the acacia will speak to you."

Although curious moments ago, Zaghran now seemed unsure of himself. He'd no doubt heard the stories of Nalamae communing with the tree, collecting memories of her past incarnations. Heard how she'd pieced herself together bit by bit over the course of many long days.

"This is ridiculous," Tanzi said, and took her husband's arm in hopes of leading him away.

But Zaghran wouldn't be moved. He freed his arm from her, then stepped forward with an expression Çeda could only describe as wary reverence. Hands held before him, his fingertips touching, mirrorlike, he stared up into the branches. He took in the colored pieces of glass hanging by threads of gold. He walked around the trunk, considering the tree from different angles. He completed one circuit, then another.

"You see?" Hamid groused. "Nothing. It's time we—"

"You will remain quiet," Shaikh Dayan said evenly. His tone was pleasant, but the threat was clear.

Hamid looked like he was about to complain but stopped when Rasime, his co-conspirator in Macide's betrayal, put a hand on his forearm and shook her head. She'd sailed the southern sands many times, and knew the tales of Dayan's mercurial nature, even if Hamid didn't.

Hamid's expression grew dark as Zaghran completed a third circuit. Çeda was becoming even more convinced she'd failed. And that for whatever reason, the tree had chosen to withhold its power from him. Or perhaps Zaghran was only feigning interest so that he could justify abandoning Çeda and the others.

Tanzi was growing more and more anxious. She wrung her hands. Her lips were pressed into a thin line. Her forehead pinched, distorting the star-burst tattoo across her brow.

She was just stepping forward, her patience apparently run out, when Zaghran's head jerked back. His eyes grew wide and filled with wonder and no small amount of fear. His hands shook as they gathered at his breast. Blinking fiercely, he drew his gaze away. How small he suddenly seemed, how haunted, as if he'd witnessed his own death.

As though still lost in the vision, he drew his gaze slowly but surely to Çeda. Suddenly he blinked and took in the rest of the assemblage, as if he'd just remembered they were there. He seemed embarrassed, as if he feared everyone had shared in the vision the acacia had granted him.

Then, with a hard look to Shaikh Dayan, he said, "The tribunal may convene." His gaze slid to Çeda. "You have one day to prepare."

Chapter 19

SHORTLY AFTER DAWN, five days after the surprise attack by the qirin warriors, Ihsan walked along the quays of Sharakhai's poor, western harbor. Tolovan, Ihsan's old vizir and most trusted servant, led him along the quays toward The Harp and Hare, a small shisha den all but indistinguishable from the dozens of others sprinkled throughout the city's western reaches. Most such dens would be shuttered this early, but the mousy proprietor of The Harp and Hare was up and sweeping the floor free of the sand and dust that had collected during the night. He nodded to Tolovan and Ihsan as they entered.

"Leave," Tolovan said, and sent a golden coin arcing through the air.

The proprietor deftly snatched the rahl and left, closing the front door behind him. Tolovan led Ihsan past the shishas and the piles of pillows into a small storeroom. On the shelves along one wall were dirty shishas, a collection of mismatched tea cups, and a variety of wooden crates filled with tea and tabbaq. Near the back wall, a man with a greasy pate was tied to a chair. He stared at them. A red vest and sweat-stained shirt covered his ample belly. His peppery beard was tangled and messy as a half-finished hawser. He had a bruise below one eye, and at its center was a weeping cut.

Near the man stood two women, both dressed in drab, west end garb. Both had shamshirs at their sides and wore turbans with veils drawn across their faces. They were Blade Maidens, assigned to Ihsan for the duration of his mission into the city. When Ihsan waved to them, they bowed their heads and headed into the front room.

Ihsan grabbed a nearby stool, set it down with a thump in front of the man, and sat. "You're Yosef."

"Yes, my lord, and there's been a terrible mistake."

Ihsan smiled. "I'll be the judge of that." He raised his hand as Yosef started to protest. "This won't take long, and no ill will befall you if you answer a few simple questions with all the candor you can muster."

"Of course, my lord, of course! I would think of nothing—"

When Ihsan raised his hand again, Yosef glanced uneasily at Tolovan's bloody knuckles, and fell silent.

"A Qaimiri woman named Meryam came to you several weeks ago about a ship." Ihsan wiped a spot of dust off the knee of his ivory thawb. "Tell me about her."

Yosef shrugged. "I *thought* she wanted the ship, but when she arrived, all she was interested in was the ship's maps and Adzin's logs."

"Toward what purpose?"

"I've no idea, my lord."

"Then why the change of heart? Why buy a ship when she'd come looking for maps and logs?" Yosef opened his mouth to speak, but Ihsan talked over him. "Take care with your answer, Yosef of the Red Crescent. I know much about this particular woman."

Yosef sobered at that. When he spoke again, his words had lost the veneer of a grifter salesman. He sounded, in fact, perfectly earnest. "My cousin Adzin was a soothsayer. When she found messages written in the curiosities aboard his ship, she became determined to buy the entire ship. She didn't so much as bat an eye when I named my price, which was twenty percent higher than what I *had* been asking. I was angry I didn't *double* the price."

"Why the interest in your cousin's messages?" Ihsan's mouth ached as he leeched power into his voice. "What was she searching for?"

Yosef's cheeks flushed, but beyond this Ihsan couldn't tell if his power was working or not. "I'd tell you if I knew, my lord, but I don't."

Ihsan added more power. His eyes watered from the pain it brought on. "You must have some clue."

"Not a one. I didn't ask her purpose. Why would I? I'd had that cursed ship for months. I just wanted to be rid of it." When Tolovan cracked his knuckles and pushed himself off the wall, Yosef's eyes went wide. "I swear! She asked of Adzin's forays into the desert, the places he visited to gather magic. She must have wanted to visit them. Why else would she have wanted his maps? But what do *I* know of such things? I was Adzin's *cousin*, not his bloody keeper!"

"And where, precisely, did your cousin go to gather his magic?"

Yosef's look was half innocence, half impotence. "I might have been able to tell you if I'd kept the maps, but I didn't. She wanted them all."

"You kept none of them?"

"Not a scrap!"

"Did you hear of her movements afterward? Any rumors of her around the quays?"

Yosef seemed relieved by the new line of questioning. "You've heard of Ibrahim the storyteller?"

"I have," Ihsan said.

"I bought him a drink one night and he told me a story. He said he was out walking one night beyond the mouth of the harbor. Said he saw a yacht anchored beside *The Gray Gull*. A crew of men were using a sleigh to transfer something big *between* the ships. A dead ehrekh, if you can believe it."

No ehrekh, Ihsan mused, *but Goezhen himself.* "Did he say what Meryam meant to do with it?"

"If Ibrahim knew, he didn't tell me."

It was clear Yosef was trying to pawn Ihsan off on Ibrahim, but that didn't mean he was lying.

"Tell me now, Yosef"—for the third time, Ihsan tried using the power given to him by the desert gods—"has all you've told me been true?"

"Of course, yes!"

"Is there anything else you can tell me about Meryam or her purpose?"

"No! Nothing!"

Ihsan nearly ordered Tolovan to beat Yosef until he was certain he was telling the truth, but doing so was tantamount to admitting his power was failing. Its strength had always waned when he used it repeatedly, and there had always been those who could resist his commands, particularly those with blood of the thirteenth tribe running through their veins, but this was different. Ever since Cahil had helped him regrow his tongue, the power had been unreliable. Sometimes he couldn't tell if it was working at all. That was the case now. His power *might* have affected Yosef. Then again, it might *not* have. It was somehow more terrifying than when he'd lost his tongue. At least then he'd had the hope of one day regaining it. Now it felt like his power was waning and that, when it was gone, it would be gone for good.

"My lord?" Tolovan was staring down at Ihsan with a concerned look.

Yosef, meanwhile, looked terrified, as if he thought Ihsan was debating whether to kill him. "By the gods who breathe, I swear I'm telling the truth!"

With a sharp intake of breath, Ihsan stood. "You're free to go."

Tolovan cut him free, and Yosef fairly fled from the storeroom.

"Is there anything the matter, my Lord King?" Tolovan asked when the door had slammed shut.

But Ihsan was in no mood to speak of it. "Find Ibrahim. Bring him to me."

"Of course," Tolovan said, "but—"

"That will be all, Tolovan."

A pause. "Yes, Your Excellence."

He left with one of the Blade Maidens in tow. The other accompanied Ihsan back to his room—a small, nondescript flat in the Red Crescent. When he arrived, he found Nayyan and the Blade Maiden, Yndris, standing beside the water basin. Nayyan held Ransaneh in her arms. She was crying, but that was hardly the most concerning thing. "Nayyan, what *happened*?"

The front of her dress was stained with fresh blood. Her right cheek was covered in it. Ransaneh was bloody too, with scrapes along her chin, nose, and cheeks. She seemed unfazed by it, however; her mismatched eyes were bright and wide, and when she locked eyes with Ihsan, she smiled.

Yndris was using a curved needle and thread to stitch a jagged gash on Nayyan's forehead. A few stitches were already in place. The one Yndris was tying off with a gleaming set of forceps and scissors looked to be the last. She cut the thread and set the instruments aside. Picking up a clean cloth from a pile beside the water basin, she wet it and began to dab the bloody wound clean.

Ihsan had never been bothered by his own blood, but to see so much of it on his Queen and his daughter made his gut twist into knots. "Nayyan," he asked again, "what *happened*?"

Nayyan didn't answer.

"She took a tumble is all," Yndris finally said.

"Go," Ihsan said to her. He'd have a word with her later about answering for her Queen.

Nayyan took the wet, bloody bandage from Yndris and nodded to her.

The scars over Yndris's brow and cheeks—remnants an old beating from Çedamihn—puckered as she frowned. She looked like she wanted to argue, to *deny* Ihsan, but then she bowed her head and left the room.

Ihsan took Ransaneh from Nayyan's arms and waited for her to say something. But Nayyan only stood there silently while pressing the bandage to the gash along her forehead.

"Were you *attacked*?" Ihsan asked.

"I fell." Tears fell down her cheeks, creating tracks in the blood. She waved to Ransaneh. "I fell and I dropped our daughter."

"You tripped?"

"I fainted." Her face screwed up and she slipped into a deep bout of crying.

"Where?"

She motioned vaguely toward the window. "A block away." She folded the bandage, dipped it into the water, and began dabbing her forehead and left eyelid, where the blood was heaviest.

"But why?"

"My moon day." She bent over the basin and began scrubbing more vigorously at her cheeks and jaw. "Its come sooner than expected, and it's been heavy. It started seven days ago and hasn't stopped."

Ihsan recalled her mentioning something about it as she'd left to visit the physic. He was embarrassed to admit he hadn't been paying much attention. He certainly was now. "What did the physic say?"

"She gave me some herbs that should help to stem the flow and alleviate the cramping."

That was a small relief, at least.

"Get cleaned up," Ihsan said gently. "Then we can rest. Just the three of us, like on the ship." Things had been so busy in the city he'd actually come to miss the slow rhythm of their desert voyage. It had been hellish when Ransaneh couldn't sleep, but the intimacy had been nice, and their worries over the desert's fate had felt distant.

As Nayyan continued to wipe away the blood, Ihsan looked Ransaneh over. The excited burble she gave was normally a heartwarming sound, but Ihsan hardly noticed it. There was something hugely distracting about seeing your child hurt for the first time.

A vision swam before him, of Ferah, his daughter with another woman. Ferah had lived and died centuries earlier, but the image of her crumpled body at the base of his throne, her wrists slit, was still bright in his mind. She'd been fully grown, but still young and married to Abdul-Azim, a man she loved, and who loved her.

Abdul-Azim had had the misfortune of being a member of the thirteenth tribe. When the Kings struck their bargain with the desert gods, he, like so many others, had been sacrificed to save the city.

In his mind's eye, Ferah stared at him in accusation. *You did nothing to stop him from being cursed. You watched him be turned into an asir, then claimed he was a holy warrior. Lies, father. All lies!*

Tears blurring his vision, Ihsan went to the small chest they'd brought with them from the desert. Stacked beside a sizable store of money were a dozen metal vials, each with a dose of the healing elixir Nayyan had crafted many months ago.

He took one of them and popped the cork with his thumb. He was just raising it to Ransaneh's lips when Nayyan snatched his wrist, forestalling him. "Don't, Ihsan."

But the need to see Ransaneh healed of her wounds was so great he jerked his arm away and tried again.

"Ihsan, don't!" She wrenched the vial from his hand, stuffed the cork into the vial's mouth, and dropped it back inside the chest with the others. With a shove from one slippered foot, the lid slammed home.

"She's *hurt*," Ihsan said, utterly baffled.

"She doesn't need it."

He tried to speak, but stopped when she went to the nearby windows and opened the shutters. She pointed toward Tauriyat. "The end is near, Ihsan. We'll need every resource we have, including those vials."

"We have enough."

"No, we don't." Her face, now mostly clear of blood, flushed red. A trickle of blood was leaking from one side of the freshly stitched wound. She went to the table with the basin, took up a fresh bandage, and wiped it away. "Ransaneh has a *scrape*. She'll heal."

Nayyan refused to use so much as a drop of the elixir on herself, either. She finished cleaning herself up and changed into a fresh dress. It was early, but she was exhausted, and so, apparently was Ransaneh. As they lay in bed, with Ransaneh napping between them, Ihsan reached out and stroked Nayyan's cheek.

"Did the physic say anything more?"

She looked annoyed by the question. "Wouldn't I have told you if she had?"

"It's only, you reacted so strongly when I wanted to give Ransaneh the elixir."

She was silent for a time. Outside, a rebab and a flute took up a song. An old woman joined in a moment later, her voice imperfect, the words soulful. Suddenly, it felt like the ancient days of Sharakhai, early in Ihsan's rule, when life had been simpler.

"You've had other children, Ihsan," Nayyan finally said. "I haven't. I worry with every step we take that we're going to ruin her future."

"It won't be ruined."

"Let's make sure by taking each step with care and by conserving what we can." She reached out and pressed her hand to his cheek. "Yes?"

"Yes," he said, and they fell asleep together.

Chapter 20

ÇEDA FOUND LITTLE sleep the night following Shaikh Zaghran's decision to allow the tribunal to proceed. Long into the night, she lay beneath her bedroll while staring at the ceiling of the tent she, Emre, and the others had been given.

You have one day, Zaghran had said.

One day to prove Hamid was a liar and a murderer. One day to bend the acacia to her will. Only after hours of worry did she manage to fall asleep, but it was fitful at best, her dreams chilling. She woke exhausted. It was still dark, but dawn wasn't far off.

Emre snored softly beside her. She wanted to let him get his rest, but she was too eager to get started, so she shook him, and he woke bleary-eyed. He seemed confused at first but then nodded and grabbed his shirt from the pile of clothes beside him. "I'll wake the others." He sat up, pulled the shirt on, then paused, looking suddenly pensive. "What do you suppose the acacia showed Zaghran to convince him?"

Çeda stood and began to dress. "I've no idea, but the acacia speaks the truth. Apparently that was enough for him."

"I suppose. Let's just hope it's enough for the others as well."

By the time everyone was roused and fed, the sun was peeking between the shoulders of the mountains to the east. A fine fog lifted off the nearby lake as they all gathered beneath the acacia. The pressure was high, but Çeda had to admit it felt good having those closest to her there to help. On her left were Emre, Sümeya, Kameyl, and Shal'alara; on her right, Dardzada, Frail Lemi, and Leorah, who had Nalamae's staff lying beside her on the wiry grass. Çeda was all set to begin when Emre glanced meaningfully toward the fort above them. Atop the walls, a woman stared down. It was Rasime, Hamid's closest ally besides Darius.

"Let her watch," Çeda said, then took in everyone in the circle. "Our goal is to ensure that I can summon visions of the past and share them. If we can do both, I can show the shaikhs the sort of man they've allied themselves with."

She hoped to use the tree to show them the danger Sharakhai and the desert were in as well, but first she needed to stop Hamid from gaining an even larger foothold on the tribal alliance. Do that using the power of the tree, and they would become receptive to more.

"Close your eyes," Çeda continued. "Open your minds. Listen to the wind through the leaves. Sense the rising heat of the sun. Breathe and feel the beat of your hearts. Be with me in this moment. The tree, I hope, will do the rest."

As the others closed their eyes and began taking deep breaths, Çeda pulled her necklace from beneath her dress, the one her mother had given her. "Be with me, Memma." She kissed the teardrop pendant. "Today of all days, I need you."

When she looked up, she saw Frail Lemi looking back at her. He nodded the way an older brother might. A smile overcame her, and the growing pressure she'd been feeling shed from her like sand off skimwood. Seeing it, Frail Lemi winked and closed his eyes again.

Çeda summoned the power of the desert, spread her arms wide, and opened herself to the tree. She felt its presence suffuse her, body and soul. She wanted the tree to show everyone Emre's past and how Hamid had betrayed him. She wanted to verify that she could share her visions with the shaikhs. But the tree had other plans.

A different sort of vision swept her up, and it was so powerful, she lost all sense of her original purpose.

A pair of Silver Spears in white tabards escorted a woman along a hallway lined in rich marble and beautiful bronze sconces. The woman was a beauty with dark hair and striking eyes. Her name was Ahyanesh, though the guardsmen and the Sharakhani King she was about to meet knew her by a different name. And while they thought her a locksmith, she was anything but.

Covering her head was a respectable, leaf-pattern kufi. Her trousers were stuffed into the tops of soft leather boots that curled at the toes. Her kaftan, made of green linen, was embroidered with thread of gold around the collar. Her clothing spoke of a woman who was well off, though not *too* well off. A russet bag made of fine leather, containing the tools of her trade, was slung over one shoulder.

Ahead stood a man in King's raiment: jeweled slippers, an ivory thawb with pearls sewn into the cuffs, and a sandstone khalat made from the finest of silks. His name was King Yusam, and he was tall, lithe, and gifted with a feral grace that was beautiful and threatening at the same time. His aquiline nose warred with his soft, rounded chin and his light beard. It was his eyes, however, that were the most arresting. He wasn't called the Jade-eyed King for no reason. His gaze seemed to pierce Ahya as she strode forward, flanked by the two Silver Spears.

Hands clasped behind his back, King Yusam led Ahya to a room lit by golden lanterns. On the far side was the door to a vault, which was swung partway open.

"You've been apprised of the situation?" Yusam's voice was calm and confident.

"I have, Excellence," Ahya replied, her nervousness masked by weeks of preparation.

"I want it done before nightfall."

And for good reason, Ahya thought. The holy night of Beht Zha'ir began at sunset. She'd chosen this moment carefully. In recent months, the

Moonless Host had used Beht Zha'ir to launch some of the most violent attacks in years. King Yusam feared his treasury had become a target, and he was taking no chances.

"I need three hours, four at the most."

Yusam considered, and then nodded. "I require four copies of the keys. Any notes you take will be given to the Silver Spears on your departure."

"Of course, my Lord King." Ahya patted the leather bag by her side. "Everything has been prepared."

Yusam considered her, his jade eyes discerning, discriminating. "The master locksmith. Is he faring any better?"

She shook her head. "I'm afraid not. He can't take food. He can hardly keep water down. He's lost half a stone in three days."

"Well," Yusam said with a spin toward the door. "The gods will provide."

Ahya bowed as King Yusam left the room. "Yes, my Lord King."

With him gone, the pressure eased, but not entirely. She had only so much time to change the lock and trick the guards to get what she wanted from the vault.

For over two decades, one master locksmith had safeguarded the locks in King Yusam's vaults and stores. Two nights ago, Ahya had broken into his home in Hanging Gardens and slipped one of Dardzada's poisons into his meal. The poison, made from sand drake venom, would see him sick as a dog for days. That same night, after he'd fallen ill, she stole into his home again and took the safe where he kept his most precious notes, those that described the configuration of the locks he maintained.

The theft, as Ahya had known it would, had been reported to King Yusam. Yusam, worried the Moonless Host was planning to loot his treasury, had asked the locksmith to come to his palace immediately to change the combinations.

"My deepest apologies, my Lord King," the locksmith had written, "but I've contracted a sickness that may be part of the plan you fear. I won't be well enough for some days. To ensure the highest safety to your valuable stores, I recommend Master Fallay attend you in my stead. He keeps his premises in the heart of the merchant's quarter."

Through careful research, Ahya knew that King Yusam's private messenger adored fine tabbaq. On his return to the House of Kings, he rode his silver-and-bronze akhala along a curving road, only to find Ahya on her knees, trying to fix the wheel of a dray that had slipped its axle.

The messenger, a rail of a man, looked ready to move past without offering help but stopped when he noticed a broken crate. Ahya had made it look like it had fallen off the top of a stack when the wagon wheel slipped. There was a spray of tabbaq all over the road. The brand on the side was from a rare house in Qaimir. All of the crates on the dray's bed were from extremely fine growers in the southern kingdom, the sort that men who knew tabbaq—men like the messenger—would kill to sample.

"Can I help?" he finally asked.

Ahya stood, dusted off the front of her dress, then wiped the sweat from her brow with the back of one sleeve. "I would be eternally grateful if you would."

He dismounted and from a box at the front of the wagon's bed pulled out the tools needed to lever the front axle high enough for the wheel to be slipped back on. As he began putting it in place, he glanced at the open crate. Even from this distance, the air was thick with the smell of it. Ahya had been educating herself on the finer points of tabbaq for years. She could detect notes of marzipan, rum, toasted almonds and, beneath it all, an undercurrent of cinnamon and black pepper. The lone crate cost as much as many households in Sharakhai made in a season.

The messenger pursed his lips and gave the crate an appreciative nod. "House Darrio."

She feigned surprise. "Why, yes."

"The mark shows it's from the tabbaqanist's select reserve."

"It is!" Ahya let a touch of excitement leak into her voice. "Do you partake?"

He waggled his head. "From time to time." He looked up, his eyes moving from crate to crate. "Remigio . . . Abrantes . . . Vartaga-Almore."

"The finest in Qaimir." She paused. "You know, I was just headed to a private tasting at an auction house."

The messenger laughed. "If only I had the funds to bid on full cases."

"But you don't have to! Many don't, in fact. I work for the auction house." She waved to an especially large crate near the front of the bed, the sort used to hold bottles of liquor. "Each of the tabbaqs is going to be paired with fine

Qaimiri brandy. I could vouch for you, say you're a buyer. Then they'll give you a bidding paddle. You'll sample the tabbaqs. You'll drink some of the finest brandy ever to find its way onto the sandy seas. And you'll go home a happy man."

The messenger stopped all pretense of working on the wheel. His eyes moved from the open crate to Ahya to the crate again.

"Please." She waved to the half-fixed wheel. "It's the least I can do."

A smile broke out across his face. "Very well, though I fear I'll be the one owing *you* by the time this is done."

From there they moved on to the auction house. The owner maintained a respectable appearance, but he'd been on the take for years, allowing the occasional crate of stolen goods to pass through the auction house. Ahya hadn't lied about the tasting, though. It was real. Ahya had paid the owner handsomely to allow her to borrow a few of the crates, on the understanding that she would return them before the auction began.

The messenger got his bidding paddle, just as Ahya had promised. A wide smile broke over his face as he smoked from the hookahs filled with rare tabbaq. He chatted gaily with the other auction goers while sipping golden brandy. He looked to be having the time of his life, hobnobbing with so many of the city's upper crust, and Ahya left him to it, calm in the knowledge that she'd have long enough to do what she needed.

After slipping five sylval to the auction house's stablehand, she found herself alone in the stables and opened the messenger's saddlebag. She took out the note from the ailing locksmith and proceeded to copy it word for word, forging his loopy script, which she'd practiced for days to master. She changed only one thing in the new letter: the identity of the locksmith he recommended. She specified a space along the Trough she'd rented a month back and had outfitted to look like a locksmith's. When word had come that King Yusam urgently needed her expertise, she'd gladly answered his call.

Now, in Yusam's treasury, she began the painstaking work of changing the vault's combination. The tricky part wasn't changing the mechanism itself—locksmithing had been a necessary part of her training, and she'd mastered it years ago—it was getting rid of the guards long enough to look through the vault's contents.

She took the set of keys and spoke to the younger guard, the one who seemed most naive. "Could you hold these?"

The guard accepted them from her, confused.

She took up the lantern, stepped inside the vault, and motioned to the reinforced jamb. "I need to make sure the tenon's setting into the mortise properly."

He shrugged, but did so with a flash of pride, the sort that came with being trusted.

With that she closed the vault door and twisted the mechanism that sent the thick steel tenon into the mortise, sealing the door. The key clanked as the guard inserted it, but nothing happened when he turned it. She'd removed the pin that let the mechanism drive the tenon, effectively locking herself inside the vault.

"It's not working," she heard the guard call.

"Try again," she called softly.

"What?"

"Try again!" she called, louder this time.

"Still nothing!"

"Ah! I see the problem. It won't be but a moment."

What followed was a series of mishaps: her making the mechanism jingle like she was doing something; the guard trying the key to no avail. She left long pauses to indicate she was thinking, or preparing her tools.

In reality, she was searching the many shelves within the vault, looking for a particular chest she'd heard rumor of years before. She found it at the back, a metal chest with jewels and golden filigree in the design of a spread-winged roc. It took her several tries with her lock picks, but eventually she had it open. Inside, she found a small jewelry box lined with red satin. Within the jewelry box was a glass vial with a brown, oval seed inside. An acacia seed. As she'd seen in a vision on one of her visits to the desert witch, Saliah.

From her pack she retrieved a silver vial with intricate designs etched along its length. Inside it was another seed, also from an acacia, this one collected from a tree in the temple district. She switched them, made all as it had been, and returned to the door just as a clanging sound came from the opposite side.

"Are you trapped?" the young one called, sounding worried. "Should we send for help?"

She replaced the missing pin she'd pulled earlier, unlocked the vault door, and swung it wide. "This is a delicate mechanism!" She scowled at the shamshir in the guard's sword hand, which he'd clearly been using to bang on the door. "You don't fix it by swinging a bloody sword at it, you know!"

He looked angry but also a bit chagrined and said no more as she went about her work.

"You'd think she'd know how to get out of a gods-damned vault from the inside," she heard the older one say. The younger chortled in agreement.

Only when she'd left the palace and returned to her fake premises along the Trough did she allow herself to take the seed from the silver vial and look at it. She held it to the sunlight streaming in through the window, wondering what it was for, wondering why Saliah's fabled tree had shown it to her.

But the mystery remained, and she put the seed back into its vial.

Chapter 21

THE MORNING AFTER Nayyan's fainting spell and the scare with Ransaneh, Ihsan was awakened by a growing din. Leaving Nayyan and Ransaneh sleeping, he went to the window. Up the street, people were rushing toward the Spear, the large thoroughfare that started at the western harbor and ended at the gates to the House of Maidens. The sound that had woke him was chanting. Ihsan had heard the sort before. Civil strife. Voices raised in anger.

"What's happening?" Nayyan said as she lifted her head and squinted at him.

"It appears Queen Sunay was successful in her attempt to foment rebellion in the streets," Ihsan said.

Nayyan propped herself up on one elbow. "Riots . . . ?"

"Net yet, from the sound of it, but with the food shortages as bad as they've been, I'm sure violence isn't far off."

An urgent knock came at the door. "My lord." It was Tolovan. He sounded worried, but Tolovan never sounded worried. The knock came again, harder this time. "My lord, please let me in."

After giving Nayyan a moment to pull on her night coat, Ihsan opened the door.

Tolovan rushed inside. He was red in the face, breathless. "He's gone, my lord."

"Who's gone?"

"The storyteller. Ibrahim. I went to find him as you asked. It took me some time before I found where he lived, but I went there before daybreak, only to find a squad of green cloaks already there. They battered down his door and took him away in chains."

Gods, no, Ihsan thought, *not when we were so close.* He threw off his night shirt and began pulling on his trousers. "Where did they take him?"

"They were headed toward the House of Kings"—he motioned at the window—"but by then people were marching. Sensing trouble, the green cloaks took him to the garrison for safekeeping. He's there still, but there's no telling for how long."

The sounds outside had been steadily rising. Mixed among them were screams of pain. Orders being bellowed. The streets were about to slip into chaos.

Nayyan's brow furrowed as she worked through the implications. "I might have said Queen Alansal is following the same sort of scent we are, but her water dancers are dead."

"True," Ihsan said, "but who knows what visions she gained before they died? We need to intercept Ibrahim before he's taken to the House of Kings. Gather the Maidens," he ordered Tolovan, who nodded and left in a rush.

With the door closed, Ihsan slipped into a thawb and donned boiled leather greaves and vambraces, which he hid beneath his slate blue khalat. By the time he finished wrapping a patterned keffiyeh and black agal around his head, garb more commonly found in the city's west end, Nayyan was tugging at the ties of her dress. It took him a moment to realize it was her violet battle dress and turban.

Ihsan raised his hands. "You need to stay here with Ransaneh."

"No," she said flatly. "I'm going with you."

"You have to take her out of the city if things get worse."

Nayyan paused with her sword belt across her hips, not yet buckled. "Is Ibrahim important to our mission or is he not?"

Ihsan hesitated, and nearly lied to her. Nearly told her there were other clues that could lead them to Meryam. But it wasn't true. "Fine. I admit it. Everything may ride on what happens to Ibrahim. But what if I'm wrong?"

"Ihsan, for the sake of all we're trying to do here, stop." She clasped her buckle and adjusted the belt. "No one in the desert sees what lies ahead and how to stop it better than you. If Ibrahim is a knife we can use to cut the net closing around us, then we need to get him." There was a great roar from the east, and Nayyan gestured toward it. "This is for Ransaneh as much as it is for us."

Ihsan didn't want to admit that he was inspired by her words—doing so would lead to his letting her come along, letting her be in terrible danger— but the truth was, he'd never been more proud of her. He'd never been more proud of *anyone.*

"Very well," he said as he buckled his own belt, this one with a sheathed fighting knife. "Let's go get Ibrahim."

After handing Ransaneh to the wet nurse and assigning two Blade Maidens to guard her, Ihsan, Nayyan, and Tolovan left with their remaining three Maidens, including Yndris. Together they wove through the city streets. They tried to avoid the crowds but, breath of the desert, there were people everywhere. Whatever Sunay had done, it had riled up half the city.

At the horde's outskirts, people were raising their fists and shouting, "Down with Mirea! Down with Malasan!"

The farther they went, the more people were waving knives, swords, or clubs in the air. Some roared. Others drummed their weapons against round shields. The sound was deafening. As they neared the collegia and its collection of ancient, sandstone halls, they passed along the edges of the esplanade. At the center of the open space, people lifted their weapons high, crying in ululations.

Ihsan didn't understand why until he stood on the marble plinth of a statue. A squad of green cloaks were trapped at the center of the mob. More than cut up and bloody, they were a travesty of human flesh. Having trapped them, the crowd was taking turns hacking them to pieces.

"Come on," Nayyan said, pulling Ihsan down from the statue and away from the horrific sight.

New shouts of pain and fear rose along the edge of the collegia grounds.

The Mirean regulars had come. Rank after rank of armored soldiers stood at the ready. Through occasional gaps in the crowd, Ihsan saw those at the front holding large wooden shields—war doors, they were called. They were meant to create a barrier for the soldiers behind the front line, who brandished long spears. Like thorns along the snaking branch of an adichara, the spears jutted outward from the makeshift wall. In lockstep, the spearmen would stab their spears into the mob. The mob, screaming in outrage, was forced back, which created space for the shield men to advance a step. Slowly but surely, they were creating the space they would need to launch a more violent assault, which was clearly about to happen. Behind the war doors and spearmen, several companies of cavalry and heavily armored soldiers bearing daos and kite shields were forming into orderly ranks.

The garrison where Ibrahim was being kept was a blocky monstrosity that lay just beyond the esplanade, though they couldn't reach it. The crowd, thick already, was growing thicker by the moment as the Mirean soldiers pressed the rioters back, trying to gain control. Making matters worse, the Mireans would have dozens, perhaps hundreds, of their soldiers inside the garrison itself.

Ihsan had seen plenty of spontaneous riots. This was more organized, no doubt due to Sunay's long and careful preparations. Gang leaders called orders. Mobs threw rocks and glass bottles. Some threw clay pots filled with kerosene, which arced through the sky, trailing smoke. They landed among the Mirean soldiers and broke, spreading orange flames.

But the Mirean soldiers were fresh from war and reacted with cool discipline. They batted out flames where they caught and retreated as needed, always keeping the rioters at bay through the quick and vicious use of their spears.

The mob tried to fight back. Some grabbed the soldiers' spears to prevent them from stabbing anyone. While the spearmen were occupied, others would rush forward, grab the massive war doors, and yank them aside. Some of the Mirean shieldsmen fell to knives or swords. A few more were dragged into the crowd, where they were given the same barbarous treatment as the trapped green cloaks. But it never came close to overwhelming the Mireans. The foreign soldiers were too disciplined, too numerous. When the rush became too much for the front line to handle, they would simply let some of the crowd through. As the swordsmen *behind* the spearmen cut them to ribbons, the shieldsmen would push hard and close the line once more.

Nayyan took in the chaos. "Do we go around? Or take to the tunnels?"

A gap had formed in the Mirean line. Through it, a full squadron of cavalry were pouring onto the collegia grounds. The bulk of them pressed back the riot line. A company of eight, however, peeled off and made for garrison.

They were after Ibrahim. Ihsan knew it in his bones.

He thought of charging the Mirean line, of using his power to command them. But his power might falter, and with the noise, they might not hear him in any case.

Ihsan scanned the faces of the Sharakhani crowd. With the cavalry approaching, many looked like they wanted to break and run. He'd never felt as though the city were slipping away from him as much as he felt it then. Bottling his fears, he lifted his hands like a prophet and bellowed, "To our shores have these jackals come!"

He poured so much of his power into those words it *hurt*. He cared little for the pain, however. What he cared about was that it seemed to be working. The crowd around them had stilled. They watched Ihsan with wary eyes.

"More of their dunebreakers arrive by the day," he went on. "They bear soldiers and weapons meant to quash rebellion, meant to silence all speech against their queen."

The looks of worry and wariness in the crowd faded, and the anger that had burned so brightly moments ago returned with a vengeance.

"They refuse to let more than a handful gather in the streets! Their queen and her generals hide behind walls *we* built. And why?" He thrust a finger toward Tauriyat. "Because they *fear* us!"

The crowd rumbled with discontent.

"They may have slipped past our Kings' fleet. They may have stolen onto the mountain to hide like frightened amberlarks. They may think themselves safe in the House of Kings. But they aren't, are they?"

The rumble became a roar. "No!"

"No," Ihsan repeated, "because they haven't reckoned with us, the children of the Amber Jewel. They haven't learned the most important lesson: what it means to invade our city. They don't realize we will *die* before we live under their rule."

A high ululation, swords, knives, and clubs rising. They were poised, a surging river held back by a crumbling levee.

Ihsan pointed to the line of soldiers. "Let's teach them."

With those words, the levee burst. The crowd rushed past Ihsan, Nayyan, and their Blade Maidens with a thunderous roar. They threw themselves at the spearmen. Some took terrible wounds and fought on. Others fell, dying. Meanwhile dozens, then hundreds, made it beyond the shield wall. It was a terrible, bloody slaughter. The Mirean foot soldiers engaged with swords. Their spearmen stabbed. The Sharakhani swung wildly with their weapons. The Mirean line was sturdy, but there were simply too many Sharakhani surging forward, their own vengeful feelings and the power of Ihsan's voice working together to drive them beyond their normal limits.

First the Mirean line buckled.

Then it broke altogether.

"Now!" Nayyan yelled to the Blade Maidens.

Ihsan would have ordered them forward himself had his tongue and jaw not been in so much pain. Spit pooled in his mouth. The hinges of his jaw felt like spikes were being driven into them. Tears streamed down his face from the sheer intensity of it. He swore it felt as awful as when Surrahdi the Mad King had cut his tongue out.

Nayyan noticed, but Ihsan chose to ignore her. He couldn't so much as move his mouth, much less speak.

Together they ran. Yndris and the other Blade Maidens went first, bulling their way through the chaos. Yndris paused along the way to pick up two fallen spears. She handed them to two of the Maidens beside her. "Take the lead."

The Maidens complied, and Yndris, Ihsan, and Nayyan followed. Ahead, the line of cavalry approached. The clop of hooves and the screams from their horses rose above the sounds of battle. At the garrison, the stout front doors had been opened. Exactly as Ihsan had feared, an old man with a long gray beard was being led out and down the steps toward the company that had broken away from the cavalry's main group. Ibrahim.

Nayyan pointed to the nearing line of cavalry. "Can you stop them?"

Ihsan shook his head no. Nayyan nodded, then pointed to the four cavalry riders that had just reined their horses toward them.

Yndris backed up and whistled a series of notes that meant *set spears*, at which point the lead Maidens slammed the butts of their spears into the ground, set their back feet on top to keep them in place, and crouched low, pointing the tips at the barded chests of the approaching horses.

One rider pulled on the reins so hard his horse came to a skidding stop. The others swung wide, clearly hoping to flank their small group from both sides.

Yndris, meanwhile, sprinted toward one of the crouched Blade Maidens. She launched herself off her sister Maiden's back to fly high through the air. The cavalryman who'd reined in his horse managed one wild swing of his dao before Yndris landed on his horse's rump. In a blur of movement she grappled with the rider, threw him from the saddle, and slipped into his place. The soldier gained his feet, his sword in both hands. But Yndris, uttering a ragged battle cry, was already swinging her ebon blade in a vicious downward blow. The soldier's helmet and skull were cleaved in two.

As the other two Blade Maidens used their spears to fend off two of the cavalrymen, Nayyan charged the third. The soldier maneuvered his horse and raised his shield, hoping to block her, but just then one of the Blade Maidens disengaged and sprinted toward him, swift as a desert hare. The soldier, clearly unused to the Blade Maidens' synchronized battle tactics, appeared unsure which of them to block. He effectively blocked neither. Nayyan swung, driving the edge of her blade into the man's knee. As he screamed in pain and dropped his shield, the Blade Maiden thrust the spear past his guard and through the underside of his jaw. His strangled cry was cut off as she advanced, sending the spear up and through his mouth, and shoved him from his saddle.

Yndris had spurred her horse toward one of the remaining two soldiers.

"Ihsan!" Nayyan yelled.

He spun and raised his knife, knowing it would do little against a mounted warrior. Indeed, the last Mirean cavalryman looked ready to cut him down, but before he could Nayyan gave a trilling ululation, "Lai, lai, lai!" and charged toward him.

The soldier spun his horse around and met her first blow with his shield. The horse's rump bashed Ihsan, and he stumbled away. He heard the rider make a clicking sound with his tongue. A moment later, the horse kicked backward, toward Ihsan. One hoof struck. It was only a glancing blow, thanks the gods, but Ihsan still went flying.

His head struck the ground hard. Through the sudden ringing in his ears came the ring of clashing steel, cries of pain, orders shouted in Mirean, and the roar of the rioters' unfolding fury. He blinked and managed to lift his head, but lay back down when searing pain flared along the right side of his chest. Probing tenderly, he guessed at least two ribs were broken.

Nayyan was suddenly there, helping him to his feet. Stars formed in his vision. He nearly blacked out. But with slow, careful movements he was able to tread toward the riderless horse. He stopped beside it and stared up at the saddle.

"That's an awfully long way for a man with broken ribs," he managed.

"A bit of pain or your life, Ihsan. You choose."

He smiled ruefully. "A *bit* of pain . . ." With Nayyan helping, he got one foot in the stirrup. Then, with a long, pain-filled grunt, he was finally, blessedly, up and sitting in the saddle. The pain was so bad his vision dimmed.

Nayyan passed the reins to him. "Follow us, but keep your distance until we have Ibrahim safely away."

Ihsan nodded as Nayyan mounted behind Yndris. Soon they and the other two Maidens were riding hard for the foot of the garrison stairs, where Ibrahim was being led toward a waiting horse.

Ihsan had never felt more useless. His broken ribs prevented his joining them in battle. And as far as his power was concerned, *swallowing* was painful; using a command to help Nayyan was out of the question.

Thankfully he was accompanied by four of the best swordswomen in the desert. Nayyan, Yndris, and the other two Blade Maidens made quick work of the Mirean cavalrymen. Five fell in moments to the swings of their ebon blades; the remaining three retreated, relinquishing their queen's prize.

Ibrahim had watched the clash unfold around him with growing horror, but as Nayyan and Ihsan approached, his looked turned to one of awe. "You're King Ihsan," he said, then slid his gaze to Nayyan, "and you're his queen."

"I am my *own* queen," she replied, and led Ibrahim toward the waiting horses.

"Of course." The manacles on Ibrahim's wrists clanked as he touched his fingers to his forehead in apology. "I only meant to ask why you, of all people, would come for me."

"We need answers to a few important questions," Ihsan managed, though the pain it brought on, to both his ribs and his throat, was terrible.

"Questions I'll gladly answer"—he held his wrists out—"so long as you can rid me of these."

"Soon enough." Nayyan mounted the nearest horse, a chestnut roan, and held one arm down to Ibrahim.

Ibrahim swung up behind her and fortunately asked no more questions. Ihsan couldn't have managed a reply anyway. They headed south, away from the fighting. Soon the sounds of battle were behind them, and they lost themselves in the streets of Sharakhai.

Chapter 22

ÇEDA BLINKED, RECOVERING from the vision the acacia had granted her. The cool stillness of King Yusam's palace was replaced by a warm wind. The stone ceiling and walls of the vault dissolved into a blue sky and the tall, dark peaks surrounding the valley below Mount Arasal. Ahead of her stood the acacia, the tree grown from the very seed her mother had stolen from King Yusam's palace.

As the acacia's branches swayed in the wind, sunlight shone through the leaves in dreamlike bursts. It was so entrancing it took her several long breaths before she realized the sun was high overhead. The savory scents of roasting meat drew her attention beyond their circle to the cooking pit, where a boy with a hopelessly dusty fez was turning a spitted lamb and tending to a dozen yogurt-marinated chickens—one part of the midday meal's preparations.

By the gods, *hours* had passed since she'd fallen under the vision's spell.

On hearing a deep exhalation beside her, Çeda turned to find Emre sitting in the same place as when they'd begun. He was staring at the glass chimes hanging from the tree. Without looking at her, he said, "You saw Ahya?"

Çeda nodded, then took in the others, who, while awake, seemed just as dreamy as Emre. "Everyone saw it? My mother stealing the seed from Yusam?"

A round of nods.

"But why would the acacia grant you *that* vision, child?" asked Leorah in her croak of a voice. "What does it mean?"

In truth, Çeda had hoped *Leorah* might know. She'd been one of the wisest in the thirteenth tribe, one of the wisest in all the desert. And she'd known Ahya well, known much of what she'd gone to Sharakhai to do, but over the past year her memory had declined sharply.

Çeda stared at the amethyst ring on Leorah's right hand. Within its facets was the soul of Devorah, Leorah's twin sister. At nightfall, the two traded places, Devorah using their body for much of the night. Then, at dawn, the two would trade again. In recent years, Devorah had been the sharper of the two—perhaps she'd have some idea.

For the time being, Çeda could only shrug. "I don't know what it means."

Neither, it turned out, did anyone else.

Frail Lemi had a pensive look on his ruggedly handsome face. "Before the ritual, you *did* ask your mother to be with you." He shrugged his broad shoulders. "Maybe the tree abided."

It was possible, she supposed, but in the moments before the vision had swept over her, she'd been focused on *Emre's* past, not her mother's.

Before she could formulate a reply, Shaikh Zaghran strode into their circle, his wife, Tanzi, by his side. "Well?" he asked.

He'd said it gruffly though not unkindly. But what could Çeda say? She had nothing to give him. Nothing at all. And worse, she didn't know if she ever would. "I need more time."

"I have very little time to give you."

"Please, if we could have a few days—"

Zaghran raised one hand, forestalling her. "May we speak alone, Çedamihn Ahyanesh'ala?"

Çeda nodded, then motioned for the others to take their leave. As they left in a group toward the tables filling with food, Zaghran pointed Tanzi toward the Tulogal tents beyond the pavilion. If Çeda was surprised, Tanzi looked like she'd been struck.

"Whatever you have to say," she said in an affronted tone, "I should hear as well!"

But Zaghran would not be persuaded. All but ignoring his wife, he guided Çeda along a path that ran around the lake. Tanzi looked as if she were ready to follow. She even took a step toward them, but then stopped and watched in brooding silence.

"I knew your grandfather, Ishaq," Zaghran said when they were out of earshot. "I knew Macide as well. They were forthright men. Hard at times, but you always knew where you stood with them. I agreed to join the Alliance because of them, and now another stands in their place, a man who will always choose the sword before the quill."

"That's precisely why you should abandon his cause."

When their path came alongside a stand of cattails, Zaghran stopped and faced Çeda. His hands were clasped before him. He looked bound, resolute. "The talks in this morning's council have progressed. No vote has yet been taken on Hamid's proposal to sail on Sharakhai, but I tell you this, it will not go as you hope"—he glanced back at the acacia, which swayed in the afternoon breeze—"unless you can prove his deception."

"Then help me convince them."

Zaghran shrugged. "I wasn't there. And neither were you for most of it. Don't think that fact is lost on anyone. Many are worried you're planning to manufacture a vision that will prove your and Emre's innocence and falsely condemn Hamid. Given your inability to command the acacia after hours of trying, even some of your allies will start to wonder."

"Then why did you vouch for me?"

"Let's be clear, Çedamihn. I didn't *vouch* for you. I voted to give you the opportunity to prove yourself."

"But if even *you* don't believe me—"

"I didn't say I didn't believe you." A look of careful consideration came over him. "Would you like to know what the tree showed me?" He didn't bothering waiting for Çeda's response. "It showed Rasime sailing west. It showed her meeting with my wife. It showed Rasime's offer. 'Convince your husband to join us,' she said to Tanzi, 'and the first of Sharakhai's plunder goes to Tulogal.' I saw Tanzi accept. I saw Hamid's smug smile when Rasime returned east with the news."

Zaghran's gaze shifted to the acacia, then to Tanzi, who was standing still as a statue in the exact place where Zaghran had left her.

"As those visions faded, I recalled how much has changed over the past months, how subtly my wife has manipulated me. I am not, nor was I ever, an admirer of the Sharakhani Kings, but I never thought to debase myself as they did. I never thought to employ their cruel methods. But Tanzi knows me well. She plucked me like a harp, striking just the right notes. She reminded me of every transgression, large and small, that our tribe suffered under the Kings' rule. And I grew angry from it, angry enough that I was willing to join Hamid's cause."

"Why are you telling me this?" Çeda asked.

"To make something clear to you: as this dawned on me, I grew embarrassed, not only from my wife's manipulations but because others *recognized* I could be manipulated in such a way. It was a painful set of facts to face, yet never once did I doubt that the tree had shown me the truth." Zaghran paused, letting the words sink in. "No mere words are going to convince the shaikhs of Hamid's guilt, but get the *acacia* to show it to them and you'll have what you want."

"I understand," Çeda said, "but I need more time."

Zaghran considered while, somewhere on the slopes above, a rock hawk cried.

"I'll see if I can gain you the morning. After that, we'll likely hold a vote on Hamid's proposal. If that vote is taken and we agree to sail west to make war, it will be too late. No one will wait for your proof once the decision is made."

With that he walked away. Curiously, as he passed beneath the acacia's broad limbs, the wind settled for a moment, and the tree went perfectly still.

"Please, give me what I need," Çeda whispered to it.

As if in answer, the wind kicked up, stronger than before, making the tree sway so much it looked tortured and helpless in the gale.

Çeda ate lamb and flatbread with the others, but every bite she took felt like time wasted. She wolfed it down in moments, then pressed the others to do the same. When it was done, they all returned to the acacia and settled themselves.

For a long while, Zaghran's words weighed on her. *Show them the truth and you'll have what you want,* he'd said. It added so much pressure she was having trouble finding the right mindset.

The only thing that calmed her was the memory of her mother. It was truly a gift, seeing her again. It led to more pleasant memories. Meals shared. Stories told. The few times her mother had embraced her and made her feel loved.

Soon, she was swept away by the acacia again.

The vision began with sunset over Sharakhai, with Ahya weaving her way along the streets of Roseridge toward the small, one-roomed home she shared with her daughter, Çeda. She'd just come from Yusam's palace. The acacia seed was in the small leather bag at her side. She was so aware of its presence it felt as if everyone she passed was watching her, and that if they stared at her long enough, they would learn of her wrongdoing.

So blinding was her paranoia she didn't at first recognize the old woman with the shawl walking toward her. It was Old Yanca, a neighborhood woman who watched Çeda from time to time. Ahya had left Çeda with her that very morning, but now Çeda was nowhere to be seen.

Yanca's shoulders curled inward as she shuffled closer. "It's Çeda," she said, wringing her hands, "she's gone."

Ahya shook her head, confused. "Gone where?"

Yanca waved back the way she'd come. "I fell asleep in my rocking chair. When I woke, she wasn't there."

Ahya rolled her eyes. "That child will be the death of me."

"I—" Yanca's wrinkled face pinched, prune-like in her embarrassment. "I think I heard her whispering with someone at the window. It's only, I haven't slept well lately. It's my ankles—"

Ahya was already moving past her. "It was Emre. It must have been."

"I thought about going to find her myself, but my ankles, you see."

But Ahya was hardly listening. "I swear by Bakhi's bright hammer I'm going to tan his hide so badly the boys in the bazaar could make a saddle from it."

They checked Yanca's home and found it empty. Çeda was no doubt off with her little flock of gutter wrens, probably running a scam cooked up by Tariq, or worse, the dead-eyed one, Hamid.

She was just ready to leave and head to her own home when Yanca caught her sleeve. "The whispering . . . They said something about the western harbor and a dare."

Just then a distant wail fell over the city, sending a terrible chill down Ahya's spine.

"Oh gods, not now."

She'd been so high on winning the acacia seed, a treasure she'd been seeking for the last decade, she'd all but forgotten it was Beht Zha'ir, the night the asirim stole into Sharakhai to take tribute. Some nights they came early, some they came late, and their numbers varied greatly, depending on how long it had been since they'd last feasted and how many King Sukru had marked with his cursed whip. Whatever the number, when the full moons rose, those who felt the call would lift themselves from the blooming fields and descend on the city in packs.

"Yanca, I have to go."

As Ahya fled out the door and down the stairs, Yanca called after her, "Can I help you look?"

Ahya didn't answer. She flew along the street to her home, praying she was wrong, praying she'd find Çeda there, praying this was all nothing but a terrible scare.

Over the last several months, rumors had been flying through the west end. Youths, mostly part of gangs, were daring one another to stay out on Beht Zha'ir to tempt fate—in essence, daring the asirim to take them. Ahya suspected it had started with some fool who'd been caught out on the holy night, survived, and *claimed* he'd stared death in the face. The young being the young, others had risen to the unspoken challenge and done the same. Now it was an outright epidemic. Surviving Beht Zha'ir outdoors had become a badge of honor. It was like thumbing their nose at the Kings and all their power. They were practically begging King Sukru to make an example of them.

As Ahya feared, Çeda wasn't home.

After throwing off the fine clothes she'd worn to King Yusam's palace, she put on her battle dress and turban and pulled the veil across her face. She buckled on her sword belt and climbed out the back window, the one that looked onto a narrow chute between the three poorly built dwellings. Knowing Çeda and her friends would almost certainly have gone to the western harbor, she climbed up and headed in that direction.

She made her way over the blocky and blessedly empty landscape of rooftops of the neighborhood known as the Red Crescent. She'd not gone far when a terrible keening rose up. Other wails rose up as if in consolation. *Fear not, sister,* those haunting calls said, *for soon we feast on the blood of the promised.*

Like their number, the path the asirim took into the city was like a roll of the bones. Ahya could already tell Çeda had rolled very, very poorly—a horde was approaching from the west. They'd reach the harbor in minutes.

By the time Ahya reached the quays, the sun had set and the twin moons had risen. There was light yet in the west, but it wouldn't be long before it failed entirely. Ahead, the harbor was a bay of sorts, with long, crescent-shaped quays running along its inner edge. Its outer edge was defined by a scattering of rocks that jutted from the sand. Word was, to complete their *dare,* the foolish youngsters were to hide behind the stones for at least an hour when the asirim began to wail. Few lasted that long, they were so afraid of being out in the open while the asirim prowled.

Ahya scanned the quays, the many docks, and the harbor itself for signs of Çeda or her gutter wren friends. Seeing nothing but the silhouettes of ships and empty sand, she sprinted to the end of the quays and leapt down to the rocky soil. She'd no sooner landed than she spotted two forms hunkered along the wharfs.

Lo and behold, it was Emre and Hamid.

"Where's Çeda?" Ahya asked them.

Emre was the first to answer. It seemed to take some courage for him to stand and point to the sea of black rocks beyond the mouth of the harbor. "Out there."

She grabbed him by his kaftan and shook him hard. *"Where?"*

"I don't know!" His voice was small and pitiful. "We split up like you're supposed to!"

She shoved him so hard he stumbled and fell. "You're not *supposed* to be out here at all!" She loomed over them both. "Get to the nearest ship and take shelter." When they remained, she drew her shamshir. "Now!"

They scrambled up to the quay and ran, though with the surfeit of sense the gods saw fit to give them, Ahya guessed they'd circle back when they thought she was gone. She couldn't worry about them, though. She had to find her daughter.

She peered into the night, scanning for any signs of wrens hiding behind the rocks. "Çeda, you stupid, stupid girl."

Her words were a bare whisper, and yet, only a moment later, a howling rose up not ten paces away. It was pained and heartfelt, a dirge for those who could not die.

Ahead, Ahya saw a form hunkered low, its arms spread wide. It stared at the city as if the last thing it wanted to do was enter. But it knew its fate. As the asirim had been forced to do for four hundred years, it would kill and drag whoever fell to its rending claws to the blooming fields, where it would throw them to the twisted trees.

Ahya ducked low behind a rock as the asir's head swiveled toward her. Its eyes glinted, diamonds on kohl, searching for whoever was foolish enough to be out on the holy night. The mark of Sukru's whip might be urging it to continue into the city, but that didn't mean it couldn't kill another before fulfilling its obligation to the Kings and the desert gods.

The asir's chest swelled and contracted. Its head shifted back and forth like a black laugher searching out its next kill. Ahya, meanwhile, stilled herself. Made her breath go shallow as she hoped, prayed, the asir would move on.

Please, Nalamae, I have so much more yet to do.

A moment later, the asir gave a sharp huff and turned back to the city. With a howl that made Ahya's skin crawl, it dropped to all fours and sprinted across the harbor floor, sand kicking up behind it in plumes.

When the sounds of its passage had faded, Ahya moved on, deeper into the rocks, as the asirim wailed.

Chapter 23

UNDER A HOT sun and with a favorable wind, Ramahd and his crew sailed the swift, three-masted clipper Hektor had given him, a ship named *Alu's Crown*. A week had passed since he'd left Mazandir. He and his crew had reached the area where the dead cooper said the Hollow would be found, but the desert was a big place. They'd stumbled across three sandy reefs already, and none held a circle of stones.

"Are you sure the cooper knew where it was?" Ramahd asked Fezek, who was sitting on the foredeck across from him.

Fezek shrugged, which was particularly infuriating after everything Ramahd had risked. "Who can say?"

"*You* can. You're the one who spoke to him."

"Yes, but I hardly knew the man. And let's recall, he *had* been dead for more than a century. Memories do tend to fade."

Ramahd closed his eyes, fighting the urge to rail against Fezek. It was his own fault, really. He should have pressed Fezek harder when he said he knew where to find the Hollow. "Was there anything else, some clue we might use to find it?"

Fezek's cloudy eyes went distant. "He said the stones were quite tall."

Fezek had an unreasonably optimistic look as he touched his nose. "He mentioned a noxious smell. The Hollow's very scent may lead us there!"

"If the wind is right."

Fezek's famous optimism held for a moment, deflated slightly, then collapsed altogether. "Well, that's true, isn't it?" A moment later, he added in a quieter voice, "At least it's *something* to go on."

The following two days saw them taking random paths in hopes of stumbling across the Hollow. Ramahd himself spent nearly the whole third day in the vulture's nest, scanning the horizon. He'd been so optimistic when they'd started their journey, but was starting to think it was a lost cause.

As the sun was lowering in the west, Cicio called up to him. "There's a plate of food for you."

Ramahd stared down, but made no move to descend, effectively ignoring Cicio's implied request to trade places.

"It's my turn," Cicio went on, "and when you're tired, you start to miss things. Come down. Eat. Rest a while. It'll be dark soon."

Ramahd finally relented. He climbed down and ate the prepared dish of salt pork, dates, and stale biscuits. He downed it as if he were starving, not because he was particularly hungry, but because it tasted so bad he wanted to get it over with. *Mighty Alu how I miss sea bream drenched in butter, capers, and lemon.*

Within minutes of finishing, he was restless. A few minutes more and he found himself standing at the bow, gazing at the way ahead.

"Rest!" Cicio shouted from above.

Cicio was right, he knew. To keep himself from going mad, he returned to the tradition he'd started early in their journey: he sat on the foredeck and read a few pages of Fezek's journal.

The journal, written in Fezek's uniquely shaky script, was an interesting piece of ordered chaos. On its lefthand pages were stanzas from the epic poem he was writing. Many stanzas had been crossed out and rewritten—Fezek's attempts at narrowing in not only on the story's substance but also its best expression. On the righthand side were dates, times, and various notes on the fantastic set of events he'd born witness to since being raised by Anila. Much of the earliest pages were dedicated to Anila herself, how she'd been abducted by Hamzakiir, one of the desert's most infamous blood magi;

the frostbite she'd suffered when Davud used a spell to douse the flaming ships in Ishmantep; and her eventual death in the cavern below the Sun Palace, a sacrifice she'd made to save Sharakhai.

The poetry wasn't half bad, Ramahd decided. Fezek had come a long way since his early and rather horrible attempts. More than that, Fezek's love and admiration for the people he'd met along the way was clear. Anila and Davud were quite obviously the foremost in his heart, but there were plenty of others, people like Çeda and Emre, Ramahd and Cicio, Frail Lemi and Esmeray. Even King Ihsan and Queen Nayyan were mentioned in a positive light.

As the deck tilted over a shallow dune, Fezek thumped his way over the foredeck and sat across from Ramahd. For a time he stared at the sunset, but occasionally his eyes slipped to Ramahd and the journal.

"Come to watch the sun set?" Ramahd asked.

"Yes, and why not? I don't know how many more I'm likely to get." He smiled his earnest smile, which Ramahd had once thought grisly but now found touching. "And you, Lord Amansir?" He tipped his head toward the journal. "Have you found anything of interest?"

"Some, yes."

"Some . . . ?"

"I'm speaking of the content, Fezek, not your prose."

"Oh, yes, of course. Me as well."

He *hadn't* been referring to the content. He was always fishing for Ramahd's thoughts on his style. Ramahd didn't blame him for it—words a writer didn't fret over were words they weren't proud of, after all—but really, Fezek needn't worry in that regard.

"It's good." He touched his fingers to the lefthand page. "Truly."

He gave Ramahd a theatrical tilt of his head. "Well, thank you for saying so."

Ramahd continued reading and soon stumbled across a page that mentioned one night in Sharakhai when Fezek had been out watching the stars. In it, Ramahd had just woken from a dream in which Meryam was hunting him mercilessly. Fezek, in helping Ramahd to digest it, had told a story of his mother and how she used to unweave the ribbons in baskets and reweave them to suit some new inspiration. It had led to a watershed moment in Ramahd's quest to stop Meryam.

That wasn't what attracted him to the page, though. At the bottom, Fezek had written, *How I wish I could have met him in true life.* And with that insight, he recalled all the passages in the journal where Fezek had made note of Ramahd's clothing, his hair, even how closely his beard was trimmed. He'd been infatuated, maybe in love.

Looking up, Ramahd realized *that* was the reason Fezek had been watching him so closely. For his thoughts on his prose, yes, but also for Ramahd's reaction when he eventually, inevitably, came across this particular passage.

Fezek, clearly nervous, met Ramahd's eyes. Somehow, his ashen cheeks darkened.

"You know," Ramahd told him, "I wish I could have seen one of your performances. I would have been proud to sit in the audience, perhaps speak to you and the troupe afterward."

Fezek's gruesome smile returned. "It would have been a grand night, indeed. And who knows? Perhaps there's still time for me to make my long-awaited return!"

Ramahd smiled. "May the fates permit it."

Fezek put on a look of mock horror. "Oh, no, no, no!" he said in his hoary voice. "Wishing a thespian good luck is the worst thing you can do! We promptly forget a line or trip from the stage."

"In that case, may you catch cold and cough through all your lines."

Fezek tipped his head. "Now your horse is headed in the right direction. Again, but this time with more gusto."

"May the stage cave in and the theater catch fire!"

Fezek's enthusiastic smile was a horror show. "*Now* you've got it, my lord!"

They both laughed. Above them, Cicio rolled his eyes and went back to scanning the horizon.

That night, Ramahd dreamt of Meryam. She stood in a cave on the shores of the Austral Sea near Viaroza, Ramahd's ancestral home. The cave was one they'd visited several times together, first when Ramahd had been married to her sister, Yasmine, and later when she'd been trying to dominate Hamzakiir, who'd proved more difficult to break than Meryam had imagined.

The final trip, mere days before Meryam had broken through Hamzakiir's defenses, had been a pleasant experience. It was near sunset. The cave's walls and roof had been lit in glittering, geometric patterns as the sunlight reflected off the incoming waves, the sound of which was like the world sighing. It had done much to ease Meryam's troubled mind.

In the dream it was different. The skies outside were slate blue, a squall threatening. The waves rushing into the cave were chaotic, the water foamy and churning, a deep green beneath. The tide was rising. Each fresh set of waves brought the water higher along the walls.

Meryam stood at the back of the cave along a narrow stone shelf. Her ankles were chained to iron rings driven into the stone and there was so much blood covering her arms that it looked as though she were wearing tattered crimson gloves. Concentrating on the water, she drew sigils in the air. Her breath came heavily. She was scared. The water was going to drown her, and she didn't know if she could slow it. She didn't know if she could save herself.

The water continued to rise, the sound becoming an ever-present roar as it rose above the cave's entrance. When the entrance was lost to the rising water entirely, the waves quelled and the cave plunged into darkness. In the faint light coming in through the water, Ramahd saw Meryam's desperation. The water was lapping at her knees and still rising.

As it reached her hips, she cried out, rejecting her fear. Ramahd had seen her do it before. The energy released seemed to give her a renewed sense of purpose: the fear in her eyes was replaced by a look of pure determination.

As the water continued to rise, reaching her neck, she drew a new combination of sigils. The water began to slow . . . then it stopped altogether. Finally, it began to recede.

When it dropped low enough that the sea beyond the cave's entrance was revealed once more, the clouds had begun to break in the distance, sending shafts of light down against the dark water. Eventually the water dropped below the stone shelf, and the sea became calm. When it did, Meryam lowered her hands, closed her eyes, and breathed deeply, as if she knew how close she'd come to drowning.

Her energy spent, she lay on the stone shelf and fell asleep.

When Ramahd woke, it was morning and they were already under sail. "Why didn't you wake me?" he asked Cicio when he reached the clipper's main deck.

"I tried," Cicio said, and sipped on a cup of steaming kahve. "You were dead to the world."

The air was still cool from the night but the heat was already starting to build. In the distance, the desert shimmered with it. It reminded him of the water, the dream of the cave on the Austral Sea. "I was dreaming," he finally said to Cicio.

Cicio took an especially noisy sip. "Do tell."

"I saw Meryam."

At this, Cicio frowned. "Like when she was hounding you in Sharakhai?"

"Yes, I suppose."

Nearby, Fezek had his journal to hand. He suddenly started flipping through the pages, then handed the journal to Ramahd, pointing to a particular section. In the notes along the righthand side, Fezek had written, *Ramahd is despondent, feeling he'll never be rid of Meryam. He said, 'It feels like she's created a link between us that will never be broken.'*

"There's no link between us, Fezek."

Fezek motioned to the journal. "You said there was. You believed it then."

"Yes, but that was then. This is now."

But Fezek seemed adamant. "What would have changed?"

"Meryam's magic was burned from her."

"But the link between you, if it existed, was made when she *had* magic."

Ramahd had a sharp reply ready and waiting—that Fezek didn't understand the nature of his bond with Meryam—but the words died on his lips. Back then, when Meryam had been hounding him, Ramahd hadn't been sure if it was something Meryam had consciously created or that had been born out of the many times Meryam had used him as a conduit for her magic. That link *had* existed. He'd been certain of it. And if it had, it was certainly possible it *still* existed.

As he'd done countless times during their harrowing game of cat and mouse, Ramahd felt for that link. There, on the very edge of his perceptions, he sensed her. "Fezek," he said softly, hoping not to disturb the tenuous feeling, "you're bloody brilliant, you know that?"

Fezek beamed, and this time there was nothing gruesome about it. It was pure, unadulterated joy.

Ramahd pointed off the starboard beam. "Meryam's that way."

Chapter 24

AFTER THE BLOODY riot, it proved difficult for Ihsan, Nayyan, and their small host of Blade Maidens to leave the city—a strange twist of fate given how easy it had been to sneak in. That same evening, hours before the violence had truly quelled, Queen Alansal ordered a cordon placed around all four harbors, including King's Harbor, which meant that no ship, large or small, could leave the city without being searched. By morning, the mouths of the harbors were tight as drums. Even sleighs were being stopped, and riders on horses were eyed more suspiciously than ships. Who, after all, would choose to leave the city on horseback but those who intended to conspire with the Sharakhani Kings and Queens?

Ihsan managed to get a note to Queen Sunay, hidden in the neighborhood known as the Well. Sunay had planned to ignite more violence all across the city, but on Ihsan's urgings focused her efforts instead on the northern harbor, the one most precious to Alansal, the one that housed many of her supply ships.

As the Mirean regulars shifted their focus to meet the threat on the northern harbor, Ihsan, Nayyan, Tolovan, their Blade Maidens, and Ibrahim waited along the skirts of the southern harbor. When the forces seemed thin, they galloped away from the city. A warning horn was sounded, but not a single soldier gave chase.

They reached Ihsan's galleon, the *Miscreant*, among a scattering of rocks several hours later. After ordering the crew to remain onboard, Ihsan built a fire in a small clearing among the rocks and set fringed carpets around it. Soon he, Ibrahim, and Nayyan were sitting around the fire while Ransaneh, swaddled in a pretty blue blanket, slept in the hollow of Nayyan's crossed legs. As Nayyan absently stroked her baby's hair and munched on olives, Ihsan poured three goblets of araq from a tall, hourglass-shaped bottle. He handed the first to Nayyan, wincing at his cracked ribs as he did so. The second he offered to Ibrahim, who immediately held his hands up, declining.

"I appreciate all you've done for me, truly, but the danger must be past by now. If you but give me a few skins of water and a bit of food, I'll make my way back to the city and leave the great game to you."

"It's funny you should mention the great game"—Ihsan, his ribs grousing from the movement, gave the goblet a swirl—"those who play it well study their opponents carefully before making their next move."

Ibrahim, clearly uncomfortable, offered up a miserable smile and accepted the goblet.

"Word has reached us," Ihsan went on, "that you were spying on Queen Meryam."

Now Ibrahim winced. "I wouldn't say *spying*, Your Excellency."

"Then pray tell what *were* you doing?"

A moment ago Ibrahim looked like he wasn't planning to have *any* araq. After Ihsan's question, he downed the lot. He bared his teeth from the alcohol burn, then set the goblet down on the carpet, noticeably farther away than he needed to. "My wife died some months ago," he finally said.

Ransaneh stirred at a loud snap from the fire. Nayyan rocked her gently, and Ransaneh burbled, squirmed a bit, then fell back to sleep.

"I'm sorry to hear that," Nayyan said.

"Thank you"—Ibrahim shared a sad smile with her—"but I didn't mention it for sympathy. Drink nearly cost me my marriage, but Eva stuck with me. It was through *her* strength that I avoided it for many long decades. After she passed . . . well . . . I tried to remain strong for *her* sake but did a rather poor job of it. One night, I decided to sit in my favorite oud parlor and have one drink. Maybe two. Things went a bit further than that, however. I became not merely *tipsy*, but good and proper, tripping-down-the-dunes drunk. Somehow I got into my head that a walk beyond the rocks of the western harbor would be good for me. *To clear my mind,* I told myself, before returning to the bed I once shared with Eva."

"Is that where you saw Meryam?" Ihsan asked.

Ihsan had been careful about speaking too much since the riots. The pain was mostly gone, but just then, for whatever reason, it came back in a rush. Spit gathered in his mouth. He swallowed and relaxed his jaw, willing it to pass.

Nayyan, perhaps noting how strangely his words had come out, furrowed her brow at him, but thankfully her eyes drifted down to his goblet. Better she thought it was the araq than the real reason.

"Yes," Ibrahim said, "but I saw little enough. A sleigh being dragged toward Adzin's old sloop. A few men and women speaking Qaimiran. My drink-addled mind was convinced it was Queen Meryam, but truth be told, I'm not certain."

"Then why did you spin a tale about a Qaimiri Queen?" The pain in Ihsan's mouth had mercifully eased to a dull ache.

Ibrahim's toothy smile was like a west end tenement, hastily constructed and likely to crumble. "A man has to earn a living."

"Do you speak Qaimiran, Ibrahim?" Ihsan asked in the Qaimiri tongue. Ibrahim didn't even need to reply. The fact that he looked suddenly nervous gave Ihsan his answer. "Tell me what they said," he went on, switching back to Sharakhan. "Tell me what she has planned."

Ibrahim's eyes turned haunted. "I'm but a humble storyteller, my good King." His voice was thin as a wight's wail. "This is all too big for me."

"What harm is there in saying it when there's only us"—Ihsan waved to the desert—"and the Great Shangazi to hear it?"

"Don't you see? She'll *come* for me."

"She doesn't know you're here."

"She's a blood mage."

"No longer. Her power was burned from her."

"Not if she succeeds in her goals. Then she'll have all that and more."

"What do you mean?"

Ibrahim stared into the fire. He took up his empty goblet and held it out. Ihsan was debating on whether to give him any when Ransaneh began to writhe. She cried until she released a bit of gas with the sort of wet sound that made parents wince at the changing that awaited them. From a cloth bag beside her, Nayyan took out a fresh diaper and changed her with efficient ease.

Ibrahim watched as Ransaneh returned to silent slumber. Ibrahim lowered his goblet. His expression faltered, as if he couldn't decide whether to laugh or cry. He settled on an earnest smile, though tears were gathering in his eyes. He blinked them away and regarded Nayyan, then Ihsan, and his smile became a look of calm acceptance. "What do you know of Ashael the Fallen?"

Ihsan's fingers began to tingle. He felt his ears turn red. He'd witnessed the passing of four centuries in the Great Shangazi. Empires had come and gone in that time. Cities had burned. New ones had risen from their ashes. He'd played the great game and played it well. He'd bargained with gods and lived to tell the tale. There was little left that could strike fear in his heart, but the name Ashael did.

Nayyan looked confused. "Who is Ashael the Fallen?"

"One of the elder gods," Ihsan said. "Legends say he was struck down and left behind when the others departed this world for the next."

Ibrahim nodded. "His name is rarely mentioned in the old texts. When they mention him at all, it's usually to say how wicked he was, how reviled, especially by his fellow elders."

Nayyan shook her head, confused. "Why are you bringing up a myth?"

"Because Meryam spoke his name. And the body on the sleigh was Goezhen's, slain by Nalamae in the desert. She said she planned to use it to reach Ashael, to awaken him"—Ibrahim paused—"as the goddess meant for her to do."

"The goddess . . ." Nayyan echoed. "Which one?"

Ibrahim shrugged. "Meryam didn't say."

Ihsan, staring into the fire, was already working through the implications. "It certainly wasn't Nalamae, and whether it was Tulathan or Rhia is immaterial. The fact is they're using Meryam to raise Ashael."

"But why?" Nayyan asked.

Ihsan peered into the darkness beyond the fire. "What do you suppose Ashael's overriding emotion will be once he's risen?"

"Anger," Nayyan replied easily.

"Precisely," said Ihsan. "He will feel, much as the young gods do, that he was robbed of the world beyond, that he's been kept from it unfairly. He will widen the gateway. He will step through to the world beyond and seek his revenge, or remake it in his image, or do whatever it is an elder god does when he gains a place long denied him. *That* is the moment the young gods maneuver toward. They plan to follow in his wake, the world they leave behind be damned."

Ibrahim looked stunned, as if he were on a collision course with what he'd been trying to avoid.

Nayyan looked shocked as well, but she'd always been a pragmatic woman. "Where are they going?" she said to Ibrahim a moment later.

He shrugged. "They were looking for a place named the Hollow."

Nayyan shook her head. "What's that?"

"It's a pit in the desert," Ihsan replied, "surrounded by a circle of ancient standing stones."

"You know it?"

"The Kings have known about it for centuries," Ihsan replied. "Word came years ago that Adzin was using it, attracting useful demons from its depths."

"And you never looked into it?"

Ihsan shook his head. "It was more Sukru's province than mine. And the things Adzin was doing seemed innocent enough. I recall Sukru thought him more madman than mage."

Nayyan asked, "Do you know where it is, this Hollow?"

"Roughly. It may take a bit of finding." Were the wind up, Ihsan would have ordered them to sail that very moment, but it wasn't. "We'll sail for it in the morning."

It was with a distinct feeling of unease that they retired to the *Miscreant*. Unsurprisingly, Ihsan couldn't sleep. He left the ship and wandered the desert for a time. He stared at the stars, stared at Tulathan and Rhia as they trekked across the sky. He wondered if the twin goddesses were staring down at him, laughing. "You won't win," he said to the chill night air. "I refuse to allow it."

A short while later, Ihsan heard footsteps. He thought it was Nayyan, but it was Yndris. "My Lord King," she said in greeting.

For a time, Yndris merely stood with him and stared at the star-filled sky, but Ihsan could tell she was working up to something.

"Is there something you wish to say, Maiden?"

Yndris had become more circumspect since her father Cahil's death. Her brashness still raised its ugly head from time to time, but more and more she thought before she spoke, which Ihsan gave her credit for—*any* amount of introspection would be more than her father had ever managed. Ihsan thought she might have come to talk about Meryam or Ashael, so it surprised him when she cleared her throat and said, "I don't mean to involve myself in your personal life, Your Excellence."

"But . . . ?"

"But I think you might want to speak to your Queen."

Ihsan spun to face her. "About what?"

"About whatever it is that might concern her."

For a moment, Ihsan had no idea what to say. "Is she worried about Ransaneh?"

"Yes, but not for the reasons you might think."

"What then?"

Yndris took a deep breath. "It really would be better if you talked to her, Your Highness." With that she turned and headed for the ship.

Left in her wake was the sort of cold unease that grew the longer it went unaddressed. It was with heavy steps that Ihsan returned to the *Miscreant*, and to the cabin he shared with Nayyan. In the bunk, Nayyan was curled on her side while Ransaneh fed at her breast.

Her soft smile faded as he stood there stiffly. "What's wrong?"

"Yndris said I should talk to you." It was an inelegant opening at best, but he couldn't help it. Yndris's refusal to speak plainly had set an indescribable fear gnawing at his insides.

Nayyan kissed the top of Ransaneh's head, pointedly ignoring Ihsan, which only made matters worse. "I told her not to bother you with it."

"Bother me with what?"

She looked up, her eyes red and glistening. The silence between them yawned wider and wider.

"Nayyan, what is it?"

She beckoned Ihsan. He moved closer, but the fear inside him was threatening to consume him. When she flicked her fingers at his hand, he froze, unable to take this final step. He was terrified of the truth. But after seeing his own terror echoed in Nayyan's eyes, he named himself a coward and held his hand out for her to take. She did, and pressed it against her belly. She moved his fingers to various places and pressed hard.

Breath of the desert, there was something *unnatural* below the skin. It wasn't apparent to the casual touch, but with her pressing so hard he could feel it, a growth of some sort. It felt so alien Ihsan recoiled from it, but then he relaxed and let Nayyan guide his fingers along the extent of it. It went from her pelvis to her rib cage, and was nearly wide as her hips. It was lumpy and hard, like a demon growing inside her.

Nayyan's tears flowed freely now. "The black mould," she said. "The physic confirmed it. She examined my birth canal as well. The flesh there is dark. Malignant. It's growing, Ihsan, and quickly."

"There must be something we can do. The elixirs . . ." He stopped himself, suddenly cold. Her insistence that they *not* give an elixir to Ransaneh now made perfect sense. "It was the elixirs," he said numbly, "*they* caused the mould."

"I wasn't sure at first," she replied, "but yes, I think so."

Ihsan felt like he was falling down a bottomless well. He went to the chest where they kept the vials of elixirs.

"They're gone, Ihsan. I woke late in the night after visiting the physic, after I'd fainted. I emptied them all and buried the vials."

He opened the chest anyway, to find them missing. A terrible thought dawned on Ihsan, and his eyes drifted to Ransaneh, who was feeding at Nayyan's teat. Without saying a word, he reached down and snatched their daughter from her breast.

"What?" Nayyan looked shocked, but then she stared down at her bared breast, then her belly. "Oh, gods, no!"

Ihsan wanted to console her, but how could he? Mothers passed many things to their children through their milk. Their temperament, their fortune, their health or lack thereof. Ihsan saw his fears echoed in Nayyan's tortured eyes.

That their folly, their desire to live forever and rule the desert alone, had been doomed from the start was bad enough. It was made infinitely worse by the realization that their efforts could deliver their daughter to the grave. They inspected Ransaneh carefully, checking her belly, her chest, her throat, and her limbs, looking for any signs of similar lumps. The fates be praised, they found none.

"She's young," Ihsan said. "She's strong. And we don't know that your milk will have passed the disease to her."

But Nayyan was inconsolable. Ihsan lay with them both long into the night, until Nayyan fell asleep at last. He'd hidden his fears—Nayyan had enough to worry about—but now they were returning, stronger than ever.

From a desk drawer he took out a mirror. He held the lantern up and adjusted the mirror until he could see inside his mouth. Then he lifted his tongue. There, on the underside, was a misshapen brown spot. Moving his tongue around, he saw another, then a third along his inner jaw. He probed the largest of them with one finger. It was lumpy underneath. Hard.

Part of him had known the moment he'd felt the lump in Nayyan's belly. She wasn't the only one who'd been doomed when they'd created their elixir of life. He had been too.

The vision he and Nayyan had read in the Blue Journal, just before Queen Alansal's surprise attack, was suddenly fresh in his mind. *A grinning demon invades,* Yusam's passage read, *making straight for one of the falcons— the one with the faltering call, the one who's meant to die.*

The faltering call was an obvious reference to him—the power of his voice had been unreliable since Cahil had helped regrow his tongue—but he'd thought the last part of the passage, *the one who's meant to die,* was referring to the orders Alansal had given the qirin warrior. He would surely have been told to take Ihsan and Husamettín's lives if he could.

Now Ihsan understood the truth. The passage was a harbinger of his death. It had been referring obliquely, not to the sudden attack by the qirin warrior, but to the black mould.

Ihsan knew he should wake Nayyan and tell her. But he couldn't. Not just then.

Instead, he blew out the lamp, lay by her side in the darkness, with Ransaneh between them. And wept.

Chapter 25

ÇEDA BLINKED FIERCELY as she returned to herself. The valley's imposing mountains stood in a ring around her. Before her, the acacia swayed in the breeze. Gods, it was already near evening. The others were all there in the circle. Sümeya was speaking in low tones with Kameyl, Shal'alara, and Dardzada. Emre was staring at her with a look of concern. Leorah smiled in the supportive way great-grandmothers did. Frail Lemi was walking away, probably to find food.

"You're back?" Sümeya asked as she broke away from Kameyl.

"Yes," Çeda said, with no real confidence.

"Good," Sümeya replied, "because you have to concentrate. Memories of your mother may be alluring, but they aren't what you need to find. You're letting regret over her death, maybe even guilt, guide you."

Çeda had no idea what she was talking about at first. But then it all came rushing back. Sharakhai cloaked in darkness. Her mother finding her gone, then rushing to the western harbor to save her.

Çeda waved impotently to the acacia. "It won't give me what I want."

"Because you aren't trying hard enough."

"I am."

"No, you're not." She crouched and stared directly into Çeda's eyes, then spoke softly, so that only Çeda could hear. "Everything rides on this, Çeda. Zaghran came by a short while ago. He moved the heavens to win you the morning, so you have until then, no longer. The tribunal votes on Hamid's proposal to sail on Sharakhai at high sun." She paused. "Visions of your mother are intoxicating, no doubt, but you can't give in to them. You need to focus, as you did with the asirim. *You* must guide the *tree*, not the other way around."

She felt like such a failure. She'd promised them she would expose Hamid's crimes and bring him to justice. "I'll try harder," she said. "I'll find a way."

"If you'd only let me help you," Sümeya said.

Sümeya had made the offer before, but Çeda had been convinced, was *still* convinced, that it would only muddy the waters.

"Thank you," Çeda said, "but I can't add another mind to mine. I need to find the way alone or I'll never find it."

Çeda stood and stretched. Frail Lemi returned with a massive platter of flatbread, hummus, and spicy olives. They ate and quenched their thirst with lemon-laced water. As before, Rasime stared down from the walls of the fort. Others watched from the shores of the lake. And in the meantime, the talks in the pavilion continued.

They were just starting another session, likely their last before being forced to sleep and to present what they could to the tribunal in the morning, when Leorah tottered toward her.

Gods, how frail you look, grandmother.

The tremors that plagued her seemed to be getting worse. The glint in her eyes, though, was strong, seemingly eternal. "I believe in you, child." She waved to the tree with a trembling hand. "Search your heart and find the truth. Find that truth and the tree will listen."

"But there are many truths, grandmother."

Leorah smiled as she took Çeda's hand and squeezed. "And the tree knows them all."

The words sounded like nonsense, the ravings of an old woman, but they also felt true.

Beyond the tree, at the far end of the lake, children swam while their mothers and fathers conversed on the bank. High above, thin white clouds passed one another, some compressing into solid-looking shapes, others attenuating like spindrift. All around her were the sounds of her tribe—conversation lifting, the acacia's leaves blown by the wind, water lapping at the lake shore. It made her acutely aware of the tree and the power within it. She felt as if she were standing at the very nexus of past and future, countless threads behind her leading to countless threads ahead.

It made her intimately aware of how integral past and future were. An event in the here and now was born of innumerable decisions and actions from the past, and would lead to innumerable futures. The notion was dizzying, but also clarifying.

"Come," she said to the others. "I would see the end of my mother's tale."

Sümeya frowned. "Çeda—"

She stopped when Çeda held up a hand. "The tree chose it for a reason. Let's see what it is."

Sümeya's gaze shifted to the pavilion. "You risk everything."

"I must see where the trail leads."

Sümeya looked like she wanted to argue, but in the end she only stared up at the tree. At the glass chimes. "Very well," she said, and took her position in the circle.

Soon they were all seated, their eyes closed. With but a reach toward the tree, they descended into darkness.

The twin moons were full, bright lamps in a star-filled sky. The asirim wailed as Ahya searched among the rocks. She moved carefully from one to the next, wary of the asirim but doubly alert for any sign of Çeda.

Ahead of her came the crunch of sand. She drew her sword as a dark shadow came rushing toward her. The silhouette was slender and shorter than most asirim but she was still wary—there were children among those tortured souls, and they could wreak as much havoc as the adults. But she could see it wasn't moving like an asir. It was weaving from rock to rock, scanning the way behind for signs of pursuit.

Reckoning the figure was a boy, she stood and held her hands up to forestall him. It was Tariq, she realized. He screamed bloody murder and slipped on the sand while trying to avoid her, then scampered away, shouting all the while.

Ahya leapt on top of him and clamped one hand over his fool mouth. "Be quiet!" When he didn't, she cuffed him. "It's *Ahya*, you bloody idiot. Çeda's mother!"

He finally calmed, but now his eyes were everywhere but on her. Perhaps realizing how much noise he'd made, he was peering beyond the nearest stones with a terrified expression.

Seizing his lower jaw, Ahya forced him to look at her. "Tell me where my daughter is." When he remained silent, she set the blade of her shamshir across his throat and leaned in until their eyes were locked on one another. "Can you feel the chill of my blade, Tariq?"

He nodded slowly.

"Good, now tell me where my daughter is before I run the edge across your useless, thieving throat."

He lifted one hand and pointed deeper into the desert. "She went farther than the rest of us. We told her not to. She didn't have to go so far, but she did anyway."

Tariq pointed to a dense litter of rocks, as a fearful yipping rose up from that direction. Another followed, this one pained, bordering on a squeal. Then a chorus of howls. Dear gods, there were dozens more asirim coming in from the west.

"Where?" Ahya asked Tariq.

He shrugged. "I don't *know*." He pointed again. "That way. I lost sight of her."

By the gods who breathe, how she wanted to strangle him for his stupidity, for the part he'd played in putting Çeda in danger. Instead, she let her sword drop from his throat. "Go. Stay low until you reach the wharfs, then hide on a ship."

Tariq nodded and rushed away in a half crouch. Ahya, meanwhile, turned on hearing a whimper. She'd spoken too loudly. Fifty paces distant, a form scuffled closer, an asir moving from rock to rock, coming ever nearer to her position.

Suddenly the asir's head shot up. It tracked Tariq's movement. Releasing a long bay, it sprinted after him.

Tariq sent one wild glance back, then abandoned all pretense of stealth and sprinted headlong for the nearest wharf some two hundred paces distant. He was never going to make it. The asir was already galloping like an akhala, sand kicking up as it drove toward him in powerful strides.

Hunkered low behind a rock, Ahya waited. She controlled her breathing lest it give her away, and when the sound of the asir's galloping stride came near, she leapt out and swung her shamshir across the asir's path. The power of the swing combined with the asir's own momentum allowed the sword to cut through skin and bone. The blade lodged deep in its chest, cutting the wretched creature's surprised squeal short.

The asir fell, but the sheer violence of the blow twisted Ahya's shamshir from her grip. Black blood flew and sand kicked up as the asir came to a rolling, loose-limbed halt. Ahya picked up her blade and stood over its twitching form. The asir had been a girl once, no older than Çeda when she'd been cursed by the desert gods.

Ahya crouched down until the two of them were eye-to-eye. "I'm sorry," she said to the poor, lost soul. "You didn't deserve this." The asir's eyes began to glaze. "You didn't deserve any of this."

When she fell slack, Ahya wiped the blade on the asir's tattered clothes and moved on in the direction Tariq had indicated. By the time she was nearing the cluster of rocks, the yips and howls of the larger group of asirim were loud and getting louder. She scanned the rocks for any sign of movement.

"Çeda," she hissed. She worried that any noise would attract the asirim, but if Çeda *was* hidden in the rocks, she'd likely be silent, curled up tight, hiding from the asirim to prove to the boys she wasn't afraid. "Çeda, there's nothing left to prove. The boys have all gone." Hearing no reply, she went on. "You're the last one. You outlasted them all."

Not far away, a large group of asirim approached the rocks. Their leader wove among them, moving with no great haste. The two behind it dropped to all fours and sniffed the sand like hounds.

"You have to call out to me, girl." She waited for several long breaths, worried Çeda's reply would be spoken too softly to hear. "Çeda, you *have* to call to me."

The asirim approached. Goezhen's sweet kiss, there were a score of them roaming the rocks.

"Çeda, hear me!"

Several heartbeats later, a small voice called back. "I'm here."

Ahya ran toward the sound and found her hiding in the lee of a tilted boulder. She held Çeda tight as tears streamed down her cheeks. Çeda trembled like a lamb before the slaughter. "It's all right," Ahya whispered softly. "Memma's here."

As Çeda held her tight, her shivering grew more pronounced. "It was stupid, memma. I shouldn't have come."

"Shhhh. Everything's fine now."

It was a lie, but Ahya would say the words a thousand times over if it would quell Çeda's fears. She'd been a hard mother. She'd come to Sharakhai with a mission, a mission filled with righteous purpose, but she should have been home today. She should have been more aware of what her child was up to, who she was friends with. If she had, she would have caught Çeda *before* she left on some foolish dare, and neither of them would have been in danger.

Instead, both their lives were at risk, and she had no idea how to make it better.

The sounds of the asirim's snuffling grew louder. One passed a tall, thin rock to Ahya's left. Another scuttled across the ground like a scarab to her right. A third howled so loudly it rattled Ahya's bones. Çeda whimpered by her side as a tall, thin asir with lanky hair and yellow eyes rounded the rock they were hiding behind. Another, this one missing an arm, approached from the opposite side. More followed, like a pack of black laughers who'd stumbled upon their next kill.

Ahya positioned herself in front of Çeda as the asirim closed in. The nearest of them, the one with only one arm, was low, practically crawling. It sniffed the air, moving steadily toward the hem of Ahya's fighting dress. A soft mewling sound escaped it, while a low growl came from the tall one beside it.

It was the blood, Ahya realized. They smelled the blood of the asir she'd killed.

Instead of drawing her shamshir, she drew her knife and ran the edge across the palm of her opposite hand. She held it up to them. "I am blood of your blood!" She waved it before the tall one, then the one crawling low. "We are both blood of your blood!"

They paused. She was convinced the words meant nothing to them, that they would tear her and Çeda limb from limb for killing one of their own. But then the hatred in their jaundiced eyes faded. Their aggressive stances eased. They shrank before her eyes, as if the presence of two of their descendants somehow shamed them.

They scuttled backward. They turned away. As they headed en masse toward Sharakhai to fulfill their duty, they released a long, combined keening, a lament for the cursed lives they were forced to live by the will of the gods and the Sharakhani Kings.

As they left and the sounds of their passage faded, Ahya held Çeda close, and the two of them wept.

———————⟵●⟶———————

Çeda woke to the soft rustle of leaves. Above her, the acacia swayed. The sky was a brilliant salmon pink, but the sun was behind the mountains and the valley itself lay in shadow. As had been true of the other visions, hours had passed.

She realized she felt a yearning of sorts, a pull toward the past. At first it felt as though it were coming from all directions, tearing her apart, but the more she became aware of the valley around her, the more she realized it was coming from the acacia.

Around her, the others were waking as well. Emre looked dumbstruck. Dardzada was pensive, as if he were comparing the vision to his memories of that earlier time. Frail Lemi was bawling, his chest wracking in great heaves. The rest seemed unsure what to think of what they'd just witnessed.

Leorah was the first to recover. "I'll make some tea," she said, and shuffled off toward a nearby campfire.

Emre, meanwhile looked confused. "You told me you and your mother hid in the stones. That you weren't discovered."

Çeda felt as if she'd betrayed Emre by hiding the truth, but there was a simple reason behind it. "She told me never to speak of it."

"Well, you could have told *me*."

"I'm sorry, Emre, but I couldn't. I owed her that much. She saved me."

Emre looked wounded, but a moment later, he nodded. "You're right."

Just then dozens began to file out from within the pavilion. Many of the shaikhs and their viziers glanced toward the tree. Hamid and Rasime looked smug. Shaikh Zaghran looked dour. Many of the others did as well, none more so than Aríz.

"Given how long you were taking," Aríz said when he came near, "Hamid pressed to advance our talks."

"And?" Emre asked.

"Enough agreed that we spoke of our collective plans for Sharakhai. I must tell you, most have already made up their minds about Hamid, and whether or not to sail on Sharakhai."

"Hamid deserves death," Çeda said.

"I agree," Aríz said calmly, "but he's been convincing. He's given up concessions. Sharakhai will be given notice. They'll be allowed to flee to neighboring lands, should they so choose." Çeda began to argue, but he talked over her. "You're only going to have one chance to change their minds."

"One chance is all I'll need," she said firmly. The vision of her mother and that harrowing night had revealed not only how to delve into the past, but how to share it.

"You're certain?" Aríz asked. "Because—"

"I'm certain."

Aríz seemed relieved. "Then you should try tonight. I can call the council—"

"No," Çeda said firmly. "I'm too tired. We need to do this right."

Aríz finally relented, and the valley quieted. Exhausted, Çeda soon found herself beneath a blanket with Emre. She worried over many things that night, but her mastery over the tree wasn't one of them.

In little time, she'd fallen into a deep, deep sleep.

She woke what felt like moments later to a thunderous sound. Another came a moment later, then another—a cascade of explosions accompanied by flashes of yellow light against the tent's canvas roof. Gods, it sounded like the mountain was falling down.

She and the others were up in a flash. They rushed from the tent as the largest explosion yet shook the earth.

Çeda gasped at the sight before her. The acacia was broken, blackened. Several large boughs had fallen to the ground. Flames licked along the fallen boughs and the branches high above.

The entire tree was lit aflame, a blinding torch burning in the night.

Chapter 26

NIGHT HAD FALLEN when Meryam left *The Gray Gull* and walked to the fathomless pit known as the Hollow. She knelt beside its yawning mouth while Tulathan, the silver moon, hung half-lidded in a dark, scintillant sky. Amaryllis and the crew, save for a lone watchman, were sleeping. Meryam had tried to sleep as well, but her dreams had been haunted by the death of her crewman, Ernesto. She woke with visions of the winged demon, wrapping its thin limbs around Ernesto's frame. The dream eventually faded, but not before she saw the demon clamp its jaws over Ernesto's neck and plummet into the depths of the pit.

Kneeling on the hard rock, she stared up at the bright moon. "Come to me." She used her thumb to draw Tulathan's holy symbol, a crescent shape, over her heart. "Come, for I need your guidance."

The cool wind gusted, sending scree skittering along the rocky plateau.

"Come, Tulathan." Though it felt like a betrayal to her patron god, Alu, she made Tulathan's sign again. "I don't know what to do."

Somewhere in the distance, a ridge owl screeched.

"*You* wanted this," Meryam said, louder this time. Her voice sounded desperate, even to her. "You wanted it as much as I did. I need but the smallest of clues to do the rest."

But the desert remained deaf to her pleas. It stung to have come so close only to be abandoned by Tulathan. What was there to do but forge ahead? She couldn't force the hand of the gods.

How very droll, Meryam, when forcing the hands of the gods is precisely what you're trying to do.

It was her sister's voice, Yasmine. She'd been gone a long while—for good, Meryam had thought.

"Leave me alone," Meryam grumbled.

But why, dear sister? Don't you miss me?

"Why would you return after all this time?"

Because your gambit has failed. When you come to grips with that fact, I expect you'll throw yourself in that pit, and the two of us will be reunited at last.

"Shut up, Yasmine."

She stared down as Ernesto's terror-filled eyes appeared in the darkness. He'd left behind a wife and three children. He'd been a veritable wizard with rope and string. He'd used that skill to make intricate hemp bracelets. He was gone now because Meryam had pushed too far, too fast. She should have taken her time. She should have learned more about Ashael.

Despite the admission, she took the leather bag she'd brought with her and tugged its mouth open.

Take care, Meryam, lest everything fall apart.

Meryam couldn't tell if it was her own voice or Yasmine's. Barely had the thought registered when Yasmine laughed, long and hard. Meryam felt her cheeks redden. Ignoring the feelings of inadequacy, she reached into the leather bag, took a pinch of the ivory powder within, and threw it into the cavernous gap.

Down the powder floated. The moonlight made it looked like a gossamer net spreading wide as it disappeared into the void. Only then did she sniff what remained of the powder from her fingertips. Its subtle power filled her lungs, made her eyes flutter momentarily.

She blinked and the edges of the deeper shadows began to shimmer. She blinked again and those edges grew bright. Having performed this ritual several times over the past few days, she'd grown accustomed to the feeling, but it still felt heady, as if a well of power lay just beyond reach.

Minutes passed as the moon cast its silvery light over the desert. Meryam became aware of the creatures below, the many demons that fed like lampreys off Ashael's dreaming form. Even as they feasted, they hungered for Meryam, especially the one that had risen and taken Ernesto. But no demons rose from the depths. They were too comfortable near the elder god. It would take a good deal more powder for them to rise.

The demons represented but the first of the dangers of trying to awaken the fallen god. Even if she found some way to protect herself and her crew from the demons, how could she safely use Ashael for her own purposes?

The answer surely lay in Goezhen's body. Tulathan had given it to her for a purpose. What, though? What was she supposed to do with it? She'd been struggling with that question from the moment Tulathan left her beside that stinking pool in Mazandir. She'd thought she had an answer, but the tragedy of her first attempt at raising Ashael from the pit had left her scrambling for some other solution, some other purpose for Goezhen beyond simple sacrifice.

As had been true during her previous attempts, glimpses of an ancient world came to her. They were from Ashael's dream, delivered to her through the powder she'd sent down into the pit. She saw the world as it was millennia ago. A world unpopulated by mortals, when only gods walked the earth. Having long since abandoned his attempts at creating new life, Ashael found amusement in maligning the creations of others, destroying beauty, perverting perfection.

Time passed. Meryam saw humanity progress. Tribes formed. Villages arose. Then came cities made of stone. Civilizations blossomed only to crumble to dust, often because of Ashael. How he adored debasing mortalkind, torturing them. He was the heart of evil, a darkness that spread to many of the young gods, Goezhen first, then Naamdah, Sjado, and Odokōn.

When Ashael's fellow elders saw his rot spread to even the most powerful of their creations, they knew something must be done. They'd already begun making plans for the creation of a new world. They would continue those plans but without Ashael. They would bury him instead, send him deep into the earth. Leave him behind as they went to create a world that would be pure and unsullied by his malevolence.

When Ashael's dreams faded, Meryam woke folded over her knees, tears streaming down her face. Mortals weren't made to experience the dreams of elder gods. Despair flooded through her. She was no closer to solving this riddle than when she arrived. She feared she never would be.

As dawn blazed bright along the eastern horizon, Meryam wondered about Ashael's influence over the young gods. Goezhen had been created by Iri, but corrupted by Ashael. His body would have meaning for Ashael, surely, but if she took that step, if she sacrificed his corpse, there would be no getting it back.

Sacrifices aren't really sacrifices unless they're permanent, she told herself.

When dawn arrived and Amaryllis came from the ship, Meryam said to her, "Have Goezhen's body brought to the pit."

Amaryllis had two cups of steaming tea, one of which she held out to Meryam. "You're sure?"

"I'm sure."

Amaryllis stared down into the nearby pit, then nodded. "As you say."

It took the crew some time, but soon enough, as the morning sun warmed the dark stone, it was done: Goezhen's massive form rested at the very edge of the pit.

Six crewmen stood at the ready, poleaxes to hand, ready to lever Goezhen's emaciated body into the pit.

"You need but give us the word, my queen," said the captain.

He had on a brave face, as if it was for Meryam's benefit alone, but the way he kept glancing at the pit made it clear that he was torn. He'd be pleased to be rid of Goezhen's corpse but feared what would happen next.

Meryam's doubts, meanwhile, were starting to creep back in. The moment Goezhen tipped into that pit, there would be no turning back.

"We don't have to do it now," Amaryllis said. "We can wait."

"I know," replied Meryam, "but the very fact that it means so much to me means the sacrifice will have more power."

What could Amaryllis say? She was out of her element, and they both knew it.

Meryam wished the bloody goddess had told her outright what to do. She wished Hamzakiir hadn't been freed. She wished Ramahd hadn't found her. She wished her magic hadn't been burned from her. She wished Yasmine were still alive.

I told you to stop using me as your excuse.

Meryam ignored Yasmine's voice and steeled herself. "Throw it in," she ordered the captain.

The captain nodded. "At once, my queen." He waved to his men. The crew spiked the butts of their poleaxes beneath Goezhen's corpse and levered it forward in concert. "Through the gates may he pass," the captain intoned, "whole and hale, to haunt this world no more."

It was a prayer for the dead, used often in Qaimir and sometimes in the desert. Though often spoken in an endearing manner, at its base it was a plea for the dead to leave this world and to bother the living no more. That was surely how the captain meant it, but it sparked a memory in Meryam, a passage from the Al'Ambra:

Ivory is the key to the wakeful mind, horn the key to dreaming.

She'd been using ivory powder for the past week because of the first half of the cryptic passage. She'd fooled herself into thinking that *waking* Ashael was the correct next step. It wasn't. Ashael was dreaming, which was precisely why she needed to use the other material mentioned: *horn*. Horn was the key to dreaming.

The men had Goezhen's body halfway over the lip of the pit. All Meryam could see in that moment was the one remaining horn: black, curving, arcing around Goezhen's head and his crown of thorns.

She hurtled forward, screaming, "Stop!"

Most of the crew did. One, halfway through his movement, kept levering, and the desiccated body started to slip over the edge.

"Save him!" she cried again, and fell upon Goezhen's chest, hoping to pin it down. She was too slight of frame, though, and the body kept tipping.

Suddenly Amaryllis was there, grabbing Goezhen's nearest arm. "Help us!"

Gravel crunched beneath Goezhen's body as it slipped further over the edge. The captain fell upon the nearest ankle. Another gripped one stiffened wrist. A third grabbed the horn. With all of them on it, its movement arrested. Dust and rocks sifted down into the pit. For several frightful moments, no one did anything but make sure the body wasn't slipping any further.

Then they were tugging it backward. It took long, harrowing moments—Meryam felt as if they would all plummet to their deaths—but soon they were back on solid ground.

Meryam's breath was on her by then. "The horn," she said while panting. "I need it shorn off and ground like the ivory."

The captain's look was sour. If he wasn't so loyal, he might have kicked Goezhen over the edge. "You're sure, my queen?"

"I'm sure."

He nodded. "Then it shall be done."

The horn itself was so strong it took nearly an hour to saw free. It took another two before any amount of powder was ready to use. Only when she had several handfuls did she accept the leather bag and command everyone to join her at the pit.

They stood as they had before. This time, however, Meryam took a handful of the horn's powder and threw it into the dark opening before her. The sun was high by then, and Meryam watched the powder fall until it was swallowed by shadow. Seeing it gone, she motioned to Goezhen's corpse.

"Now," she said. "Feed him to the pit."

The captain traded glances with Amaryllis, who seemed just as unsure. "You're certain this time, my queen? There's no hurry."

Meryam shook her head. "Do it now." She'd never been more sure of a thing in her life.

They did, and soon the monstrous, black corpse was tipping end over end into the darkness. When it, too, was lost to the shadows, Meryam took a pinch of the horn powder and breathed it in.

Earlier, when she'd taken the ivory, it had taken a long time to become in sync with Ashael's dreams. Not so with the horn. She felt in tune with the elder god immediately, so much so that the bag of powder slipped from her fingers. It spilled. Amaryllis rushed forward to collect the bag, but Meryam paid her no mind. Her mind's eye was already elsewhere.

She saw Ashael striding over a windswept sea. Crashing waves sprayed water over his sandal-covered feet. The white, knee-length shendyt he wore, bunched at his waist, was so bright it looked like freshly fallen snow. His well muscled chest and lithe arms were bare, but the golden armbands, the embossed cuffs that covered his wrists and forearms, and the torc wrapping his neck glimmered brightly in the sun. His cheeks were drawn, his mouth small and pinched, his eyes nearly lost within deep, sunken hollows. Most striking were the two broad horns that curved from the back of his skull and spread horizontally near his temples. They were the color of bone, an unsettling complement to his bloodless skin.

Many would feel small before the god, but not Meryam. She felt made for this moment. She'd spent *years* dominating others. She'd invaded dreams. Stolen secrets. She'd manipulated others by altering their reality, altering their memories, altering their very sense of self.

So it was that Meryam willed herself to appear on the sea's surface. "Come to me," she called.

Ashael had been calling to Alu, whom he was displeased with. In the dream, Alu hid in the depths below, smug in his place of power. At Meryam's words, the elder god turned, confused.

"Come to me," Meryam repeated.

And Ashael turned and strode across the water.

Outside the dream, Meryam stared down. She saw nothing at first, but then a lighter shadow appeared. Something was rising from the depths. Around her, the crew backed away. So did Amaryllis. They watched in stunned silence as Ashael rose.

The elder god was tall as a watchtower. He still wore the armbands, the cuffs, the golden torc. His sandals were scuffed and torn. His eyes, though, were hidden, wrapped in bands of dark, fraying cloth similar to his tattered shendyt. His body was gaunt, emaciated, his ribs clearly visible. His skin, pale before, was so ashen it looked as if a strong wind would see him eaten away, bit by bit, until nothing of him remained save bones and his two broad horns.

Strangest of all was the misshapen spike piercing the center of his chest. No rust marked the ebon steel. Dark, crusted blood caked around the point of entry. She recalled her vision of Iri driving it through him, recalled how the spike itself was one element of the spell that bound him to this earth.

Tall and proud in the dream earlier, *this* Ashael was bowed over that ancient wound. It weighed on his soul, caused unyielding pain, yet Ashael made no move to touch it—she felt his fear at the very thought of doing so.

Within the dream, Meryam said, "Come, Ashael, for there is a task that befalls us."

She'd taken the guise of a being with immense power. She made Ashael think she was one of the fates themselves, those who'd created the elder gods—one could do anything in dreams, after all.

Ashael believed her. He'd been dreaming for millennia, caught in the spell the other elders had laid upon him. He'd seen countless variations on reality. Why question this one?

He didn't speak in the real world, but in the dream he bowed his head and in a deep, liquid voice said, "Shall I call my children as well?"

Meryam's head jerked back. She'd been so focused on raising *him*, she hadn't considered his children. "Yes. We will soon have need of them."

"As you wish."

With this, both in the dream and without, Ashael raised his slender arms to the sky. Below, a great fluttering could be heard. A chittering came, a cacophony of screams, a cloud of beating wings. They burst from the pit's mouth in a great gout, swarming around Ashael as they went. Other, wingless demons crawled up along the pit's walls to reach the circle of stones. On and on they came, more and more flying upwards, or crawling from the pit to spill across the rocky terrain.

The captain, the crew, and Amaryllis stared in abject horror. Meryam grinned. By sea and by stone, how frightened she'd been these past many weeks, how uncertain. No longer. Now she felt potent, triumphant, all but a god herself.

As she took in the demonic host, a giddiness welled up inside her. "All of them, Ashael!" A laugh burst from her lungs. "Bring them all!"

The sheer number of them was dizzying. Eventually, however, the flow slowed, sputtered, and stopped altogether. Only then did she realize the demons had arrayed themselves in a pattern. It was in the sigil Ashael had made of the dead bodies in the dream Meryam had witnessed when she first arrived at the pit. She suddenly recalled its meaning. It was a sign of repentance. What it meant in this context she had no idea, nor did she care.

"What now, my lady?" Ashael asked in their shared dream.

"We go to Mazandir."

Ashael's head swiveled south. Though his eyes were masked, he was gaz-ing straight toward the caravanserai, the place where Tulathan had promised Meryam power. Like a seed borne by the wind, Ashael drifted toward it. His demons rose from the rocks and flowed in his wake.

Meryam turned to her crew. "To the *Gull*. We set sail immediately."

Amaryllis looked worried. "My queen—"

Meryam cut her off. "Not a word, Amaryllis. We sail for Mazandir to take my fleet. Then we move on. To Sharakhai, the desert, the world."

Soon *The Gray Gull* was sailing across the dunes behind the elder god and his host of dark demons. Meryam stood on the foredeck, bearing witness to the beginnings of her rule.

Chapter 27

As DAWN BROKE over the mountains, Çeda stood beside the burned remains of the acacia. She knew she should feel angry. Part of her was. She knew that Hamid or one of his toadies had set fire pots into the tree and ignited them. But in truth she felt numb, as if they'd reached the end of a road. She had no idea where to go from here.

The entire valley had gathered around her, people from all thirteen tribes. They waited, watching expectantly, as the shaikhs and their vizirs stood in an arc.

Çeda was well aware how the vote would go when the tribunal was convened. She'd insisted on it anyway. At the very least, all would know the story of Hamid's treachery. Whether they chose to believe it or not was now out of her hands.

As the people of the desert tribes watched, Çeda approached the trunk. The fire had only gone out an hour ago. The charred bark was still hot to the touch. When they'd finally managed to put it out, she'd hoped she might still call upon the tree's power. There had still been some life left—she could feel it flowing through the roots—but the faint sensation had faded as the sun rose. As much as it pained her to admit, the acacia was dead as the mountains around them.

Carpets were laid out. The shaikhs sat on them and listened as witnesses were presented. Çeda spoke of what had happened in Mazandir. Emre spoke of how Hamid had tried to kill him, how he'd fled when confronted. Shal'alara spoke as well, as did Shaikh Aríz. But Hamid was allowed a defense, and he called just as many witnesses to speak to his innocence. Rasime vouched for him, as did others in the thirteenth tribe, most of them the old guard of the Moonless Host, men and women thirsty for the blood of the Sharakhani Kings. A few shaikhs stood and spoke to Hamid's character. They were the ones most harmed by the Kings' ruthless policies, the ones most hounded by the royal navy, the ones punished most heavily through taxes on trade. They had been the Moonless Host's staunchest allies, and as such were sympathetic to Hamid's cause.

For a time the tribunal devolved into a shouting match, an airing of all grievances the tribes had against the Kings. Çeda tried again and again to bring them back to the subject of Hamid and how unfit he was to rule, but each time she did, one of Hamid's allies would steer it away again. It was a tactic, plain and simple. Get the crowd thinking about how cruel the Kings were, and it would diminish the perception of Hamid's own cruelties, or excuse them altogether.

"And where is Sehid-Alaz that he may speak his own truth?" Shaikh Zaghran asked as the conversations wound down and the vote neared.

"He's in Sharakhai, protecting the trees," Çeda said. "He and the asirim are keeping them alive until we come to their aid."

"He didn't come," Hamid bellowed, "because there's nothing for him to tell. Do you think for one moment the ancient King wouldn't come if he felt I had treated his memory and the memory of all the asirim poorly?"

There came a chorus of low voices, a smattering of nods.

"He's giving his life to protect us," Çeda said. "They *all* are!"

"Enough bickering," Zaghran said. "Do you wish us to take a vote now, Çeda?" His eyes slid meaningfully to the blackened ruins of the acacia. "Or do you have more to show us?"

Everyone was standing by that point, their blood up. "Please, sit," she bid the shaikhs.

It took time, and there were grumbles, but eventually they all did.

Çeda, meanwhile, stood beside the tree. She placed her hand on the warm, dragon-skin char. She reached out to it, tried to summon the dreamlike state that now felt familiar to her. There was the smallest glimmer of it, but it was like a lone star in the sky. It sat on the very edge of perception, too dim for her to see by, much less share. She pushed herself, thinking she wasn't trying hard enough, but it was no good. Too much of the tree had been burned.

Please don't let it end here.

"This has gone on long enough." Hamid stood, then strode away in that cocksure way of his, calling over his shoulder as he went. "Vote if that's what you're going to do, but I'll not sit through this any longer. My tribe has a war to prepare for."

The others stared at one another, then stood as well. Zaghran gave Çeda a sympathetic look, as if he wished things had gone another way, then his expression hardened. "So we vote. All those who wish to acquit Hamid Aykan'ava of wrongdoing?"

"Wait!" came an aged voice.

All heads turned to see Leorah, making her way through the crowd with Nalamae's staff in hand.

Many of the shaikhs looked on in confusion. Shaikh Zaghran seemed both tired and displeased. "What's the meaning of this, grandmother?"

Leorah said nothing until she reached Çeda's side. "You asked for the truth." She placed one hand on the burnt tree and regarded Çeda with a kind, motherly expression. "Be prepared to witness it."

"What are you doing?" Çeda asked so that only Leorah could hear.

Leorah patted her shoulder. "Wait and see, girl."

With that she closed her eyes. The tendons along her wrists tightened. The crystals worked into the staff's charred head began to glow. The most striking aspect of the strange turn of events wasn't the staff, but the amethyst on her right hand. It glowed brightest of all. The ring had always reflected light in a way that made it seem alive. Now it was doubly so, trebly. It was a burning star, brilliant and beautiful to look upon.

Several in the crowd gasped. Gazes shifted from Leorah and her ring to the acacia. Here and there the charred bark was splitting, falling away. All across the tree, green shoots pierced the blackened wood. They spread outward like vines and grew leaves, more and more growth spreading, lifting, creating a lush green crown on a thing everyone thought was dead.

Çeda felt power return to it. With it came the sense that she stood in the doorway between past and present. Leorah had done it. She'd given Çeda what she needed. But something was wrong. The amethyst was still glowing, bright as the sun.

With a sound like crystal breaking, the gemstone shattered. Çeda recoiled from it, felt a stinging sensation along her right cheek a split-second later. Others cried out as the amethyst's shards bit. When Çeda turned back, Leorah was on the ground, her staff just out of reach. Çeda rushed to her side and saw the mess the stone had made of the right side of her face. She was bleeding from a hundred tiny cuts.

She blinked up at Çeda, took in the others standing nearby: Emre, Frail Lemi, Shal'alara, and more. She looked as though she didn't recognize a single one of them.

"Leorah?" Çeda asked.

Voice trembling, the old woman lying on the ground replied, "I'm afraid not."

It took Çeda long moments for understanding to dawn. When it did, tears formed in her eyes. "Devorah?"

Devorah nodded and with Çeda's help stood. "Yes, child."

Shal'alara unwound her cream-colored head scarf, plucked the amethyst's shards from Devorah's skin, then pressed the cloth to the many small wounds along her face. Devorah's stature was more upright than only moments ago. She shook less. For decades, Devorah and Leorah had shared the same body. Through the magic of the amethyst, they'd traded places at sundown. Leorah had seen more life through this strange union, and it had shown in how much wearier she had seemed in recent years. And while Devorah might have experienced less than her sister, it was for that very reason she was the more vigorous of the two.

"She knew she was going to die," Çeda said breathlessly.

"We both did. She gave herself that you could make a difference." Devorah waved to the tree. "She gave herself that we could see a brighter day."

Çeda had felt numb earlier. Now she felt deep regret as she blinked away tears. She stared at the acacia's green shoots as the loss threatened to overwhelm her. But then she caught sight of Hamid, staring up at the tree with naked shock. He knew. He knew Çeda had the power to destroy him.

He stormed toward the other members of the tribunal and retook his place on the carpets. "We take the vote now."

Zaghran looked at him with disgust. "We will see what the tree has to say."

Hamid's face reddened. With a flash of his right arm, he drew his sword. He'd actually taken a step toward Zaghran before he collected himself and looked about, working his mouth, as if it had become suddenly dry. He shoved his sword back into the scabbard, but seemed to have trouble finding words. "She controls it," he said finally. "All she'll show you are lies."

"How do you know before you've even seen them?" Zaghran replied evenly.

"Because she's jealous. Çeda has wanted the mantle of shaikh since the day she set foot in the desert."

"Be that as it may"—he turned a cold shoulder to Hamid and waved Çeda toward the acacia—"Çedamihn will proceed."

The shaikhs took their places on the carpets. Even Hamid. The crowd closed in. Çeda, meanwhile, pressed her palm against the bark of the tree. It suddenly felt as if she were standing at the mouth of a well. Through it, Çeda reached into the past and summoned the truth. Hamid's truth. She shared it with those standing around her, not just the shaikhs but the entire crowd.

Hamid drawing his sword against Emre, who barely managed to block it. Hamid digging a grave for Emre in a small, sandy bay and rolling Emre's limp form into it. Hamid stealing up to the window of a captain's cabin, preparing to suffocate Emre where he lay unconscious in a coma. A girl, Clara, entering the cabin and interrupting his plans, prompting Hamid to seriously contemplate killing her as well. Hamid pulling on Sehid-Alaz's heartstrings, convincing him he'd been betrayed by Çeda and Macide.

A hundred more visions came, glimpses into Hamid's past, the damning mosaic of a self-serving man who would do anything to secure his own power. Çeda hated experiencing it, but she kept going until the story was told in full.

When the sound of the wind blowing through the acacia's leaves returned, all knew what Hamid had done. All understood the sort of man he was. None would defend him, not even those who most wanted to see Sharakhai fall.

And Hamid knew it. The fear was plain on his face. He opened his mouth several times, but did not speak. Darius, standing behind him, had gone pale.

Zaghran stood and stepped away from Hamid. So did Shaikhs Aríz, Neylana, and Dayan. The others followed suit until they were standing in an arc, leveling their glares at Hamid, who had yet to rise.

"So we vote," Zaghran said. "All those in favor—"

Çeda wasn't sure what else Zaghran might have said, for just then she was swept away again by the acacia. She stood in the desert before the mouth of a yawning pit, around which stood a circle of towering stones.

Çeda knew this place. She'd gone there with Emre, years ago, when she'd had trouble with the ehrekh, Rümayesh. The soothsayer, Adzin, had taken them there. It had felt foul at the time, but the feeling in this strange, sudden vision was infinitely worse. She felt as if her gut had been filled with a mixture of malice and spite.

An otherworldly being with long limbs and ashen skin rose from the pit. Tall as a titan, he had two broad horns that fanned horizontally from either side of his head. Ragged bandages covered his eyes. A black spike pierced his emaciated chest.

An elder, Çeda realized.

"Come, Ashael," said a woman standing beside the pit, "for there is a task that befalls us." It was Meryam, and she was staring up at the elder god with a look of unbridled joy.

Ashael's shrouded gaze swiveled toward her. "Shall I call my children as well?"

"Yes," she replied. "We will soon have need of them."

"As you wish," Ashael said, and raised his hands to the sky.

From within the pit, a dark presence grew. It rose like bile, then spewed forth, spilling into a deep blue sky. Dozens, hundreds, thousands of demons flew up, occluding the sun, casting a pall over the desert landscape.

"All of them, Ashael!" Meryam cried with joy. "Yes! Yes! Bring them all!"

The river of demons continued to flow, but Ashael seemed to be ignoring

Meryam. Instead his head turned until he seemed to be staring straight at Çeda.

Suddenly the only thing she could see was the god himself. From his forehead, a bright white light emanated. It grew and grew, and pain came with it. She felt as if she'd been thrown into the sun.

She woke on the ground holding her head. The others around her were doing the same. Her eyes met Zaghran's, who looked every bit as worried as she was.

"Did you see it?" she asked him.

He nodded. The other shaikhs, though she hadn't asked them, nodded as well.

Frail Lemi was turning around and around. "Where'd fucking Hamid get to?"

He was right. Hamid was nowhere to be seen. Now frantic, Çeda scanned the crowd for Hamid's stocky shape, his sleepy eyes, but it was no use.

Hamid was gone.

Chapter 28

WHEN THE *MISCREANT* set sail shortly after dawn, Ihsan set them on a westerly course for the Hollow. Nayyan leaned against the mainmast, bouncing Ransaneh in her arms. Ihsan still hadn't told her about his own affliction. It didn't feel right.

It likely never will.

He knew it was so, yet still he remained silent.

Perhaps tonight after we anchor and take our evening meal.

Ihsan took the stairs up to the foredeck, where Ibrahim sat with his back to the bulwark. He was absently stroking his long, gray beard while reading a Blue Journal.

Inevra, their stout old buzzard of a captain, was there as well. Eyeing Ihsan, she doffed the leather, sweat-stained monstrosity she referred to as a hat and wiped her brow with the back of one sleeve. "I've never sailed this stretch of sand," she said in her craggy voice. "The navy had orders to avoid the Hollow since well before *I* became a sandswoman, and I've been sailing for fifty years." She fanned herself with the hat then returned it to her head, situating it just so. "The caravans avoid it too. And not just because of the reefs. It gives off a *feel*, they say."

"A feel," Ihsan repeated.

Inevra nodded while pointing to Ihsan's belly. "They say it's like some-one's trying to pull out your insides through the button your mother gave you. We'll make for the center of that stretch. Unless I'm the beetle-brained fool my father always told me I was, *that's* where we'll find the Hollow."

She seemed strangely excited by the prospect, as if they were hunting for hidden treasure like Bahri Al'sir. Ihsan didn't fault her for it. It was just her way. Whatever the task, Inevra threw herself into it, and neither storm nor slipsand nor fallow wind would stop her.

"Can you feel it," she bellowed to Ihsan near midday, "your gut sinking?" She was peering intently off the starboard bow, toward a broad stretch of rocky reefs. "We're getting nearer!"

He felt it a bit, but in truth, Ihsan was having trouble concentrating on anything but the future that awaited both him and Nayyan. There were no two ways about it. It was only a matter of time before the black mould saw them dead. He doubted even Azad's fabled draughts, assuming any still ex-isted, could save them now.

At the mainmast, Nayyan noticed Ihsan's stare. She looked as if she were ready to say something, then let her gaze drift back to the way ahead.

"We'll stop Meryam," she'd said that morning. "We'll stop her, and we'll save Sharakhai. We'll leave our daughter a desert that is whole, not fractured by the gods."

Nayyan seemed to be clinging to that notion like a rock in a storm-wracked sea. Though she didn't realize it, Ihsan was clinging to the very same rock. The game that had begun on Beht Ihman four centuries earlier was tilted in the gods' favor, but there were moves yet to make, and if anything had been proven over the past several years, it was that the gods were not infallible. They'd stumbled more than once. It was up to Ihsan and Nayyan to make sure they stumbled again.

As the *Miscreant* sidled along the lee of a dune, the uneasy feeling in Ihsan's gut intensified. It felt like someone had poked a meat hook through his belly and was rooting around, trying to snag his innards.

"My Lord King?"

The summons had come from Yndris, who had a spyglass pressed to one eye. She held the glass out for Ihsan to take, but he could already see what was worrying her. Two points off the starboard bow, a dark cloud billowed along the horizon. When he peered down the spyglass's length, he saw it wasn't formed of sand and dust, but individual shapes, winged forms.

"Demons," he breathed. "Hundreds of them, thousands." They swirled in a gyre like a colony of bats.

Ibrahim snapped the Blue Journal closed and stood. Using a ratline to steady himself, he squinted into the distance. "Queen Meryam's found the Hollow then?"

"Meryam is a queen no longer," Ihsan replied, "but yes, she surely has. We may have arrived in time, though. She may not have used Goezhen's body to—" His words trailed away, for just then the cloud erupted like a geyser. "By the great beyond . . ."

Nayyan gave Ransaneh over to her wet nurse, then took the spyglass from Ihsan. "Bloody gods," she breathed a moment later.

As the *Miscreant* eased over another dune, the entire crew stared, mouths agape. The column lifted higher and higher into the clear blue sky, a murmuration of inconceivable scale complete with an attenuated sound, a screeching, a wailing that pierced the air, intensifying the already ill feeling in Ihsan's gut.

After long minutes, the column began to settle and the demons were lost from view.

No one moved. No one said a word. It felt as if to do so would rile the demons anew.

"What are the chances," Ihsan ventured, "that they've all gone back into their hole?"

Nayyan looked unamused. "She's done it, then. She's found Ashael."

"It appears so, but finding a lost god and controlling him are two different things."

"Did the journals say anything about this?" She motioned to where the demons had risen. "A fount of some sort? A column of darkness? Smoke rising from a pit?"

"Nothing that I can recall."

A silence passed, broken by a question from Ibrahim that echoed Ihsan's own thoughts. "What will she do now that she's raised him?"

Ihsan shrugged. "I imagine she'll march on Sharakhai. But she's entering a bargain with an *elder*. It may take days, weeks to get what she wants from him."

No sooner had he said the words than Yndris called again from the gunwales, "It will take neither weeks nor days, it seems."

The cloud had picked up again. It was no great column in the sky now, but a simmering shadow along the horizon. Part of the cloud was breaking away, and was heading toward the *Miscreant* at great speed.

"Draw in the sails!" Inevra called. "Anchor the ship!"

They crew worked smartly, and then filed down the stairs belowdecks. "Batten down the hatches!" Inevra bellowed. "Prepare for battle!"

The hold plummeted into shadow as they secured all hatches, doors, and shutters. They prepared weapons—swords and shields, bows and arrows, which the Maidens and soldiers aboard could use through the arrow slits built into the hull.

They watched the skies through those same slits as the demons approached. Some were small as cats while others were large as mastiffs. Some few were taller than men. These bore crude black iron weapons. Tridents. Spears. Bent swords with dull blades that could nevertheless kill a man if swung with enough force. Their eyes were wild with glee. Their mouths were split wide, revealing rows of needle-like teeth.

The sound of flapping wings rose up, grew louder. Ransaneh began to cry. Then the demons arrived.

They threw themselves against the ship. They crashed against the hull, creating dull, pounding thuds that sounded like a tumult of Kundhuni war drums. The demons with spears and tridents attempted to stave in the arrow slits, to widen them, to give the lesser demons greater purchase. And indeed, as the wooden planks gave way beneath the repeated blows, long black claws reached in. They tore at the hull. Bit by bit the openings widened, and more demons rammed the hatches. Ihsan saw them fly high into the air, then streak down to throw their weight against the doors.

The sound was deafening. The demons' high-pitched screams blended into a maddening dissonance. Ihsan could hardly think from the sheer intensity of it. And the longer it went on, the more fear spiraled within him.

"Begone!" he yelled at those near the arrow slit he was manning. "Leave this ship unspoiled!"

He poured all the power he could manage into his words. The searing pain along his tongue, throat, and the roof of his mouth was proof that his power was flowing, but the commands had no effect.

The crew loosed arrows. They stabbed through the openings with sword and spear. The demons were not invulnerable. Some fell, their flesh cut deeply, black blood flowing from their wounds. But when one dropped, there were always more to take its place.

From the top of the stairs at the aft end of the battle deck came a hard thud. Light streamed down and soldiers screamed.

"To me!" came Yndris's rally cry.

A dozen soldiers and crewmen rallied to her position at the base of the stairs, ready as demons gushed in.

Behind Ihsan, across the open deck, one of the openings was now large enough that smaller demons were slipping through. Light flooded the ship's interior as a spindly demon ripped several hull boards away. The sound of them, their screams, became deafening.

A great roar came from Ihsan's left. Captain Inevra rushed forward, holding an overturned table. Her burly cuss of a first mate was there with her. Together, they rammed the table against the opening. Other crewmen were close behind with hammers and nails at the ready. They pounded the nails quickly and efficiently, securing the table against the hull. It was a temporary measure at best, but it seemed to have worked—the pounding against the table ceased, and the demons swarmed to the other exposed arrow slits.

The rest of the crew focused on demons that had squirmed their way through the opening. One soldier was lost when a demon tore a great hunk of flesh from his neck. A Maiden fell screaming when another sliced her leg at the back of one ankle. A small demon with two sets of wings writhed in the air around Ihsan. Ignoring the pain in his ribs, Ihsan drew his fighting knife and swung for it. The demon avoided him with sinuous ease, and when he advanced and struck wildly, it slid past him and fell upon Ransaneh's wet nurse.

"No!" he shouted and dove forward. Heedless of the demon's claws, he ripped it from the wet nurse's neck before it had a chance to sink its teeth into her, then he slammed it down on the deck and stabbed its writhing form over and over.

By the time he was done, the flesh along his forearm and wrist was a shambles. Bloody furrows ran deep, some cutting into muscle, but at least the thing was dead. The others had dispatched the remaining demons, at the cost of three more soldiers.

Forward, the sounds of struggle had faded. Yndris seemed to have stemmed the tide for now.

"We can't go on like this," Nayyan said.

Ibrahim was nearby. He was staring at the arrow slits, the expression on his face an odd mixture of fear and calculation. "I need silver."

Ihsan stared at him. "What?"

"There's no time to explain. Bring me all the silver coins you can find."

Ihsan didn't know what he was on about, but he was aware there was a special connection between demonkind and silver. "The coffer," he said to Captain Inevra. "Bring it."

As the fighting continued, she rushed with her first mate toward the armory at the fore of the ship. They returned a short while later carrying a heavy chest between them. Inevra unlocked it and threw the lid back to reveal several leather bags. Ihsan pulled one out. It jingled as he set it hard onto the deck. After tugging the mouth open to reveal a not-inconsiderable sum of silver coins, he looked to Ibrahim. "Your silver."

Ibrahim nodded and scooped up a handful. "Help me. Everyone aboard takes one coin. They wish upon it, then hand it back. Quickly now."

"Wish for what?" Ihsan asked.

"No one can be guided in this. They'll wish for what they may, though I rather think many will wish for salvation."

As the battle waged on, Ihsan and Nayyan did as he asked. The three of them moved from soldier to soldier, crewman to crewman. Ibrahim insisted that the wounded were included. Anyone who was conscious took a coin, closed their eyes, and made a wish. After kissing it, the coins were collected. Nayyan, Ihsan, and Ibrahim were the last to complete the ritual. They had thirty-three in the end.

The distraction of performing the ritual with the coins threw their defense into disarray. The hatch at the top of the stairs, hastily repaired, was sundered completely. More boards near the aft end of the deck gave way. The screams of the demons came louder. It made it nearly impossible to think of anything but fighting to the death or fleeing.

Ibrahim cupped the coins in his hands. "Now help me!" he cried as he rushed aft.

Ihsan didn't argue. Nor did Nayyan. They, along with the captain, her first mate, Yndris, and the remaining Blade Maidens, slashed their way past the demons.

Ibrahim, gripping the coins tightly, motioned to the large ramp, the one that could be lowered to the sand to lade and unlade cargo. "Open it!" he cried over the sounds of battle.

"That will let all of them in!"

Ibrahim took in the carnage around them. "They're already in."

Swallowing hard, Ihsan nodded. He lifted one of the two levers that would lower the ramp while Nayyan worked the other. The ramp dropped with a thud. The sound of flapping, of demons screaming, came louder.

Ibrahim sprinted down the ramp and onto the sands as quickly as his aged frame would allow him, his beard trailing behind him like a scarf.

Demons followed. They streaked past him, slashed at him with their claws. One tugged sharply on the hem of his thawb, sending him tumbling. He got up again immediately and continued on. His flesh took slash after slash from claws and teeth, but still he went on, shouting his fear and pain as he went. One of the larger demons hovered into view. It raised a bent trident and launched it toward Ibrahim with a heave and a piercing cry.

It caught Ibrahim in the back. Down he fell, and the coins spilled everywhere. They glinted through the air, diamonds set ablaze by the sun. They pattered against the sand, kicking up tiny clouds of dust that settled immediately.

And still the battle raged on. They'd failed. Ibrahim had sacrificed himself for nothing.

"Close the ramp!" Captain Inevra called.

"Wait," Ihsan ordered.

The larger demon, the one that had thrown the trident, was hovering closer to Ibrahim. Ihsan thought perhaps it wanted its weapon back, or wished to feast on the man who writhed slowly, his hands grasping at the sand. But no. The demon flew beyond Ibrahim's prone form to the coins. It landed, staring at the nearest of them. It crouched, transfixed, and picked one up. It licked the silver with a forked tongue.

It was just reaching for another when a second demon came streaking in and snatched the coin away. When the first fought for it, the other slashed back with its crude iron sword. It created an opening for more demons to grab the fallen coins. A half-dozen came at first, each snatching up a piece of silver to call their own. Others fought for the tiny treasures. The small, cat-sized demons seemed to fare better at first. They would snatch one up and fly away, but others would catch them, tear into them, leaving them broken, dying, their black blood spilling on the amber sand.

Soon hundreds of demons were fighting. Some fled from the suddenly intense battle and flew hard for the main host in the distance. Others chased them, screeching as they went. The few demons still attacking the ship seemed to lose interest. They broke away, one by one, to chase after the re-treating host. Soon none were left but those too wounded to fly, and those were quickly dispatched.

Ihsan ran to Ibrahim. Others brought metal-working tools and cut away the tooth of the trident that had pierced his abdomen and carefully removed the weapon from his flesh. They stuffed two lumps of black lotus between his cheek and gums for the pain, then let the ship's surgeon stitch him as best he could.

"How did you know?" Ihsan asked Ibrahim.

The old storyteller's eyes were languid. With no small amount of effort, he drew his gaze from the sky and focused on Ihsan. "It was one of the legends of Bahri Al'sir. A sultan had assigned a demon to guard Bahri Al'sir for having stolen a piece of his magical bread. Bahri Al'sir used the silver to escape."

"You bet your life on a *fable*?"

Ibrahim smiled. "All stories have a kernel of truth in them, my King."

Ihsan couldn't help it. He laughed. "You're a stupid, bloody fool, you know that?"

Even with his eyes glazing over from the black lotus, Ibrahim looked proud. "Well, we had to do *something*."

"Yes, we did." Ihsan studied the fluttering black cloud in the distance. "We still do."

Chapter 29

I N THE VALLEY below Mount Arasal, Emre stood at Çeda's side. The shaikhs were all present, with one notable exception: Hamid. He'd somehow managed to break the vision's spell and fled the scene. They had hundreds of potential witnesses, but no one admitted to seeing him escape. Most had surely been caught up in the vision of Meryam and Ashael, but *someone* must have seen him leaving.

"Go," Shal'alara said to three of her best warriors. "Find him."

No one argued with her. Not even Darius, Rasime, or the shaikhs who'd sided with Hamid only a short while ago. Emre was tempted to join them, but there was too much unfinished business with the shaikhs, so he remained.

Çeda stared up at the acacia with a confused expression. "How could he have awoken?"

Emre had been struggling with the same thing. "The visions you showed the shaikhs of his treachery," he finally said. "They would have terrified him. It's possible his fear broke the vision's spell."

"I suppose." A serious look overcame her as she took in the shaikhs anew. After a brief pause, she stepped closer to Emre, took his hand in hers, and spoke in a low voice. "I hope you can forgive me, but we can't worry about Hamid. Now right now. Sharakhai is what matters."

Reliving the terrible things Hamid had done had only enflamed Emre's desire to see him pay for his crimes, but Çeda was right. Ashael and his demons had risen. Time was running short.

"Thank you for saying so," he said, "but there's no need for forgiveness."

She squeezed his hand, then turned and addressed the gathered crowd. "Hamid deserves justice, but the question before us is no longer what we should do about a traitor to his own people. It's what we plan to do about Ashael."

Shaikh Zaghran was still visibly shaken. As were Neylana, Aríz, Dayan, and several others. The shaikhs who had been ready to align themselves with Hamid seemed reticent.

It was the comely and normally taciturn Shaikh Damla who spoke first. "The council should meet."

Valtim, the baby-faced shaikh who outweighed Emre by at least ten stone, nodded in agreement. "There's much to consider, including Hamid's fate."

"Much to *consider*?" Çeda cast her gaze over them all while pointing west. "For the love of all that is good, open your eyes. We must sail for Sharakhai. We must stop what's about to happen."

"If things are as dire as you say," Damla countered, "it's all the more reason for each of us to weigh in and, if we decide your counsel is wise, discuss the best way to go about it."

"We can decide on the way to Sharakhai."

Damla's face turned hard. "You will not dictate how the council conducts its business."

"By rights," Shal'alara said, "Çeda is now shaikh of the thirteenth tribe. Her voice counts as much as any of yours."

"As much, perhaps," Damla said, "but not more. She is but one out of thirteen."

Çeda held her hands up in a sign of peace. "I'm not dictating. I'm asking you to see reason."

"Sharakhai has much to answer for." Though the words had come from Shaikh Valtim, Damla was nodding her head in agreement, as were several of the other hardline shaikhs.

Emre could tell Çeda was furious. "We have no time to waste. We *must* be on our way. I implore you to make ready. We'll have days of sailing ahead of us, why not make them days of sail and debate?" Çeda paused, but when neither Valtim nor Damla seemed receptive, she went on. "An hour ago, you were ready to set sail to make war on Sharakhai. Why won't you sail now, when the entire desert is threatened?"

"Who's to say anything beyond Sharakhai is threatened?" Damla replied in an easy tone.

"You know it is. You saw it. You *felt* it."

"I would expect a child of Sharakhai to say nothing less," said the hulking Valtim, "but the tribes deliberate in our own time, and in our own way."

Çeda stared at them both as if she couldn't believe her ears. She looked as if she were ready to argue, but then her gaze shifted to the acacia, to Nalamae's staff on the singed grass. After a deep, cleansing breath, she nodded, as if she'd just come to a decision. "I'll not stand by and watch," she said, "as you gamble my birthplace away."

Valtim seemed unimpressed. "Then go."

Emre, knowing Çeda was about to harden their minds against her, stepped forward and took her by the elbow. "Çeda, please—"

"No, Emre." With a calm he'd rarely seen in her, she drew her arm from his grasp. "This isn't something to be reasonable about." She faced the shaikhs. "If we sit here, thousands upon thousands are going to die."

"They may die if we go," Valtim replied, "only then it will be us with them."

Çeda spat on the ground. "That is the coward's path. Take it, and may the gods damn you all."

With that she stalked away. Sümeya, Kameyl, Jenise, and the Shieldwives followed. Frail Lemi watched them go, then looked to Emre questioningly, asking whether they ought to follow.

Emre shook his head no. Part of him was glad Çeda had put pressure on the shaikhs to do the right thing, no matter their attitudes toward Sharakhai. But the vote was far from certain. Someone had to remain. Someone had to try to sway them further.

"Who speaks for Tribe Khiyanat?" Shaikh Zaghran asked. His gaze alternated between Emre and Shal'alara.

"I will," Emre said, "for now."

Emre thought Rasime would argue, but she looked like a cornered fox, ready to bolt or to fight.

"Very well," Shaikh Zaghran said, and headed for the pavilion.

The other shaikhs and their vizirs followed. Emre beckoned Shal'alara to follow him into the tent. The shaikhs settled themselves, but Emre hardly let them rest before addressing the assemblage. "The only question before us—"

"You are not recognized to speak," Valtim said.

"Let him speak," Shaikh Aríz said immediately. "Or are the Standing Stones suddenly afraid to hear truth when it's spoken?"

Valtim bristled. "The Stones are afraid of nothing, but Emre son of Aykan has already shown himself to be biased."

"Not biased," Emre said. "Merely a man with a different perspective than yours. There is a city to our west that needs our help. You no longer see those people as children of the desert, but they are. I know that here in the desert the night of Beht Revahl is despised. You consider it the day the tribes were defeated by the Kings."

"It *was* the day the tribes were defeated."

"It was, yes," Emre said, "but none in the city see it that way, not any longer. They *revere* the desert and the tribes." There came snorts of derision and rolled eyes, but Emre went on. "There are those who saw things as the Kings did. The highborn. Their families. But I tell you now, the people of the west end, people all over the city, take pride in their heritage. They dream of sailing the sands as you do. They dream of traveling to the Great Mother's farthest corners and learning her secrets. They know of her beauty because of the stories you passed down. Bahri Al'sir. Fatima the Untouchable. Jalil the Bold. Bashshar of the Innumerable Tribes. We tell all these tales and more. And do you know why? Because the people of Sharakhai feel, as you do, they are part of the desert. We are part of the same tribe."

Valtim sneered. Many of the others glanced around, apparently unsure what to think. Shaikh Neylana, a woman who'd told Emre in no uncertain terms he would one day sway the hearts and minds of many, gave him a respectful nod. Aríz was smiling from ear to ear. He stifled it quickly, but not before sharing a wink with Emre.

Before anyone could say another word, Çeda stormed into the tent, and

Emre was left speechless. She now wore her armor from the pits, the guise of the white wolf, which Mist had led her to in the desert. Her battle skirt and leather breastplate were dyed white. So were her greaves, bracers, and finger-less gloves. They'd all seen better days. The leather's natural, tawny color was showing through, but it made the armor seem like an artifact discovered in some ancient crypt, evidence of a hero that words in a story could never capture. The helm with the mask of Nalamae was held under one arm; the white wolf pelt affixed to it stared accusingly at the gathered crowd. Her hair, bound earlier, was now wild, black, and curly as it fell over her shoulders and down her back. River's Daughter, her ebon blade, stood out starkly. The sword, a weapon of a Blade Maiden, not a pit fighter, looked incongruous, yet it somehow made the wild stories about Çeda loom all the larger.

Staring at her, as all in the pavilion were, Emre's heart swelled. Çeda could be standing beside Bahri, Fatima, Bashshar, and Jalil, and none could say who the greatest of them was.

"I'm going to Sharakhai. Now. All those who wish to make a difference should join me."

With that, she turned and left.

As the tent flap closed with an audible *thwap*, the mood in the pavilion changed from one of calculation to one of uncertainty and introspection. The very act of declaring her intent had called their courage into question. Çeda had the right of it, Emre reckoned. There was no debate over what they should do. Not really. If they still had questions over what the right thing was, they would one day answer for it, either to themselves, their children, or their ancestors when they reached the farther fields.

Frail Lemi stared at the pavilion's entrance, eyes pinched, brow furrowed. Then he locked eyes with Emre. "Time to leave, Emre?"

"Time to leave, Lem."

Emre, Frail Lemi, and Shal'alara left the pavilion together. They caught up to Çeda, who smiled as they came near. She took Emre's hand, curled his arm around her neck, and kissed the backs of his fingers. No one said a word as Çeda and Emre led the way down the winding path toward the desert. Frail Lemi, Sümeya, Kameyl, and the Shieldwives came next.

By the time they reached the sandy bay with its array of ships, the path above was still empty. "So be it," Çeda said as she boarded the *Red Bride*.

They pulled anchor and were just making way when Frail Lemi pointed aft and shouted. "There they are! There they are!" He was jumping up and down and pointing. "I knew they'd come!"

Indeed. It soon became clear it wasn't just a handful of tribes joining them. Shaikh Aríz and Tribe Kadri came first. Then Neylana and the Rushing Waters of Tribe Kenan. Shaikh Zaghran and the Raining Stars of Tribe Tulogal came next. Then the Black Wings of Tribe Okan, the Red Wind of Tribe Masal, the Bloody Manes of Tribe Narazid. And on and on. Valtim of Tribe Ebros came last, but they came. All twelve remaining tribes were making their way down from the valley.

The shaikhs gathered on the sand before the *Red Bride*. Zaghran stepped forward and stared up at Çeda, who stood on the foredeck. "The Alliance joins you," he said.

Çeda drew River's Daughter and lifted it into the air. "May the desert's fortunes be shaped by the edges of our blades."

It was an ancient saying, one Zaghran and the others recognized. Zaghran drew his shamshir, and the other shaikhs did as well. "By the edges of our blades," they intoned in unison.

And so, the greatest host the desert had seen in four hundred years set sail, the *Red Bride* at their lead.

Chapter 30

As the *Miscreant* anchored near a broad plateau of rock, Ihsan watched the standing stones in the distance, alert for any sign of movement. It was likely the demons had all moved on with Ashael, but assuming so could cost a life. Worse, it might be his.

When he judged it enough time for any curious demons to have arisen from the pit, he waved to the crewman standing ready with the gangplank. "Lower it."

The gangplank dropped with a thud against the sand. Yndris and three other Blade Maidens went ahead with shields and swords in hand. A score of Silver Spears followed. Most bore spears. Others held bows with arrows nocked, fingers on the strings as they cast their gaze about. Ihsan and Nayyan came last. Ibrahim remained aboard as his body fought off infection from the stab wound of the demon trident.

All were on edge as they paced toward the standing stones and the scent of brimstone grew strong, so much so that the Blade Maidens drew their veils over their faces. Others raised their arms to cover their noses.

Here and there, demons lay unmoving on the red rock.

"How did they die?" Yndris asked.

"If the way they fought one another for the coins was any indication"—
Ihsan crouched beside one of the fallen demons—"I suspect they were victims
of their own aggression." The demon had an eyeless face with long slits where
the nose on any normal desert creature would be. Its skin was riddled with
ragged tears both deep and shallow. "I suspect their attrition rate will be high."

"Little matter," Yndris said. "It looked like they have more than enough
to take on the royal navy *and* the combined might of Malasan and Mirea."
She waved east. "She's likely halfway to Sharakhai by now."

Seeing no immediate threat, their group approached the standing stones.
They were just heading inside the circle when Nayyan grabbed Ihsan's wrist
and pulled him to a stop. "We're not alone."

Hidden from view earlier, Ihsan now saw a clipper in the distance, Qaimiri from the look of it. Three men were approaching their position.

Yndris and the Blade Maidens moved to intercept, but Ihsan motioned
them to stand down. "Let them approach."

"By the gods who breathe," Nayyan said, "is that Lord Amansir?"

Indeed, Ramahd was at the lead. Behind him was Ramahd's second,
Cicio, a short, curly haired man who walked with a cocky stride. The third
was a fellow with a ridiculous, wide-brimmed hat who shambled more than
he walked.

"Will the wonders of the desert never cease?" Ihsan breathed.

It was Fezek the ghul. Ihsan thought he'd died when his creator, the
necromancer, Anila, passed through the crystal.

Ihsan and Nayyan met Ramahd and Cicio in an area blessedly clear of
demon corpses. Fezek, meanwhile, continued toward the pit. On reaching
the edge, he stared straight down, leaning out so far Ihsan had half a mind
to go and yank him back.

Ramahd waved toward the mangled bodies of two nearby demons. "I see
my sister-in-law has been here before me."

"Been and left, Lord Amansir," Ihsan said.

"How long ago?"

"She and her horde departed yesterday."

Ramahd took in the scene around them with an expression of awe. "Even
knowing Meryam, I didn't think it was possible. Part of me thought she'd
die here."

"It helps when the desert gods are looking over your shoulder," Ihsan said. "It helps when you have the body of a god as an offering as well."

Ramahd didn't seem the least bit fazed by the news. "You're well informed."

"As are you."

Ramahd told them about the long and winding path that had led him from the crystal's breaking to the Hollow. That King Hektor was still preparing to leave the desert was a far from happy development. They could have used his help.

As Ihsan launched into his own tale, Fezek wandered back from the edge of the pit and listened, rapt. He might be grisly to look upon, but there was a certain wonder in his clouded eyes that reminded Ihsan of children in the bazaar as they listened to storytellers spinning their tales. Ihsan finished relating their harrowing journey to the Hollow, their fight against the demons and their miraculous rescue by Ibrahim and his silver coins.

"We just need more coins, then, ah?" Cicio smiled his cocky smile. "Throw them down the hole, let the demons follow."

Nayyan, ignoring the jape, ambled to the edge of the pit. "I still don't understand how she could have managed it. A woman, her magic burned from her, managed to raise an elder god?"

As Ihsan joined her, the warm wind played with his hair, made the cloth of his thawb snap. "Let's not forget that the young gods knew their elders intimately. It doesn't surprise me that Meryam managed to wake Ashael. It's *managing* him now he's awake that's the real trick."

They spent hours there, searching for clues to answer either of the riddles. Ihsan debated sending a team into the pit to look for Goezhen's body, but in the end decided against it. As curious as he was, it was simply too dangerous.

Past midday, Yndris crouched near the edge of the pit. "There's something here, my Lord King."

Ihsan came near, and Yndris motioned to a hollow in the rock near her booted feet. A black substance was pooled there. A powder. Ihsan pinched a bit of it between his thumb and forefinger. The smell was odd, like burnt pine and myrrh.

Ramahd took a pinch of it as well. After smelling it, he sniffed it like some did with black lotus powder.

Ihsan followed suit. And felt himself being carried away . . .

Ashael floated over a green landscape dotted with hills and copses of white-barked trees. Mortals would no doubt admire the artful way the wind swept over the grass. They might remark on how perfectly blue the sky was. Ashael wanted to tear it all down, see it laid to waste, which confused the god for a time. His roiling hatred felt sourceless, directionless, but he soon realized it was focused on the village in the distance.

Yurts made of animal skin littered the landscape. Pools of water lay nearby, each with a lush verge that felt achingly familiar. On seeing his approach, the villagers ran in fear, for they knew the fate that awaited them.

With a wave of his hand, a host of black, eyeless demons flew forth. They fell upon the village and harried the mortals, who fled in every direction. In the end, they stood no chance. One by one, the demons wrapped their wings around the head of a man, woman, or child, and attached lamprey mouths to the backs of their necks.

Like ghuls, the mortals lumbered to the village square, where a stone altar lay. Ashael forced them to kneel before him. He savored their building terror for a time, but his hunger was unquenchable and he soon wanted more. From the arms of a mother he took a naked babe, a writhing form with downy hair the color of wheat. He lifted the babe as the mother shook her head and screamed to the heavens, smiled as the father ripped the demon from around his head and charged forward with a spear. Ashael killed him with a wave of his hand, then set the babe on the altar.

The infant went rigid as his mother stared into Ashael's deep-set eyes. Her heartbeat trilled, its beat rapid as the wings of a startled amberlark. Reveling in the wild quality of her fear, he placed a thumb against the babe's chest and slowly pressed. The cries grew louder, more frantic.

"Ihsan!"

Ihsan shivered. He blinked hard as the grasslands and yurts dimmed and the sound of the babe's crying faded. The desert came back into focus around him. A hot wind blew, whistling through the standing stones. Nayyan stood before him, gripping his arms, forcing him to face her while the others watched with concern, all save Ramahd, who was staring about as if he were recovering from the same dream.

"You saw it too?" Ihsan asked him.

Ramahd nodded.

Ihsan told the others what they'd seen. Breath of the desert, the sheer power Ashael had commanded. His first thought was that the black powder was a psychedelic of some sort. But no. That couldn't be it. Or at least, it wasn't the *whole* story.

"It was Ashael's dream," Ramahd said, echoing Ihsan's thoughts, "but it wasn't his alone."

"It was Meryam, wasn't it?" Ihsan guessed.

Ramahd nodded. "I could sense her, guiding him."

Ihsan stared at his fingertips, smudged and blackened by the strange powder. "It's the powder. That's how she's controlling him."

"Yes," Ramahd said. "She hasn't awoken him at all. He's still asleep, lost in dreams, dreams that Meryam controls."

It was true, Ihsan realized. And if Meryam had become the master of his dreams, she could control Ashael. Craft his reality, and she could manipulate him like a puppet.

He stared numbly at those standing near the pit, then swung his gaze to the *Miscreant*, anchored in the distance. His *daughter* was on that ship. Suddenly everything around him felt fragile, a landscape made of glass, ready to be shattered or altered as Meryam saw fit.

"Meryam must know she has a tiger by the tail," Nayyan said. "She may have found a way to control Ashael temporarily, but she must see it cannot last."

"Maybe it doesn't have to," Ramahd said.

Nayyan frowned. "What do you mean?"

Ramahd pointed to the mouth of the nearby pit. "The other elders drove Ashael down into that pit. Meryam might be planning to use him, then lay him down to sleep once more."

The idea sent chills down Ihsan's spine. "Collect the powder," he said to Yndris. "All of it."

"Yes, my Lord King."

As Yndris set to work, Ramahd suddenly turned south. He looked like he'd seen his own death.

"What is it?" Ihsan asked.

"The village from the dream. What did it remind you of?"

Ihsan thought back. The configuration of the pools of water he'd seen in the dream. It had seemed so familiar. "Mazandir," he said. "It reminds me of Mazandir."

"Yes," Ramahd breathed. "She's not going to Sharakhai. She's going to Mazandir."

"But why?" asked Fezek in his hoary voice.

Ramahd's face had gone slack, his skin pale. "She wants her fleet back." He looked like he'd been punched in the gut. "I have to go," he said, then turned to Cicio and Fezek. "We have to warn them."

Ihsan was not unsympathetic to Ramahd's cause, but he and Nayyan had their own mission to complete. After calling for a second leather purse, he poured half of the measly quantity of black powder Yndris had gathered into it. "We sail to meet the royal navy. Take this." He held the bag out to Ramahd. "There isn't much, but it may help."

Ramahd accepted it. "My thanks."

"You know the hills southeast of Sharakhai?"

"I do."

"Join us there with any ships you manage to rescue."

"My thanks again."

Ihsan nodded gravely, then held out his hand. He felt a little hope as he stared into the Qaimiri lord's eyes. "May the sun shine on our next meeting."

Ramahd clasped forearms with him. "As it has on this one."

It was the time-honored reply, but Ramahd seemed to mean it. Ihsan had as well. The days ahead looked bleak. Having another ally could only help Sharakhai's chances.

Ramahd returned to *Alu's Crown* with Cicio and Fezek and set sail immediately.

Chapter 31

WITHIN EVENTIDE, DAVUD stood in the hall where Chow-Shian and the others had once danced beneath the falling water. The bamboo pipes still hung from the vaulted ceiling. The sound of the trickling water reminded Davud of a hidden mountain stream. Queen Alansal sat on her throne. Her dress was silver silk accented in black pearls, but the braziers spaced about lent everything a ruddy hue, making her look like a piece of steel fresh from the forge. Alansal herself, her hair fixed high, her war pins stuck through it at sharp angles, looked like a storm ready to be unleashed.

"You requested an audience," she said in clipped tones.

Davud stood at the foot of the dais. "I've come to thank you for the news about the gateway. The information could prove valuable." Word had come to him that morning that the guards, as instructed by Queen Alansal, had been keeping a watch on the slopes of Tauriyat. Not only had they seen evidence of the gateway, they'd seen it brightening over the days since. It was not good news. If the light was growing brighter, it meant the gateway itself was continuing to widen.

"And my granddaughter?" Alansal said tersely. "What news of her?"

Davud had spent the last several hours with Chow-Shian trying to heal her, to no avail. "I'm no physic," Davud admitted. "The poison is beyond my ability to cure—beyond anyone's, I suspect. I fear Chow-Shian has little time, which is why I'm asking permission to use her to reach the farther fields, to learn more about the gateway."

Alansal's face grew piqued. "My granddaughter is not a tool for you to use as you please."

"I understand, but time grows short, Your Highness. The gateway widens by the day. The longer we wait, the more we risk catastrophe."

Alansal sneered. "Catastrophe."

Davud stared at her, incredulous. "Your granddaughter herself recognized the danger. She *asked* me to do this."

"You know what I think, Davud Mahzun'ava?" The queen leaned forward, her eyes piercing. "I think you use Chow-Shian's name all too freely. I think your loyalties extend well beyond *her* welfare, well beyond Mirea's."

"I've admitted as much from the beginning. I am a child of the Amber Jewel, but I can still care about Chow-Shian."

"My granddaughter is sick."

"And will not recover. Let her death have meaning."

"Her *life* has meaning!" Alansal flung a dismissive hand at Davud. "Find another way."

"There *is* no other way."

She jutted her chin toward the heavy tapestries that hid the windows. "Return to your bloody trees." She leaned back in her chair with an imperious look. "You say your powers do not extend to my granddaughter's health? Fine. But I will not allow her to become some instrument that furthers your own agenda. She will be given the time she needs to wake, or she will pass in peace."

Juvaan was suddenly there, taking Davud by the arm and leading him from the great hall.

Davud didn't resist, but called over his shoulder, "Your excellence, I beg you—"

"Out!"

The doors boomed shut behind them as Davud stopped and tried to appeal to Juvaan. "Please, you *have* to convince her to change her mind."

Juvaan's smile was infuriatingly calm. "I would urge you to follow her advice for now. It will take her time to see reason."

"We don't *have* time."

"Push her and you will have no chance at all."

"And if she never changes her mind?"

Juvaan had taken a step back, ready to return to the audience hall, but paused at Davud's words. "Then you're back where you began."

With that he turned and strode away, his crisp footsteps echoing along the high halls. Davud stood there for long moments, shivering with impotent rage. How could Queen Alansal be so blind to the dangers that faced them?

But as the queen's sentries watched him, he realized how prescient Juvaan's words were. With Alansal's refusal, he *was* back to where he started—with the asirim and their passage to the farther fields.

"Gods, why didn't I think of it before?"

The words had hardly escaped him before he was running toward the stables.

Leagues beyond Sharakhai, Davud rode an akhala with a coat of brindled iron. Ahead lay a grove of adichara, part of the blooming fields that ringed the city. Their branches clacked in the breeze as he slipped down from the saddle, headed toward an opening in the grove, and took the now-familiar path to Sehid-Alaz's clearing. Thorns and twigs lay everywhere, evidence that the trees, brittle in death, were slowly grinding themselves to dust.

Soon he'd reached Sehid-Alaz's tree. Unlike its colorless brethren all around, the ancient King's tree was still alive. There were fewer of the tiny, gray-green leaves, though, and the branches were bent, giving it a defeated look.

When Davud called to him, Sehid-Alaz rose from his sandy grave. Like the adichara that sheltered him, he was bent, hunched over, but he listened as Davud explained his plan. Then he spoke in his hoary voice, *"You wish to follow the asirim in death."*

"I do," Davud replied. "Your people are strong and brave. They've been protecting the trees and the city for weeks, but their strength is fading. We cannot save them, so let me accompany them into the land beyond, to shed light on the gateway's nature."

From the pits of his dark eyes, Sehid-Alaz stared at Davud angrily, *hungrily*, and for the first time in a long while Davud was reminded of the asirim's darker nature, how they used to roam the city streets and take tribute on the night of Beht Zha'ir. *"Their strength may be fading,"* the ancient King said, *"but I will not allow them to be used."*

Davud wasn't particularly surprised, but he was disappointed. He had a half-dozen arguments at the ready, but before he could voice even one, a second voice echoed within his mind.

It isn't your choice, my King.

Sehid-Alaz's head turned sharply, and Davud heard the sounds of sand sifting, the branches of an adichara rattling, both muffled by the sea of dead trees. From the meticulous surveys he'd conducted, Davud was certain he knew the asir who'd spoken. His name was Jorrdan. He'd been a soothsayer for Sehid-Alaz centuries ago, and had held much sway in his court.

"The choice is mine," Sehid-Alaz said.

Not in this, Jorrdan replied. *In this, the choice is ours. Each of us must make our own, for there is no time left.*

Sehid-Alaz pulled himself taller. *"I still rule, son of Jerran, not you."*

Behind Davud came the sound of footsteps. Their pace was uneven, as if the one approaching was limping. A moment later, Jorrdan's reed-thin voice filtered through the trees. *"My time is near, my King. Let my death have meaning."*

When Jorrdan entered the clearing, his back was bowed, and his head hung low, but the set of his jaw told Davud how deeply he believed in his words.

Perhaps Sehid-Alaz saw it too. He looked suddenly afraid, as if all his efforts to shelter his people over the centuries was about to amount to nothing. *"But so few of us remain. Your passage will only make it harder for the rest to aid the twisted trees."*

"A delay will mean nothing if we cannot find a way to close the gateway." His jaundiced eyes shifted momentarily to Davud. *"We need to help, not hinder him."*

For long moments, Sehid-Alaz stood there, resolute. Then a wave of emotion shook him and he bowed his head. Tears fell from his cheeks and pattered against the sand at his feet. Jorrdan, tears welling in his own eyes, went to his King and embraced him.

Davud, suddenly an unwitting interloper, averted his gaze until Sehid-Alaz recovered, broke from Jorrdan's embrace, and took a deep breath. His eyes shifted to Davud, then back to Jorrdan. *"It will be as you wish,"* he said, his tone defeated, *"but know that I'll be with you."*

Jorrdan smiled, and for a moment, the guise of a monster was stripped away, replaced by a mortal man who stood at death's door, fearful but ready to face his fate. *"I'll be waiting for you on the other side."*

Sehid-Alaz kissed his forehead, then stepped toward Davud. *"Since you take one of my own"*—he held one wrist out—*"my blood will be used to fuel the ritual."*

For a moment Davud could only stare. He felt a fool for not having considered it earlier. "Thank you, grandfather."

Sehid-Alaz smiled sadly, his lips a ragged line, as Davud pierced his skin with his blooding ring and sucked up the black blood that oozed from the wound. The taste was coppery but also acerbic, like a lemon gone bad, and there was something more: a note of burnt cinnamon or star anise.

On seeing his reaction, Sehid-Alaz laughed bitterly. *"What you taste is the curse of the gods."*

No sooner had Davud sealed the wound than a deep power began to fill him. It felt familiar, but also foreign, like visiting a bazaar in some distant land that reminded one of home.

Without another word, Sehid-Alaz stepped back and allowed the roots of his adichara to draw him back down into the earth.

———————◆———————

Jorrdan accompanied Davud to Sharakhai, where they were joined by Esmeray. By the time night fell, the three of them were standing on a plateau along the mountain's highest shoulder. Tulathan was freshly risen in the east. Above them, the vault's grand curtain glimmered, a curtain that brightened and dimmed, sometimes occluding the light of the firmament beyond.

Davud stared at the gateway, a column of light spearing upward from the rocky soil, and wondered if this was the very same place where the gods and the Kings had stood on the night of Beht Ihman. Shaking off his musings, he and Esmeray worked together to craft a meshwork of spells. Some focused on Esmeray. Grounding her to the real world as they did, they would allow her to draw Davud back if necessary. The other spells were focused on Davud, and would allow him to follow Jorrdan's weakened soul to the land beyond.

When they were done, Davud said to Jorrdan, "We're ready when you are."

Since the time of the crystal's breaking, the asirim had fought to remain alive, fought to protect the adichara trees and prevent the gateway from opening. They'd done so valiantly, driven by their love of Sharakhai and its people, but it was all too easy for them to give up the fight and let their souls pass. So it was for Jorrdan, who simply released his hold on life and drifted toward the farther fields.

As before, Davud became aware of Anila, Brama, and Rümayesh. He tried to speak with them, but it remained impossible—beyond the vague awareness that they were present, there seemed to be no way to communicate with them.

When the time felt right, Davud triggered the spells he and Esmeray had crafted in hopes of closing the gate. He faced the same problem he'd had from the beginning, though. He'd found no way to bind himself to the gateway, to gain purchase. Only if he did that could he find a way to close the gateway itself. It was the key to all that followed.

Over the course of an hour, he tried over and over again, but each time, he failed. He felt no movement in the gateway, no sense it was closing. The brightness of Jorrdan's soul dimmed, the adichara he'd lain beneath died. Near the end, when Jorrdan's soul was dim as a distant star, Davud sensed other souls brightening.

They're the asirim, Davud realized, *those who've already fallen.*

That they were welcoming Jorrdan with open arms came as no surprise. What *was* surprising was the sense Davud got that they were supporting Sehid-Alaz and the others in the blooming fields. Not content to simply pass to the farther fields and begin their new life, they were *helping* those on the other side.

One of them—a woman—shone brighter than the rest. She seemed familiar, somehow . . . and she was reaching out to Davud.

Before he could wonder why, he was swept away to another time, another place.

A much younger Davud stood in Sharakhai's bazaar beside his sister, Tehla. They were in her tiny stall, and Davud was forming sweet, saffron-and-lemon buns from a bowl of dough. The bazaar was busy, patrons running to and fro on a scalding day made all the worse by the mouth of the dung-fired oven at Davud's back.

Tehla was gabbing with a customer, Old Yanca, who said she'd come for buns but had clearly come for companionship. She lived alone and enjoyed trading gossip with Tehla, Seyhan the spice monger, or anyone else who would sit still for long enough.

After exchanging three freshly baked buns for a few copper coins, Yanca put them in her basket and left. Tehla turned and her eyes went wide. "Davud!"

Davud spun toward the oven. The batch he'd put in a while ago were burning, the tops already charred black.

Tehla speared a wooden peel into the oven, scooped up the buns with a deft swipe, and held them beneath his nose.

Davud's nose crinkled from the acrid smell. "I forgot."

"Well, *stop* forgetting." She turned the peel over and dumped the burnt buns into a basket that was already partially filled with a batch of almond and raisin fekkas Davud had ruined that morning. Those burnt buns and fekkas would be Davud's next several meals, as Tehla ensured the lesson was learned.

Davud felt his face go red when he realized an older couple had stopped to watch, amused. He was about to put his head down and use a razor to cut the shape of amberlarks into the sweet buns—the one and only baking skill he had—when he noticed a woman walking briskly down the row.

It was Ahya, Çeda's mother, and she was moving with purpose. "Can I borrow Davud?" she asked as soon as she was near.

Davud didn't know Ahya well, but he could tell she was distressed. Her long black hair was wrapped loosely in a bright lemon turban. She had half-healed scrapes along one jaw, fading bruises along the opposite cheek. Her eyes were what struck Davud the most, though. She was worried and trying not to show it.

"He's working," Tehla said sharply.

"This won't take long."

Tehla was already back to her mixing bowl, measuring out flour from a cloth bag. "I have a business to run, Ahya."

Ahya slapped down three sylval—full silver coins, not the six-pieces bazaar patrons often spent. "You'll have him back in an hour."

Tehla's eyes narrowed. "What do you need him for?"

"To run a simple errand. But it has to be done now, Tehla."

"Then why don't *you* do it?"

"Because I have to be elsewhere."

Tehla paused. "What sort of errand?"

"I need someone to collect Çeda." She slapped down another silver coin. "Now can I have him or not?"

Tehla looked from Davud to the coins. "Nothing dangerous. I've heard the stories."

"Nothing dangerous," Ahya confirmed.

After a breath, Tehla swept the coins into her dusty cloth purse, waved her dismissal, and went back to mixing dough. "Hurry back, Davud."

And so it was with no small measure of fear that Davud accompanied Ahya along the rows of the bazaar. He'd heard the stories, too. People who talked to her the wrong way winding up with bloody lips or a slash from her knife. People who'd threatened her going missing for good. Gang leaders found lying face down on the bed of the River Haddah after hurting Çeda.

When the stall was out of sight, Ahya turned and snatched Davud's wrist. "You know Dardzada's apothecary?"

Davud nodded, afraid to speak.

"I left Çeda there, but she ran off, probably with that idiot, Emre. They're likely running some scam. Find her, Davud. Tell her I sent you. Tell her not to go home. She's to meet me at Bent Man Bridge at nightfall. Understand?"

Davud nodded.

"Hurry." As she skipped backward along the dusty street, she pointed to the center of Sharakhai. "Check the Wheel first. They like gulling the tourists."

With that she sprinted in the opposite direction. The last Davud saw her, she was pulling the veil of her turban across her face, then leaping against a wall that abutted one of the densest and poorest sections of the Shallows. She was up and over it in moments.

The vision of that hot day faded, replaced by the piercing cold near the gateway. Davud felt himself floating, halfway between the worlds, and suddenly realized how close he'd been to slipping through entirely.

Esmeray was clearly worried. "Who was that?"

Davud, still disoriented, said, "Who was who?"

"The woman in the yellow turban."

For a moment, he couldn't speak. "You *saw* that?"

Esmeray shrugged. "I caught a few glimpses."

"She was Çeda's mother."

He explained the vision in full, and what came after. He'd gone to the Wheel, as Ahya had asked, found Çeda, and given her Ahya's message. Çeda had laughed so hard his ears had gone red. She thought it was a joke Tariq was pulling on her, but then she suddenly sobered.

"Oh, gods," she said, and sprinted away, not toward Bent Man Bridge, but toward the Shallows.

"Çeda!"

"What did you *tell* her?" Emre had asked.

But Davud only shook his head. There was no way he was going to reveal Ahya's secrets.

He left soon after. The following day, rumors floated around the west end. A back alley near the packed tenement where Ahya and Çeda had been living had been found covered in blood. No one knew why. No one had heard screams or sounds of a struggle. Davud didn't see Ahya or Çeda again for another two months, and when they *did* finally show up again, Çeda refused to talk about what had happened.

It seemed important somehow, but Davud couldn't say how, and his thoughts were interrupted by the sound of distant clanking. He and Esmeray walked toward the sound, to the edge of a drop-off where, far below, the whole of Kings Harbor could be seen. The clanking came from the harbor gates. They were opening, and the Mirean fleet, comprised of dozens upon dozens of dunebreakers, ponderous ships with four masts and league upon league of canvas, was preparing to sail into the desert.

"What's happening?" Esmeray asked.

Davud could only stare at the dunebreakers and the staggering number of soldiers standing in formation on their decks. "Alansal's been scouring the desert for the royal navy for months," he finally said. "I guess she's finally found them."

Chapter 32

WITH EVERY LEAGUE that passed, Ramahd worried he would reach Mazandir too late to make a difference. He was increasingly certain that by the time he arrived, every last soul would either be dead or in thrall to Meryam.

"Will it work?" Fezek asked, his cloudy gaze intent on the purse in Ramahd's left hand.

Ramahd hefted it. There wasn't much black powder within it—two or three pinches at most. "I don't know," he said, wrapping its cord around his belt.

"I wonder if they're part of the dream," Fezek mused.

Cicio stared at him hard, then asked in his broken Sharakhan, "What you mean?"

Fezek waved to the sand, where a massive demon with four arms and anvil-like fists lay in the trough between two dunes. It had a thousand tears in its skin. Black blood stained the sand around it in a pattern that reminded Ramahd of a cressetwing moth. "Do they fight because the dream Meryam crafted shows them fighting?"

"Perhaps," Ramahd said. "Or perhaps, now that their god is awake, they're vying for his attention."

Fezek was uncharacteristically somber. "For all we know it's *Meryam's* attention they're vying for, not Ashael's."

As the wind blew harder, making the ship's hull creak, Ramahd gripped a ratline and stretched his arms and shoulders. "I doubt they're even aware of her."

Suddenly, Cicio's expression turned mischievous, the way it did in the oud parlors when he was fixing for a fight. "Maybe you *make* them see?" He jutted his chin at the purse hanging from Ramahd's belt.

He meant Ramahd should try to give the demons some insight, thereby exposing Meryam's presence. "Better yet," Ramahd said, "I could make *Ashael* see."

Cicio's grin widened. "Now you on to something, ah?"

Ramahd released the ratline as the ship passed another wingless demon lying broken on the sand. "I might make Ashael aware, but what then? What happens if he wakes?"

Cicio's grin collapsed, then he seemed to grow angry. "Fucking Meryam."

Fezek's cloudy gaze was distant, his waxen face pinched in concentration. He shrugged in answer to Ramahd's question, then sat and began writing furiously in his journal—his way of working through the problem, perhaps.

In a bit of good fortune, the winds were favorable, and they made good speed toward their destination, sailing into the night. It was risky, but with this part of the desert largely clear of reefs and shoals, Ramahd considered it worth the risk.

The next three days of sailing saw more demons left for dead, a pattern that only changed on their fifth day out from the Hollow. When morning's light arrived, they saw no demons at all, making Ramahd fear they'd lost the trail.

It was early on the sixth day when Cicio pointed off the port bow. "See there."

Along the horizon was what looked to be a black cloud. Meryam's horde was nearing Mazandir. *Alu's Crown* could close the gap if she kept her current pace, but the demons would surely spot her.

Cicio stared at him grimly. "Skirt wide?"

Ramahd nodded. "We can't risk confronting them directly."

"Agreed," Cicio replied, and began calling out course adjustments.

They sailed hard along a path well wide of the demons, but made sure to always keep them in view. They gained ground, but Ramahd could already tell it wasn't going to be enough. The horde kept its pace through sunset and beyond, and as the moons rose, they lost sight of the cloud entirely. Ramahd was certain Meryam meant to continue on through the night and assault Mazandir in the morning.

They stretched the sails as far as they could. They lightened their load by tossing as much cargo, food, and water as they dared in hopes of reaching Mazandir in time to warn the fleet. Ramahd ordered the crew to sleep in shifts. He tried to find sleep himself, but the night was as cold as any he'd spent in the desert. The warmth seeped from his bones like he'd fallen into the Austral Sea.

Giving up on sleep entirely, he returned to deck and stood at the bow for a long while, holding a stay line, praying to the one true god, Mighty Alu, that they would reach the caravanserai ahead of Meryam.

When dawn brightened the horizon ahead, it created an idyllic glow that felt absurd in the moment. The geometric shapes of Mazandir broke the monotony of the sandy terrain. When Ramahd spotted Ashael's black cloud, his heart sank. It had already reached the nearest harbor and was sweeping through the moored ships, moving into the streets.

Cicio peered through his spyglass. "King Hektor's fleet still lies to the south."

He handed the spyglass to Ramahd. Sure enough, the fleet lay beyond the shoulders of Mazandir. They had yet to make sail. They had no idea the sort of threat they were facing or the danger they were in.

"Skirt west," Ramahd said, knowing that to sail too close to the horde would doom their mission from the start. "We'll sail to meet them."

The helmsman pulled at the wheel and the ship creaked while the crew made subtle adjustments to sails and rigging. Ramahd, meanwhile, sat on deck, leaned back against the foremast, and took out the leather purse Ihsan had given him.

"May Mighty Alu guide you," Cicio said.

Ramahd smiled ruefully. "I never took you for a religious man, Cicio."

Cicio smiled his cocky smile. "In death's shadow does the beacon of religion shine brightest."

Ramahd chuckled, and Cicio set off to see to the ship while Ramahd pinched some of the powder between his thumb and forefinger, lifted it to his nose, and inhaled sharply. He'd hardly cinched the purse before he was lost to a vision.

Ashael stood before a city by the sea. The gray strips of cloth over his head were gone. So was the misshapen spike of ebon steel that, outside the world of dreams, pierced his heart. His eyes were open, two diamonds all but lost in deep pools of shadow.

The city had been built for the mortals by the elder god Raamajit the Exalted, and they adored him for it. They worshipped him. Raamajit himself was gone, flown to the northern wastes to build great palaces of glass among the ice. He might stay there for another day or another age. It was impossible to tell with him.

But the city itself remained, a testament to Raamajit's power, and to Ashael, its very existence was offensive. It was long past time to tear it down, to prove that Raamajit could neither protect it nor the mortals within.

Ashael stormed the city. With a wave of his hand, roots rose from the earth. They devoured the roads, consumed the crumbling walls. They knocked down buildings and choked those who survived. At another wave, a murder of ravens swept over the people who rushed from their homes and from their temples. They saw him and despaired. Some ran, but it mattered not. The ravens descended, wrapped black wings around necks, tore with beaks, with claws, with talons.

The streets turned red with blood.

"Ramahd!"

Ramahd blinked. He hardly knew where he was, so strong was the vision of Ashael and the golden city. As it faded, Ramahd saw Cicio standing beside him. He was pointing to Mazandir, now less than a league distant—much closer than it had been when he'd inhaled the black powder. Judging from the sun's angle, over an hour had passed.

The sound of screams drifted to them. The demon horde was sweeping through the streets, as the ravens in his vision had been. There were hundreds, thousands, of them breaking through the feeble line of defense the Silver Spears and a ragtag militia had managed to mount.

"Concentrate, Ramahd! Stop her!"

Mighty Alu help me, I don't know how.

But the patron god of Qaimir was, as ever, silent. Ramahd stared at the purse in his hands. He'd hoped to save some of the powder, to use another time if needed. But there was nothing for it. He had to take the rest and hope it would be enough.

He pinched more between his fingers and sniffed. Then again with the last of what was easily accessible. The visions were already sweeping over him as he turned the purse out and sniffed one last time, getting all he could from the material.

His perceptions shifted, and Mazandir melted away.

Ramahd watched as Ashael floated over the streets of the city by the sea. The perspective was different this time. He was himself, not Ashael. The realization made him feel as though his existence had just been exposed.

Indeed, Ashael's head turned, his broad, bone-white horns sweeping through the air as he did so. For a moment the elder god's gaze searched for Ramahd.

The sense Ramahd had of the dream world was not so different from the weeks he'd spent hiding from Meryam in Sharakhai. She'd been a queen then, and had considered Ramahd a traitor. She wanted him brought to justice, wanted the threat he represented nullified. Her arcane searches rarely bore fruit, but when they did she sent Silver Spears or Blade Maidens to capture him. Through the stalwart actions of his most loyal men, Ramahd had

had escaped her time and time again and, each time, grown more adept at avoiding her spells. The skills learned then were likely the only thing that saved him from being seen by Ashael in Mazandir.

The god's piercing gaze passed over the village square where Ramahd hid, then focused on a nearby well. It shifted to a statue of Raamajit, the god clearly alert for something. Then, Alu be praised, Ashael moved on.

Ramahd followed him toward the blue waters of the harbor, where scores of ships were moored. He was aware enough to know that the harbor was Mazandir's, not some port city of old, and that the ships were King Hektor's. If Ashael reached them, Hektor and his entire fleet would be taken. Ramahd had mere moments in which to act, but he didn't know what to do.

Outside the dream, he was vaguely aware how close his own ship, *Alu's Crown*, was to the fleet—they'd rounded Mazandir's southwestern edge and were heading toward it fast. Ashael and his horde had already swept through half the caravanserai.

Find her, Ramahd told himself, *reveal her to Ashael.*

He sunk back into the dream, saw Ashael approaching the ships in the seaside harbor. Their crews fought the elder god. There were some among them who wielded magic, but what were they to him? He was an elder, and what the elders had given to mortal kind could be taken away.

In the real world, demons flew ahead of the host and fell upon King Hektor's fleet. Time was running out.

In the dream, Ramahd searched for signs of Meryam—any sign at all. Finding none, he grew desperate. The sounds of terror filled the desert sky and the seaside city, both. The battle had hardly begun and he'd already failed.

As small, winged demons, ifins, attacked the Qaimiri crews, it struck Ramahd. He'd been trying to pierce the veil of dreams Meryam had created, but he was a *part* of that dream. And dreams could be altered.

He needed to take control. To take the fight to Meryam.

He imagined the harbor was smaller than it had seemed. He visualized it with fewer piers, fewer ships, fewer soldiers on the decks . . .

. . . and it worked. Some of the demons that had flown toward the farther reaches of the Qaimiri fleet winged over and began concentrating on other ships, leaving the farthest reaches of the fleet alone. Ramahd reduced the numbers again and, lo and behold, the demons concentrated on the ship nearest to Mazandir.

No sooner had he managed that small victory than the vision altered again. Ships wavered into existence, sailed in from the sea to join the battle. Sunlight glinted off Ashael's golden armband and cuff as he waved a hand toward the farthest ships, and a flight of winged demons headed toward them. And just like that, Ramahd's gains were erased.

Meryam had sensed his meddling, he realized. He could feel her anger burning like a brand in the fog. It was fitful at first but grew stronger, as if she were searching for him. He'd found her signature at last.

And if I can sense you, Ramahd thought, *so can Ashael.*

Drawing on the dozens of times they'd been linked to one another, he listened for her heartbeat. He felt for the panic that swept over her when she felt like the walls were closing in.

Moments later, he had her. She stood on the wooden docks among hundreds of demons, only paces behind Ashael.

He focused on her, noting everything about her. Her frail limbs, her bony cheeks, the wicked gleam in her sunken eyes. As he did, the elder god slowed, then halted. He turned and stared down at Meryam. Around him, the demons flew into the sky, forming chaotic patterns.

By then, *Alu's Crown* was sailing through the harbor alongside the Qaimiri fleet. Cicio, bless him, had set a course that would bring them close to King Hektor's capital ship. Ramahd saw Hektor on the foredeck holding a sword. He stood wild-eyed, breathing hard, his face slick with black blood.

Basilio was just stepping onto the maindeck from the aftcastle. He took in the carnage with a stunned look. Qaimiri and demons alike lay dead across the deck. Then he spotted Ramahd, his eyes filled with confusion and wariness, as if Ramahd were somehow to blame for what was happening.

"Follow us, my king!" Ramahd shouted across the gap.

Basilio ran toward Hektor while waving his arms. "Your Highness, we must go home!"

"No!" Ramahd called. "Sharakhai needs us. We must sail north!"

Basilio said something too soft to hear. Moments later, Hektor, to Ramahd's complete horror, nodded. "We sail south, Lord Amansir! You will follow us."

"Your Highness, I beg you not to do this! King Ihsan is waiting for us with reinforcements."

Ramahd had said it to lend hope, but it was clearly a misstep. The mention of a Sharakhani King only seemed to harden Hektor to the benighted city. Horns were sounded, the king's orders being passed. Some ships moved to obey. Others did not. Ramahd saw why a moment later. The crews on the ships closest to Mazandir stood like statues. Around their heads, ifins were wrapped, their twin sets of wings flapping lazily. The demons' mouths were clamped to the backs of crewmen's necks, pacifying them, enslaving them.

Twenty ships had soon set sail, headed south for Qaimir. As their fleet slid over the sand, *Alu's Crown* included, Ramahd stood on the aftcastle and faced the docks.

He could no longer see Meryam. She was lost in the cloud of demons, which had gathered tightly around Ashael. The god, meanwhile, stared down, unmoving.

Ramahd tried to reenter the dream, but the moment he did his mind was flooded with so much chaos he was forced to retreat. As the ships curved around a cluster of red rocks to the south of Mazandir, the cloud of demons tightened further. It was so dense even Ashael was lost among them.

And then the harbor was lost from view, and they were sailing hard, away from Sharakhai.

Chapter 33

A WOMAN ONCE KNOWN as Varal sat beneath a dying acacia. The tree stood in a garden that had once been lush. She remembered tending to the tree and to the garden itself. She remembered planting the valerian, the Sweet Anna, the veronica. She remembered planting the oleander bushes that had attracted so many songbirds—reed warblers, finches, saddlebacks, even the occasional amberlark. Now the garden was dead. The birds were gone. Only the acacia remained with its chimes: from the branches she'd hung hundreds upon hundreds of crystals using thread-of-gold that they might grant her visions.

Varal remembered all of this, and yet it felt foreign. She knew who those memories truly belonged to. When she was a young girl growing up in Sharakhai, she'd heard of Saliah the desert witch who lived far from the city with a lone acacia. She'd heard stories of how Saliah lured young men and women to the desert and devoured their souls. She'd had no idea at the time that Saliah was actually Nalamae. Even Saliah herself hadn't known who she really was. Like Varal, when she'd worked for the Kings of Sharakhai as a shipwright, Saliah had thought herself her own woman. But then one day Nalamae's presence had swept into her and everything changed.

Varal still remembered her husband, whom she'd married young. She remembered her five children, three of whom had died before their time. She remembered every ship she'd ever designed, every curve and edge of the twenty-seven ships she'd built for the Kings of Sharakhai. She remembered her hopes and dreams, all of them taken from her by the river goddess reborn.

"I want it back," she said to the hot desert air.

The tree didn't answer. Nor did the desert. She went to the well and drew a bucket of water. She poured it around the base of the tree. She refilled it three more times and repeated the ritual. It never helped. She was certain the tree wouldn't survive the coming days.

As the thirsty ground drank the offered water, she sat in the shade beneath the tree's broad branches. She couldn't see beyond the stone walls, but she felt deeply connected to the desert. She remembered using a gnarled wooden staff to summon visions from the chimes. But the staff was gone, burned in the mountains to the east. Now she used her sister's adamantine spear.

"Not *my* sister," Varal said softly, "*Nalamae's* sister."

Your sister, countered Nalamae within her mind.

Varal shrugged and stabbed the spear's tip into the runnels of the acacia's rough bark. She knew she shouldn't resist Nalamae—doing so only seemed to dull her divine powers—but she couldn't help it. She'd always been stubborn. And besides, Nalamae had been running from her brothers and sisters for centuries. Perhaps what the goddess needed was a bit more stubbornness, an irascible will to take the battle to them.

If you truly believe that, Nalamae said, *then why are you still here?*

Varal looked up at the chimes, which were beginning to sound. "Because I don't know what else to do."

There were so many possibilities. So many ways the future might unfold.

Now you see the real issue, Nalamae said with sisterly affection. *It was never the will, but the way.*

"Be quiet," Varal said. "I'm trying to concentrate."

The chimes glinted in the sun. The sound they made was easy on the ears, but disturbing all the same. They gave the barest hint to the chaos playing out beyond the garden's rough stone walls.

Through the chimes she caught glimpses of the desert's past, glimpses of its future, glimpses of events that were unfolding at that very moment. She sifted through the visions, searching for the ones her sibling gods hoped would come to pass, then for ways to prevent them.

She saw a thousand pasts hurtling toward the future. She followed their trajectories, saw them twist and bend as other threads cut across them. She heard many voices. She saw children being born, armies being sundered. Again and again, she saw a city burning, then crumbling to dust.

"No!" Varal shouted, and gripped her spear tight.

So many paths led to that dark future, which the other gods had hoped for and counted on from the moment they made their pact with the Sharakhani Kings. But she refused to let it happen.

How to stop it, though? That was the question. She might kill Bakhi or Thaash. She might murder Tulathan or Rhia. She might rid the world of them all or bind them to this earth, and still the gate might open, destroying Sharakhai and its people, her children.

My children, Varal thought.

She'd had five, hadn't she? Her memories of them were beginning to fade as other memories rushed in. The memories of the generations of people she'd given aid to. People she'd broken bread with, those she'd sung with around countless fires. The elder gods may have created the desert, but Nalamae had made it her own. She'd sheltered it from the foreign gods who coveted it. She'd fought her brothers and sisters for centuries to protect it.

Now all her work was about to be undone.

Gripping the haft of her spear tightly, she stabbed the tree again, and this time she saw something new. She was at the edge of a golden city by the sea. She stood on the docks. Ships were arrayed before her and a battle raged. Massive ravens with knife-like talons swooped toward the soldiers aboard the ships. Yet more attacked the people from the city who'd run to help them. They fought in vain, for the ravens were driven by the hand of an elder.

Ashael, tall and terrible to behold.

Then Ashael saw her. He hove closer, wondering who she was, how she'd come to be there. Was she another of the elders in disguise? Or one of the fates themselves?

In that moment, she feared for her life as never before. She'd come so far. Nearly all she'd ever wanted was hers. She need only control the one before her, the one who dreamed—

She blinked and found herself standing on the outskirts of a caravanserai. Sandships lay in the harbor, besieged by a host of demons. More and more of the demons were inexplicably giving up the fight. They flew up into the air, twisted in wild patterns, converging around the elder god and around her. Closer and closer they came, the cloud tightening, becoming denser, occluding the sky above.

As Ashael loomed over her and his glinting eyes stared into her soul, she knew.

She knew what she had to do.

The vision of Mazandir faded. The cacophony of flapping wings and screaming demons did as well. They were replaced with a kaleidoscope of chimes, a soft tinkling sound, and the soughing of the wind through branches all but bereft of their tiny green leaves.

Nalamae blinked. Took in a deep, cleansing breath and stood. The woman in her vision had been Queen Meryam. At last, the tree had shown her the path that was likeliest. It had shown her the part she, Nalamae, would play.

It wouldn't be easy, and the price would be dear. If all went as she predicted, she would never see her children again.

"So be it," she said to the dry desert air.

Spear in hand, she turned into a column of sand, which collapsed, coughing outward.

Then all was still in the garden once more.

Chapter 34

IHSAN STOOD AT the mouth of the Hollow, watching Lord Amansir's clipper sail away. "May Alu grant you favor."

Behind him, Nayyan approached holding Ransaneh. "If you truly wished them well, you should have convinced him to join us."

Ihsan shrugged. "He goes to save his people."

"I understand, but if Meryam truly *has* set her sights on Mazandir"—she stopped several paces away and began bouncing Ransaneh on one hip—"he's likely just consigned himself and his crew to death."

"Don't sell Lord Amansir short. He's weathered much when it comes to Meryam." The clipper was but a wavering smudge along the horizon. "Besides, if things are truly so hopeless, you could say the same about us."

Nayyan, holding Ransaneh tight to her chest, made no reply. Her eyes were red. Not from emotion, he suddenly realized, but the physical pain of the black mould, eating away at her. Nayyan didn't like his calling attention to it, but Ihsan still found his gaze drifting down toward her belly. Almost subconsciously, he tongued the hard spots inside his mouth. He still hadn't told Nayyan about his own illness. It wasn't yet visible to the passing glance, but it wouldn't be long before it was.

"Is it bad?" he asked her.

"Yes." She swallowed hard. "But it'll pass."

It was a testament to Nayyan's distress that she allowed Ihsan to take Ransaneh. She stared at their daughter afterward with a forlorn expression.

"Go and rest," Ihsan said. "Ransaneh and I will go for a walk."

The wind tugged at the tail of Nayyan's violet turban. "I feel so useless lying in the ship."

"I know you hope to see Sharakhai liberated before you die"—he stared down at Ransaneh's round face—"but you can't do that if you're weakened when your strength is called upon."

Still she paused, tears gathering at the corners of her eyes. "I really did think we'd live forever, Ihsan."

Ihsan smiled, but it was a feeble, fleeting thing. "So did I."

"Promise me you'll protect her."

The words made Ihsan feel horrible for hiding his sickness from her. He nearly confessed it right then and there, but the way she was looking at him, as if he were her only hope, convinced him to remain silent. *Soon,* he vowed, *when the time is right.* "Of course I'll protect her," he said.

She leaned in and kissed Ransaneh's head, gave Ihsan a longer kiss on the lips, then headed for the *Miscreant.*

For a time, Ihsan was lost in guilt, but he'd never been one to stew in his own misery. He preferred to be active, mentally if not physically. *If the fates have decided our days are numbered, so be it.* He rubbed Ransaneh's back. *See Sharakhai safe. Make that your focus.*

As he walked away from the Hollow with Ransaneh, his thoughts wandered to Meryam. He knew the former queen had long coveted Sharakhai. He hadn't realized the lengths she'd be willing to go in order to get it. She'd cast all caution aside, which made him wonder whether she was thinking about anything beyond the conquest itself. With Ashael by her side, there was little doubt she could conquer the city. She could conquer the desert as well. She could retake Qaimir, then move on to the other three kingdoms bordering the Great Mother.

What then? Did she imagine she could set Ashael aside like some unwanted artifact from the days of the world's making? Perhaps. She'd have all the power she'd need to retain hold of her burgeoning empire. And none would dare stand against her, knowing she could call upon Ashael again if needed.

"And what of the abandoned god himself?" Ihsan mused.

As Ransaneh took a sudden, halting breath and released it in a sigh, Ihsan stared south, toward Mazandir.

If he and Ramahd were right about Meryam—that she was controlling Ashael through his dreams—she'd likely try to return him to the Hollow. He'd lain there for an age already. Who was to say he wouldn't lay for another when Meryam no longer had use for him?

It was a brilliant, if very dangerous, plan, but it neglected one thing: the young gods and *their* plans. Meryam might think she could use Ashael's power against them if needed, but she didn't understand them as Ihsan did. She didn't realize how far they saw, how subtly they tugged on the threads of fate. If they'd given her the power to raise Ashael, it was because her doing so was a crucial move in the game they played.

So did they want Ashael to awaken or not? And if they *did* want him to awaken, what would *Ashael's* first move be?

His first thought was to return to Yusam's journals, but they contained little to nothing about Ashael. He'd taken the journals as far as he could. There was another possibility, though it had its dangers as well. But he'd been playing the game with a handicap long enough. It was time he had a word with his opponents.

Late that night, after Nayyan and Ransaneh had fallen asleep, Ihsan dressed and crept quietly from the cabin. He waved to the pair of guards on deck—men well used to his peculiar nighttime routines—and made his way to the standing stones. Above, Rhia shone brightly, casting her soft golden light across the desert.

On reaching the pit's mouth, he knelt at the edge and opened the small leather purse that held a little of the black powder. He'd deduced that it was made from the filings of Goezhen's horn. Horn was used in many rituals in the desert, some of them to honor Rhia herself. And the powder had already proven it was related to dreams. In fact, it was so perfect an offering it felt as if Rhia were summoning *him*, not the other way around.

He pinched what powder he could between his thumb and forefinger, then lifted it to his nose. Worried he'd be drawn into Ashael's dream, he kept his eyes fixed on the moon's mottled surface above him and sniffed, first one nostril, then the other.

The world shifted. He soon found himself standing not in the desert, but on a plateau on the shoulders of Mount Tauriyat. He and his fellow Kings, including Sehid-Alaz of the thirteenth tribe, stood in a line. Kiral King of Kings was pleading with the gods for help to save Sharakhai from the tribal invaders. Bakhi and Tulathan listened with calm expressions on their graceful faces. Thaash stood behind them, silent and grave, his well muscled arms crossed over his chest. Goezhen stood apart, his twin tails beating strange rhythms against the mountain's dry, rocky ground. Yerinde, casting her gaze over the gathered Sharakhani men and women, looked hungry, as though she wanted to devour the entire assemblage—devour them, or bed them.

Rhia, the one Ihsan cared about most, peered down the line of Kings with a quizzical expression, looking from King to King until she landed on Ihsan. The look in her moonlit eyes, so dreamy a moment ago, became piercing.

She took a half step toward him and spoke within his mind. *Where dost thou stand?*

That fateful night, four centuries earlier, was still clear in Ihsan's mind. He didn't remember Rhia speaking to him in this way. Even so, it dawned on Ihsan that this was no dream, but a visitation. "I stand in a different place," he said, "a different time."

Her eyes relaxed and understanding dawned. *Of course.*

Ihsan motioned to Kiral, who continued to speak. "I've come to ask you about the end. About Ashael."

Rhia blinked. Her lips parted, opening in the shape of a circle as if she'd forgotten what she was about to say. *He hast risen.*

"He has."

Her face softened. *The end draws nigh, then.*

Nearby, King Kiral fell silent, and the Kings waited for the gods' answer to his plea. Tulathan spoke, but the words were soft and distant. None seemed to notice the conversation taking place between Ihsan and Rhia.

"The end is very near," Ihsan said, "but you have yet to reach the gate. You have yet to reach the farther fields. There is still much that remains in doubt."

Rhia's eyes narrowed. Her nostrils flared. *What is it that remains in doubt?*

"A woman of royal blood, Meryam, controls Ashael. What will she do with him? Will the elder wake from his dream? What will he do if he does?"

Why hast thou come, oh King of Deepened Vale?

"Because the desert stands on the very brink. Its fate could tip either way. I know the danger you run by meddling in the affairs of mortals. I understand you don't wish to be bound to this earth. Even now, you're uncertain whether what you've done will prevent you from crossing."

Goezhen's jaundiced eyes passed over Ihsan. A low growl emanated from his throat. Thaash's jaw worked while his sword hand flexed.

Rhia glanced at them, then returned her dreamy gaze to Ihsan. *Tell me what you wish.*

"*I* want to be the one to open the gateway." Ihsan's heart had never beat so rapidly as it did then. "*I* want to pave your way to the farther fields."

All eyes turned toward Ihsan and his conversation with Rhia. The silence stretched on and on.

If what thou sayest is true, Rhia said, *if the desert indeed stands on the very brink, what need do we have for another?*

"The woman you chose is unstable," Ihsan said easily. "Ramahd, her dead sister's husband, is on his way to stop her now, and he has with him some of Goezhen's horn, the very thing Meryam is using to control Ashael. Ramahd may very well succeed. But if *I* went, with your blessing, I could stop him with but a word and take Meryam's place. You could be assured that I would work to see you pass to the land beyond."

Why wouldst we do so, oh King?

Ihsan steeled himself. They'd arrived at the most dangerous part of his plan. "Because you made a bargain: you gave the desert to me and my brother Kings. I'm asking you to fulfill that bargain. I would go forth willingly, to protect your long investment with no need for you to interfere. It would guarantee you reached the land beyond, to be reunited with the elders."

Rhia's gaze drifted from his eyes to his lips. *And thou wouldst survive the mould that threatens to devour thee, as wouldst thy queen and thy child.*

"Yes," Ihsan said, suddenly more aware of the ache inside his mouth. "Ashael can heal us of our affliction. We can live for as long as we wish."

Yet thou must know the fate of Sharakhai. Rhia's gaze deepened. *Thou must know what happens to the desert at the moment of our parting.*

Ihsan stood taller. "We would have Ashael to protect us."

Sharakhai would still perish. Not even Ashael can save all. Wouldst thou live without thy home?

"We can remake Sharakhai, this time in *our* image. People would flock to it."

Why dost thou think anything from the gods is owed thee?

Ihsan laughed. "Was I not instrumental in your plans? Did I not help you in your manipulations of Ahyanesh and her daughter, Çedamihn? Did I not aid in the Moonless Host's rise to prominence? Did my actions not lead to the thirteenth tribe's rebirth and the conflicts that followed? I *ensured* the crystal would shatter, thereby forging the pathway to the land beyond. I *ensured* the desert was led to a point where you and your fellow gods stand on the very doorstep of your dreams, your entry to the farther fields."

For long moments Rhia was silent. As the cold desert wind toyed with her golden hair, three of the other gods moved to stand behind her— Tulathan, Bakhi, and Thaash; those who, outside of the dream, yet lived. Goezhen and Yerinde, meanwhile, stepped back, deeper into the darkness.

"The gate has been opened. Your dreams might yet be fulfilled." Ihsan paused, composing himself. Everything rode on his next words. "Or they could crumble before your eyes. It all depends on what *I* choose to do next, and whether or not you agree to help me."

Rhia's face turned cross. *Nay, King of Three. The events we've set into motion can no longer be denied.*

"You chose to awaken Ashael because he has power. You chose him because you think he will widen the gateway. I can stop him, should I choose. My voice still carries power. One word from me and Meryam will lose her place as Ashael's puppet master. One word from me and your dreams will turn to dust."

Rhia blinked, then drew breath so sharply it sounded like a sword being stabbed into the sand. She cast her gaze about, over the Kings, her fellow gods, the gathered mortals, as if she were reevaluating everything that had happened since Beht Ihman.

Her eyes finally drifted to the leather purse in his hands. *Dost thou think thyself ready to wield the key to dreaming?*

"I've already proven I can."

Rhia laughed and waved to the plateau around them. *Dost thou think* this *akin to the subtleties required manipulate an elder? That the stuff of dreams is akin to the truths found in the waking world?*

"Meryam mastered it."

For years hath she walked the ways of the slumbering mind, whereas thou . . . Despite thine own dreams, thine ambitions, thou hast always been rooted in reality.

The scene around Ihsan began to dissolve.

"Stop!" he said desperately. "I can learn!"

No, she said, and the dream faded altogether.

"Wait!" Ihsan cried, stepping toward her.

But it was too late. She was gone, and Ihsan was teetering on the edge of a bottomless pit. He swung his arms and managed to catch himself. Knees shaking, he dropped to the ground and rolled away. For long moments all he could do was stare at the night sky while his breath came in short, rapid bursts.

Only when his pounding heart began to quell did he realize that Rhia's moon was gone from the sky, replaced by Tulathan's bright silver coin. Ihsan lay on the stony ground a long while, recounting the conversation and what it meant. He kept returning to the question she'd posed: *Dost thou think thyself ready to wield the key to dreaming?*

He was certain he'd heard it before, but he couldn't put his finger on where. He focused on what he'd learned instead. He'd gone into the conversation hoping to find something, anything, that might help him stop the gods from achieving their goals. He'd hoped to threaten them, provoke, knowing he was taking his life into his own hands by doing so, but feeling it was necessary to determine where the gods stood.

The effort had been far from fruitless.

The fact that Rhia wouldn't consider replacing Meryam with him, a willing participant in their plans, was an indication that they felt their plans secure. More revealing was Rhia's reaction to his threat to stop Meryam if they didn't agree. Had Rhia had any room to maneuver, had she been able to prevent him without endangering their goal of reaching the farther fields, she would have done so.

The gods had reached a point where they were no longer willing to perform even the smallest of acts that might bind them to this world. It wasn't much of an edge, but it was something.

The powder now gone, Ihsan tossed the leather bag into the pit and made for the ship. It was time to return to the royal navy. Meryam might have gone to Mazandir to retake her fleet, but she would soon set her sights on Sharakhai. At most, Ihsan had a handful of days to find a way to stop her *and* Ashael. Fail in that and the streets of the city would be bathed in blood.

Chapter 35

THE BUZZING THAT so often plagued Hamid's thoughts had all but vanished during his escape. It returned with a vengeance near midday, when a line of warriors appeared along the slopes of Mount Arasal.

He watched through a gap between two massive boulders as hundreds upon hundreds of men and women, all geared for war, walked the path down toward the desert's grand basin. Tribe Khiyanat came first with Çeda, Emre, Frail Lemi, and the she-devil, Shal'alara, at their lead. Tribe Kadri came next, then Kenan, Narazid, and Okan. On and on they marched, tribe after tribe.

All bloody thirteen of them. The buzzing in Hamid's head intensified. *The alliance has held, and on the word of two craven fools.*

The tribes were preparing to sail for Sharakhai, where they would no doubt throw their might against the city's occupiers, Mirea and Malasan. And for what? To help the city's highborn, people who'd stood by for centuries while the Kings pressed their knees to the necks of the desert tribes?

Hamid spat onto the dry earth next to him. "Let them burn," he said in a low voice. "We'll drive out what remains and put the city to the torch."

But the tribes marched on, oblivious to his wishes.

He ducked as a woman with a spyglass scanned the slope where he was hiding. He waited for several breaths, then peered carefully between the rocks and saw her spyglass swing elsewhere.

Likely she was searching for him. He needed to take care over the next few days. He'd barely escaped the valley earlier. He'd seen the visions Çeda had summoned up from the acacia. He'd felt the surprise and anger of those watching, then seen it on their faces when the visions faded. Moments later, he'd been drawn into the strange vision of Meryam and the tall being, clearly a god, and the demonic host that had issued from the black pit's open maw.

There was no denying that vision's power—for a time, he'd been as entranced as everyone else—but his anger over having his past laid bare for all to see had thrown him from it. For long moments, he'd stood there while those around him remained stock still, eyes wide, mouths hanging open. He considered slitting Çeda's throat, Emre's too, but feared the moment he did the visions would end, and he would be caught red-handed, literally, so he'd sprinted away instead. He'd only just made it to the tree line when the shaikhs and all those around them had awoken bleary-eyed.

They searched for him, but he knew the valley well and escaped along little-known paths. He made his way toward the desert, planning to hide on Rasime's ship until she returned. He'd even made it halfway there when the first of the warriors took to the path leading down from the valley. Caught on the slopes, he'd had no choice but to wait until they passed. It took nearly three hours.

Then came a new surprise: a line of twenty men and women, chained together, being led down to the sand. All of them were ardent defenders of Hamid's plan to burn Sharakhai down, so it came as no surprise when Hamid spotted Darius and Rasime among them. Darius looked defeated, Rasime defiant. The others looked as though their anger was burning so brightly they hoped to storm their captors and die fighting.

Hamid lost sight of them as they were led into the fleet of ships. They were the core of his support, the ones who'd helped him overthrow Macide and the elders who bowed to him. It was unclear why the shaikhs would have decided to take them on this journey. Perhaps a combination of wanting to give them a proper trial and *not* wanting to leave them in the valley with those who remained. Whatever the reason, it was a stroke of good luck—if he could free them, all might not be lost.

By midday the tribes had boarded their ships. An hour later, they sailed away. Hamid was bitter, but gods, the sheer scale of it. A single fleet comprised of warriors from every corner of the desert. It was an awesome display of power.

"And it should have been mine." The buzzing rose so high it made Hamid cringe. He closed his eyes and pinched the bridge of his nose, willing it to pass. "It should all have been mine."

By the time the fleet had diminished in the west, dusk had arrived. When it was fully dark, Hamid hiked to a bay where he'd secreted a skiff stocked with enough water and rations for two weeks' sail. As Rhia rose, a slanted sickle in the east, he lifted the skiff's mast into position and set sail.

The buzzing finally started to fade, and as the winds bore him over the desert he began to calculate. There was a good chance it would be several days before anything happened to Darius, Rasime, or the others. The shaikhs would be consumed with planning their arrival in Sharakhai. Then they'd hold some sham trial, which might also take a day or two. In that time Hamid could free Darius and possibly Rasime.

Together, they might reach out to Shaikh Valtim and secure his allegiance. Three, maybe four other shaikhs would follow. What happened in the valley wasn't the end. It was a delay, a temporary reprieve for Emre, Çeda, and that brainless stack of muscles, Frail Lemi.

He made steady progress over the next two nights. Each morning saw him closer to the fleet than the previous. On the third day, worried the trials would happen soon if they hadn't already, he braved the sands early. It was a risk—he might be seen by scout ships—but he needed to catch up and still have enough time during the night to find Darius.

He kept near the taller dunes when he could. Twice he saw scout ships cutting a line across the desert. Both times he steered behind the nearest dune and laid the skiff's mast down. Neither ship, thank the gods, appeared to have seen him, and when night fell, he sailed quickly on.

The gods smiled on him again as he neared the fleet. A thin layer of clouds blanketed the heavens, reducing Tulathan to little more than a glowing wisp in the fog. He anchored a quarter league away from the fleet and proceeded on foot. The camp had not yet settled: he could hear music, tambours and ouds and mournful doudouks. Fires stitched a haphazard line across the fleet's nebulous shape.

He made his way toward the head of the fleet, where the Khiyanat ships would likely be anchored, and spotted the *Red Bride* near the *Amaranth*. The buzzing, so faint these past few days, returned with a vengeance.

Between the two ships, sitting around a fire, were Emre, Çeda, Frail Lemi, the two bloody Blade Maidens, and several shaikhs, Neylana, Dayan, and Aríz among them. Dardzada waddled near and plopped his bulk down by Neylana. The two held hands briefly, then Dardzada launched into some tale while the others looked on with amused expressions. They laughed when Dardzada threw his good arm into the air and made a sound like a fire pot exploding. A few clapped their knees. Several women trilled a high ululation. Then one of the Maidens—the big one, Kameyl—began a tale of her own.

How he wished he could sneak up behind them and take his kenshar to their throats. He wanted to feel the resistance as the keen edge slid through their flesh, feel it ease as each stroke neared its completion. He wanted them to watch their own lifeblood pour onto the sand.

The buzzing rose so high he felt rattled by it and pressed his fists against his temples. He beat his skull, willing it to go away. His breath was coming so rapidly he was forced to retreat lest he be heard. He left them to their stories, their camaraderie, and hid alone in the darkness until the revelry wound down.

Eventually the music faded. Sand was kicked over flames. Fires winked out, one by one, until only a few remained. Hamid waited for the heavy silence of a fleet at rest before heading toward the *Burning Sand*, the ketch that had once been Rasime's. The ship had been altered. The shutters along the forward cabins had been replaced with iron bars. Goezhen's sweet kiss, they'd turned it into a prison ship.

As sure as the desert was dry, that was where Darius and the others were being kept. He watched it for a while, wary of guards, but saw none. Likely they were onboard, perhaps in the captain's cabin. He'd go there first. Slit their necks before—

Someone climbed on deck and walked down the gangplank. He could see only his silhouette, but he would know Darius's gait anywhere. He walked stiffly, his right arm held close by his side. It was from an old wound, an arrow he'd taken after they woke Hamzakiir from the dead and tried to carry him away from the Wandering King's hidden desert palace. His right shoulder had healed poorly, limiting the movements of that arm ever since.

But how was it he was free? Why wasn't Darius in the ship, awaiting trial?

Hamid followed him as he wove between the ships toward one of the few fires still lit. Darius apparently meant to sit with the group gathered there. It was comprised of men and women from many different tribes. Presently they were singing an old war ballad. Poorly. Most of them were drunk.

Hamid needed to approach before Darius stepped into the firelight. "Darius?"

Darius slowed, then stopped. He turned and peered into the darkness. He seemed to deflate before Hamid's eyes. "I was hoping you wouldn't come."

Hamid felt his entire body tighten. "Why would you say that?"

"You need to go, Hamid. Leave while still you can."

Hamid stepped closer, only then realizing why Darius had been favoring his right arm so much. His arm ended at the wrist. There were spots of blood on the bandages wrapped tightly around the stump. "What have they done to you?"

Darius lifted his bad arm as far as he could, which was not very far. "This was the price."

"The price for what?"

"To stay, to fight with them."

Hamid felt his breath leave him. "You would *fight* with them?"

"I know you hoped for something different. I know you had grand visions for the desert. But you *saw* what's ready to befall Sharakhai. We all did."

"You don't care about Sharakhai."

"No, *you* don't. Sharakhai is all I've ever known."

"You hate what became of it. Your father died penniless working for that cunt of a horse trader. Your mother was raped and murdered by a filthy Kundhuni dog!"

By the fire, two men snorted in laughter, distracting Darius momentarily. When he turned back to Hamid, he lifted his maimed arm higher. "I gave my hand so they wouldn't kill me. I gave it so I would have a chance to fight for the people of the Shallows." He paused, as if searching for the right words. "There are people you loved there. Your little sister."

"My sister is dead."

"Others like her still live. The least you can do is walk away now so we can stop the coming slaughter."

For long moments Hamid didn't know what to say. "You were with me every step of the way. You watched it all happen and said nothing. You wanted it all. You wanted to rule the desert as much as I did."

By the fire, Jenise, one of Çeda's Shieldwives, kicked several logs, sending a burst of embers into the air and bringing renewed life to the fire.

"You went too far, Hamid, when you gave Macide up to Queen Meryam. You went too far when you used the asirim against the other tribes. You went too far when you tried to kill Emre."

"When *we* tried to kill him."

Darius closed his eyes, then nodded. "When *we* tried to kill him."

"How can you *defend* him?"

"Emre isn't the problem. Your blind hatred is."

"*My* blind hatred?" Hamid barked a laugh. "You mean to tell me you've seen the light? That you're some holy priest who thinks he can walk to the farther fields with his head held high?"

Darius's back straightened. "Held high, no. But higher than when we were together."

The buzzing at the back of Hamid's head was so loud he could hardly string two thoughts together. "Think carefully, Darius."

Darius's head jerked back. It was his easy smile, though, a smile that didn't reach his eyes, that enraged Hamid. "Don't think for a moment you can bully *me*, Hamid Malahin'ava."

"If it weren't for me, you'd be a nothing in the Shallows, just like your father, or you'd be dead like your whore of a mother."

Darius's face went blank. "Better to be nothing than to die in the desert having made nothing. *Done* nothing." He gestured to the fleet around them with his good arm. "It must burn to have all your dreams stolen from you. To have nothing left save bitterness and bile."

The buzzing had become a tumult of sounds and memory and screaming voices, echoing inside Hamid's skull. They deafened him. Blinded him to everything save Darius, who laughed—*laughed*—then turned away and strode toward the fire as if Hamid meant nothing to him.

No, Hamid thought as he drew his kenshar. *It's you who are nothing.*

He stepped lightly over the sand, closing the distance.

He lifted his free hand as the buzzing and screaming and laughing in his head threatened to reach his own throat. It was just there, ready to burst from him as he reached for Darius's shoulder. It was all he could think of, that on seeing Darius's blood the clamor might be quelled for a time.

A small laugh escaped him as he took a fistful of Darius's thawb. He was just ready to pull him back, clamp a hand around his mouth, and send the knife into his back, when something fluttered through the air to his right.

He was punched hard in the chest and staggered back as pain blossomed. An arrow was sticking out of his shoulder.

Darius turned at the sound. He stared wide-eyed at the arrow, at Hamid.

Hamid roared, his pain and anger driving him. He lunged for Darius and lashed out with his knife, going for the throat, but Darius took a staggering step back. Hamid was ready to charge him when another arrow came streaking in.

This time it sent Hamid stumbling sideways. He fell in an awkward, sand-spraying heap. He groaned, struggling to breathe. The second arrow had taken him through the chest.

Darius approached carefully and stared down at Hamid with an infuriating mixture of anger and pity. Behind him, other figures resolved from the night. First Emre, then Frail Lemi.

The buzzing in Hamid's head had inexplicably ceased. The world was as silent as he could ever remember its being. "You set a *trap* for me?" he said to Darius.

"He didn't know," Emre said as he dropped his bow onto the sand. "We spotted your skiff. I knew you'd go to Darius first."

Hamid struggled to understand how everything could have fallen apart so quickly, so completely. He tried, but he couldn't piece it together. It was too confusing. And he was too taken by the hard look on Emre's face.

"You're pitiful," Hamid said to him in a long wheeze. "You'll go to Sharakhai. Throw yourselves against her walls. But you're all going to die."

Uncaring, Emre straddled his hips and prised Hamid's knife from his enfeebled hand. "You first," he said, and pressed the knife through Hamid's ribs, piercing his heart.

For a long while, Emre held the knife to Hamid's chest. He felt Hamid's breaths become more shallow. Felt them cease altogether as his body went slack.

Only then did he stand, leaving Hamid's knife where it was. Were it anyone else Emre might have wondered what those unseeing eyes saw and what sort of life awaited them in the farther fields. In Hamid's case, he found he didn't care to think about it. He'd spent too much of his life worrying about Hamid.

They had a city to save. A whole desert.

Those from the nearby fire had come to see what had happened. A ring of onlookers formed around them, talking in low voices. Emre heard Hamid's name being passed among them.

Frail Lemi, meanwhile, stared down at Hamid's lifeless form. Emre couldn't tell if he was furious or relieved. Maybe he was both. Emre never learned which; Frail Lemi turned and walked away without a word, leaving Emre alone with Darius.

Emre wasn't quite sure how Darius was feeling. He'd cared deeply for Hamid at one time, and though he'd renounced his former lover's ways, Emre could tell he was battling with his emotions.

"Do you wish to say anything?" Emre asked him.

Darius couldn't seem to take his eyes from Hamid. When he finally did, he blinked away tears and shook his head. "No."

A moment later, Frail Lemi returned with two shovels and handed one to Emre, who accepted it with a nod. As the two of them began digging Hamid's grave, Darius turned his back on the still form and wove his way through the encircling crowd. As the grave deepened, the sound of the shovels rhythmic, others did the same.

By the time they rolled Hamid into the hole and covered him with sand, none were left to witness it.

Chapter 36

MERYAM STOOD ON the docks of Mazandir's southern harbor. Ashael loomed above her, staring down with bandaged eyes while his demons swarmed around the two of them. The vortex they created was strong. The wind tugged at her clothes, whipped her hair against her face and eyes. It felt as if she were in the center of a sand devil, the shrieking demons grains of sand swirling ever tighter around her.

Even through her panic, she knew this was Ramahd's doing. He'd somehow made Ashael aware of her. Her saving grace was that Ashael was still lost in the land of dreams. She could see him as he stood beside the ocean and stared at the lapping waves and the fleet of waterborne ships. Meryam herself was still hidden, but thanks to Ramahd, Ashael had sensed her, become curious about her. He was moments from seeing through the illusion and waking fully.

In the dream, his gaze pierced. His two broad horns fanned like wings. She felt naked and exposed, as she had when the blood mage, Meiying, had burned her magic from her. As then, her failure felt like a certainty, a foregone conclusion.

How you thought you could stand against an elder I'll never understand. It was Yasmine's voice, taunting her.

Meryam's right hand reflexively clutched the leather pouch at her belt, holding the filings of Goezhen's horn, which had caught Ashael in a dream of Meryam's making.

"All is not yet lost," Meryam said under her voice.

Yasmine's laugh was biting. *Well of course it is, sister.*

"No, it isn't," Meryam vowed, louder this time. "The god has not yet awoken."

As if drawn by her thoughts, Ashael crouched, his sandaled feet still hovering off the ground. The scent of brimstone, charred myrrh, and desert sage grew stronger.

Meryam had been forced to abandon her guise as one of the fates— Ashael's will was simply too strong to maintain it. She played the part of the harbor master instead. "Why have you come, Ashael the Terrible?" As she spoke, she tugged at the pouch, reaching for more of the powder. "How have we angered you?"

The pallid skin of Ashael's brow furrowed. He reached up and touched the skin around his eyes, where in the real world tattered bandages covered them. He was so close to piercing the veil—if he did, Yasmine's dire omen would prove true.

"I beg you to leave," Meryam shouted over the din of flapping wings. "Your servants have taken enough!"

Ashael made a low, deep sound like the horns the Kundhuni used to mark the moons' rising. Meryam reached into the pouch and grabbed a handful of powder. Several demons approached, curious. One hovered between her and Ashael. It had a ravenous look, as though it wanted to sample her flesh. At a wave of Ashael's hand, it screeched and returned to the gyre.

Meryam thought of throwing the powder at Ashael, but to do that would be to alert him to its existence.

Give up, Yasmine urged. *Give up your fool dream and join me in the land beyond.*

Ignoring her, Meryam let the powder sift through her fingers. So strong were the currents formed by the cloud of demons around her that it was borne up into the air. She saw it curling, blooming subtly like drops of ink in water.

Ashael's eyes, so sharply focused a moment ago, went distant. He stood and considered the demons around him, then the ships in the harbor.

You have enough, Meryam willed him. *Take your ships and the mortals within them. Go to the city that has always been your goal, where Iri himself lies hidden.*

He would, she felt him decide. He would take his army and destroy the golden city as proof to Iri and all the rest that he was not to be taken lightly.

Decided, Ashael rose from his crouch and floated across the waves. His murder of ravens followed. The fleet would come last, the soldiers in his righteous crusade.

Meryam found herself blinking, breathing hard, alone on Mazandir's sandy docks. Ashael floated above the caravanserai, heading toward Sharakhai. His horde of demons followed. She took in the Qaimiri ships that were still in the harbor. It wasn't as complete a victory as she had hoped, but it was enough.

Ramahd surprised you, didn't he? Yasmine asked.

He had. Ramahd had somehow entered the dream she'd crafted to manipulate Ashael.

Well, what did you expect? Yasmine went on smugly. *He spent years linked with you, watching you manipulate the minds of others.*

"Be quiet." She considered having Ashael turn around, kill Ramahd, and take what was rightfully hers.

Do that and he might take it all from you.

"I said be quiet!"

Yasmine laughed and might have said more, but just then Meryam's thoughts were interrupted by *The Gray Gull*'s approach. She'd take time to consider Ramahd, to find ways to prevent his manipulating her dreams in the future. In the meantime, she had what she'd come for: ships and soldiers to protect her while Ashael and his host fell upon the forces gathered around Sharakhai.

The Gray Gull glided to a halt in the center of the harbor. As Meryam climbed down the stone stairs to the sand and headed toward it, the other ships, all with crews controlled by Ashael, began to set sail. By the time Meryam gained the *Gull*'s deck, they were underway and sailing after the demonic host in the distance.

As the *Gull* trailed after them, Meryam went to the foredeck, stood beside Amaryllis, and marveled at the sight of it: thirty ships and two thousand soldiers to call her own. "We're nearly there," she said, more to herself than Amaryllis.

The long silence that followed was uncharacteristic of Amaryllis. Meryam turned to find her staring restlessly at the fleet ahead, her gaze flitting from ship to ship to ship.

Among her newly formed fleet, only the *Gull*'s crew retained free will. The rest had their heads wrapped by the small demons, the ifins, their lamprey mouths clamped to the base of their victims' necks while twin sets of wings wrapped their heads. Between the wings, their victims' eyes peeked through. Without exception they were wide as saucers, as if the trapped man or woman were living a nightmare.

It's like a grand net, Meryam mused. *The ifin control the minds of the mortals. The ifin, in turn, are controlled by Ashael. And I am Ashael's master.*

Yes, came Yasmine's distant reply, *but for how long?*

Ignoring her sister, Meryam turned to face Amaryllis. "What troubles you, dear Amaryllis?"

Amaryllis shook her head as if nothing were the matter, but then said, "Couldn't they be freed now that we've won?"

"Freed?"

"Yes." Amaryllis pulled her gaze away and regarded Meryam with a neutral expression. It was a composed look, meant to convey that her request was driven by simple prudence, not emotion. "Surely they'll see they cannot stand against you."

"But they already *have* stood against me."

"Some of them did. Hektor. Ramahd. Mateo."

"Basilio," Meryam added.

"Basilio," Amaryllis acknowledged, though she seemed reluctant to do so. "But the bulk of them merely take orders. They'll follow you. I'm sure of it."

"And what if Hektor returns? Who would they follow then?"

Amaryllis knew she was caught, yet she still shrugged and waved to the ships ahead where, all across the decks, ifins flapped their wings lazily. "Surely there are some who are loyal to you."

"How could I tell the difference between them?"

"You *know* them. *I* know them. I could give you a list of fifty right now."

"Yes, but allegiances shift."

"Only among the weak. We'll choose the strong."

"Are *you* strong, Amaryllis?"

Amaryllis blinked as if just realizing what Meryam was hinting at—an act, Meryam was sure, but a good one. "My queen," she said, "of course I am! How could you think otherwise?"

Meryam smiled easily and reached one hand up to stroke Amaryllis's cheek, her comely chin. "You may be right. Let me think on it."

"Of course, my queen."

Seeming relieved, Amaryllis left to help the crew. They sailed on, and Mazandir shrank behind them. Focusing on the horde ahead, Meryam took a pinch of black powder and sniffed it. Her mind was suddenly alive with the dream she'd given Ashael. They sailed across an achingly beautiful sea with white-tipped waves. One day, she'd return to the sea, not as a queen, but as a conqueror.

A conqueror, she mused, *because queen is not enough.* She saw that now. No one could be trusted. Not Ramahd. Not Basilio. Not even Amaryllis.

Ahead, the elder god floated over the sea with his cloud of shrieking ravens. With but an urging from Meryam, a small flock broke away and flapped toward her.

"My queen?" Amaryllis called. She saw no ravens, but ifins approaching *The Gray Gull.*

"I've thought on it," Meryam said.

The ifins reached the ship and winged through the rigging.

"My queen!"

That was all she managed before one of the ifins descended on her, wrapped its wings around her head, and clamped its mouth onto the back of her neck. Moments later the same happened to the rest of the crew.

Some struggled, their limbs thudding against the deck and making hollow wounds. Then all was silence once more.

On they sailed.

First Sharakhai, Meryam mused. *Then the desert. Then the world.*

Yasmine laughed harder than ever.

Chapter 37

ÇEDA STOOD ON the *Red Bride*'s foredeck as the tribes sailed west. Along their starboard side she could see Sharakhai's famed aqueduct, a marvel of engineering. Its tall stone columns, elegant arches, and water channel cut a perfect line through the desert. Where the line faded in the distance, the tip of Mount Tauriyat could be seen, wavering over the vast field of amber.

If the strong winds held, the following morning would see them landing at the blooming fields, where Çeda meant to speak to Sehid-Alaz, to learn how he and the other asirim had fared, and what state the gateway was in before they continued toward King's Harbor.

At a groaning sound, Çeda turned to see Dardzada climbing up from belowdecks. It was already mid-morning, but he looked like he'd just awoken from a dead sleep. He'd come aboard last night, saying he wanted to speak to Çeda. About what, Çeda wasn't sure. She'd been pulled away at the last minute to speak to the other shaikhs, and by the time she'd returned, Dardzada was already snoring in a bunk. She was exhausted herself and didn't much feel like launching into another conversation, long or short, so she'd laid a blanket over him and gone to sleep.

As he navigated the side deck toward the foredeck, he teetered several times. In his path, Emre was resting in the hammock Frail Lemi had hung between the foremast and the cabin's roof. As Emre had done to Frail Lemi not so long ago, Dardzada gave him a shove in passing. It was with markedly less humor, though. Dardzada was a notorious grump in the morning.

"Get enough sleep?" Çeda asked with a wry smile.

He glowered at her. "I never get enough sleep these days." His voice creaked like an ancient door. He jutted his chin toward the sand as the *Bride* crested a dune and the foredeck dipped. "To tell the truth, I never liked sailing much."

Çeda loved sailing, but telling Dardzada so would only darken his mood, and she didn't feel like bickering. "You wanted to talk?"

Dardzada groaned in affirmation, then jutted his stubbly chin toward Tauriyat in the distance. "Yes. About what happens when we reach it."

Çeda shrugged. "We speak to whoever happens to be sitting on Tauriyat that day."

Dardzada nodded in mock seriousness. "It *is* rather difficult to keep up, isn't it?"

"It's like a bloody carousel."

"So we *speak* to them. Perhaps we win our so-called argument. What then?"

Çeda stared back at the massive fleet behind her. "You mean what happens to us? The people of the desert?"

Dardzada tipped his head, half an affirmation. "To them. The people of Sharakhai. The Kings."

It was a fair question. If the tribes could ally themselves with what remained of the Royal Navy, they had as good a chance as they would ever have at saving the city. They might manage to stop Ashael. They might oust Queen Alansal from Tauriyat, without allowing the Kings to retake their power. What then? What would Sharakhai even look like without the Kings?

"One thing at a time, Dardzada."

He looked as if he wanted to argue, or chastise her for not looking far enough ahead, but then his discontent eased and he nodded. "One thing at a time."

"Is that really what you wanted to speak to me about," Çeda asked him, "Sharakhai's future?"

He looked suddenly and uncharacteristically self-conscious. "In truth, I wished to speak to you of the visions the tree gave you."

She had suspected as much. Seeing Ahya would have stirred up a host of memories in Dardzada. "What about them?"

"You went to the acacia asking for help with Hamid. It showed you visions of Ahya instead."

"And?"

"The tree grants prophecies."

"We saw visions of the *past*, Dardzada."

"I know, but I wonder if it was meant as a lesson of some sort, or a warning." He waved toward Tauriyat. "Something to prepare us for what's to come."

Çeda shook her head. "You're reading too much into it. I was focusing on Hamid, and the tree showed me a vision that *included* Hamid."

Dardzada put on a skeptical frown. "You really believe that's all there is to it?"

"Does there need to be more?"

"Nalamae's acacias have helped to protect us for centuries. I think it was trying to tell us something."

"They've helped to protect us, yes, but the trees are always guided by those seeking visions."

"And did you *guide* the tree when you first visited Saliah's acacia?"

"Not consciously, no. But Nalamae did when she collected her memories and began piecing herself back together. *I* did when I exposed Hamid's treachery to the shaikhs."

"It just didn't feel like a coincidence," Dardzada pressed. "Your mother went to Yusam's vault. Maybe there was something else there? Or maybe she did something else *after* the theft."

"Maybe," Çeda conceded, "but if so, I have no idea what. And without the acacia—"

Çeda stopped talking as a sour feeling wrenched her gut.

Dardzada frowned. "What is it?"

She swallowed the spit that had gathered in her mouth. Pressed one hand against her belly. "Can you not feel it?"

"Feel what?"

"It feels like the blooming fields used to. The curse on the asirim."

"Are they being attacked?"

She flexed her right hand, concentrated on the sensation. "No," she realized, and swung her gaze over the *Bride*'s port bow. "It's coming from the south."

The feeling suddenly intensified, and she remembered where she'd felt it before. The vision of Ashael lifting from the black pit in the desert felt precisely like this.

"It's Ashael," she said breathlessly.

Dardzada stared at the horizon with a fatalistic look, as if he'd already made peace with the fact that they would have to face the fallen god. "So what now?"

Her first inclination was to continue toward Sharakhai, but her sense of the desert allowed her to feel more than Ashael, more than his vast horde. She felt mortal souls huddled in the desert, those who all too soon would be threatened.

"We go to face him," Çeda replied.

Without so much as a flinch, Dardzada nodded to her. It was a simple thing, an expression of fatherly approval, but it gave her heart.

After nodding back, she began calling orders for the fleet to turn south.

Chapter 38

L ESS THAN AN hour after the battle in Mazandir's harbor, Ramahd sailed south on *Alu's Crown* with the remains of King Hektor's fleet. Everyone, including Ramahd, had been terrified Meryam and her demonic horde would give chase and ensnare them with the winged ifin. They hadn't, though. They'd headed north so Meryam could claim her prize.

Ramahd was preparing to swing over to King Hektor's ship to convince him to change course and lend aid to beleaguered Sharakhai.

"It won't be easy," Cicio said. "Basilio's words are like poison. He's made Hektor almost as craven as he is."

Ramahd didn't wish to speak ill of his king, but he knew Cicio was right. "Hektor will see reason. He must."

When *Alu's Crown* was sailing alongside Hektor's capital ship, Ramahd, Cicio, and Fezek swung over, and King Hektor met them on the main deck. Basilio and several naval officers, including an admiral and two commodores, stood behind him. Ramahd and Cicio held fists over their hearts and bowed to their king. Fezek, meanwhile, put on a serious face and performed an overly dramatic bow.

The ship groaned as it heeled over the dunes. The sun glinted off King

Hektor's crown. His chestnut hair flapped in the stiff wind. Though he'd grown somewhat in his role as king, Hektor was still a young man and was visibly shaken by all that had happened. "That was you, wasn't it?" he asked with a wave toward Mazandir. "You forced her away."

"By Alu's grace, yes."

"But how?"

Ramahd explained all he knew of Meryam and Ashael, how the elder god dreamed, and Meryam was manipulating him. He told them of the black powder from the Hollow, how he'd used every last grain of it to invade Ashael's dream. Ramahd finished with a plea to give chase. "The lives of our soldiers depend on it, my king."

It was Basilio, looking haggard and scared, who answered. "But you said yourself you have no more powder. What would we accomplish beyond sacrificing everyone who survived the attack by that bloody horde?"

It was with no small amount of effort that Ramahd ignored Basilio and focused on King Hektor. "Two thirds of your fleet has been taken, the ships' crews and soldiers dominated by Ashael's servants. Meryam will use them to take Sharakhai."

"It's unfortunate, to be sure—" Basilio began.

But he stopped as Cicio, red in the face, stormed toward him, one finger pointing over the nearby gunwales. "Interrupt one more time—ah?—and I throw you from the ship."

Basilio pulled himself tall. "My king, I will not stand for—"

He'd no sooner said the words than Cicio, in a blur of movement, grabbed him by his shirt and dragged him toward the gunwales. It took no small amount of effort—Cicio had been serious about his threat—but eventually Ramahd pulled him away and waited until he'd calmed.

Ramahd had never seen Cicio so angry. He'd been horrified over what had happened to the fleet, and that horror had turned to fury when King Hektor chose to sail south while the rest of their fleet was enslaved by Meryam.

"I will not stand for this!" Basilio shouted, then turned to the admiral. "He will be thrown into the brig this instant!"

The admiral, a willowy man with thick sideburns, looked like he wished he were on another ship entirely. He was just waving toward the ship's master-at-arms when Hektor raised a hand.

All fell silent. Everyone, including the master-at-arms, went still. As they waited for their king to speak, the mainsail fluttered, then filled with an audible *whump*.

Hektor had been a brash, even reckless, young man before wresting the crown of Qaimir from Meryam, but the king's mantle lay heavily upon his shoulders. He'd begun second guessing every move he made, always choosing the safest approach. The trouble was, the safest approach wasn't always the *right* approach.

Basilio, clearly sensing Hektor's mood, was the first to speak. "Excellence, our people are depending on us. Meryam wants the desert so badly? I say let her have it."

"You think she'll be content with the desert?" Ramahd said. "You think she won't come for Qaimir when she's done with Sharakhai?"

"That"—Basilio smoothed down the wrinkles on his shirt Cicio's man-handling had caused—"is a problem for another day."

"She'll be stronger then! She'll have the power of Sharakhai behind her, *plus* our soldiers and ships."

"Meryam is being used by the desert gods," Basilio countered. "Do you really think she'll survive whatever fate awaits the city?"

Ramahd paused as the ship eased over a dune. "What did you say?"

"I said Meryam is lost, Lord Amansir. And good riddance."

But that wasn't what Ramahd had been getting at, and he could tell by Basilio's shifting eyes that he knew it.

"You *know* what's about to happen to Sharakhai," Ramahd said. "You know, and you're willing to let it happen."

"Not *me*!" Basilio shouted. "Nor our king, nor you, nor anyone else. The *gods* are the ones who are about to let this happen, and there's nothing any of us can do about it. Not anymore. It's too late, Lord Amansir!"

"Sharakhai is a city of *hundreds of thousands*." Ramahd paused, let the statement sit between them. "All will perish if the desert gods have their way."

"And *we* will be safe in Qaimir under Mighty Alu's protection when they do."

Ramahd was so angry he nearly drew his sword, but he knew the moment he did, he would lose King Hektor. "When we were in Sharakhai," he said to Basilio calmly, "shortly before the crystal broke, you saw through

Meryam's lies. You saw that she threatened us all and came to warn me and the Sharakhani Kings. I saw bravery in you that day, Basilio Baijani. I saw a man ready to fight for Qaimir." He stared into Basilio's scared eyes. "What happened to that man?"

Basilio's face turned splotchy red. His gaze slid to Cicio, who'd been there as well. Basilio had nearly been assassinated by Amaryllis, which had scared him enough to betray Meryam, but there had been genuine bravery as well. It had vanished, however, the longer he'd been with King Hektor and his position grew more and more secure.

"I have *children*," Basilio said. "I have a *wife*." He waved around the ship. "We all have families who await our return. Don't you want to see them again?"

Ramahd shook his head. "I could never look them in the eye again, if I took the coward's path home."

"I am a *realist*," Basilio shot back, while the redness in his cheeks and neck deepened.

"No," Fezek said sharply, startling Ramahd. He'd been so quiet Ramahd had all but forgotten him. King Hektor took a half step back as Fezek approached.

Basilio stared at Fezek. "Pardon me?"

Fezek replied with perfect calm. "You are no *realist*, as you claim, but the man your wife and children will be ashamed to speak of."

Basilio looked to King Hektor, as if he expected him to order the ghul to remain silent. Hektor didn't, though, and Fezek went on. "You are the man *their* children will try to strike from the family annals as a stain on your house, because even after everyone has forgotten your name, your house will be plagued for generations, because *Baijani* will become a synonym for *craven*."

"You're *dead*," Basilio said, as if that proved anything at all.

"I may be dead," Fezek said with a flourish, "but I'm also a poet, and I recognize a story that will refuse to fade with time. They are populated with only two types of characters: those who manifest heroism"—he looked Basilio up and down—"and those who try to steal it from others."

Basilio was shaking. He seemed to be avoiding King Hektor's gaze. Before Ramahd knew it Basilio had drawn the ceremonial dagger from his belt.

Ramahd was ready to pull Fezek back, but Basilio never made a move. He merely stood there, breathing hard, his gaze passing *through* Fezek. The officers watched in stunned silence. Even the crew had stopped what they were doing.

King Hektor, meanwhile, had undergone a transformation. Unsure of himself only moments ago, he now stared at Basilio in disgust.

The flush of Basilio's anger faded from his cheeks. Then they turned bone white. After an interminable silence he turned to King Hektor and whispered, "My King, *please*. We must go *home*."

King Hektor motioned to the nearby hatch. "Lord Baijani, you will retire to your cabin and remain there until summoned."

Basilio's mouth worked. He looked lost. Then all the energy seemed to leave him at once. Without another word, he turned and walked stiffly away.

King Hektor turned to Ramahd. "Basilio's question remains. How can you hope to fight Meryam without that powder?" He motioned aft, toward Sharakhai. "What lever can you pull that might slow that dark machine?"

In reply, Ramahd reached into the small bag at his belt and retrieved a necklace made of red beads that were worn at the edges, showing the white ceramic beneath. "We have this."

Hektor stared at it in wonder. "Meryam's necklace."

"Yes."

Hektor looked like he wanted to say more, but was distracted by something behind Ramahd. Ramahd turned to see sand swirling on the hatch's lid. More sand gathered, creating a column, which solidified into the form of a woman. Suddenly, a goddess stood among them. Nalamae, in her new incarnation, with graying hair and bright armor, and a magnificent spear in one hand.

As she stepped down from the hatch lid, she focused not on King Hektor, but on Ramahd.

Ramahd bowed his head. "Goddess . . ." For long moments, words failed him. "Why have you come?" he finally managed.

"I've come to lend aid." She pointed to his right hand, which still held Meryam's necklace. "You've chosen the right message, but you're going to need help if you hope to deliver it."

Chapter 39

IN THE CAPTAIN's cabin of the *Miscreant*, Ihsan sat in a rocking chair. On the floor before him was Ransaneh. With Ihsan's help, she was making a passable though rather comical attempt at standing on her own. She would stand tall, topple like a stack of wooden blocks, then stand again.

When she managed to hold the pose for several breaths, Ihsan smiled. "Who's that I see standing like a big girl?" Speaking was still moderately painful, but the palliative he'd mixed in with his water and wine that morning, a combination of cloves and red nettle, was helping. Still holding her wrists, he gave Ransaneh more of her own weight. "Can you try on your own?"

For a moment, just a moment, she stood tall. She burbled and blinked her mismatched eyes. Then her legs buckled from underneath her.

"Not quite ready, I see." Ihsan propped her back onto her feet and winked. "Perhaps tomorrow."

No sooner had he said the words than she waddled toward him. It was only a few steps, and he was still holding her hands, but she did it with such a heartbreakingly beautiful smile on her face that Ihsan smiled too.

"Well, there we are!" he said. "Soon we'll need to tie a rope to you to keep you from climbing over the gunwales!"

A knock came at the door, and Ihsan's joy all but faded.

"Come."

The old storyteller, Ibrahim, entered the cabin and closed the door behind him. In one hand he held a tiny ceramic cup. The foamy liquid inside it smelled of rich kahve. After taking a stool near the bed, Ibrahim lifted the cup to his nose, breathed deeply, and took a sip. "Are you sure you don't want some? It's surprisingly good."

Ihsan shook his head no and held Ransaneh against his chest.

After another noisy sip, Ibrahim regarded Ihsan. "Now, you were saying?"

"I was speaking of my dream"—Ihsan rocked slowly back and forth—"my visitation with Rhia." They'd started the conversation earlier, but Ibrahim had insisted that he couldn't think straight without his second cup.

"Yes," Ibrahim said. "My apologies. Do go on."

"Rhia and I spoke of Meryam and how she's using Ashael. I told her I was prepared to take the helm, to finish what Meryam had started."

"And what made you think she would let you?"

Ihsan shrugged while rubbing his daughter's back. "That isn't the point." Ransaneh released a wet burp. "When I offered, she said, 'Dost thou think thyself ready to wield the key to dreaming?'"

"The key to dreaming . . ." Ibrahim's eyes were narrowed, his cup of kahve poised halfway to his mouth. "She was referring to the powder from Goezhen's horn, yes?"

Ihsan nodded. "I've heard the phrase before, but I can't put my finger on where."

Ibrahim frowned. The moments that followed saw his bushy eyebrows creep toward one another like fellow conspirators. "Keys are for locks," he finally said.

"And locks are on doors. The question is: the door to what?" Ihsan paused, frustrated at his inability to solve the riddle. "Rhia gave us something she didn't mean to. I'm sure of it."

Hunched over his cup of kahve, Ibrahim was like a granite statue—all save his eyes, which roamed ceaselessly. Suddenly his eyes lit and he stared intently at Ihsan. "Locks are also for gates."

Ihsan paused, trying and failing to understand. "And?"

"'Ivory is the key to the wakeful mind,'" Ibrahim intoned, "'horn the key to dreaming.' It's from the Al'Ambra, part of a passage that speaks of the two gates the first gods used to step through to reach this world."

"That's all well and good, but our concern is over the *next* world." Ihsan adjusted Ransaneh, who was getting fussy. "Does the Al'Ambra mention their leaving?"

"Of course," Ibrahim said.

". . . Through similar gates?"

"There are passages that speak of the elder gods' feelings that they'd done all they could in this world, that it was time they let their creations stand on their own. There are others that speak of the elders' visitations with the young gods, who were predictably upset. There are more still that speak of their final gathering before the great exodus." He shrugged. "None that I recall gives specifics about their passage to the next world. Only that the day was 'the fairest the world had yet seen.'"

Ihsan scoffed. "Yes, that always seemed a bit much."

Ibrahim finished his kahve, dregs and all, and smiled. "Call it poetic license."

Ihsan's thoughts drifted back to his conversation with Rhia. "The goddess and I spoke of dreams and waking. She said Meryam had walked the ways of the slumbering mind, while I'd always been rooted in reality, implying I couldn't control Ashael as well as Meryam could."

"We all have our strengths," Ibrahim said.

At those words, Ihsan sat bolt upright, startling Ransaneh. He felt like he'd been struck by lightning. The notion of everyone having their strengths put the two halves of this strange equation—dreams and waking—into stark relief. "Ashael is dreaming—"

Ibrahim's eyes narrowed. "We already knew that."

"—and ivory is the key to the wakeful mind."

Ibrahim was clearly confused, but then his eyes lit up. "Ivory . . ."

"Rhia *fears* Ashael's waking," Ihsan said. "If we could awaken him—"

"Dust ahead!" bellowed Yndris from the deck above.

A cold fear washed over Ihsan. *Dust ahead* was the telltale signs of a fleet of some sort, the ships not yet over the horizon. They were currently southeast of Sharakhai, far from the traditional shipping lanes. No ships would normally sail there, none but pirates, but even pirates knew that stretch of desert was occupied by the remains of Sharakhai's fleet, the royal navy. They'd been steering clear of it for months.

Yndris had spotted the royal navy, Ihsan was sure of it. Except they weren't meant to be sailing, not unless they had to.

After calling for Ransaneh's wet nurse, Ihsan and Ibrahim rushed from the cabin. By the time they reached the foredeck, Nayyan was already there. Yndris stood near the bowsprit, a spyglass to one eye.

"There's a battle underway," Yndris said, confirming Ihsan's fears.

Nayyan took the spyglass from Yndris and peered through it at the cloud of dust along the horizon. Within it, Ihsan could barely discern the dark hulls, the lighter shapes of sails.

The looks of the crew turned flinty. This was something everyone had feared, the day Mirea and Malasan finally managed to pin down the royal navy.

"Ready ballistae," Nayyan called, handing the spyglass to Ihsan. "Load catapults with firepots. Have cat's claws at the ready."

"Aye!" called the crew.

Peering through the spyglass, Ihsan saw dozens of royal galleons spread out in a long line. Behind them were taller ships, Queen Alansal's dune-breakers. Even from this distance they looked fearsome. They couldn't match the pace of the galleons, but they didn't have to. The fleet was being harried by what looked to be hundreds of smaller ships—the junks and dhows that made up the bulk of the Malasani fleet.

As the *Miscreant* sailed on, a horrifying pattern took shape. Time and again, one of the royal navy's ships would be slowed enough—by cat's claws or by damage inflicted against their rigging or sails—that one of the dune-breakers would catch up to them. Grappling lines would snake out from the dunebreakers to fall against the galleons' rigging. A few ships escaped when their crews managed to cut the lines. But more often than not the ships would be drawn inexorably toward the dunebreakers.

The Mirean crews aboard the towering ships outnumbered those on the galleons three-to-one. They would swarm across the decks of the Sharakhani ships, subduing them in little time.

"Dear gods," Ibrahim said. "It's going to be a slaughter."

For weeks the royal navy had been hiding in bays sprinkled throughout the nearby hills. Some had been found, but King Husamettín had been defending against such attacks for centuries. He used the galleons' maneuverability to great effect, sometimes to flee but as often to spring a trap, turning the tables on their foes.

The enemy had never sailed in such numbers, though. Somehow they'd been able to find the fleet and fall on them unawares.

As the Sharakhani galleons approached, Ihsan used the spyglass to survey the pennants along their mainmasts. "There!" he said, and pointed along the windward wing of the navy's long line.

It was the *Bastion*, Husamettín's capital ship. It was an impressive craft, but dozens of Malasani ships were approaching it. Some were already harrying the galleons along its wings. Several of the enemy ships were soon engulfed in flames as the *Bastion* and other nearby galleons counterattacked, but for the most part the Malasani ships brought the fires under control quickly. Those that didn't simply drifted from the pack and were replaced by others. It was only a matter of time before the rightmost wing of the navy's fleet succumbed.

"We sail for the *Bastion*," Ihsan called.

"Aye!" called the ship's helmsman.

Nearby, Ibrahim gripped a shroud for balance. His knuckles were white, his brow furrowed. His throat convulsed over and over as he took in the harrowing spectacle before him. The reaction was one Ihsan had seen a thousand times before: a man of peace being confronted with war for the first time.

"Why don't you go belowdecks?" Ihsan said to him.

Ibrahim blinked. Looked about the ship and all the preparations being made. "I would stay," he said at last, "see it with my own eyes."

Ihsan considered ordering him to retire, but then shrugged. "Just don't get in the way."

The distance between the *Miscreant* and the approaching fleets narrowed. The battle beyond the royal navy's front line intensified. More and more ships became locked in battle as they succumbed to the steady rain of cat's claws or the harassment of the Malasani ships. The bulk of Sharakhai's royal navy was still on the move, but it wouldn't be long before the entire fleet was embroiled in battle.

But the navy was far from toothless. The galleons were filled with seasoned Blade Maidens and Silver Spears. When the smaller Malasani ships became locked with theirs, the Sharakhani forces would sweep across the decks, slaying dozens in moments. They'd cut the lines tying the ships to one another, clear their galleon's skis of cat's claws, and sail on.

The tactic cost the Malasani dearly, but the goal wasn't to overwhelm the royal navy. It was to slow them down enough that the dunebreakers could catch up. As Ihsan watched, three dunebreakers drew even with a pair of hobbled galleons. Mirean soldiers in blue uniforms swarmed over the gunwales and dropped down onto the galleons' decks. The first to board were felled in moments, but the Mirean soldiers were just so numerous. In the time it took for the *Miscreant* to sail another half-league, both galleons had fallen to the enemy.

"What do we do?" Nayyan asked.

Ihsan had been asking the very same question. What *should* they do? Adding the *Miscreant*'s meager strength to the royal navy's would make little difference in the battle's outcome. Ihsan would likely have ordered them in anyway, but there were Meryam and Ashael to consider. The gateway on Tauriyat was on the brink of opening wide. Should he and Nayyan risk Sharakhai in the slim hope that the *Miscreant* might save one or two ships?

Before he could come to a decision, he noticed something strange. "The Malasani ships," he said to Nayyan. "They're breaking."

Indeed, to either side of the royal fleet, the smaller Malasani ships were beginning to peel away.

"But why?" Nayyan asked.

"They're preparing for something."

No sooner had he said the words than he caught movement along the dunes ahead. The sand was mounding. Soldiers were rising up, throwing aside the amber tarps that had hidden them. Bloody gods, the number of them. More and more stood from their hiding places until there was a line an eighth-league long, then a quarter-league. They were pulling iron beams from the sand and assembling them, leaning them against one another, interlocking them to form a barricade, which would foul the skis of any ship that had the misfortune of running across them. Breath of the desert, the barricades were stout enough that they might shatter the oncoming galleons' struts.

"Queen Alansal laid a trap," Ihsan said breathlessly. "She knew they would come this way."

Nayyan swept her gaze across the line. "Dear gods."

The urge to flee was becoming overpowering. What could they do against so many? The rear of the fleet was being picked off, one by one. And the barricades had been erected so quickly, the vanguard no longer had room to maneuver around them. The navy had only two choices: ram the barricades or drop their rakes and stop. Either decision would be disastrous.

Retreat, a voice inside Ihsan said. *Live to fight another day.*

But if the navy was destroyed, they stood no chance of stopping Meryam and Ashael at all. He knew he risked much with decision he was slowly coming to, but he refused to leave so many to die.

"Make for the center of the line!" he called to the helmsman.

"Ihsan," Nayyan said with a hand on his wrist.

He ignored her. "Sail hard," he said to the crew, "sail smartly, and prepare to turn along the line of barricades!"

For the briefest of moments, looks were exchanged among the crew. Then a grim look overcame them, and the *Miscreant's* heading shifted toward the *Bastion*.

"You're sure you want to do this?" Nayyan asked as she squeezed Ihsan's hand.

It was no lack of bravery that spurred her to say it, but rather the instincts of a mother. Their daughter was aboard the ship. Ihsan's decision risked not only *their* lives, but hers as well.

Ihsan squeezed her hand back. "I'm sure."

Nayyan nodded, and Ihsan called for Yndris to bring him a bow and quiver. When she complied, Ihsan accepted the bow, but took only one arrow from the quiver. Yndris stared at him quizzically.

"One will do," Ihsan said with a wry smile.

"Do we turn, my Lord King?" the helmsman asked. The *Miscreant* was coming closer and closer to the barricades.

"Not yet," Ihsan called, "but be ready."

They neared the line of barricades. They were a quarter-league away, then an eighth. Soon it would be too late to avoid them.

"My Lord King?" called the helmsman.

"Hold . . ." He gripped the bow and nocked his lone arrow. "Hold . . ." When he sensed they had no more room to maneuver, he shouted, "Now!"

The helmsman and the ship's first mate cranked the wheel. The *Miscreant* turned sharply starboard, groaning as the skis and hull fought the wind and the ship's momentum. The crew moved quickly, shifting the lines attached to the booms to better catch the southerly wind.

Ihsan stood along the port bow. As the Mirean soldiers on the sand began launching arrows, he drew his bow, aimed, and let fly. As the arrow arced through the air, Ihsan summoned the power of his voice. Pain came with it, but he ignored it, gathering every ounce of power he could.

His arrow struck the sand near the barricades. As the enemy's arrows streaked in against the *Miscreant*, Ihsan cupped his hands to his mouth. "Clear the way!" he shouted in Mirean. "Disassemble all barricades around that arrow!"

A beat passed, then two—the soldiers struggling with a sudden compulsion to obey.

Then all the soldiers within earshot dropped their weapons and ran toward the nearest barricades. The *Miscreant* curved, narrowly missing the barricades themselves. The Mirean soldiers, meanwhile, pitched themselves into pulling the barricades apart, dragging them out of the vanguard's path.

By then the *Miscreant* was close enough to hear orders being called on the *Bastion*. King Husamettín's voice boomed. Ihsan saw him standing on the foredeck in his black armor, calling orders to the *Bastion*'s helmsman. Bells rang in sequence, sending orders to other ships, which closed the gaps between them, a few coming so close the hulls butted up against one another. Their booms reached beyond the gunwales of neighboring ships, creating all sorts of hazards. Some ships slipped behind others in hopes of skirting the barricades that had yet to be broken down and dragged away.

Like a school of fish navigating a channel in a raging river, the vanguard passed though the gap. The ships were too numerous, however, to avoid the hazard entirely. Those at the edges ran afoul of the barricades. Their wooden skis crashed against the stout metal. In some cases, the struts held and the ship sailed on, but the barricades acted like cat's claws, slowing the ships precipitously, causing the ships trailing them to crash into their sterns.

The struts of some ships were compromised entirely. One such galleon listed port, then curved sharply as the struts' shattered remains gouged the sand. Another dipped prow-first into a dune, spraying sand in two great fans.

The *Bastion* sailed through and curved so that its path would eventually coincide with the *Miscreant's*. Other ships followed. More than a score had made it through, but that was a poor number considering they'd started with over two hundred.

The other ships were either besieged, had run aground, or were trapped in the net created by the long line of barricades. The Mirean dunebreakers, meanwhile, sailed ever closer. Some were engaging the galleons that had fallen victim to the Malasani ships' delaying tactics. Others were closing in on the grounded ships.

Worse, the *Miscreant*, *Bastion*, and other ships that *had* made it through were still not in the clear. Knowing about the trap ahead of time, the Malasani fleet had split in two. Each group steered wide of the barricades to catch any of the Sharakhani ships that managed to slip the noose.

As the *Miscreant* came in line with the *Bastion*, Husamettín stood at the gunwales, a dozen Blade Maidens behind him. "Impeccable timing," he bellowed, "almost as if you'd planned it."

"Believe me," Ihsan replied, "there are safer ways to paint oneself the hero."

Husamettín smiled grimly. He used his two-handed shamshir, Night's Kiss, to point toward the ships that hadn't made it through. "We're going back for them."

Ihsan tipped his head. "I thought you might"

Husamettín seemed surprised. "And *I* thought you'd argue."

"Here, at the end, I see the reality as well as anyone. If we fall, Sharakhai falls."

Husamettín didn't seem convinced of his sincerity, but apparently decided it didn't matter. "Follow our lead," he said, and began calling crisp orders to his crew.

In her planning, Queen Alansal had made a critical error. Her trap required that the Malasani fleet split in two, in order to pass around the barricades. It left the nearest wing of the Malasani fleet vulnerable.

The *Bastion*, the *Miscreant*, and the trailing galleons descended on them with a vengeance. They launched a fusillade of fire pots, sent cat's claws twisting through the air. Some of the royal galleons were capped with battering rams, which they used to great effect, crashing into the smaller Malasani dhows, shattering their skis and sundering their hulls.

Other enemy ships were caught with grappling lines. A storm of arrows decimated the enemy as capstans drew the ships closer to one another. When they were near enough to board, Silver Spears and Blade Maidens stormed over the gunwales and slaughtered the enemy's crews.

The skirmish was over in minutes, the Malasani ships destroyed, subdued, or fled.

Husamettín ordered them around the barriers, and while it became clear they would reach the wounded ships before the Mirean dunebreakers did, it was going to be a near thing.

As the distance was closed, Husamettín ordered their ships to aim for the very gap they'd just sailed through. They slowed their pace, threw rope ladders over the gunwales, and helped hundreds of survivors to climb to safety. The *Miscreant* alone took on fifty additional crewmen and soldiers. Other ships rescued as many or more.

But slowing their ships meant that the dunebreakers had had time to narrow the gap between them, and now they'd be on the royal navy in moments.

But here they made another mistake. They'd ordered themselves into a column, planning to follow the royal navy through the gap in the barricades. Husamettín, anticipating it, ordered the three rearmost galleons to come in lengthwise, to drop their rakes and stop themselves in a line, effectively closing off the gap in the barricades.

Those ships had already been reduced to skeleton crews, the rest having swung over to other ships, and the few still aboard dropped the rakes, cut the sails, then abandoned their ships and ran over the sand to the waiting galleons ahead of them.

Husamettín had managed to save well over half the soldiers in their fleet, something which had seemed impossible only a short while ago.

But by then, the second half of the Malasani fleet, the group they'd avoided earlier, had sailed ahead and set up a defensive line. They couldn't hope to stand against what remained of the Sharakhani fleet, but their goal was to delay, not defeat them outright.

The lead dunebreakers crashed into the abandoned galleons. So massive were the Mirean ships that they pushed the galleons along the sand like sledges. The ships at the lead came to a sliding stop, but maneuvered the galleons wide of the central path while doing so. Ihsan heard the Mirean soldiers cheer as a narrow lane was created for other dunebreakers to sail through.

Husamettín, meanwhile, called for their galleons to punch through the Malasani line. In some cases they succeeded, but much of the fleet became mired in the conflict. Ship after ship was brought to a halt, either by cat's claws, enemy boardings, or the Malasani dhows throwing themselves into their path.

After a valiant effort, the tide was beginning to turn against them again, and horns called for all ships to stop, to gather in a defensive circle, and to prepare to fight the enemy to the death. Ihsan feared this moment, as the Malasani ships closed in and arrows began to thud against the deck. Nayyan's eyes met his. She had a bow in hand, an arrow nocked. *We can escape on a skiff if need be,* she'd said earlier.

Ihsan tipped his head aft, where the skiffs were lashed to the side of the ship. "Take her. Save our daughter."

Nayyan was already shaking her head. "Even if I escape"—she glanced down at her belly—"I'll not be able to protect her tomorrow. But you can use your power. You can see her safe."

The fates preserve him, he nearly commanded her to take Ransaneh and sail away. But it wouldn't be right. She deserved to choose the manner of her own death. She deserved to know the truth about him as well. He'd hidden it from her long enough. The confession was right there on his lips: *I'm dying. The black mould has found me as well.*

Before he could utter a word of it, Yndris pointed to an approaching dhow with the bow. "Beware!" she cried. "Look to the catapult."

On the dhow's deck, a strange contraption had been set up. It was indeed a catapult, but much larger than those used for cat's claws and fire pots. In the cradle, ready to be launched, was a wiry looking soldier, curled up in a ball.

"Let fly!" called the Malasani captain, and the catapult's lever was released.

The arm arced forward, then thudded against the stanchion, but the soldier flew on. His arms windmilled as he soared toward the *Miscreant*'s stern. Yndris shot an arrow, catching him in the thigh. Nayyan did the same and clipped his left arm.

It didn't stop him, though, and he held a long, curving fighting knife in one hand. As Yndris drew her shamshir and sprinted toward him, he landed awkwardly on the quarterdeck, just in front of the transom. Ihsan thought he was going for the helmsman, but he wasn't.

"Halt!" Ihsan cried in Malasani.

He put power into the word. A terrible pain burned his tongue, his jaw, even his teeth. Worse, the command failed. The saboteur kept going.

Ibrahim was suddenly there. He threw himself on the soldier, hoping to stop him, but Ibrahim was old and frail and the soldier tossed him aside like a child. As Ibrahim crumpled to the deck, the soldier slashed at the rope that held the ship's rake in place. Yndris was on him a moment later. Her blurring shamshir cut deep into his neck, and a fount of blood issued from the wound, but the damage had already been done.

The rake fell against the sand and cut deep furrows, slowing the ship precipitously until it came to a sudden, mast-shuddering halt.

"All hands retreat to the *Bastion*!" Ihsan called. "Prepare to fight your way through!"

The crew gathered on the sand, preparing to charge for the cluster of Sharakhani galleons. Nayyan and Yndris led the way down the *Miscreant*'s gangplank. Ihsan followed, with Ransaneh's wet nurse, who held Ransaneh tightly against her chest, coming last. With their crew leading the way, they ran toward the *Bastion*.

What followed was sheer madness. The Malasani had ordered many of their ships stopped as well. They came in a screaming wave, scimitars in hand. Nayyan was a demon with a blade. With fire in her eyes, she cut down enemy after enemy. Ihsan fought as well, but he'd never been gifted with a sword and could do little. As three brutes carrying war clubs closed in on them, Yndris flew in and cut one down from behind. Felled another as the enemy turned to meet the new threat. Nayyan took the third, dodging two clumsy blows from his war club, then slicing through his gut with such speed all Ihsan saw was the blur of her dark blade and the crimson burst trailing behind it.

They'd gained themselves a few seconds but, gods, the nearby dunes were thick with the enemy already. More were leaping over the sides of the dhows by the moment, and the dunebreakers weren't far off. Soon, they would disgorge hundreds of fresh soldiers. It was going to be a massacre.

The Malasani nipped at their heels. Others sprinted ahead, hoping to cut them off. Many slowed, however, when they saw King Husamettín leading a dozen Blade Maidens and a hundred Silver Spears toward them.

"Husamettín!" came the cry from the Malasani.

They seemed eager to be the one to slay the fabled King. But Husamettín cut down all enemies who stood before him. Night's Kiss buzzed and rattled, eager to drink the blood of its enemies, to cut through sword, shield, and flesh alike. The Blade Maidens fanned out around their King, dealing death, while the Silver Spears joined with those from the *Miscreant* to form a defensive line against the Malasani.

And by the gods, they held. The Malasani were driven back as they made an ordered retreat toward the *Bastion*. Soon, Ihsan, Nayyan, Ransaneh, and her wet nurse had gained the deck, a miracle in and of itself.

"Ram!" came a cry from behind Ihsan.

He turned to see a dunebreaker with an iron-capped prow and grinning dragon figurehead coming straight toward them. It crashed into the *Bastion* moments later. Intermingling with the great boom of the two ships colliding were the sounds of hull boards snapping, wooden beams shattering. As the galleon was shoved sideways along the sand, everyone aboard was thrown to the deck.

The ship hadn't even come to a halt before blue-uniformed soldiers carrying round shields and tassled dao swords were leaping from the dunebreaker's bowsprit to the *Bastion*'s main deck. The Silver Spears engaged, in a fight for their lives, and extracted a heavy toll from the Mirean invaders, but already more of the enemy were leaping down or sliding along ropes.

The battle quickly spread to the foredeck and quarterdeck. Husamettín fought. Nayyan and Yndris too. Hundreds more were locked in battle beside them, but they had no hope of stemming the tide.

It was as another dunebreaker approached that Ihsan realized an inexplicably fierce wind had kicked up. Dust and sand blew. Began to bite. It felt as if the desert itself had turned against them, as if it wanted to cover them with dust, bury them beneath the amber sea, and forget they ever were.

A hundred ships were now engaged in battle, with more being drawn in by the moment. Mounted Qirin warriors felled all who stood before them. A charge of small Mirean ponies fell upon a regiment of Silver Spears, tearing them to pieces.

And all the while the wind continued to rise. It stung the skin. A haze lifted, turning all to amber, and the sounds of battle decreased as more and more soldiers lowered their weapons and tried to shelter from the biting sand.

A distant horn blew a series of notes—two short low notes, one long high note. The sequence was echoed by a second horn, then more and more. It was coming from the Mirean dunebreakers. It had been a long while since Ihsan had studied their signals, but he remembered this one. It meant *enemy sighted*.

The battle on the *Bastion* devolved into chaos. The dead lay across the decks and the sand below. The clash of steel rose high. The cries of soldiers were everywhere, shouts of anguish, the desperate roars of those besieged. Arrows peppered the biting, dust-streaked air.

Nayyan took down a Mirean soldier with a tassled helmet just in front of Ihsan as another horn called, this time from the dunebreaker that loomed above them, the one that had crashed into the *Bastion*. Soldiers on the dunebreaker's decks turned away, and Ihsan followed their line of vision, but saw nothing save dust, soldiers, and the hulls of nearby ships.

Then he caught a glimpse of bright sails in the sea of amber, a dark hull growing more and more substantial. Ihsan knew that ship. It was Çeda's: the *Red Bride*. The yacht was followed by the larger *Amaranth*, and more ships besides. As more Mirean horns sounded the alarm, ship after ship resolved from the liquid backdrop of the sandstorm. A score of ships, then two score. Then a hundred or more.

It was the tribes, Ihsan realized. Çeda had rallied them to her cause.

A sound rose above the battle. Desert warriors lining the gunwales beat their swords against their shields in an incessant rhythm. *Throom, throom, throom.* It grew in volume the closer they came. Soon the vastness of their fleet was revealed. The tribes had brought close to five hundred ships with thousands of warriors, all of them eager to wage war.

At their head, standing at the bowsprit of the *Red Bride*, was a warrior clad in white armor. She bore a buckler and River's Daughter, an ebon steel blade. The leather breastplate and battle skirt, the armor she'd once used in the pits, was nicked and worn. The steel helm she wore had a wolf pelt atop it, and a mask of shining bright steel in the guise of Nalamae. It was Çeda, the White Wolf once more.

Like the others, she beat her shamshir against her shield. The sound was already deafening, but as their line of ships approached, the desert warriors added their voices. They roared while quickening the drumbeat of their weapons.

Behind Çeda stood two Blade Maidens: Sümeya and Kameyl. Emre was there as well, a bow in hand, and the hulk they called Frail Lemi, who bore the greatspear, Umber. They all waited as the *Bride* sailed swiftly toward the *Bastion*. When it came near, Çeda leapt aboard and tore into a group of Mirean soldiers. Sümeya and Kameyl followed. Frail Lemi thumped onto the foredeck and swung his spear in a mighty sweep, sending three Mireans over the gunwales.

Arrow after arrow streaked in from Emre's bow. With surgical precision, they lodged into the throats or chests of the Mirean officers. Others from the thirteenth tribe followed, all screaming and wielding bows, shamshirs, or spears, pushing the enemy back. With a cry born of hope and desperation, the Blade Maidens and Silver Spears joined them.

Beyond the *Bastion*, the desert was awash with the ships and warriors of the desert tribes. Ship after ship hemmed the lead dunebreakers in. Ihsan understood the tactic immediately: overwhelm the lead ships to give the impression of an indomitable enemy. Debilitate enough of the Mirean vanguard, and the rest would flee in hopes of regrouping before all was lost.

In little time, a half-dozen dunebreakers and half the Malasani fleet were overwhelmed. Above the sounds of battle, Ihsan heard a lone word being called in Mirean over and over, the word for demon. It had come from high up, the lookout in their vulture's nest, he realized. Moments later the ship's horn sounded again. This time it gave one long note followed by three quick ones—the signal for *retreat*.

More horns followed, the signal passing along the Mirean line. It spurred the royal navy and the desert tribes, both. An unlikely, unified force, they fell upon the enemy with renewed zeal and turned the battle. The enemy ships were fleeing. The desert tribes, smelling blood, harried their flanks, grounding a dozen more ships and falling upon them with no mercy.

A heavy drumbeat sounded, a signal from the tribes to regroup. By then the battle on the *Bastion* was slowing. Mirean soldiers had leapt overboard and fled. The same was true of many other ships, both Mirean and Malasani, the soldiers hoping to reach the safety of their fleeing ships.

As the sounds of battle ebbed, Çeda reached Ihsan's cluster, removed her helm, and approached. Husamettín was there, as were Nayyan and Yndris. Sümeya and Kameyl came to stand behind Çeda, then Emre and Frail Lemi. The wind, so strong earlier, was ebbing now. Sand was falling like rain, pattering against the deck, against their helms, turbans, and armor.

"Well met," Çeda said.

"Well met," said Ihsan.

For once, he was all but speechless. So was everyone else, apparently. The desert tribes had just saved the royal navy. They'd saved a pair of Kings they'd once hoped to destroy—and might still.

"Hey, Emre"—Frail Lemi lifted one massive arm and pointed south—"what's that?"

All eyes turned. The air had cleared enough to see the horizon, which roiled like heat lifting off the desert. But it was no mirage. Ihsan had seen the same sort of vision as the *Miscreant* approached the Hollow days earlier.

"It's Meryam," Ihsan said. "And Ashael."

Chapter 40

ÇEDA, WEARING THE armor of the White Wolf, stood on the deck of the *Bastion*. Her breath was on her from the pitched battle that had just ended. Sümeya and Kameyl stood beside her, swords still drawn, their chests heaving too. Not far away, Emre, wearing a beaten scale armor breastplate, stood beside Frail Lemi and Shal'alara. Husamettín, Ihsan, Nayyan, and Yndris were gathered near the mainmast. Circling them were dozens of Blade Maidens, hundreds of Silver Spears, and the warriors of the desert tribes. As the dust from the windstorm Çeda had summoned continued to settle, all eyes stared at the dark cloud in the distance.

"Gods," Sümeya said, "the size of it."

Çeda flexed her right hand, shaking away the burning pain. The old wound felt hot, even infected. What had started as a sour sensation in her gut when she'd first sensed the horde's approach now felt painful, like a disease spreading. The acacia's vision of Ashael floating above the ground while his host poured into the sky had terrified her, but it was nothing compared to what she felt as she watched the horde bearing down on them.

"We have to stay ahead of them," Çeda said.

There was much Çeda needed to discuss with Husamettín and

Ihsan—she needed to share what she'd learned, and she needed to learn all they knew of the horde—but any delay would see their ships overrun.

Husamettín nodded to a Blade Maiden who wore the First Warden's insignia, a shield with a lone shamshir beneath it, on her right shoulder. She immediately began bellowing orders to make all sandworthy ships ready to sail. As the orders were passed, Blade Maidens, Silver Spears, and ships' crews moved to obey. Emre, meanwhile, passed the same orders to the warriors of the desert tribes, and the crowd on the deck quickly thinned.

"The royal navy sails north," Husamettín said to Çeda, an unspoken request for the desert tribes to join them.

Çeda had known Husamettín as a commander—he was also her father, though she didn't view him as such. She'd never known him to be a circumspect man, but admitting that the royal navy needed their help was apparently a bridge too far for him.

"Bloody gods," she said, "can we agree that for the time being we're united?"

Husamettín stood there, warring with himself, then gave her a sharp nod. "We'll send orders once we're under sail."

"Send *us* orders?" Frail Lemi barked a laugh at Husamettín. "*We* saved *you!*"

Çeda held Husamettín's gaze, letting the words sink in. "We take no orders from the Kings of Sharakhai. The shaikhs will meet on the *Amaranth*. I hope you'll join us." She waved toward the approaching cloud on the horizon. "We have much to discuss."

Frail Lemi began walking away. "*We* saved *you!*" he repeated, louder this time, as he reached the gangplank and headed down toward the sand.

Color rose in Husamettín's cheeks as he stared at Lemi's retreating form and took in the desert tribes' vast fleet. Without another word, he spun on his heel and strode away into the captain's cabin and closed the door behind him.

Çeda stood there, furious. She nearly went after him. She'd kick the door in if she had to. But suddenly Ishan was there, his hands held up in a sign of peace.

Çeda waved toward the cabin. "Get him to come, Ihsan. We need him."

"He'll come"—Ihsan began backing away—"even if I have to give up my Kingdom to do it." He winked, then headed for the cabin.

With that, a small amount of tension was released, enough that Çeda realized she needed to leave the ship and begin making her own preparations. She left the *Bastion* with Emre and the others and headed for the *Amaranth*.

Over the next hour, the Alliance fleet and the royal navy rushed to collect their wounded and make ready to set sail. The shaikhs gathered in the *Amaranth*'s hold. The shutters were opened to let in light. Barrels of food and water, and crates of fire pots and cat's claws, were stacked along the hulls, leaving only a cramped space in which to hold council.

Calls from other ships could be heard through the hull. Horns sounded. Men and women barked orders. Others wailed in pain. True to his word, Ihsan reached the *Amaranth* with Nayyan and Husamettín in tow. Yndris and her hand of Blade Maidens joined them. And in a strange twist of fate, Ibrahim the storyteller was with them.

Çeda went to him immediately and embraced him. "By the Great Mother, how did you wind up *here*?"

"That, dear girl," he said in a low voice, "is a story for another day."

As the *Amaranth* lurched into motion, Husamettín broke the relative silence. "Who speaks for the desert?"

"I do," Çeda said. The others had agreed that her history with the Kings positioned her best to lead the discussions.

She returned to her place beside Emre. To either side of them were the other twelve shaikhs. Behind them, Frail Lemi, Kameyl, Sümeya, and a dozen other vizirs and advisors stood in ranks.

"Sharakhai is grateful for your help," Husamettín began, "but a greater task lies before us." He focused his attention on Çeda and Çeda alone, as if expressing gratitude to the entirety of the Alliance was beyond him. "Meryam of Qaimir moves quickly toward our fleets. She hopes to take us, then move on to the city. I ask that you cede authority to us until—"

His next words were lost as the entire assemblage of shaikhs began to shout. Arms flew in the air, some with fists clenched. They might have agreed to let Çeda speak for them, but ceding authority to the Kings, Husamettín especially, was asking too much. Çeda and Emre tried to calm them, but their words were drowned out.

Suddenly Ihsan stood in the center of the hold, hands raised, his palms facing the shaikhs in the Kadri sign of peace. "Please, my good shaikhs!"

Slowly, the shouting quelled.

"Let's have no talk of ceding authority," Ihsan went on. "Let us agree instead that we offer council, with the best interests of the desert in mind, a starting point for negotiations."

It was an interesting ploy. He hadn't asked Husamettín's permission, and now that the offer had been made, Husamettín couldn't easily retract it without making himself look the fool.

"Can we just get on with it?" Nayyan said. Her brow was furrowed and her expression pinched. She didn't look wounded, but she seemed to be in a good deal of pain.

Ihsan looked to Çeda, waiting for her assent.

He had changed so much in the past few years, Çeda genuinely believed he wanted a partnership with the desert tribes, at least until the war was decided, which was about as far ahead as any of them could see anyway.

She nodded, urging him to continue, and Ihsan went on to tell them how Meryam had raised Ashael. How she used powdered horn to manipulate him through his dreams, and how Ramahd had sailed to Mazandir to try to use the same black powder against her.

"Well, he's surely failed." Emre waved vaguely aft. "Meryam is still coming for the city."

"True," Ihsan said, "but I cannot say what became of Lord Amansir."

"We have a battle to prepare for," Çeda said, "and you have a plan, so let's hear it."

It was Ibrahim who responded. "We use ivory," the gray-bearded storyteller said.

"Ivory?" Çeda asked.

Ibrahim looked to Ihsan, who nodded. "Meryam relies on powder from Goezhen's horn to keep Ashael in a dreaming state. In this way, she controls him. But the Al'Ambra speaks of a second powder: ivory, the key to the wakeful mind. If we cannot wrest control of Ashael from her, our best option is to awaken him from his dream."

A rumble of confused, worried conversation suffused the hold.

"Can it be done?" Çeda asked Ihsan.

"I believe so."

"And what if we *do* wake him?"

Ihsan smiled wryly. "I rather think he'll be angry with the woman who manipulated him."

"Maybe," Çeda said, "or he could destroy everything in sight. We can't predict what Ashael's reaction might be."

"Granted, but the alternative is allowing Meryam to continue unchecked."

An uncomfortable silence followed. Çeda tried to weigh the odds, but how could she? She hardly knew the first thing about Ashael. "It's dangerous, Ihsan."

"Very. But we have no other way to stop him. And at the moment, events are following the young gods' plan to the letter."

"How do you know?"

"Because I spoke to Rhia, who all but sanctioned Meryam's actions. Tulathan *gave* Goezhen to her, along with clues, no doubt, on how to use his horn to control a dreaming god. They *want* Meryam to succeed. They believe her actions will lead to the gateway being opened. That's reason enough to stop her. If that means waking Ashael, then so be it."

Çeda's first instinct was to disagree. The plan felt foolish in the extreme. But the sour feeling in her gut was still growing. If they didn't find some way to stop Ashael, all would be lost. "Assuming the desert agrees, what would you need?"

"Ivory of any sort," Ihsan said. "Jewelry, statues, carvings. Anything that can be filed down to a powder. As much as we can find."

"And in the meantime?" Çeda asked.

It was Husamettín who replied. "Our options are to flee into the desert or sail for Sharakhai in hopes that Alansal will open King's Harbor to us."

"We cannot flee," Ihsan said adamantly. "The events of this next day will decide Sharakhai's fate."

"And do you suppose," Çeda said, "that after the battle we just fought, Queen Alansal will simply welcome us into Sharakhai?"

"There's no way of knowing," Ihsan replied, "which is why we've sent envoys ahead, one to her fleet, another to the city, both requesting that she do exactly that."

"Do you think she'll agree?"

Ihsan shrugged. "No, but the effort must be made."

"And if she refuses?" Çeda asked.

"Then we fight our way into the city," Husamettín said.

The rumble of conversation resumed, louder than before, but Çeda didn't join in. The ever-present ache in her right hand had suddenly deepened. Something was wrong. Terribly wrong.

"Quiet!" she shouted. "Be quiet!"

"What is it?" Ihsan asked.

Before she could reply, a heavy thud sounded on the deck above them. Then came a cry of surprise and pain, followed by a voice raised in alarm.

"To arms! To arms!"

Chapter 41

ÇEDA SPRINTED UP the stairs to *Amaranth*'s maindeck to find a winged demon with its arms around the ship's helmsman, an aging woman with freckles and kinky red hair. She was swiping at the demon with a knife as it flapped its wings and lifted her off the deck. She screamed as the demon clawed her wrist, and her knife went spinning beyond the gunwales.

Something dark loomed to Çeda's right. She would have sworn the skies had been clear only moments ago, but another demon was attacking the leader of the Shieldwives, Jenise. Çeda ran toward her, but the demon was too fast. With a mighty beat of its wings, it launched itself over the side of the ship. Jenise twisted and squirmed in its grip, fighting to free herself, to no avail. The demon was too strong, its grip too sure.

Many had bows to hand and were sighting along arrows, the strings drawn, but none let fly. They were as likely to hit Jenise as they were the demons.

"Give me that," Emre said.

He took a bow from one of the warriors, drew, and released the arrow in a motion that made it look easy. It caught the demon holding Jenise in the neck. It gave a high-pitched wail and flailed, clawing at the arrow and releasing Jenise. As she fell to the sand with a hard thump, three of her fellow

Shieldwives jumped overboard and ran toward her. The demon, meanwhile, twisted through the air, crashed against a dune, and lay still.

The demon holding the helmsman flapped away, screeching as it went, weaving wildly to avoid the arrows that were finally streaking toward it.

All across the fleet, demons appeared out of thin air. Several winked into existence over the *Bastion* and began attacking the company of Silver Spears on the foredeck. Two more with curving tusks jutting from their bat-like snouts materialized several ships over. One attacked the ship's helmsman while the other fell on the ketch's mainsail and began tearing at the canvas.

Çeda's heart pounded. Her first instinct was to draw her shamshir and join the fight, but what good would that do? The demons were being concealed, the spell lifting only when they attacked. If they didn't find a way to combat it, the fleet would be decimated. At the very least these attacks would slow their fleet down, allowing the approaching horde to overtake them.

Çeda took a deep, calming breath and balled her right hand into a fist. She pumped it over and over to heighten the pain and, with it, her sense of the desert. Casting her awareness over the desert before her, she felt for the hidden demons. She sensed one flying toward the *Amaranth*. Another hovered above the *Red Bride*. More were distant, closing with every moment. An arcane veil concealed them.

As more demons appeared and attacked, Çeda raised her hand, squeezed it as if she were gripping the edge of a sheet, and yanked down sharply.

In a blink, a hundred demons appeared all across their fleet. A great shout rose up from the crews and warriors alike. But, though they were surprised, they were no raw recruits. Nearly all were battle-hardened. Arrows flew, filling the sky like dragonflies along the Haddah in spring. Spears were set against the approaching demons. Swords and shields were raised when they swooped too close. On the *Bastion*, a Blade Maiden snapped a whip toward one demon headed toward the rigging, caught it around the neck, and yanked down. Where it fell to the deck, a dozen soldiers in white tabards stood ready. They stabbed it with their spears, killing it in moments.

Demon after demon fell to the assault but, breath of the desert, it wasn't enough. Some of the demons were utter terrors. Dozens of soldiers perished. Worse, ship after ship was coming to a sliding halt as sails and rigging were torn.

And all the while the horde itself was catching up.

Ashael could be seen clearly now, towering above a host of six-armed demons that skittered over the sand like scarabs. Countless thousands crawled around them, seemingly tireless. And behind the horde came a fleet of Qaimiri ships.

"It's Meryam," Çeda said to Sümeya, who had just felled an attacking demon. "She must have taken King Hektor's fleet in Mazandir, as we feared."

Orders were called to bring the *Bastion* and *Amaranth* closer, and Husamettín, Ihsan, Nayyan, and their entourage returned to their capital ship. They'd just swung over when a cloud of small demons descended on them. They were ifins—small, eyeless demons with two sets of wings. Many of them were felled with sword and spear. Others were struck through with arrows. They plummeted to the decks or the sand and flopped about like fish in the bottom of a boat.

But there were so many of them. And when one managed to slip by a warrior's defenses, the demon would wrap its wings around their head. Some were torn free. Others clamped their circular mouths filled with needle-like teeth onto their victims' necks. Immediately, whoever they'd bitten would go still. Moments later the demons threw themselves against any who stood around them. Their movements were wooden but effective, for the simple reason that no one wanted to fight them.

The soldiers and crew mates all across the fleet soon realized their mistake and fought back in non-lethal ways—grappling, tripping, or throwing nets over their compatriots. But that created another problem: with fewer soldiers left to fight the ifin, more and more of the small demons were finding victims to latch onto.

Emre released arrow after arrow, taking an ifin with nearly every shot. Others on nearby ships did the same. Çeda hoped she might use the power of the desert to force them away, but she was weakened after the earlier battle and from banishing the demons' spell of hiding.

Instead, she drew River's Daughter and slashed at the incoming ifin. Frail Lemi manage to bash one, but another dropped onto his head with a slap from behind. He went still a moment later, his brown eyes going impossibly wide as the ifin's wings hugged his head. Kameyl ran to him, tried to pull the ifin off, but the next moment another one caught *her* from behind.

Emre had an arrow aimed at them, but held his shot. The risk of harming either of them was too great. "Get off them!" he shouted in fear and frustration. "Get off them!"

As a frenetic battle took place on the quarterdeck against several larger demons. Sümeya ran forward and threw a cargo net over Kameyl.

Emre dropped his bow and sprinted for Frail Lemi.

"Emre, stop!" Çeda called.

But Emre didn't. He slammed into his towering friend. While Emre's momentum was halted, Frail Lemi went staggering backward. He swung his arms wildly and fell into the open hatchway. A moment later there was a heavy thud, and Frail Lemi groaned.

Çeda had just turned back toward the *Bastion* when something struck her helm. She heard the sound of flapping, felt the ifin's leathery wings slapping the metal. She was fortunate she had the wolf pelt trailing down her neck to her back. Even so, she could feel the ifin's head and neck slither beneath it. She felt the burning pain of scrapes and cuts as its needle-like teeth fought for purchase.

Shal'alara was suddenly there. She gripped the ifin with one hand and tore it free, but the demon immediately clamped its teeth onto her forearm. Gritting her teeth against the pain, Shal'alara swept her shamshir through its neck.

The head was severed, but the mouth remained tightly clamped and it took a fierce tug for Shal'alara to free it. Even then, a hunk of flesh went with it and the wound started bleeding freely.

Everywhere Çeda looked it was chaos. The winged demons had been slicing through more and more rigging. Sails were starting to fall, useless now, and the *Amaranth* was slowing as more of the crew were falling victim to the ifins. The *Bastion* was similarly under siege. Indeed, it was slowing to a crawl, its sails all but useless. Only a few on the quarterdeck, including Ihsan, Nayyan, and Husamettín, were still free and fighting. The rest of the crew had all been taken.

All across their combined fleet were similar scenes—ship after ship succumbing to the attack as Ashael loomed. The horde's forward line pulled even with the trailing ships. Some still had crews aboard. Others had fled across the sand. Both were overrun by larger demons, torn limb from limb, feasted upon. The sound of it was horrific.

"What do we do?" Emre asked, his voice strained.

"I don't know," Çeda said.

How could they hope to stand against an elder? They couldn't. It had always been folly, she realized.

As the horde nipped at the *Bastion*'s heels, a light came streaking down from the sky. Like a comet it fell toward the dunes and struck along the leading edge of the vast horde. A great plume of sand lifted into the air and black demon bodies were thrown wide of the impact.

As sand rained down and the dust cleared, a woman stood alone in the crater. She looked small compared to the demons, and minuscule compared to the approaching elder god. She looked potent nonetheless.

Çeda's heart lifted. It was Nalamae.

She held her spear against the coming horde. The demons on the sand scrabbled toward her like insects. Those in the sky descended. Some, bearing tridents, threw them down at her, shrieking as they went.

Nalamae swung her spear over her head in a circle, once, twice, thrice, and the sand lifted in a vast arc around her, more with each swing. On the third, it sprayed outward, flaying the demons' skin and flinging them wide.

The bulk of the horde, meanwhile, parted, creating a corridor between Ashael and Nalamae. Ashael floated along it. The tattered shendyt gathered around his waist fluttered in the wind. Small demons flew around the broad sweep of his horns. A spike of ebon steel transfixed his chest, the wound around it dark and crusted with blood. His eyes were bandaged, and yet his gaze was clearly fixed on the goddess before him. As her spell of biting sand rushed toward him, he lifted one hand. Like a pillar of rock standing alone against a storm-wracked sea, the sand and rock splashed against some unseen barrier. He drove his palm toward Nalamae, and the same sort of wave rushed toward her.

The wave sent her flying backward. As she rose again, a whip made of fire appeared in Ashael's hand and he lashed it at Nalamae. Though Nalamae blocked it with a swipe of her spear, a sound like thunder and a fan of flames were released from the point of impact.

Nalamae retreated toward the *Bastion* as Ashael sent lash after lash against her defenses. Flames exploded with each one and burned brightly against her armor. Some splashed over an abandoned sloop, setting it ablaze. She struggled more with each swing of her spear. One mighty lash drove her down to one knee. She dodged the next, rolling and hiding behind the stricken *Bastion*.

Staying his whip, Ashael lifted his opposite hand, and the *Bastion* burst into a kaleidoscope of pieces. Wood, rigging, canvas, shards of metal, pottery, and more spread outward in the air before him. Within those shattered remains, Nalamae floated, helpless in Ashael's spell.

"No!" Çeda cried, and leapt over the gunwales.

"Çeda, stop!" Emre shouted.

She couldn't, though. She refused to abandon the goddess. She knew she couldn't hope to make it in time, but she kept running anyway.

Ahead, Ashael held out one finger toward Nalamae. She floated ever closer to him. Her shining spear fell to the sand below. With a look like Ashael meant to do to Nalamae what he'd done to the ship, he touched his finger to her chest.

And Nalamae screamed.

Chapter 42

ERYAM WATCHED THE glorious battle unfold. The royal fleet and, apparently, the ships of the Alliance were arrayed in the distance. The two may have thought joining forces would help them, but it had only made things easier for Meryam—she no longer had to worry about hunting them down separately.

Ashael drifted toward the retreating ships, his hands spread wide, his mind still caught in Meryam's dream. Ship after ship fell to her demonic horde.

"It won't be long now," Meryam said to Amaryllis.

Beside Meryam, Amaryllis stood on *The Gray Gull*'s foredeck, motionless. The ifin wrapped around her head flapped its wings lazily, in time with her breath. Her eyes, still visible through the interlaced wings over her face, were opened wide. Her mouth worked soundlessly.

"We'll finish them, then move on to Sharakhai." Meryam pointed to a smudge along the horizon. "Just think, by this time tomorrow, the city will be ours."

Amaryllis, still as a statue, blinked. Tears trailed from her eyes, making bright lines along her cheeks and the ifin's black wings. The rest of Meryam's crew moved woodenly, steering the ship in the churned wake of the demons. The ships trailing *The Gray Gull* were the same, their crews expending the minimum effort to keep their ships on the move.

Meryam took a pinch of powder from the bag at her side, breathed it in deeply, and the dream shared by both her and Ashael brightened. In it, Ashael and his flock of ravens were nipping at the heels of a host of fleeing ships. He'd caught them at last and was hungry for revenge.

"I wonder if Queen Alansal knows," Meryam said absently. "She must. Surely her water dancers warned her of what's to come. Or maybe her hoard of artifacts contains a looking glass. She might be watching at this very moment." Meryam imagined Alansal's growing terror as she watched the horde approach the city. "Be content it was yours for a time," Meryam said to her.

Content? came Yasmine's voice. *You think she would ever be content?* Yasmine's laugh was biting. *She's as hungry for power as you ever were.*

"No." With a smile, Meryam surveyed her host. "No one's as hungry as I am."

Yasmine paused, a grudging acknowledgment of Meryam's statement. *The real question is which of you sees farther?*

Suddenly a comet streaked down and struck the sand near the front line of the battle. A newcomer had arrived, a woman in shining armor holding a spear that shone brightly in the sun.

Meryam laughed. "At last, the goddess has come out of hiding!"

Her sudden arrival presented a problem, though. Ashael might recognize her. He might start questioning the reality around him, so Meryam altered the dream, disguising Nalamae as a witch of the sea.

The witch smote Ashael's ravens. She struck down the beasts he'd summoned to his cause. Ashael would not be undone, however. He conjured a whip and threw lashes of fire against her. When the witch hid behind a ship, he raised one hand and shattered it, lifting the pieces into the sky and Nalamae with them.

Nalamae's arms and legs were drawn wide as if she were lying on a confessor's table. Her adamantine spear fell to the sand. Ashael approached, one finger raised, and touched her chest. And Nalamae screamed, the sound carrying over the vast battlefield. Meryam reveled in the sound of the goddess's pain. Her enemies' best defense was nothing compared to Ashael.

Nalamae was a *young* god, a malnourished child before a gilded warrior. It was as heady a feeling as Meryam had ever had. After all, if Nalamae couldn't stop Ashael, no one could.

But then, as Ashael stared at Nalamae's writhing form, the ashen skin along his brow furrowed . . . and in that moment, as Meryam sensed a glimmer of recognition within Ashael's mind, she saw the danger. Ashael was beginning to pierce the dream. He was beginning to see Nalamae for who she truly was.

Knowing that to manipulate him too much could shift his attention to *her*, Meryam dropped the guise she'd placed over Nalamae. As Ashael, perplexed, peered into Nalamae's soul, Meryam felt something new. There was something hidden. Something near her, either on *The Gray Gull* itself or close to it. It felt very much like the spell of concealment she'd had Ashael place on the demons that had attacked the enemy fleet.

It took great effort, for Ashael was now preoccupied with Nalamae, but she forced the elder god to search for it, suggesting it was some ploy of Nalamae's.

With a wave of Ashael's hand toward the *Gull*, the spell was removed, and there, suddenly, stood Ramahd. He was heading across the deck toward her with something in his hands. A red necklace.

Fear surging up inside her, she retreated. "Seize him!"

Amaryllis and the *Gull*'s crew responded immediately. With leaden movements, they lumbered past her and attacked.

Ramahd seemed unwilling to fight them. Indeed, he hardly struggled as they grappled with him. "Remember who you were, Meryam!" He threw the necklace toward her. It fell against the deck with a rattle, then slid to a stop against her slippered feet. "Remember who you were!"

For a moment, Ramahd managed to free himself, but Meryam's terror had summoned the attention of a winged demon. It swooped in and bowled into Ramahd, knocking him over the side of the ship. Several of the crew, including Amaryllis, jumped after him, dumbly following the orders she'd given.

Meryam, meanwhile, stared at the necklace. It was *Yasmine's* necklace, the one she'd sacrificed to liberate Goezhen's body from the pool in Mazandir.

Old memories began to swirl. Of Meryam and Yasmine being kidnapped as children. Yasmine giving the necklace to Meryam as a symbol of hope they would survive. Meryam had worn it for years, and when Yasmine had been killed by the Moonless Host, she'd often rubbed the beads, especially when she grew tired of the endless chase for Yasmine's killers. Later, it became her path to an endless well of anger, a fount where dark inspirations were born.

In Mazandir, Meryam had tossed the necklace onto the hardened surface of the pool that held Goezhen, as a signal to Tulathan that she would give up the past and focus on what she, Meryam, wanted. *What I do after this point,* she'd told herself at the time, *is for me and me alone, to fulfill* my *dreams.*

She thought she'd left Yasmine behind, and yet, as she stared at those red beads lying on the deck at her feet, her grief at Yasmine's death came rushing back. She was reminded of all those she'd hunted and killed to have her vengeance against Macide and the Moonless Host. Hundreds had died on her orders, many by her own hand.

She'd justified it because her sister had been taken from her. Even murdering her own father had felt noble at the time.

In her mind's eye, she remembered her father in the moments before the ehrekh, Guhldrathen, feasted on his heart. The terror in his eyes was echoed by his short, ragged breaths. When it was over, when he lay dead and the mantle of queen had passed to her, Meryam had prayed for her *own* death. In a strange twist of fate, it was Ramahd himself who'd helped her overcome it, who'd consoled her, unaware she'd orchestrated it all, and slowly but surely the armor she'd constructed for herself after Yasmine's death had been reforged.

She'd reinforced it many times since. But now she stood face to face with her necklace, the very thing she'd sacrificed to gain her newfound power, and it was dismantling her armor in ways she hadn't thought possible. Which was why Ramahd had brought it.

The knowledge made it all the worse. She felt frail and weak all over again, a helpless princess unable to control the forces swirling around her.

That feeling of helplessness was like the opening of a door that allowed more emotions to flood in: guilt over trapping her father, guilt over others who'd died at her command, some with only the thinnest of threads tying them to the Bloody Passage.

They still deserved it, Meryam told herself.

Did they, though? Yasmine asked.

She had a vision of two men, a father and his son, who Meryam had experimented on to perfect the spell of summoning before using it on Macide. She'd had their ears put out to be sure it was the *spell* drawing them together, not their own senses. Other visions came: of men, women, and children slaughtered in her long, unending quest for revenge.

She saw *The Gray Gull*'s crew anew, and the ifins wrapped around their heads, lazily flapping their wings. She turned a circle and cast her gaze over the crews on the other ships, all similarly enslaved. Her mouth went dry as every woman and man met her gaze with sightless eyes. She felt as if a pit were opening beneath her, the Hollow remade, and she was falling into it, to be lost until the end of time.

Yasmine's laugh echoed in her mind. *Come, sister. You can't tell me you're shocked. This is what you wanted.*

Meryam wanted to bicker with her as she once had, but she paused. Movement beyond the ship drew her attention to the horde. Sensing the wild swing of her emotions through the dream, Ashael was floating toward *The Gray Gull*. Soon the god towered above her. Though ancient bandages still covered his eyes, he seemed to regard the crew. He was piercing the veil of the dream. He was starting to understand what was happening.

Meryam felt it all slipping away. She considered ending it right then, of allowing Ashael to awaken, effectively giving up her quest for power.

But no. She'd come too far. She refused to give up now.

As Ashael bent close and inspected her with hidden eyes, Meryam took a handful of the powder from the pouch at her side and threw it into the air.

The elder god reeled and retreated. He'd breathed in a good amount of the powder. The trouble was, Meryam had too, and she'd taken too much.

As Ashael craned his neck toward the heavens, so did Meryam. Her last thought was for Ashael to save her, to protect her from her enemies. She had no idea whether the command had worked, but just then, all around her, the demons on the ship, on the sand, and in the air went wild.

Chapter 43

ÇEDA SPRINTED OVER the sand toward Nalamae, who floated in the air before Ashael. Her screams were cut blessedly short as Ashael's head turned. Çeda had no idea what had attracted his attention, not until he turned mid-air and fixed his gaze on the fleet of Qaimiri ships trailing the horde.

Çeda peered at the lead ship, a tumbledown sloop she recognized as *The Gray Gull*, and her footsteps slowed. Meryam stood on the foredeck, surrounded by her crew, who had ifins wrapped around their heads. A moment later, she realized it wasn't only *The Gray Gull*'s crew, but *all* the Qaimiri ships'—across her fleet, soldiers and sandsmen alike moved over the decks and rigging, but in an oddly stilted manner, each controlled by one of the black demons.

On the sand near the *Gull*, a man was apparently trying to flee but was struggling against several enslaved crewmen. By the gods who breathe, it was Ramahd. What he was doing there Çeda had no idea, but she suspected it had something to do with Ashael's sudden interest in Meryam. With a great shove, Ramahd broke away from his pursuers. He tumbled once, then was up again in a flash and sprinting over a nearby dune.

Ashael, meanwhile, floated toward *The Gray Gull*, leaving Nalamae and the shattered remains of the *Bastion* suspended above the sand. When he reached the *Gull*'s prow, he bent down and stared at Meryam. He seemed transfixed, a child who'd stumbled upon a curious toy, and Meryam's hand whipped upward and a cloud of dust billowed into Ashael's face. Ashael reeled. He retreated from the ship's prow and, as one, the demons burst into motion. They flew randomly, mindlessly attacking any that were near, including their own.

As Çeda cringed from the intensity of their wild screams, Nalamae dropped from the air like a stone. So did the pieces of the sundered *Bastion*. Çeda launched herself into motion, hoping to break Nalamae's fall, but she was too late. Nalamae thudded against the sand without so much as a groan. Surging forward, Çeda threw herself across the goddess's body to protect her. Pieces of falling debris struck Çeda's back and legs, and a wooden beam crashed into her helm so hard her vision went hazy. More shattered pieces of wood pounded the nearby sand, sending sprays of sand over Nalamae and Çeda.

When the hail of ship's pieces finally ended, Çeda lifted herself off Nalamae. The goddess was breathing, her heart still beat, but she didn't wake when Çeda shook her.

Çeda leaned close and spoke loudly so she could be heard over the demons' high-pitched screams. "Please, Nalamae, hear me! It's Çeda. We have need of you."

But the goddess didn't stir.

With one eye on the warring demons, Çeda dragged Nalamae across the sand, hoping to reach the relative safety of her fleet. Ten paces away, a cluster of long-limbed demons battled one another. Black blood flowed as they clawed and bit, rending one another's flesh.

Their roars and pained whoops pushed her to the brink of her flagging strength. But she was too slow. The battle was spilling closer.

A hyena-like demon with long limbs and beady eyes had just finished ripping the throat from a smaller demon. A shiver ran along its skin as it spotted Çeda. It lurched toward her with a halting gait, then rose up on its hind legs to face her.

Çeda drew River's Daughter and placed herself between the demon and

Nalamae, then met its charge with a mighty swing of her shamshir. The well-honed blade bit deep into the demon's forearm. She blocked a swipe of its claws with her buckler, then skipped back as its elongated jaws snapped. She moved quickly, instinctively, sending cut after cut into the demon's flesh.

Yet every wound she inflicted seemed only to enrage the demon further. When a downward swing of her shamshir glanced off its shoulder, it surged forward and butted her with its head.

She let the momentum carry her away, then rolled backward over one shoulder and regained her feet. She was readying to defend against another charge when the demon inexplicably turned away.

She understood why a moment later.

A demon the size of an ox was charging it. It gored its smaller brethren with the horn on its snout, tossed its head, and launched the smaller demon skyward. As it tumbled through the air, the larger one spun toward Çeda. With a thunderous, bellowing trumpet, it hurtled toward her. She was preparing to dodge from its path when a massive black spear blurred through the air and struck the demon through the ribs. A moment later, an arrow caught it in the neck. A second arrow streaked in, then a third, all of them sinking deep.

The demon collapsed onto the sand, its momentum sending it into a hissing slide that ended mere paces from Çeda.

Frail Lemi was there a moment later, placing a sandaled foot against the demon's barrel chest and yanking his greatspear free. Behind him, Emre sent another arrow streaking into the sky, felling a winged demon that was shrieking down toward them.

Kameyl, Sümeya, and a host of others stormed in behind them. Çeda was relieved but also confused—many of her rescuers had fallen victim to the ifin.

"How?" she asked Emre.

"The moment the horde went mad," he said, "the ifin released us."

Çeda looked up and saw that the air above the battlefield was thick with ifin.

Husamettín, Yndris, and Nayyan arrived, all of them wearing dark battle garb. Supporting them were a dozen Blade Maidens, their veils covering their faces, and two hundred Silver Spears in white armor.

Ihsan arrived last, huffing and puffing and bearing a litter. "Quickly," he said, and lay the litter on the sand beside Nalamae.

As the sun began to set in the west, Ihsan and Çeda lifted Nalamae onto the litter and carried her toward the *Amaranth*. With Husamettín bellowing orders, five hundred desert warriors, Blade Maidens, and Silver Spears set up a defensive line against the demons. The horde fought each other senselessly, which helped, but their numbers were staggering. All across their line, wherever their soldiers were near the demons, they were attacked, and more and more were falling.

Then something changed. Across the battlefield, demons began to collapse against the sand. Winged demons dropped from the sky, pattering against the dunes.

"Look!" Emre said.

Çeda followed his gaze toward the center of the horde, where Ashael floated in midair. He'd gone perfectly still. Though his eyes were bandaged, his head was tilted upward, as if he were staring at the heavens. Or dreaming.

Frail Lemi had his greatspear lifted high, ready to plunge it into the neck of a demon lying helplessly at his feet.

"Don't!" Ihsan cried. "Touch them and they may awaken."

Frail Lemi looked as if he was going to stab it anyway, but then his gaze lifted and he took in the horde anew. His battle rage faded, and he lowered his spear. Others stayed their swords. After the terrible shrieking and the din of the battle, the silence made Çeda's skin prickle. It felt as if any sound they made, be it cry of pain, clank of armor, or hiss of sand, would wake the demon horde.

All across the battlefield, companies of soldiers collected their wounded and made a swift and quiet retreat toward the bulk of their hobbled fleet. It felt truly bizarre, as if they weren't a retreating host, but a den of thieves stealing past sleeping guards. With every heartbeat, Çeda worried the horde would reawaken, but not a single demon roused as their soldiers navigated between the demons and returned to the waiting ships.

King Ihsan, King Husamettín, and Queen Nayyan joined Çeda on the *Amaranth*. All across the fleet, ships' crews made hasty repairs. Rigging was replaced. Rips in sails were sewn up or replaced with sets scavenged from nearby fallen ships. It was slow work. At every moment it seemed Ashael would awaken and call for his horde to renew their assault. But the elder god remained frozen.

Through some strange combination of Nalamae's and Ramahd's interventions, they'd gained a temporary stay.

One by one, then two by two, their ships began to set sail. Near sunset, the last of their fleet were finally underway, including the *Amaranth*. Çeda stood at the stern and surveyed the carnage: thousands of warriors lost, nearly a hundred ships, stripped of anything useful, foundered on the sand. She used a spyglass to search for Ramahd, but wasn't able to spot him near or beyond *The Gray Gull*.

"Mighty Alu protect you," she whispered, then swung her spyglass forward.

Along the horizon, barely discernible in the haze of amber dust, were the bric-a-brac shapes of Queen Alansal's dunebreakers. They were sailing for Sharakhai, where they'd find safe harbor. The Mirean and Malasani fleets may be wounded, but they still boasted superior numbers, even with the Alliance and royal navy combined.

"She'll let us into King's Harbor," Çeda said to no one in particular. "She must."

Ihsan, standing nearby, shrugged. "Queen Alansal may not recognize the danger until it's too late."

"Then force her to," Çeda said.

Husamettín watched their exchange with some interest. Nayyan did as well while holding her daughter tight against her chest. Emre approached while staunching a nasty cut on his right wrist with a bandage.

"You're assuming she'll come anywhere near us," Ihsan said, "but Alansal is well aware of my power. She won't take the risk."

"The soldiers at the harbor then. Command *them* to open the gates."

The smile Ihsan gave was anything but encouraging. "It's worth a try, but you must know that of late"—he sent an embarrassed glance toward Nayyan—"the power of my voice has been unreliable at best."

Çeda stared at him, then at Nayyan. "Please tell me this is another one of your lies."

Nayyan smiled sadly. "I wish it were."

"But why?" Çeda asked. "What happened?"

Nayyan shrugged while rocking her daughter. "The fates did to Ihsan what they do to us all in the end."

"Fucked him, you mean," said Frail Lemi.

Husamettín sent a withering glance Frail Lemi's way, then took in the rest of the assemblage. "Ihsan's right. If we head for King's Harbor and Alansal has no sudden change of heart, we'll be trapped."

Just then a signal horn called out the sequence for *enemy sighted*. Behind them, along their starboard side, the Qaimiri fleet was sailing around the vast, mottled patch of sleeping demons.

Emre held a spyglass to one eye. "They're calling for parley."

Çeda saw he was right. Every Qaimiri ship had a white pennant raised. And the crews were free of ifins.

"We should accept," Çeda said when she lowered the spyglass.

Husamettín eyed the approaching fleet warily, as if he distrusted the Qaimiri. But in the end he nodded. They ran white pennants up the mainmasts, signaling their acceptance.

Mere moments later, Nayyan said, "Gods, no."

A chill passed over Çeda as she followed Nayyan's gaze. The horde was stirring. Demons lifted back into the sky, creating a now-familiar cloud.

"Signal the Qaimiri ships to make all haste toward Sharakhai," Husamettín ordered.

"We should speak with them now," Çeda said.

But Husamettín was adamant. "We cannot afford a delay, not when every spare moment is needed to reach King's Harbor, enter it by any means necessary, and ready for its defense."

Çeda's first instinct was to insist, but as the black cloud billowed in the distance, she realized he was right.

"Very well," she said, "we'll meet them when we anchor."

The message was passed on, and their fleets sailed through the night, a harrowing time in which they weren't always sure whether they were staying ahead of the horde. The winged demons could have caught up to them, but none approached. Çeda could only guess that the strange encounter with Meryam had made the god wary. Whatever the case, he seemed content to keep his horde close for the time being.

Shifts were set up so that all crewmen could find at least a few hours' sleep. They'd need their strength for the coming day. Çeda tried, but she was too restless, too worried. She spent hours by Nalamae's side, hoping the goddess would awaken, but she never did. She breathed fitfully, shallowly, as if each might be her last.

All too soon dawn arrived.

By then they'd closed the distance on Queen Alansal's dunebreakers. They wouldn't catch them, though. The distance was still too great, and in only a few hours, they would reach Sharakhai.

Near high sun, they passed through a channel in the blooming fields. Çeda stared at the adichara trees in wonder. Vibrant only months ago, they were now an ashen white. Only one that Çeda could see was green. She wondered about the asirim, how many yet lived, how close to the end they were. She tried calling to them, but none responded, and she prayed it was because they were too weak, not because they'd all perished.

Ahead, Tauriyat loomed. Sharakhai and its mismatch of buildings and walls sprawled below it. The vault could be seen, glimmering even in the daylight, while the gateway speared upward into a deep blue sky. Queen Alansal's fleet split, the dunebreakers heading for King's Harbor, the Malasani ships heading for the southern harbor and the rocky channel that protected it from assault.

As Çeda and her fleet followed the dunebreakers, the horde closed in, screeching, a sea of dark shapes and flapping wings, a god floating at its center.

"What's that?" Frail Lemi asked.

Çeda turned to find him pointing toward King's Harbor. The dunebreakers had reached the harbor's interior, and the great gates were clanking shut. Below the gates, something burned on the sand. Two skiffs, Çeda saw through her spyglass. A pair of bodies burned as well, both reduced to charred husks, the skiffs surely set ablaze with lamp oil or the like.

"Your envoys?" Çeda asked Ihsan.

Ihsan nodded stiffly. "It appears Queen Alansal has given her answer."

Chapter 44

NEAR HIGH SUN on a cloudless day, Davud blinked his eyes open. His limbs felt leaden. His joints ached from disuse. He'd just woken from another foray into the lands beyond.

Before him, the brilliant light of the gateway stabbed upward through the stony ground. Esmeray knelt on his right, blinking herself awake. On his left, completing a triangle around the gateway, was the lifeless form of an asir. Her name was Bahar, and she'd been a seamstress once. Now she was the latest in a growing tally—seven so far—who'd died helping Davud reach the land beyond.

He might have felt her death had meaning had he made more progress in gaining mastery over the gate, but he hadn't, and it made the cold around the gateway feel all the more bitter. To be fair, his efforts with Esmeray hadn't been completely fruitless—the spells they'd crafted allowed him to gain purchase on the gateway—but he lacked the raw power needed to close it. He was beginning to fear it was too monumental a task and that he'd *never* be able to manage it.

As he'd done since Jorrdan's passage to the farther fields, Sehid-Alaz had given his blood before the ritual began. The ancient king had been noticeably weaker than during their previous attempts, but Davud took his blood anyway. There was too much power in it to ignore.

"This can't go on," Davud said, more to himself than Esmeray.

Esmeray smiled wanly. "We're making progress."

"Yes, but not enough." Each performance of the ritual had claimed the life of an asir while the others weakened at a noticeably faster rate than only weeks before. Only a hundred remained in the blooming fields, supporting the adichara trees that yet lived. "How long before they *all* pass?"

"I don't know," Esmeray said.

Neither did Davud, but he knew this much: when the last of the asirim perished, Sharakhai's devastation wouldn't be far behind.

When at last the fields do wither,
When the stricken fade;
The gods shall pass beyond the veil,
And land shall be remade.

That was the final stanza of the poem Willem had discovered on a clay table in Nebahat's archive. It had been made by a woman who bore witness to the bargain made between the Sharakhani Kings and the desert gods on Beht Ihman, and gave hint to the danger Sharakhai was in. Every moment of every day, Davud feared the remaking of the desert would come to pass, and that he was powerless to prevent it.

As the cold wind blustered over the top of Tauriyat, Davud and Esmeray stood and stretched their aching joints. Staring into the gateway's light, Davud puzzled over the strange vision he'd had of Ahya sending him to fetch Çeda. He hadn't had a similar vision since, nor had he been able to sense the soul who'd triggered it from the gateway's opposite side.

"What's that?" Esmeray asked, interrupting his thoughts.

Far into the desert, well beyond the city, a cloud of dust was rising. Davud described a sigil in the air, one that combined *distance* and *sight*—he was exhausted but had enough power to effect the simple spell. The air wavered before him, distorting the view beyond it, and he lifted his arms, adjusting the spell of farseeing until he could see the fleet. He couldn't tell much beyond the fact that they were Alansal's dunebreakers, along with the Malasani dhows and ketches that had sailed with them.

"Alansal's fleet returns."

He shifted the lens and Esmeray peered through it. "Yes," she said, "but look beyond."

Davud spread his arms, intensifying the spell's effect and allowing them both to see. Several leagues beyond the Mirean fleet sailed a second line of ships comprised of galleons and smaller ships with the stylings of the desert tribes. "It's the Alliance. They're sailing with the royal navy."

Suddenly Esmeray's eyes went wide, her mouth slack. "Fates preserve us."

When Davud saw it, he felt sick. Trailing the fleet was a roiling black cloud. Using the last of his power, he intensified the spell enough to see a tall, horned figure floating above the black cloud.

"Ashael," Esmeray said, echoing Davud's thoughts.

"The royal navy and the Alliance ships need shelter." Utterly exhausted, Davud let the spell go and the air returned to normal with a soft, rising whistle. "Alansal must grant it to them."

A squad of four Mirean guards stood in a cluster some distance away. Esmeray glanced at them, then spoke in a low voice. "You really think the queen will let them in?" She jutted her chin toward the desert. "This is what she's wanted all along."

"This is the end, Esmeray." He began walking toward the path that led to Eventide. "The gods' plan will come to fruition when Ashael arrives. Even Alansal must see that."

Esmeray stopped him, then held out her wrist. "Send me to Meiying's. We'll warn the Enclave."

Using his blooding ring, Davud pierced her skin and drank her blood. It gave him enough power to trigger a spell. A triangular portal opened in the air before them. Beyond it lay a quaint room with a rocking chair, a basket of balled yarn, and a half-finished throw blanket.

After pulling him close and placing a warm kiss on his neck, Esmeray stepped through the slowly spinning portal. Davud allowed it to close then rushed toward the waiting guards. "I need to speak to your queen," he said in Mirean.

They didn't argue. They had orders to bring Davud to Queen Alansal if he found anything of importance at the gateway. The five of them rushed down the nearby path. By the time the were nearing Eventide's high walls, the bulk of the Malasani fleet made for the southern harbor while the dune-breakers continued through the tall doors of King's Harbor. Sharakhai's royal navy and the tribal ships were only a few leagues away, maybe less, but the doors were already starting to close.

Davud had no idea what it might indicate, but as the harbor doors shut with an ominous boom, a trail of black smoke lifted from beyond the harbor walls.

Within the palace, the guards led him to an empty dining hall. Three remained to guard him while one left to inform Queen Alansal. Time passed, and Davud pressed the guards to speak with the queen immediately, but his pleas fell on deaf ears.

Davud had been hoping not to anger Queen Alansal by forcing the issue, but when an hour passed in that empty hall, he saw he would have to take matters into his own hands. Using the power of Esmeray's blood, he drew a sigil for *form* and *bird* and *luminesce*. He had need of the amulet that had formed the portal earlier, and the bird he'd just created in Meiying's home would deliver it to him.

He'd no more cast the spell than Alansal's advisor, Juvaan Xin-Lei, stepped into the room. "Queen Alansal is otherwise engaged, I'm afraid. She's sent me to take hear news of the gateway. We both hope you've achieved a break-through."

"I saw the fleets approaching the city," Davud said. "I beg you to give them shelter."

Juvaan's expression became flat, unreadable, which revealed a lot more than he thought. "You told the guards you had news of the gateway."

"Because I needed to speak to her," Davud said. "Please, she cannot leave them in the desert to fight the oncoming horde alone."

"That isn't for you or me to decide," Juvaan said calmly. "If you have no real news to share, then I'm afraid—"

He turned to leave, but Davud grabbed his wrist. "I saw the horde, Juvaan. I saw Ashael approaching. We have to protect those fleeing toward the city."

Juvaan twisted his arm, breaking Davud's hold. "I serve at my *queen's* pleasure, not yours."

"And your queen wants a Sharakhai that is whole, not destroyed by the elder god bearing down on us."

"The day looks to be a dark one, I'll grant you." He waved toward the door. "All the more reason I must return to my queen's side."

At this, Davud went perfectly still.

Juvaan's words—the very notion of standing by Queen Alansal's side—reminded Davud of Chow-Shian's predictions. She'd said Davud would guide Chow-Shian to the land beyond, and that he would lead Queen Alansal through the gates of ivory. He'd thought they were two separate events, but they weren't. They were one in the same.

How to make it happen, though? The answer came to him a moment later. The same way the water dancers had gained their visions: through the powder, zhenyang.

A small, glowing bluebird fluttered through the nearby doorway. Pinched in its beak was a golden amulet in the shape of a triangle. Davud had planned on sending it to Alansal's throne room. Instead, he bid the bird fly to the palace infirmary.

Clearly worried about Davud's purpose, Juvaan grabbed for the bird as it passed him by. He missed, and the bird flew into the hallway with a high-pitched warble. Juvaan then drew his sword and advanced on Davud. For the first time since meeting him, he seemed truly angry. "What do you think you're doing?"

"Your queen is making a grave mistake, Juvaan."

"You will not question her decisions!"

Sensing the bird had reached its destination, Davud triggered a spell, and the same triangular portal Esmeray had used earlier sprang up beside him. Through it, Davud could see the bamboo pipes, beneath which Chow-Shian and the other water dancers had summoned their visions. "Tell the queen to meet me at her granddaughter's bedside."

"Stop!"

Juvaan rushed toward him, but Davud was already stepping through the portal. Juvaan pulled up just as it was closing. He stared, a shocked look on his pale face, then turned and sprinted for the door behind him.

Standing in the hall, Davud shrunk the golden amulet and stuffed it into a pocket in his khalat. Chow-Shian lay on a bed nearby. Her sweet old physic was sitting in a chair at her bedside, massaging Chow-Shian's legs. She looked up, startled.

"Your queen sent me to fetch you, grandmother," Davud said in a calm voice while leading her toward the door. "She wishes to speak to you. Now."

She looked confused, but let Davud usher her from the room all the same. The two guards posted outside looked startled by his sudden presence. "Master Davud!" one said, then crooked his neck to peer inside the room.

Before they could think of trying to stop him, Davud drew another sigil, and a glimmering shield blinked into being across the threshold. Their shouts passed through the barrier, but they were muffled, as if underwater. They drew their swords and tried to hack their way into the room. Davud might be drained, but his shield was proof against their weapons.

Even so, time was running short. He moved to the corner of the room, where the inlaid box of zhenyang rested on a table. If it was empty, his plan would unravel before it had truly begun. But when he slid the top open, he found it blessedly full.

He took it to Chow-Shian's bedside and sat in the chair the physic had recently occupied. Leaning in close, he whispered in Chow-Shian's ear, "I understand now. I know what you meant me to do."

He could almost hear her reply. *It wasn't what I meant for you to do, but the fates.*

"That may be so," Davud said softly, "but I need your help all the same. I need you to concentrate, to summon the vision you and the other dancers—"

He never finished the thought.

A figure had appeared in the doorway. Queen Alansal stood beyond the glowing shield, her long hair flowing past her shoulders, her steel pins gripped tightly in her hands. One moment the shield was in place, and the next, one of the pins was blurring in a swift downward stroke. With a sound like dragonflies swarming, the shield burst in a shower of sparks.

"You dare!" Queen Alansal said as she advanced on Davud. "You *dare*!"

Davud thought he'd have time to reason with her, especially with Chow-Shian lying between them, but Alansal came around Chow-Shian's sickbed so quickly he was forced to act faster than he'd wanted. Using both hands, he grabbed as much of the powder as he could and flung it into the air.

Chapter 45

ASTIFF WIND BORE the *Amaranth*, and Ihsan, toward Sharakhai. Their fleet was now considerable. It was comprised of the remains of the royal navy, the ships of the desert tribes, and those from Qaimir that Ramahd Amansir had somehow, miraculously, liberated from Meryam. The air grew cooler as they headed toward King's Harbor, and when they passed through the vault's glimmering curtain, the temperature dropped precipitously. It felt bizarre, the heat of a summer day being so rapidly replaced by winter's chill.

Ahead, the skiffs near the harbor doors continued to burn. The corpses of Ihsan's envoys, who'd carried his offer of peace, burned along with them. That Queen Alansal had declined didn't particularly surprise him. That she'd delivered her answer in such a manner did, until he remembered how their new Crone, Shohreh, had seen to the deaths of all but one of her water dancers.

Ihsan looked to Husamettín, who stood on the foredeck beside him. "It's not too late to continue north and enter the city from the Fertile Fields."

"No." Husamettín peered at the formidable harbor doors, at the towers along the walls. The morning sun sent harsh shadows across his angular face, making him look severe. "We're taking our harbor back."

Ihsan paused, waiting to see if it was a joke. He needn't have bothered.

Husamettín never joked. "And how by the Great Mother do you expect to do that?"

"Through the doors, Ihsan. We'll go through the doors."

"If you're depending on my power—"

"You'll have your chance to sway them but one way or another, I promise you we'll gain the harbor." Ihsan was about to object when Husamettín, clearly distracted, broke away and headed toward a cluster of wardens in black battle dresses and other commanders in steel armor. He waved to the Qaimiri fleet as he went. "As we agreed, speak to King Hektor. Have him cede command to me."

"He may not be amenable—"

"I don't care how you do it, Ihsan. Send their fleet commander to me when it's done." A moment later he reached the other group and began speaking to them with a grim intensity.

"I hope you know what you're doing," Ihsan said softly.

When the fleet anchored a short while later, Ihsan disembarked and headed across the sand toward the Qaimiri ship, *Alu's Crown*. By the time he arrived, Ramahd Amansir was walking down the gangplank with his man, Cicio, and, surprisingly, the ghul, Fezek, who for some reason was wearing antiquated Qaimiri garb: a ruffled shirt, wool trousers, and a coat that, with his prosthetic leg, made him look rather piratical.

"Well met!" Fezek said with a smile.

Ihsan had seen a litany of gruesome things in his unnaturally long life. Fezek's smile was close to the very top of that ignominious list.

Cicio slapped Fezek's shoulder with the back of one hand, and pointed to the chaos around them. "Open you eyes, ah? You call this *well met*?"

"Yes, I see . . ." Fezek's smile faltered, then returned, brighter and grislier than before. "At least we managed to wrest control of the fleet from Meryam." He waved to the fleet with a theatrical flourish. "Surely *that's* worth a smile!"

"I'll grant you that." Ihsan bowed his head politely to Fezek, then to Cicio, then focused on Ramahd. "I take it you didn't manage to stab her in the heart before leaving."

"No," Ramahd said. "And I didn't intend to. Nalamae came to us before the battle. She had concerns about what might happen if Meryam was still controlling Ashael as she died. My purpose was only to break her hold on him."

Behind Ramahd came a woman with long, curly hair. Ihsan recognized her as Amaryllis, a spy and assassin for Queen Meryam. She'd been a sultry beauty once. Now she was a bedraggled husk of a woman.

"You were with Meryam on that tumbledown ship, were you not?" Ihsan asked her.

Amaryllis's nostrils flared. "I was," she said, her Qaimiran accent strong.

"A loyalty she repaid by enslaving you and her crew."

Amaryllis scowled. "I presume you have a point?"

"I'm trying to get a lay of the land, as it were."

"Well, the *lay of the land*," Amaryllis said with a sneer, "is that you have a madwoman on your hands. Meryam is nothing like the woman I once knew."

Ihsan nodded. "And where is your former queen now?"

Amaryllis gestured toward the approaching horde. "We searched for her after the ifin released us but never found her. She's out there somewhere."

"The important thing," Ramahd cut in, "is that we disrupted her plans. We have a chance to fight thanks to Nalamae." His gaze shifted to the *Amaranth*. "I saw her being taken to the ship. Is she well enough to speak?"

"She hasn't awoken since the battle," Ihsan said. "She nearly died fighting Ashael."

Ramahd touched his forehead with his right hand, a sign of prayer in Qaimir. "May Alu grant her mercy."

"Yes, well," Ihsan replied, "would that Mighty Alu had decided to come and help."

Ramahd seemed displeased by the comment, Amaryllis turned and walked away, and Cicio spat on the sand, but notably, none of them spoke against him. They, too, had likely been wondering where their patron god was.

Ihsan arranged for the leaders of King Hektor's navy to meet with Husamettín and the tribal shaikhs. Restless earlier, Husamettín was now the calm, decisive commander Ihsan had come to know during their centuries of rule together. He spoke briskly and efficiently, relaying his plan for the coming battle. Soon they broke, and orders were spread among their hastily cobbled army.

Work gangs moved their ships into a grand crescent that ran from one rocky shoulder of Tauriyat, beneath the aqueduct, to a jagged promontory south of the harbor. When it was done, the gangs proceeded to saw or chop at the ships' struts. One by one, galleons, clippers, sloops, and yachts tilted and dropped to the sand, creating a defensible wall. The line would have gaps—the ships could only be fitted so close to one another—and they didn't have enough work crews to hobble *every* ship, but it was a damn sight better than fighting on open sand.

Within the crescent, the wounded were placed on skiffs and sleighs cobbled from the recently detached ships' skis. Crewmen unfit to fight were stationed with them, ready to drag the wounded into the harbor quickly if and when the doors were breached.

From the nearby towers and atop the walls, ranks of Mirean archers watched silently. They could have sent arrows raining down if they'd wanted, but so far they seemed content to let the gathered army founder as the horde approached.

Near the wounded, Ihsan spotted Frail Lemi dragging Nalamae on a sleigh. The goddess tossed and turned, as if in the throes of a nightmare.

"Has she awoken?" Ihsan asked when they came near.

"No." It was easy to think the big man was made for fighting and little else, but Frail Lemi stared at Nalamae with a surprisingly tender expression. "She started thrashing as soon as it got cold."

"Not when it got cold," Ihsan countered, "but when we entered the *vault*." He was certain the nature of the vault, the outer boundary of the gateway itself, had done something to stir the goddess's soul.

"Ihsan?"

He turned to find Çeda headed his way. She held an engraved wooden box, the sort women in the desert kept kohl in. She handed it to him. "The ivory you asked for."

On the flight toward Sharakhai, the Alliance ships had gathered all the ivory they could find and ground it down. Ihsan opened the box and stared at the dirty white powder.

Nayyan, wearing her violet battle dress, joined them with Ransaneh, swaying the baby back and forth, consoling her as the babe cried from the raucous noises around them. "Well?" she asked while nodding toward the box. "Do we use it or not?"

Ihsan took a pinch of the powder and held it to his nose. It smelled faintly of toasted cumin and white pepper. *Please let this work.* He inhaled sharply. Over the following moments, Ihsan tried not to show his disappointment. The sounds of the fleet preparing for battle grew loud in his ears. He felt the chill air on his skin more acutely. He felt the irritation of the powder in his sinuses, and the mild pain from the tumors in his mouth deepened into an ache. But it went no further than that.

Ivory was supposed to be linked to truth. He'd expected an expansion of his senses, a certain clarity of mind, but there was nothing mystical or magical about it. He'd been so sure the powder would provide a way for them to save themselves. Now he saw it had been a fool's errand all along.

He wanted to dash the box against the sand. He wanted to scream and shout. He wanted to rail against the fates.

Nayyan, the Great Mother bless her, knew him well. Her eyes reddened, understanding that the powder was useless.

Çeda stared at them both, then nodded resignedly. "We'll find another way."

Ihsan said nothing. There was nothing *to* say. He'd been holding out hope that he could fix the world before the black mould took both of Ransaneh's parents from her, and now he had nothing.

Çeda left to prepare as she could. Nayyan pulled him in for an embrace, then went to do the same. Ihsan turned to look at the horde. They were only a league away now, a black tide that would soon crash against the harbor walls, against the city itself.

And who can stop it? Ihsan wondered.

As the sound of the horde grew, the bulk of their soldiers went to defend the line of ships. Reserves were organized into three regiments, ready to rush in and overcome the breaks in the line that would inevitably come. Husamettín had called for ship's masts to be sawed down and denuded of spars, sails, and rigging. In time, over two dozen of them lay in ordered rows. Troops made up of Silver Spears, desert warriors, and Qaimiri infantry hefted them and pressed them against the harbor doors like battering rams.

Ihsan had lost track of Husamettín's preparations, but he noted the dismantled ballistae, which had been strapped below the masts, surely to hide their presence from the archers above. More interesting were the satchels some of the Silver Spears had slung over their shoulders—they were filled to bursting with fire pots.

Frail Lemi noticed the satchels as well. "Those aren't going to budge," he said, motioning to the harbor doors. "Not in a thousand years."

The big man's thoughts echoed Ihsan's precisely. The fire pots might be used to burn the doors, or even create an explosion, but the doors would take hours to burn through, and an explosion, even a large one, couldn't hope to shatter them.

Mirean archers stared down, some with looks of smugness, others with stiff, worried expressions. The demons, meanwhile, screamed, chittered, and wailed.

Ihsan took it all in with a sweep of his gaze—the rams, the wounded on their skiffs and sleighs, the three reserve regiments, the semi-circle of ships and the thousands upon thousands of soldiers preparing to defend it. Bakhi's bright hammer, it looked hopeless. What were they now but children cornered by a pack of wolves? And that was without Ashael, who loomed like a dark sentinel in the midst of the demons.

After adjusting the positions of the soldiers and the masts they bore one final time, Husamettín handed Ihsan a white pennant. "Now's your chance, Ihsan."

Taking a deep breath, Ihsan waved the pennant at the harbor's defenders atop the wall. When he saw many of them watching, he gathered himself, cupped his hands to his mouth, and poured as much power into his voice as he could. "Open the gates!" he cried in Mirean. The pain it brought on was terrible, but he didn't stop. "Open the gates! Give us shelter!"

But the archers didn't budge, and soon the pain became too much and Ihsan was forced to give up.

In truth, it had gone precisely as he expected. Even so, in all his years walking the sands of the Great Shangazi, he'd never felt like a greater failure.

Husamettín gave him a look of deep disappointment. As he turned and headed toward a group of nearby commanders, he called over one shoulder. "Best you return to the wounded, Ihsan. Things are about to get bloody."

Chapter 46

OMENTS AFTER HUSAMETTÍN left, winged demons began harrying the archers aboard their crescent of ships. Other demons stormed the hulls and threw themselves against the soldiers. Yet more skittered over the sand, squeezing through the gaps between the ships. They were met by the defense's front ranks, who had shields interlocked and spears set for the oncoming charge.

The sound was terrible: men and women shouting, demons screeching, the ring of steel rising as soldiers fought to stem the tide.

Atop the nearby wall, all hints of smugness from the Mirean archers had vanished. Many watched the horde's approach, others stared down at Ihsan and the soldiers holding the battering rams. Their expressions were grave, as if they were finally coming to grips with the fact that their enemy's fate would soon be theirs.

The first gap in their defenses appeared. Along their right flank, demons poured between two galleons and fell upon the defending soldiers. A reserve regiment charged forward, screaming as they went, and laid into the demons, pushing them back.

The line held, but they'd no more than shored it up than another gap formed, this one along the center. As the second reserve regiment rushed in, Ihsan tried again to command the Mirean soldiers, but it was useless. His mouth burned as if molten iron had been poured into it, and he was forced to give up.

All the while, Ashael gained ground. Though his eyes were hidden, he appeared to survey the battle. His broad horns swept the air as his head swiveled, and a perverted smile lit his gaunt face, as if the struggle playing out at his feet amused him.

It wasn't long before the line broke along their left flank, and it was the worst so far. Hundreds of demons poured through. It was met by the third and last reserve regiment, led by Çeda herself. She charged forward in her white armor and the mask of Nalamae, her black sword high, and fell against the demonic horde. Sümeya, Kameyl, and Shal'alara ran beside her. A cadre of Shieldwives came next, a fighting force nearly as impressive as the Blade Maidens. Last came the warriors of the thirteenth tribe.

Çeda fought with fearsome skill, and commanded the desert to obey her as well. Gouts of sand pushed the enemy back. At one point she stumbled when she was bull-rushed by a hulking demon, and those around her swarmed to her defense, cutting the demon down as Çeda regained her feet.

As they stemmed the tide, Ihsan caught movement along the ranks of battering rams. Every third soldier was releasing their hold on the masts and unwinding the ropes that held the ballistae parts in place. Moments later, they were assembling the ballistae. Two dozen were erected on wooden pedestals that would allow them to fire their bolts straight up.

The archers above hardly seemed to notice, focused as they were on the battle with the demons.

The teams of soldiers who'd constructed the ballistae each split in two. As one soldier cranked the ballista's winch to tighten the firing cord, another ran a rope through the eye of a bolt, the sort used to catch an enemy ship's rigging. The bolt was then laid in the ballista's slider. Curiously, one end of each rope was coiled neatly beside the ballista, while the opposite end was tied to the belt of a Silver Spear.

Near the crews, Husamettín had Night's Kiss held high above his head. The sword thrummed loudly in the air, a sound Ihsan had long ago come to associate with an eagerness to taste blood.

"Now!" Husamettín cried, and brought his dark shamshir down with an angry, rattling buzz.

A score of ballistae let loose in unison. The bolts streaked upward, the ropes attached to them wavering in the air like smoke from burning incense.

As they arced over the battlements, the ballistae teams pulled the ropes tight, arresting their forward momentum, then began running *away* from the wall. The hooks caught along the wall above, the ropes sizzled through the iron eyes, and the Silver Spears tied to the ropes' opposite ends were whisked upward, flying through the air until they could plant their legs against the harbor doors and fairly run to the top. It made for a peculiar sight, like the world had suddenly been tilted sideways.

The Mirean archers, caught completely flat-footed, shouted warnings. Some drew knives and attacked the ropes, but the ropes were zipping through the eyes so quickly they had no hope of cutting them. Others were felled by archers on the sand who were targeting sections of wall where the Silver Spears were closest to gaining the top. Before Ihsan could count to five, there were a dozen soldiers atop the wall and more on the way. Some were felled by the Mireans. But the Sharakhani soldiers had all been hand chosen by Husamettín. They were the Silver Spears' elite, devils with blade in hand. They fought viciously, clearing space for others. In a blink there were three large clusters of Silver Spears atop the wall.

More hooks flew from the ballistae. More soldiers, these bearing the fire pot satchels, were lifted up. Some were struck through with arrows. Others plummeted as their lines were cut by the Mirean soldiers above. But many reached the top and joined their brothers in arms, adding to their advantage. They fought the Mireans hard, driving the enemy back to make room for yet more on the wall.

Husamettín sheathed Night's Kiss. "Be ready!" he shouted, then grabbed one of the ropes and began climbing hand over hand with remarkable speed.

The Mireans were finally stemming the momentum of Husamettín's surprise offensive and starting to push the Silver Spears back when Husamettín reached the top of the wall, slipped through a crenel, and drew his sword. Night's Kiss blurred as he blocked blow after blow from the Mireans who stood against him. Even from this distance, even through the thunder of battle, Ihsan heard the sword sizzle as enemy after enemy fell to its keen edge. Husamettín pushed into the leftmost tower. A line of Silver Spears followed him while, along the righthand side, more Sharakhani soldiers pressed toward the opposite tower.

Behind Ihsan, as the battle against the demons raged, horns blew, calling for an ordered retreat, sooner than he'd feared. The broad arc of their defenses abandoned the ships and pulled back toward the harbor doors, collapsing their lines to prevent a complete rout. Grouped by nation earlier, their fighting force had been reduced to a mad mix of soldiers, be they Sharakhani, Qaimiri, or desert tribesman.

Nayyan stood near Ihsan with her shamshir at the ready. Their stalwart wet nurse was with her, Ransaneh protected in her arms. Nayyan glanced up at the wall, the look on her face echoing everything Ihsan was feeling in that moment.

"Husamettín had better bloody hurry"—she stared at Ashael, who was just crossing the line of abandoned ships—"or it won't matter if we breach the doors."

Ihsan's mouth hurt too much to reply. And what was there to say? Nayyan was right.

The winged demons had been focusing on the front lines, but more of them were swarming over Ihsan's position. One bearing a trident with a broken tooth swooped toward him and Nayyan met it with a swing of her sword, but the demon pulled up and swept in from another direction. Another smaller demon with claws like sickles joined it, and Nayyan simply couldn't keep up. She took cut after cut. Most of the damage was absorbed by her battle dress, but not all. In a half dozen places, Ihsan saw fresh blood that stained the violet cloth of her dress black.

The one bearing the trident had just struck a nasty blow to the back of Nayyan's legs when an arrow punched into its chest. Another caught it in the neck as it tried to fly away and it fell, whirling like a waterwheel and was lost in the throng beyond the front lines.

Ihsan turned to see Emre, bow in hand, nocking another arrow. Ihsan nodded to him, and Emre nodded back, then turned to fire an arrow into an ifin hurtling toward Çeda.

Ashael floated above the crescent of wounded ships. As he cast his gaze over the death being dealt in his name, Ihsan found himself wondering where Meryam might be. Was she as amused as the elder god? Were those *her* emotions playing out on Ashael's face?

As if in answer, Meryam was suddenly there, floating over the sand in Ashael's wake. For a moment, her eyes met Ihsan's, and she smiled, as if to say, "You see? I told you it would all be mine in the end." Ihsan had never reveled in dealing pain, but now he wished he could turn invisible, as she could. He wished he could appear before her and send his blade into her heart—

—A massive explosion rent the air behind him. Meryam shook in fright, then disappeared, hiding herself once more with Ashael's power.

Ihsan turned to see rock and dust coughing outward from the leftmost tower. A moment later there was a second explosion from the same tower, this one lower down, closer to the sand. A third came near the top of the opposite tower. Stone fragments rained down. Ready for it, the soldiers below lifted shields to protect themselves.

The explosions had destroyed the mechanisms that opened and closed the gates. It was meant to allow the soldiers below to push forward with the masts and force their way into the harbor. But no one was moving. They were waiting for a signal.

Hurry, Husamettín.

Even with the demons howling around him, Ihsan was transfixed by the battle along the wall. The Mireans were mounting a stiffer defense. More of their soldiers poured toward the fight. Soon, they would regain the left tower, and if *that* happened, the doors might never be opened.

There came a metallic pounding from the tower's lower hole. Then a roar followed by a loud *clink*. Several breaths later, Husamettín ducked his head through the lower hole and waved Night's Kiss back and forth. The sword buzzed, trailing darkness as it went.

"Now!" Husamettín called. "Reclaim your city!"

As one, the teams of men and women holding the masts shouted, "For Sharakhai!" and drove forward.

The masts pressed, and the right door held, but the left one was pushed back. Farther and farther it swung, and the moment a gap appeared, a line of Silver Spears rushed through it. The Mireans had sussed out what their enemies were trying to do—Ihsan could see teams on the opposite side trying to keep the gates closed—but they couldn't hope to stand against so many.

The soldiers along the righthand side, seeing that the assault teams had failed to compromise the rightmost door, dropped their masts and ran into the gap to engage the Mirean soldiers. Soon it was an outright rush, dozens, then hundreds filing through to secure the passage of those behind them.

Husamettín slipped down along a rope from the smoking hole in the tower. Horns blew again, the signal that the doors had been breached. As hundreds more began attacking the Mirean soldiers inside the harbor, the flotilla of wounded were dragged toward the gap, and the lines of warriors fighting the demons retreated further. They did so with discipline, collapsing the lines as those behind them reached the relative safety of the harbor.

Order couldn't hold forever, though. The battle was reaching a fever pitch. The demons, sensing weakness in their enemies, grew reckless in their assault. And the Mireans had managed to form a defensive line inside the harbor, slowing their advance.

Like sand through an hourglass, more and more joined those inside the harbor, but those who'd not yet gained entry were beginning to panic. A crush of soldiers pressed Ihsan backward, together with Nayyan, Ransaneh, and her wet nurse.

As the shouts around them rose to new heights, the four of them were pushed through the gap and into the harbor's interior. It was hardly a relief. The Mireans had built a stout line of defense, comprised of not only their own soldiers, but those of Malasan and Kundhun as well. Warriors wearing grinning demons masks and mounted on qirin tore into their right flank. The legendary beasts with the head of a dragon and the rear of a horse trumpeted their strange calls, and sent gouts of blue flame over rank upon rank of Silver Spears. A Blade Maiden amongst them, acting too boldly for her own good, was gored by a qirin's horns and sent pinwheeling through the air.

For all the progress they'd made initially, Mirea had now stemmed their advance, which was nothing short of calamitous. Fully half their numbers were trapped beyond the harbor doors, unable to make their way inside.

Ihsan saw the horde through the gap in the gates. The land-bound demons fought wildly, killing with fearsome efficiency. Those with wings fought with more precision, targeting the archers and those using spears to keep the larger demons at bay.

Ransaneh, still in her nurse's arms, cried inconsolably. Nayyan stared about wide-eyed. None of them could do anything but watch as the slaughter played out.

Chapter 47

WITHIN EVENTIDE, QUEEN Alansal, holding her war pins, rushed toward Davud. The powder he'd thrown into the air began to settle, spreading as it did so. Queen Alansal was caught in it. So were Davud and Chow-Shian.

One moment, Davud was coughing from it. The next he was swept away.

———— ⟵—●—⟶ ————

A god floated over rolling sand dunes. Around him were his children—simple beasts with simple souls. They prayed for his true awakening, prayed for his release from the manipulations of the One Who Crafts His Dreams.

Through those dreams, the mortal woman used the black powder to drive the god and his children toward the Amber City. A great battle unfolded. The mortals struggled. One of the young gods joined them. But what could she or the mortals do against an elder?

The closer he came to the ancient city, the more he became aware of the spear of light rising from the slopes of Tauriyat, a gateway of some sort. It sparked ancient memories, instilled in him an anger he could not fully explain.

As he struggled to remember, his dreams changed. He saw visions of other gods—elders, not the young gods who came after. He saw how he was shunned. He saw how his creations were condemned. He saw how the other elders conspired, then struck him down, before leaving this world for the next.

They robbed him of his long-awaited reward. Turned *this* world into a prison. It would have remained so if not for the ambition of a lone, mortal woman, one whose skill with the red ways was taken from her, who found a way to awaken him nonetheless.

Through the light ahead, he sensed the world beyond. Saw glimpses of it. It was just there, mere steps away. All he need do was to walk through. And why not? He deserved the next world as much as the others.

So it was that he floated up the mountain toward it. The gateway was too narrow for one such as he, but what matter was that? He need only widen it.

As he did so, he sensed others nearby: four of the young gods. He knew their names—Tulathan, Rhia, Bakhi, and Thaash—but paid them little mind as he stepped through and was lost to the world beyond.

The young gods wasted little time. They followed as the gate was closing, heedless of the damage its imperfect seal would cause to the world they left behind.

In the wake of their passage, a rift was formed, an imbalance between the two worlds. A bright, wavering miasma flowed from the gate. It spread outward, consuming all within the city. Lost were those who call the city home. Lost were those from the desert. Lost were those who hail from foreign lands. In its indiscriminate hunger the miasma consumed man, woman, and child, desiccating their bodies in moments, their screams attenuating as their flesh turned to ash.

The miasma spread beyond the city, consuming the caravanserais, the oases, the tribes who sail the amber sea. There was nothing but ruin, a desert torn asunder, a swath of devastation that would last another age as the gate slowly mended itself.

Davud slowly came to. Above him, suspended from the stone railing, was a lattice of bamboo pipes. It took him long moments to shake off the horrific vision of the miasma, the lost lives, the devastation that extended well beyond Sharakhai.

Near him, Queen Alansal lay on the cold stone of the empty hall. She blinked and pushed herself to a sitting position. Her gaze shifted to the sickbed beside her, where Chow-Shian lay still, unmoving. She was dead, a victim of the poison, the potency of the dream, or both.

Her gaze slid to Davud with a look so emotionless that Davud couldn't say whether or not she would take up the steel pins that lay on the floor beside her and plunge them into his heart.

"I didn't understand," she said slowly. "As powerful as Chow-Shian was, I thought the vision of Ashael a farce, some trick Meryam was playing on us all, or a ruse of the Sharakhani Kings."

"And now that you know the truth?" Davud asked.

Queen Alansal tilted her head and softened her gaze, as if she were listening for something. Davud heard it as well. It was the clash of steel. The shouts of soldiers. The battle for King's Harbor had begun.

Alansal stood, twirled her ankle-length hair into a ball, and speared her hairpins through it to keep it in place. "We must go, you and I." She held her hand out to Davud. "We must save them."

Davud accepted her hand, and the queen of Mirea pulled him to his feet. Then the two of them were running through the palace toward the patio that overlooked King's Harbor.

Chapter 48

ÇEDA STOOD BELOW the gates of King's Harbor and realized that Husamettín's gambit had failed. The doors to the harbor remained closed. *This is where we die,* she thought, *caught between two forces, each greater than our own.*

As she fought desperately beside Sümeya and Kameyl, a bell began to toll. At first it was barely audible over the sounds of battle, but more bells rang until the mountain was alive with it. They were the palace bells, echoed moments later by those in the harbor master's tower. For hundreds of years the Kings had rung those bells to celebrate holy days or to relay simple messages between the palaces, the harbor, or the House of Maidens. Now they were being used by Mirea, in a particular rhythm: one long note followed by three short ones, the signal for retreat.

The Mirean soldiers faltered, then stopped fighting altogether. More and more of them stared at something higher along the mountain. Çeda turned and caught movement along the slopes of Tauriyat. A qirin was heading down toward the harbor, leaping from stone to stone with liquid ease. The beast had a broad golden head, a flowing mane, and forelegs that reminded Çeda of the great, flightless birds the Malasani sometimes raced. The coat along its rump and long tail were a bright, shimmering silver. It was the size of an ox but moved with the grace of a yearling oryx.

A woman rode the qirin side saddle. Her jet black hair was held in place with two large pins. Her dress was made of golden silk. Çeda had thought her a qirin warrior but soon realized her mistake: It was Queen Alansal herself. Sitting behind her, holding tight to her waist, was a young man wearing a desert thawb and a thick winter khalat. By the gods, it was Davud. With three jaw-dropping leaps, the qirin bore them both to the harbor's sandy floor.

By then the Mirean forces had not only ceased fighting, they'd backed away, letting the throng push through the harbor doors. When all had made it through, every available soldier began pushing on the door with the ruined hinges. But the demons were both numerous and inhumanly strong. They prevented its closing, then began pushing it back. Some were starting to sneak through the gap.

Everything, all their efforts, would be for naught if the demons entered the harbor. Spotting a pair of spears lying on the sand nearby, Çeda scooped them up and tossed one to Sümeya, who understood immediately. Sheathing her sword, Kameyl retrieved another and handed it to the man in front of her, a bloodied Silver Spear.

"Take up the spears!" Çeda yelled as the three of them pushed their way through the crowd of soldiers toward the gap. "Help close the doors!"

All across the line near the broken harbor doors, spears were passed forward. Çeda stood behind the frontmost ranks, those who heaved against the door with their shoulders. There, she placed the spear against the door and pushed. So did Kameyl, Sümeya, and a hundred more. Frail Lemi was suddenly beside her, roaring while putting everything into heaving with his greatspear. It still wasn't enough. There were too many demons working against them.

Çeda turned at an odd trumpeting sound. Charging toward the door with surprising speed was a staggeringly large beast. The thing was big as a house with a bumpy shell, a long neck, and steel-capped horns jutting from its bony head. It was a gui shan, brought all the way from the forests of Mirea for Alansal's invasion of Sharakhai. On its back was a wooden platform with a rider's bench, upon which sat a single Mirean soldier, a woman who held the gui shan's reins and a long crop. She was using the crop to strike the gui shan's broad head. As the gui shan came closer, the rider yelled a single word in Sharakhani over and over. "Away! Away! Away!"

The soldiers near the gap scrambled from the gui shan's path as it lowered its head and rammed the door, trampling demons as it went. Its legs churned. Its beady eyes rolled in their sockets, and it gave a loud trumpeting call.

A second gui shan followed, this one ridden by a man with only one arm. The gui shan added its efforts to close the gate to the first's. Soldiers joined in the effort, and slowly, slowly, the door began to close, and the tide of demons was stemmed. Emre and a group of archers sent a rain of arrows into the gap, preventing more demons from entering the harbor. Finally, with a great, collective roar, the door boomed shut.

Near the harbor's quays, Queen Alansal and Davud had dismounted. Alansal drew on the qirin's reins, the beast lowered its head, and she spoke into its ear. A moment later, it rose up on its hind legs, clawed the air, and breathed a gout of blue-white flame. A sound issued from its throat, a warbling, high-pitched peal that went on and on.

The demons had begun flying over the wall, but on hearing the strange call, they winged over and fled, screeching. In moments they were gone, leaving the harbor a safe haven, proof against the darkness beyond the gates. A ragged, triumphant cheer rose up. Even the Mireans joined in. All knew the horde weren't defeated, but they'd gained a moment's peace.

By the time Çeda made her way through the crowd and entered an open stretch of sand, she found Alansal and Davud standing beside a cluster of Mirean commanders. Thousands were gathered nearby, but a circle was kept clear to allow Alansal to parley with her enemies.

Husamettín, Night's Kiss gripped tightly in one hand, was first to enter the circle. Çeda followed with Emre. Across from them, Ihsan broke through the crowd with Nayyan. Young King Hektor, bloodied and looking more than a little shaken, came next. Ramahd, standing at the circle's edge, nodded to Çeda, and Çeda nodded back.

Queen Alansal spread her arms to the six of them and spoke imperiously, "I declare our hostilities ceased." She motioned to the harbor doors, making the long sleeve of her yellow dress flare. "At least until this battle is fought."

Husamettín stood still as a statue, though Night's Kiss swayed from side to side, as if he were having trouble sheathing it. The sword buzzed, as if it yearned to taste the blood of a foreign queen.

Beside him, Ihsan spoke softly. "Will you *put* that bloody sword away?"

A beat passed, then another, and Husamettín sent Night's Kiss into its scabbard with a clack. "Why now?" he asked Queen Alansal.

"Because with the help of one of your own"—Alansal waved at Davud—"I saw the destruction of this city. I saw the desert and its people laid to waste, a victim of the young gods' conspiracy."

"You *saw* it?" Husamettín pressed.

Alansal's face was stony, emotional through its utter *lack* of emotion. She clearly didn't want to answer *how* she knew, and in the end, she didn't. She glanced to Davud, who answered for her.

"Chow-Shian shared a vision of it using zhenyang."

Husamettín seemed to take this news in his stride, but Ihsan looked dumbstruck. "Zhenyang?" he asked.

"Yes," Davud replied. "It's a powder that binds the water dancers to one another and reveals truths to them."

"And what, may I ask, is zhenyang made from?"

Like Davud, Queen Alansal seemed intrigued by Ihsan's strange reaction. Çeda suspected the queen understood how important the answer was, not only to Ihsan but to them all, or she never would have answered. With a wave toward the massive beasts whose legs were still churning to help keep the harbor door closed, she said, "We grind it from the tusks of the mighty gui shan."

Ihsan, focused on Alansal, was more intense than Çeda had ever seen him. "Do you have more of it?"

"Yes," Alansal said stiffly. "Why do you ask?"

"Because I believe we can use it to awaken Ashael."

Alansal's eyes narrowed. "*Awaken* him?"

Ihsan nodded. "At the Hollow, I spoke to the goddess, Rhia. I offered to take Meryam's place, in a gambit to learn more about this very day. She declined my offer, but I came to understand that the young gods *fear* Ashael's awakening."

"With good reason." Alansal waved toward the harbor doors. "Who can predict what Ashael might do if awakened? The way to end this is not to awaken a sleeping giant, but to kill Meryam, then lead the god back to his resting place."

"But how?" King Hektor asked. "And who's to say Ashael won't awaken when we *do* kill her?"

"Precisely," Ihsan said while peering intently into Alansal's expressive eyes. "How do you suppose an elder god will react when awoken in such a violent way? If *we* wake him, though, he may see us as his liberators. We could reason with him. He might return to the Hollow so that he may find his rest once more."

"Or he may finish what he's begun," Alansal countered, "and complete the work of the young gods for them."

"Perhaps," Ihsan conceded, "but if so, then we'll be no worse off than we are now."

There was a long silence. Husamettín was the first to agree. "I can prepare an assault against the horde in case this fails."

Nayyan nodded. For Çeda's part, she'd already agreed to this approach after the battle in the desert, so she gave her assent for the desert tribes. King Hektor followed for Qaimir.

Finally, Queen Alansal bowed her head. "I'll have the powder brought here."

"This is all well and good," Çeda said, "but it doesn't solve the larger problem." She motioned to the glittering column of light on the slopes of Tauriyat above them. "*Whatever* happens with Ashael, the gateway is still open."

"Sadly, that's true," Davud said. "I've been trying to find a way to close it since you left the city." He told them of his recent experiments, and how the asirim had given their lives in hopes of finding the secret. "I even saw a vision of your mother," he said to Çeda.

Çeda went suddenly stiff. "My mother?"

He nodded. "You probably don't remember, but Ahya came to me once in the bazaar. She sent me to find you."

"I remember, but"—Çeda felt so confused; first the acacia granted visions of her mother and now this—"why would you have seen a vision of *her*?"

"I thought one of the asirim triggered it at first, someone who'd known her in life, but now I think it was just my subconscious dredging up memories."

"Did you have any other visions of other people?"

Davud, looking helpless, shook his head. "No."

"Then why—?"

Before Çeda could finish the thought, Frail Lemi bulled his way into the circle. He towered over everyone present, even Husamettín. "It's Nalamae," he said breathlessly. "She's awake." He pointed toward the wounded on their skiffs and sleighs. "She just opened her eyes, looked about, and started walking toward the gates."

Emre looked completely flustered. "Did she say anything?"

"She said she's buying us time"—Frail Lemi turned awkwardly toward Queen Nayyan—"and that she'll be ready for *you* when it's time."

The blood drained from Ihsan's face. "She said *what*?"

Before Lemi could respond, a thunderous boom came from the harbor doors. Nalamae stood before them, holding her adamantine spear. She pointed the spear toward the doors, and its head grew bright as a newborn star. The soldiers nearest her cringed and averted their gaze. Some retreated. As the space began to clear, Nalamae pressed a hand to the shell of the gui shans, and the beasts trumpeted, then lumbered away.

Another boom came, and this one cracked the foundations of the towers to either side of the gates. The third sundered the doors themselves. They broke apart and flew inward in lethal splinters, revealing the horde beyond, although none rushed forward. The demons had cleared a path for Ashael, who floated into the gap where the doors had once stood.

He stared down with bandaged eyes and the strange black spike sticking out of his chest. Nalamae stood defiant, her spear raised. As she'd been in the desert, Nalamae was lifted into the air, but this time she seemed ready. She held her spear across her body with both hands. The light from the spear's head grew brighter, then brighter still, like a comet ready to strike.

For the first time, Ashael spoke. His words were resonant, spoken in an elder tongue now lost to the desert. A deep, mystical feeling came with it. Çeda's eyes fluttered from it. She became aware of her musculature, her bones, her blood as it coursed though her veins. It made her right hand ache so much she groaned from it.

Whatever Ashael was saying, it was clear from the tenseness in Nalamae's frame she was fighting him, but how long could she possibly last?

Realizing the others were caught in the same spell of wonder, Çeda spoke in a loud, clear voice, "Nalamae said she's giving us time." As their eyes regained clarity, she motioned to Queen Alansal and Davud. "Best we make use of it."

Chapter 49

IHSAN RETURNED TO himself with Çeda's words. Like others, he'd been
lulled to inaction by the timbre of Ashael's sonorous voice. Indeed, the
thousands of soldiers around him stood spellbound. But as more awoke and
roused their neighbors, their ragtag fighting force was returning to action.

The message Frail Lemi had relayed from the goddess still echoed in Ihsan's mind. Why would Nalamae be waiting for *Nayyan*? His first thought,
the one that frightened him the most, was that it was to do with the black
mould, the fact that she was dying. He was about to ask Nayyan about it when
he noticed Davud drawing a sigil in the air. A few paces ahead of him, a triangular portal opened. Through it, Ihsan saw a large, empty hall, once King
Kiral's audience chamber in Eventide. In the hall's center, a delicate woman
lay unmoving on a bed. A grid of bamboo pipes hung from the ceiling.

Davud stepped through the slowly rotating portal, picked up a wooden
box from the floor and returned the way he came. The portal shrunk behind
him. "The zhenyang," he said, holding the box out to Ihsan. He jutted his
chin toward the struggle playing out between Nalamae and Ashael. "Whatever you plan to do, you'd better do it now."

The group of leaders had dispersed, each to prepare as they could and to relay orders. But Nayyan had remained close by and so had Çeda. The two were speaking—what about, Ihsan couldn't say.

He accepted the box from Davud. "What will *you* do?"

The wind gusted, momentarily plastering Davud's curly hair to his head. Behind him, the spinning portal reopened. The view through it now showed the gateway itself, bright and shimmering like a waterfall. "I'll keep the gateway from opening for as long as I can." Davud stepped through the portal. "I'll leave this open so that you or any of the others can follow."

As Davud was lost from sight and the portal continued its slow rotation, Ihsan looked at the peacock design on the wooden box's lid. His heart beat madly as he levered it open. A high-pitched tone began to ring in his ears, temporarily occluding Ashael's percussive speech. He took a healthy pinch of the white powder and lifted it to his nose. It smelled of cedar and myrrh and musty root vegetables.

He inhaled it, and the world around him changed.

All about, the soldiers, the horde, the gods struggling against one an-other, the dunebreakers, the sweep of buildings beyond the piers and quays became sharper. Shapes were limned in rainbow hues, bright, almost painful to look upon. The cold air prickled against his skin. Ashael's words felt so much deeper, so much more meaningful. He felt as if he were on the very verge of understanding them.

"Ihsan?"

He shivered and turned. Nayyan stood several paces away. In one hand she held a crossbow, its string already cocked. In her other she held a headless crossbow bolt and a piece of cloth, used to create a bolt known as a powder-head. The cloth's seams were sewn with thin thread so that its contents, when affixed to an arrow or crossbow bolt, would burst on impact. Blade Maidens used them to deliver various powders: some burst into clouds to hide their movements, others burned their victims' eyes and throats.

"We should prepare," Nayyan said.

After setting the loaded crossbow onto the sand and pinching the bolt beneath one arm, she cupped the cloth in both hands. "Pour some in here," she said, jutting her chin toward the box.

Ihsan was about to comply, but paused. The clarity the zhenyang had granted him had put several things in stark relief. Nayyan's movements were

clipped, as if she were anxious. Her lips were pressed together, as she sometimes did when she hadn't yet worked up the courage to tell him something.
Coupled with the way Çeda was flexing her right hand, and the way Nayyan
was favoring her left side—undoubtedly pained by the malignant growth
inside her—their purpose became suddenly and abundantly clear.

Ihsan had planned to use the powder against Ashael himself. He could
see now *Nayyan* wanted to be the one to do it. And Çeda, having summoned
the power of the desert, was there to ensure he didn't stop her.

Ihsan closed the inlaid box. "You're not going," he said to Nayyan. "*I*
am." Çeda stepped forward, and Ihsan stepped back, keeping her at a distance. He spoke again. "Do you hear me, Nayyan? *You're* not going. *I* am."

Nayyan smiled sadly. "I'm sorry, Ihsan, but this once, you're not getting
your way."

On some unseen signal, the two of them darted toward him.

The pain in Ihsan's mouth had eased to a dull ache, but it flared back to
life as he summoned his power. "Stop," he commanded them. "Stop!"

It worked to a degree. Nayyan slowed, but Çeda was able to resist and
kept coming. Ihsan tried to avoid her, but Çeda was too strong, too fast. She
grabbed his wrist and though he attempted to wriggle free, he was no match
for her. She was just wrenching one arm behind his back when Nayyan recovered and snatched the box from his opposite hand.

In a blink, Çeda had him in an arm lock. She wrenched it painfully to
keep him in place. "I'm sorry, Ihsan."

Her words sounded dull and meaningless. He focused on Nayyan. Only
on Nayyan. "Please don't do this," he said to her. He didn't bother using his
power. A command would only delay what was happening.

Eerily calm, Nayyan laid the cloth on the sand, poured a helping of powder onto it, and wrapped it carefully. Only after she'd tied the payload to the
end of the crossbow bolt and set the bolt into the crossbow's channel did she
lift her gaze to meet his. There was no regret in her eyes, only sadness and
tears.

Her gaze flitted up to the gateway's bright, shining column. "See this
done, Ihsan"—she caressed his cheek—"then take care of our daughter."

Ihsan searched for the right words. He would say anything to go in her
place. He nearly confessed his secret—the words were right there, begging

to be spoken: *I have the black mould, too, and one day it will consume me as it nearly has you.* He could prove it. He could show her the inside of his mouth, and she might relent.

And yet the confession died on his lips. He didn't need the clarity of zhenyang to recognize two inescapable truths: first, that Nayyan was dying, and second, that *this* was her dying wish. She was sacrificing herself that others, including Ihsan, including their daughter, might live.

With that knowledge, he reached a calm acceptance. "You're the most obstinate person I've ever met," he said with a smile. "You know that, don't you?"

The quip was one he'd leveled against her often over the years. "And you're the most devious," she said with a smile that matched his own. Then their smiles faded, and she was stepping forward and kissing him. "I'll be waiting for you," she whispered, "you and Ransaneh, both." She kissed him again, then stepped back.

"Go well," Ihsan said.

With that she turned and jogged toward the fray. Only when she was out of earshot did Çeda release him.

Nalamae still hung in the air before Ashael. Her spear suddenly glowed brighter. Ashael's deep, unknowable words paused, and he seemed transfixed, oblivious to Nayyan's approach. But then his bandaged head swiveled until his gaze was fixed on her, as she set her stance and sighted along the crossbow.

"No!" Nalamae screamed as Ashael raised one hand high.

A flash of light came from her spear, so bright it burned. Ihsan was forced to throw a hand up against it, and Ashael reeled.

Nayyan's crossbow twanged. The bolt sped through the air and Ashael lashed out. A wave of darkness spread from his hand, striking Nalamae, Nayyan, and many beyond.

Nalamae dropped to the sand. Nayyan crumpled and lay unmoving.

But the crossbow bolt continued its flight and struck Ashael in the chest, just above the black spike and blood-encrusted wound. A cloud of white powder burst into the air. Ashael staggered backward. He threw his head from side to side, his horns sweeping the air and his arms waving wildly, as if he were fending off an unseen foe.

A heartbeat passed. Then two. Ashael's movements stilled. He rose upright, still floating above the ground, still bowed over the terrible wound in his chest. Reaching up, he touched the bandages covering his eyes, as if he'd only just realized they were there.

Then, with slow, deliberate care, he began to unwind them.

Chapter 50

ERYAM FLOATED IN the midst of the horde, borne through the air by the spell Ashael had cast after she'd lost her fleet to Ramahd's pathetic gambit. The necklace had made her question herself, but she'd found clarity in the moments that followed. The experience reminded her of who she was and what she wanted most. The memento of her past meant to destroy her now gave her hope. She wore the necklace as a badge of honor, a remembrance of *her* past, *her* dreams, and no one else's.

She heard sounds of echoing laughter, but ignored it.

Ahead, Ashael lifted Nalamae into the air, spoke to her in an ancient tongue. It was a dangerous turn of events. Very, very dangerous. Meryam didn't understand the tongue they spoke, but she bid Ashael to view Nalamae's answers as defiant, aggressive, even bellicose. Ashael reacted with ill temper at first, but more and more his mood was turning to one of curiosity, reflection, and, worst of all, suspicion. He was starting to unravel the dream Meryam had built around him.

Fearing that leaving him to his own devices would see all her plans unraveled, Meryam toyed with Ashael's emotions. She made him think the goddess was biding her time, gathering her power, and that she would soon strike. *Kill her,* she willed him. *Kill her and be done with it.*

It was a terrible mistake.

In the dream, Meryam had cast herself as Ashael's high priestess, a woman eager to witness the sacking of the golden city. It had worked thus far, but the moment she urged Ashael to kill Nalamae, he stopped speaking, swung his head toward Meryam, and stared down with his sightless gaze. The demons around Meryam turned as well.

She had no choice but to play the part of the submissive priestess. Ashael would tire of Nalamae. Or Nalamae *would* attack him. Only a little while longer and he would destroy the goddess and Sharakhai would be Meryam's. So she remained quiet, she remained still.

Ashael eventually returned his attention to Nalamae but his discontent grew the longer they spoke. There was a tinge of fear as well, which sparked memories of deep pain and anguish. Just what had caused that pain, Ashael wasn't certain, but he was scratching at it, picking at the scab to uncover the wound.

It won't be long now, Yasmine said.

Be quiet, Yasmine.

Soon you'll join me.

I said be quiet.

Then we'll go and see father together. Won't it be grand?

"Be quiet, Yasmine!" she shouted.

The demon near her, an eyeless monstrosity that smelled like a charnel, turned her way.

Meryam ignored it. Her offensive had come to a complete standstill. The horde had retreated, cringing from the bright light of Nalamae's spear. And Ashael was close to piercing the veil of his dream.

She had to find a way to make him angry once more. She needed him to lay waste to Sharakhai's defenders, including Nalamae, and she saw the perfect excuse mere moments later. Queen Nayyan, wearing a violet battle dress, was sprinting toward Ashael with a crossbow. She stopped, lifted the crossbow to her shoulder, and sighted along it.

Worry flared in Ashael's mind. He cast his hand before him, and a dark wave rushed outward, striking Nalamae and slaying Queen Nayyan. It killed many beyond her as well, felling them like the sweep of a mighty scythe. But it didn't touch the bolt streaking toward him. Nalamae had used her power to protect it.

The bolt struck Ashael high in the chest and a white powder burst from the point of impact in an uneven cloud. The elder god reeled from it. He shook his head as if he were being assaulted, but what Meryam felt *within* him was worse. The veil of his dream was being torn to shreds. Ashael was confused at first—struggling to discern reality from dream—but he was starting to piece it together. Memories ordered themselves within his mind: his struggle with the other elders, his abandonment, his long sleep followed by an awakening and a journey to the edges of a city that had been born half an age after the other gods had left the world.

Asleep no more, Ashael unwound the bandages around his head and stared with sunken eyes at the forces arrayed in the harbor. He gazed up at the brilliance of the gateway on Mount Tauriyat.

"No!" Meryam screamed, and ran forward.

She took the bag of black powder, the filings of Goezhen's horn, tugged the drawstring open, and threw it at Ashael's head. It made it only halfway there before Ashael lifted one hand and the bag halted mid-flight. Black powder coughed from its mouth, but none came near him.

Ashael turned toward Meryam and crouched. The scent of brimstone and charred myrrh grew stronger. The setting sun shone off the ridges of his broad horns. As he considered her, a swirl of emotions swept through Meryam. She felt exposed, vulnerable, useless. There was fear as well, but it was soon eclipsed by an unbridled fury. She had claimed Sharakhai for her own. The Great Shangazi was *hers*, no one else's. She was on the cusp of ruling the world.

Ashael's breath rasped, its rhythm slow as the tides. She was certain he was preparing to kill her. He would slay her for manipulating him, then leave her corpse to be swallowed by the sand.

But he didn't.

As the demons around Meryam stirred, Ashael rose from his crouch and turned his back on her. He floated into the harbor, surveyed the ships, the thousands of mortals struggling against his demons, then fixed his gaze once more on the gateway, the glimmering pillar of light on the slopes of Tauriyat.

The demons around Meryam, which had been watching her with a sort of hunger, turned away as well. Most followed Ashael. Many returned to the fight against the soldiers in the harbor. Some few peeled away from the horde's main body and fled into the desert. But none touched Meryam.

She had become an island, a woman alone in the world.

A high-pitched laugh echoed in Meryam's mind. It went on and on and on. "In the end, you're nothing, Meryam! Nothing!"

Meryam paused. The words had come from her own throat. Never before had Yasmine's words been spoken aloud.

Meryam shook her head. "Stop it, Yasmine."

"You aren't even worth the effort to kill—"

"Stop it!"

"—not even the lifting of a finger to end your miserable life!"

Meryam beat her head with balled fists and shouted to the sky, "I said, *stop it!*"

But Yasmine only laughed and Meryam screamed until . . .

"Meryam?"

Meryam opened her eyes and stared at the nearly empty landscape around her. The demons were gone. She could hear the sounds of fighting but couldn't be bothered to look for the source of it. Not with Ramahd standing before her, staring at her with a revolting combination of pity and disgust.

His look, coupled with the sudden and complete absence of Yasmine's voice—no, of her very *presence*—made Meryam feel hollow, a delicate ceramic vase ready to crack at the least pressure.

"Well, Ramahd?"

He strode toward her, a sword in one hand. "Well, what?"

"Come to gloat?"

"No, Meryam. I haven't."

With that he drew the sword back and slashed it across her line of vision. She felt a moment of pain, then the world went tumbling through the air. In the passage of a lone heartbeat, the red beads of Yasmine's necklace, cut from their string by the swing of a sword, pattered against the sand.

Chapter 51

CEDA WATCHED NALAMAE fall. She watched Nayyan succumb to the terrible black wave. She watched the crossbow bolt strike.

Ihsan stood nearby, dumbstruck. He blinked away tears and strode toward Nayyan on unsteady legs. Ashael, meanwhile, probed the cloth over his eyes with his eerily long fingers. He unwound the blindfold, regarded the bloody tableau before him, then spun and crouched before a woman. It was Meryam, revealed moments after the powder had awakened him.

Ihsan had reached Nayyan's ruined body. His throat convulsed as he stared down at her. He shook his head violently, a man trying to order his thoughts, then stared up at the god who towered above them. "Hear me, Ashael!"

But Ashael didn't. As he rose from his peculiar, levitating crouch, he turned toward Tauriyat with complete disregard for Meryam, Ihsan, Çeda, and everyone else. He was focused on the gateway and the gateway alone. It was strange, though. His expression seemed one of naked wonder, but the way his brow creased and his deep-set eyes kept shifting gave the impression he was troubled.

Around Ashael, the horde stirred. The demons fought, but their mood had changed. Gone was their hunger, their brutality. Instead, they seemed defensive, confused, as if they too had woken from a dream and were lashing out in response, rather than as a directive from their god.

"Ashael!" Ihsan shouted. "Ashael!"

Çeda and Emre ran to Nalamae, as did Frail Lemi, Sümeya, and Kameyl. Frail Lemi lifted the goddess in his arms while the others fought the demons back.

Soon they'd reached Ihsan, still standing by Nayyan's unmoving form. In his hands, all but forgotten, was the box of powder Davud had given him.

"Come," Çeda said to him, tugging on his sleeve.

Ihsan yanked his sleeve from her grasp. "It didn't work," he said in a flat, dispassionate tone. "He won't listen to us."

"I know"—she pointed to the demons—"but we have to leave."

He stared at her as if she'd gone mad. "Where can we go when all is lost?"

A cry rose up nearby. Shal'alara, striking in her flame orange battle dress, was leading a valiant charge with the Shieldwives. Hundreds more followed them, all fighting viciously to prevent demons from spilling unchecked into the harbor. They were buying precious time for Çeda and the others, but the cost was dear. More warriors and soldiers were falling by the moment.

Çeda pointed Ihsan's attention to Ashael, who was floating beyond the line of Mirean dunebreakers. He continued onto the harbor's curving quay then entered the shipyard. All the while, his gaze fixed on the bright gateway.

"He's going to the summit," Çeda said, guiding Ihsan toward Davud's spinning portal, "and so are we."

Ihsan didn't follow so much as allow himself to be led. They stepped through the portal into a bitter cold Çeda felt not just on her skin but in her nostrils and at the corners of her eyes. Her entire body tightened from it, which only seemed to deepen the chill.

"Bloody fucking gods." Emre, having stepped through behind her, was hugging himself. "I thought the end of days would be hotter."

They stood on a broad plateau near the top of the mountain, the very clearing where the twelve Sharakhani Kings had met with the desert gods on Beht Ihman. Clouds had formed above them. Snow was falling, a thing Frail Lemi seemed to distrust. He stared at it, brow furrowed, while laying Nalamae carefully on the rocky ground.

The gateway's shining light speared upward only ten paces away.

Standing in a circle around it were Davud and seven others from the Enclave. The wild-eyed Esmeray and the pretty Mirean blood mage, Meiying, were among them, and there were three women and two men besides, all of varying ages and nationalities. Their arms were spread wide, and they stared directly into the light. They were working, Çeda understood, to prevent the way to the farther fields from opening, but they looked tired. Some already seemed on the brink of collapse.

Closer to Çeda, Ihsan paced back and forth. His gaze was restless. His fingers drummed ceaselessly on the lid of the wooden box. Husamettín, meanwhile, had joined Queen Alansal and King Hektor. Others were clustered near them, including Yndris and several hands of Blade Maidens.

"Coming?" Emre asked, pointing to the gathering of Kings and Queens.

"Yes, it's just"—Çeda waved toward Davud—"before Ashael broke the harbor gates, Davud told me about his vision of my mother."

Emre shrugged. "He said it was a memory, drummed up from his past."

"Yes, but a memory with no meaning at all?"

"Must every vision have a deeper meaning?"

"This one does," Çeda said, recalling her discussing with Dardzada. "I'm convinced it's related to the visions the acacia gave me. They're too similar for coincidence."

The first of Çeda's visions in the valley had shown Ahya stealing the acacia seed from King Yusam's palace. The second had shown the heist's aftermath, Ahya returning to her home in Roseridge only to find Çeda missing. The third had shown Ahya searching for Çeda along the edges of the western harbor, persuading her to call out so that she could save her.

"The visions in the valley," Çeda went on, "ended with my mother coming to find me. Davud's vision showed the same thing."

Emre's gaze went distant. "That's true," he said in a slow, cautious voice, "but they also ended with you calling out to her."

"No, they didn't."

"Yes, they did. In your last vision, you overcame your fear, called out, and she found you. In Davud's, he told you to go to Bent Man Bridge at nightfall. I joined you, remember? Ahya didn't show. You got nervous and started calling out for her. You were shouting by the time she turned the corner of the old tea shop."

Gods, he was right. "You remember that?"

"Like it was yesterday." He shrugged. "I was nearly as scared as you were."

Çeda had been terrified her mother was dead. Her relief had never been greater on seeing her mother turn that corner and yell at her to stop acting like a fool.

As Çeda stared intently at the gateway, everything became clear. "My mother sent the visions."

Emre gave her a doubtful look. "You think *Ahya* sent them?"

Çeda nodded. "Davud said someone had spurred his vision. He thought it was an asir, but it wasn't. It was memma. She wants me to find her. She *needs* me to."

She thought Emre would argue—it sounded ridiculous, even to her—but he didn't. He nodded to her, the way one does when stumbling on a fond, half-forgotten memory. "I think you're right, Çeda."

For the first time in a long while, Çeda felt hope.

But Ashael was already halfway up the slope, oblivious to the battle raging in the harbor. He was passing King Cahil's palace, where some few Mirean soldiers stood on the walls and fired crossbows. All were felled with a wave of Ashael's hand.

Nearby, Çeda heard a groan, then the rumple of thick winter clothing.

"Davud!" cried Esmeray.

Çeda turned to find Davud collapsed in a heap on the frost-covered ground. The gateway was noticeably brighter than moments ago, and she swore the tugging sensation inside her felt more powerful as well.

As Esmeray and Meiying rolled Davud onto his back, his eyes fluttered open. He blinked up at Esmeray, then Meiying. When his eyes met Çeda's, he could hardly hold her gaze. He was *embarrassed*, Çeda realized.

"There's nothing to be ashamed of," she said as Esmeray helped him to his feet. "You did what none of us could have."

"I was so close. I just didn't have enough power. I was certain Chow-Shian's vision—"

Davud stared up at the sky, at the falling snow, then took in Çeda's armor.

"What is it?" Çeda asked.

"The water dancer, Chow-Shian, had a vision of me leading a snow queen through the gates of truth. I thought it meant that Queen Alansal would help close the gateway, but I was wrong. Chow-Shian saw me leading *you*."

Combined with the realization that her mother had reached out to her, Davud's words warmed Çeda's heart, gave her a sense of hope when everything had seemed so bleak moments ago. "Let's do it, Davud. Lead and I'll follow."

"I would, but . . ." His look of embarrassment deepened. "I don't know if I can. I don't have enough left in me."

"Davud?" came a deep voice. It was Frail Lemi. He was crouched beside Nalamae, who lay prone on the snow-covered ground.

Davud and Çeda approached, both with wary looks. Others gathered around. Nalamae was awake but her skin was ashen, her breath dangerously shallow.

"Take *my* blood," she said to him, "and close the gate if you can."

Davud looked terrified. "Take *your* blood?"

"All that you can, yes." Nalamae paused as a pained look swept over her. "It's all I have left to give."

"But I failed."

"Only because you lacked the power. Take my blood and go with the asirim." Nalamae motioned to the well-worn path that led down the mountain. "They'll help you find the way."

A line of bent shapes approached along the path. They were the last of the asirim, Çeda realized, mere dozens of them, and they were clearly weakened. They staggered toward the light with bowed backs and pained looks. Many walked two by two: one with some remaining strength helped another who couldn't walk on their own. The very fact that they had abandoned the trees meant that the end was near, one way or another.

Sehid-Alaz, ever proud, led them, but he could hardly put one foot in front of the other. Çeda rushed to his side and slipped his arm across her shoulders. The Sehid-Alaz of old might have declined her help. This one, the one nearing the point of collapse, didn't, and his people formed a rough circle around the gateway, several ranks deep.

"They will lend you their strength one last time," Nalamae said, "as you make your final stand."

"As *we* do," Çeda said hopefully.

Nalamae no longer looked like a goddess, but like the aging shipwright Çeda had abducted from King's Harbor. "I'm too weak," she said. "I'm ready to embrace whatever the fates have in store for me, but I would go knowing I've helped."

Shouts drifted up from further down the mountain as Ashael passed Eventide. It wouldn't be long before he reached the plateau.

"Make haste," Nalamae said.

Davud looked spent, but as he took in the wounded goddess and the Kings, Queens, and shaikhs around him, he pulled himself tall. "I'll need your help," he said to Meiying, Esmeray, and the other blood magi, who nodded readily.

Nalamae, her eyes heavy, held out her wrist and Davud tried to use his blooding ring to pierce her skin, but failed, the goddess's skin proof against mundane weapons.

"My spear," she said.

Hands trembling, Frail Lemi took up her adamantine spear, placed the point against her wrist, and slowly applied pressure. Her skin was pierced, blood flowed, and Frail Lemi snatched the spear away with a look of child-like awe. Nearby, the ghul, Fezek, was on his knees, watching intently while writing furiously in his journal.

Davud took Nalamae's arm and drank from the flowing wound. He reeled from it. His eyes rolled back in his head and he looked as if he were going to pass out, but he recovered as Esmeray held him steady. He nodded to her and then stood with her help. Meiying repeated the ritual. She'd seemed calm and confident as she knelt by Nalamae's side, but her eyes fluttered worse than Davud's when she took the blood.

When the other magi had done the same, they wove together through the circle of asirim and retook their positions around the gateway. Nalamae watched them go, her wistful smile hinting at the pride she felt for those she knew would outlive her.

Çeda knelt beside Nalamae and kissed her hand. "Go well," Çeda said.

Nalamae, her eyes growing heavy, patted Çeda's hand in return. "Hurry, my child."

A moment later, the goddess went still.

Steeling herself, Çeda left her on the cold ground, stepped through the gathered asirim, and returned to the gateway where Davud was finishing a complex sigil. Çeda, one hand held up against the gateway's brightness, watched as Davud completed the sigil and spread his arms wide, summoning the spell into being. The light suddenly dimmed, bearable to look upon once again.

Çeda became vaguely aware of Ashael cresting the nearby ridge but ignored the elder god as best she could and stared into the light. She felt the gateway's power, felt it tugging on her soul. She felt as close to death as she ever had, as if—were she to let all the air from her lungs—her soul would detach from her body and drift to the land beyond.

The notion was alluring but terrifying in the same breath and spurred her to ground herself in the mortal realm, to reach out to her mother as she had with the asirim in the past.

Hear me, memma. Hear me, for I have need of you.

Little changed save her awareness of the world beyond. She sensed the asirim on the opposite side helping the asirim who stood on Tauriyat.

Memma, please hear me.

But she felt nothing. And Ashael drifted ever closer. She saw him from the corner of her eye, hovering closer to the plateau where she and the others stood. It felt as if everything were falling to pieces. All her plans, her efforts, and those of everyone around her.

"Ahyanesh Ishaq'ava," she shouted. "You will come to me!"

But she heard no reply.

And then, Ashael reached them. Ignoring them all, the elder god stared into the light and spread his arms.

Chapter 52

IHSAN HAD STOOD in awe, truly in awe, only a handful of times in his improbably long life. The day Suad, the Scourge of Sharakhai, had come to destroy the city four hundred years earlier, had been one. That same night, Beht Ihman, when the desert gods had come to strike a bargain with Ihsan and the other Sharakhani Kings, had been another. More recently, there had been the Night of Endless Swords, when the Moonless Host broke through the doors of King's Harbor and assaulted the House of Kings. Then the shattering of the crystal in the cavern beneath the mountain.

Now this: the blooding of a god to close the gateway that had been created when the crystal broke. Ihsan watched in silence as Davud and the other blood magi pressed their lips to the wound on Nalamae's wrist and drank of her blood. Though he didn't partake of Nalamae's blood himself, Ihsan felt integrally linked to the ritual. It was the zhenyang, he knew—the sheer potency of it still coursed through his veins. It also made him feel linked to Ashael, who, like Ihsan, had breathed in a good amount of the powder. The zhenyang had created a deep connection between them, just as it had with Queen Alansal's water dancers.

So it was that Ihsan felt Ashael's anger over what the other elders had done, leaving him to rot in this world. So it was that he felt the god's uncertainty over whether he'd be able to cross over. So it was that he sensed the dark god's many calculations, and his fear and eagerness to see his fellow elders again.

Davud drew sigils in the air, and Ihsan recognized the symbology, not because *he* understood the language of spells, but because Ashael did.

As Ashael approached, more and more of the elder god's memories returned. He began cataloging his mistakes, which in turn made Ihsan catalog his. Chief among his regrets, the most bitter tincture of all, was how spectacularly he'd failed to protect Nayyan. Bad enough his own orders had led to Nayyan's developing the elixir that had given them the black mould; he'd also failed to foresee her sacrificing herself in hopes of awakening the elder god so they could bargain with him.

And it was all for nothing.

Ihsan stared down at the inlaid box in his hands. He'd been so certain the zhenyang would see an end to this long nightmare. It had awoken Ashael, as they'd hoped, but done nothing to make him listen to reason, or even acknowledge them.

Instead, Ashael had immediately become captivated by the shining gateway. It was the worst possible outcome, and he was beginning to understand that Rhia had known it would happen. She'd seen it and set him up for failure from the start.

Dost thou think thyself ready to wield the key to dreaming? she'd asked Ihsan in their shared dream. *Dost thou think* this *akin to the subtleties required to manipulate an elder? That the stuff of dreams is akin to the truths found in the waking world?*

She'd known Ihsan had hoped to stop Meryam manipulating Ashael. She'd known he would recognize her words as having come from the Al'Ambra. She'd planted a seed, knowing it would grow and lead step by step toward one logical, unavoidable result: Ihsan using the ivory powder to awaken the god.

Rhia had wanted—indeed, *all* of the young gods had wanted—precisely that. They knew Ashael wanted to reach the farther fields. They knew he would want his revenge on the other elders or, at the very least, to prove he could not be tossed aside like chattel.

Ihsan tried to share that knowledge with Ashael, tried to show he was being manipulated again, but Ashael ignored him. To the god, Ihsan was the very definition of inconsequential.

Soon Ashael reached the plateau. He towered over Davud and the blood magi, over Çeda and the asirim, over Ihsan, Husamettín, Yndris, Alansal, and everyone else who stood near the gateway. Ignoring them all, Ashael studied Davud's spell with something approaching wonder. It was stronger than he'd thought a mortal's could be, and moments later he realized why. The goddess, Nalamae, who'd stood against him in the harbor, lay dead, having given her blood to the mortals who stood around the gateway.

And there was more. The undying creatures around the magi held another sort of power. They were reaching out to others of their kind beyond the gateway. Together, they held the gate closed, foiling his attempts to widen it and step through.

But what was made could be unmade. It would only take time, and what was a few moments compared to the age he'd spent sleeping below the earth?

It took great effort for Ihsan to free his mind from Ashael's. The zhenyang's power to unite them was strong, nearly undeniable. But Ihsan's fear and anger over what the young gods had done drew him back to himself. It was dizzying to contemplate, all the levers the young gods had pulled to bring everything to this moment on the plateau, the gateway shining brightly, ready to forge a path to the farther fields. It made him wonder: where are they?

Everything over the past four centuries had been done to ensure that they would be present at the bell's final tolling. So why weren't they here? Why weren't they preparing to step through to the farther fields?

They are, you bloody fool. You just can't see them.

Suddenly, he was acutely aware of the land surrounding the gateway. The plateau was broad—mostly flat but uneven in places. The young gods could be anywhere along it, watching, waiting.

Nearby he heard Çeda calling to her mother, "Ahyanesh Kirhan'ava, you will come to me!"

Davud, his fellow blood magi, and the asirim were trying to close the gateway, but they were failing. They would succumb to Ashael's will sooner or later, even with Nalamae's power added to theirs.

Ihsan knew he had only moments in which to act. He thought of Nayyan, standing in the world beyond, watching, willing him to find a way. *I'm sorry, my love, it's too much. I don't know what to do.*

But thinking of Nayyan made him think of how she'd died, how Ashael had awoken, how Ashael had taken long moments to understand his connection to Ihsan, Meryam, and the world around him. He'd practically dismissed Ihsan and Meryam, but how would he react if he knew the young gods were involved? How would he react if he knew he'd been a part of their machinations?

It might not change Ashael's intent, but he might pause as he considered it. It might give them the time they so desperately needed . . . but only if Ihsan could put him on their scent. How, though?

The answer came as he stared at the box of zhenyang. *The question isn't where they might be found, but how to force them to reveal themselves.*

Could he do it? Could he force their hand?

There's only one way to find out.

He was acutely aware there was little time, but he took what time he could. He summoned the power of his voice. He drew on his fear over what was about to happen to Sharakhai, to the desert, and its people. He used his frustration at being manipulated for so long. He used his anger at Nayyan for giving herself to this cause and dying in the process. He thought of all the plans they'd made together, all of which had withered to dust. He thought of their daughter, Ransaneh, whose future hinged on his actions.

The pain it brought on was terrible. It drove him to one knee, and he let it come until he could take it no more. Then, gripping both hands into fists, with all his power, he shouted in the old tongue, "Reveal thyselves!"

And there, suddenly, were all four gods, standing mere paces away: Thaash in golden armor, arms crossed over a broad, muscular chest; handsome Bakhi watching with a wary gaze; silver-haired Tulathan peering into the light, either unaware or ignoring that she'd been exposed; and golden Rhia who gazed at Ashael with reverence.

Rhia was the one Ihsan had been worried about the most, but Ashael's very presence seemed to have undone her. It was Bakhi who saw the danger first. He began backing away as Ihsan lifted the box of powder, but it was too late. Ihsan flung it toward them. The box's lid flipped back, the powder flew into the air, and scattered into a cloud which enveloped the young gods.

In the moments that followed, their fears blossomed in Ihsan's mind. They didn't know precisely why he'd done it, but they worried over what the powder they'd worked so carefully to see delivered into Ihsan's hands would do to them.

Thaash, his legendary wrath flaring, drew his golden sword and stalked over the frost-rimed ground toward Ihsan. But he'd not taken three steps before Ihsan felt Ashael pause in his dismantling of Davud's spell. Thaash's footsteps came to a stop as Ashael floated toward him. Ashael's eyes glinted, starlike, from within the depths of their hollows. It felt hypnotic as the elder god regarded Thaash, then Bakhi, then Tulathan and Rhia.

Worried Ashael might dismiss them, Ihsan planted a lone question in Ashael's mind: What if the young gods had planned to leave *him* behind? Might they have concocted this scheme so that they could reach the farther field while Ashael, an affliction on the ancient world, once again remained?

Ashael's gaze slid toward Ihsan. His dark eyes blinked once, and Ihsan was laid bare.

Ashael rummaged through Ihsan's mind, but found no deception. The worry Ihsan had placed in his mind was entirely possible, and Ashael needed the truth before he unwittingly triggered some snare of the young gods' making.

And so he silently questioned the young gods. They were terrified. They resisted, an all too predictable result.

Ihsan turned to Çeda, who stood beyond the circle of blood magi, mere paces away from the gateway's blinding light. She met his gaze, looking utterly lost.

A strange calm had overcome Ihsan. It felt completely unjustified, but it was there all the same. "Go on," he said to Çeda. "You can do it. I believe in you."

Chapter 53

NEVER IN A thousand years did Çeda think she'd be inspired by King Ihsan. He was called the Honey-tongued King, the King of Lies, for good reason. He was a man she'd vowed to see dead. And yet she was heartened by his words.

Calmer than she'd been moments ago, she returned her focus to the gateway's beatific light. She knew the gateway was a tear in the fabric separating her world from the next. She knew that if the young gods had their way, that tear would lead to Sharakhai's destruction. But for the time being she ignored the weight of those facts and focused on Ahya. Hoping her mother might recognize her daughter, Çeda reached *through* the gateway. It wasn't easy—the gateway's nature was foreign to her—but the asirim helped. She felt them reaching to others on the opposite side, to those who'd already passed. Hundreds of them were helping the asirim who stood around Çeda to gain some small amount of sway over the rift between worlds. And not only those who'd died recently.

Çeda recognized Havva, the asir who expressed her anger through her bond with Çeda, and had been killed in cold blood by Mesut the Jackal King. There was Kerim, Havva's husband, with whom Çeda had fled Sharakhai into the desert before stumbling across Onur the Feasting King. There was Mavra with her children, who'd helped Çeda break the asirim's centuries-old curse. And many more besides.

It's all of them, Çeda realized.

The very notion made her intimately aware of the tattoo across her back. It depicted an acacia but was made up of the names of all the asirim. Sehid-Alaz, their King, had inked it shortly before Çeda had broken their curse once and for all.

But while she could feel each of the asirim intimately, she couldn't feel her mother.

"Memma, please," she whispered.

She heard no reply.

Nearby, Ashael whispered ancient words. It made her think of the myriad paths that had led to this time and place, made her think of the visions her mother had sent, both to Çeda through the acacia and to Davud when he'd traveled to the land beyond with Chow-Shian.

If those visions had been messages of a sort, then maybe Çeda needed to do the same and summon a memory they shared, an instance where Çeda needed her and they were reunited. She raked her memories, but her mind kept returning to their final parting at Dardzada's apothecary when she was eight.

Ahya had already taken hangman's vine, the drug that had made her forget everything but her mission: to go to the House of Kings and kill King Azad. Çeda hadn't known it at the time, but it had created a nearly impenetrable wall between them. Ahya was ready to leave Çeda behind with Dardzada but hesitated and stared at her daughter. She was abandoning Çeda to ensure the Kings wouldn't find and kill her for her mother's crimes and for the threat Çeda represented.

"Please don't go, memma."

Ahya was stark in her purple dress, dusty from the day's sailing in the desert. She hadn't taken Çeda's hands in an act of care and concern; she'd gripped her by the arms, an act of control. She blinked, an early sign of the hangman's vine beginning to work its magic on her. "Be good for him, Çeda."

Ahya had said those words before, but this time was different. This time she was leaving Çeda with Dardzada forever.

Çeda felt the world around her begin to crumble. "Memma, no!" Their life had never been stable. They'd always moved from place to place, barely staying ahead of the dangers Çeda had only the vaguest awareness of. But her mother had always seemed so resilient, an unyielding rock in the windstorm of their lives. Çeda never thought she'd be forced to grow up alone.

Ahya released Çeda and with effort focused on the front door. She'd already taken two steps toward it when she stopped, shook her head as if clearing it of a dream, then returned to Çeda and knelt on one knee. This time, she took Çeda's hands. "Be good for him," she said, and kissed both of Çeda's hands, "and remember what I said in the desert." Then she stood and walked away.

In the desert, earlier that day, Ahya had taken Çeda to see Saliah, the desert witch, who was Nalamae in disguise. On the way there, Ahya had seemed fatalistic. She'd told Çeda to read the books she'd given her, to practice with sword and shield. She'd said not to take her affinity for the blade for granted, to take her bladecraft seriously. She'd said to go to Dardzada if she ever had need.

When Çeda scoffed, Ahya immediately replied, "He is blood of your blood, Çedamihn."

"He isn't, either!" Çeda said back, adamant.

"He is," Ahya replied calmly. "And you'll understand that one day."

Çeda had wanted to be strong for her mother, but just then all she could think about was Ahya leaving. She grabbed her mother's wrist and begged, "Please don't go!"

Her mother resisted, and then lifted her opposite hand and slapped Çeda across the face so hard it sent Çeda reeling. Dardzada took her by the shoulders, thinking Çeda might try to stop Ahya again, but Çeda didn't. She stood there, stunned, while Ahya left, the bell above the door jingled, and the darkness in the street beyond consumed her.

Çeda had wanted to find a different memory. But now that this one dominated her thoughts, it felt the perfect one to use.

The light before her was blinding. The air was so cold it stole her breath. She held herself tight, feeling eight years old all over again. "Please come back," she whispered, allowing all her feelings of love and loss for her mother to well up inside her. "I need you."

She felt the asirim around her like never before. She felt those beyond the gateway as well. She felt as if she were one of them, not some distant descendant. She felt as if all of them, those few in the mortal realm and those in the land beyond, could meet in the light and hold hands with one another.

And then she felt one more. A newcomer.

A lump formed in Çeda's throat.

In the light ahead was a glimpse of gray. A shadow that grew into the form of a woman. She resolved from the light, Ahya, her mother, wearing a dress that seemed to change by the moment, woven of different cloths, different patterns. Ahya herself seemed an indeterminate age. She was young, then Çeda's age, then the intense woman who'd been tortured and hung by her feet after going to slay a King. As she came nearer, however, she resolved into a woman in a cream-colored abaya, the very dress Ahya had worn when the two of them had gone deep into the desert to witness the flock of blazing blues.

"Çeda," she said.

Her voice brought tears to Çeda's eyes. "Memma."

Ahya looked around the plateau, stared up at Ashael, then gazed at the four desert gods who stood transfixed, children before their elder. She turned a circle and took in the asirim, especially Sehid-Alaz. She stared at the men and women beyond. For King Ihsan, she had an appraising look. A displeased, even resentful one for King Husamettín, which softened to one of regret, making Çeda wonder at all that must have passed between them as she inveigled her way into his life, and as he seeded her with her one and only child: Çeda.

At last, her gaze returned to Çeda. "I'm so sorry, Çedamihn."

Çeda blinked and tears fell, hot rivers along her cheeks. "We need your help."

"I know." And with this she took Çeda's right hand. "You've forged the path, child. Now you just need to hold it."

She touched the old, puckered wound on the meat of Çeda's thumb, where Çeda had poisoned herself on the thorn of an adichara. With that touch, the old wound came alive. It warmed, then burned. The feeling traveled up Çeda's arm to her other tattoos. It wrapped around her back, rushed along her opposite arm. Soon, everywhere that was touched by ink burned with a bright energy.

Smiling, Ahya released her hand and began backing away.

"Wait!" Çeda said. "Where are you going?"

"Hold the way, Çeda."

"Memma, stop! I don't understand!"

"Hold the way." Ahya continued stepping backward until she was swallowed by the light. "Don't let Ashael or the young gods tear it open."

Nearby, Ashael seemed to be considering Ahya's final warning. Tulathan, Rhia, and Bakhi seemed enthralled, unable to do more than stare into Ashael's deep-set eyes. Thaash was different. His breath came hard and heavy. His gaze kept slipping to the bright gateway, to the blood magi and the asirim around it.

With a roar made of rage and frustration, he broke away, raised his sword high, and laid into the outermost circle of asirim. Many asirim, either too weak or too unaware of what was happening to stop him, fell to his blade. But Thaash wasn't focused on them. He pressed beyond them to reach the innermost circle and cut down one of the blood magi, a spindly man with goggly eyes. The arc of his broad swing caught Esmeray across the face, and she crumpled with a sharp cry.

As Thaash rounded on Davud, Çeda rushed forward. Her tattoos, still aflame, granted her a power she'd felt only hints of in the past. She felt alive like never before, a goddess in her own right. She deflected Thaash's initial blow. Then did so again while sliding left, blocking the god's path to Davud.

She'd managed to surprise the god of war, but he was recovering. His swings became mightier and the two of them fought viciously over the frost-covered ground. Çeda held her own for a time, but each of Thaash's ringing blows put her farther back on her heels.

Then a swing came that was too powerful to block. Çeda was lucky to escape with only a ringing strike to her helm. Her vision swam. Her heel caught on the body of the slain blood mage and she tumbled to the ground. As Thaash stalked toward her, ready to end her life, a dark shadow rushed in. Something buzzed angrily: Night's Kiss. Husamettín was suddenly there, trading blows with the god of war.

As Çeda regained her feet and tried to shake off the wound, Husamettín and Thaash fought. The King of Swords fell when he took a powerful kick to the chest, but by then he'd maneuvered the god of war around so his back was to the bulk of those gathered around the gateway. It left an opening for

Frail Lemi, who rushed in with his greatspear, Umber. Thaash spun and blocked him, and the two fought, both releasing thunderous battle cries.

Arrows tipped in ebon steel came blurring in from Emre. One clipped Thaash's ribs. Another bit deep into his thigh.

Çeda and Husamettín were both preparing to attack Thaash from opposite sides when the god roared and lifted his left arm high. Gripping his hand into a fist, he pulled his arm down, and suddenly Çeda's limbs felt heavy. She felt as if ten stone, then twenty, had been added to her weight.

She was driven to the ground. As was Husamettín and the others nearby.

The last one standing was Frail Lemi, who cried out, muscles bulging, his neck straining, his skin bright red as he fought the spell.

In the end it proved too much. Frail Lemi collapsed. Everyone—the blood magi, the asirim, the kings and queens, those fighting Thaash—were laid flat on the cold ground, unable to lift so much as a finger. As Çeda fought for breath, she struggled to maintain her link to her mother. It already felt tenuous, near to breaking, and was growing thinner by the moment.

When Thaash returned his attention to Davud, Çeda felt it all slipping away. She was certain that everything she'd fought for, that they'd *all* fought for, would be lost when Thaash slew him—Davud, after all, was the lynchpin to the spell that kept the gateway from being torn open, thereby preventing Sharakhai's destruction.

Thaash apparently knew it. His spell complete, his warlike gaze shifted to Davud. He was just stalking toward him when Çeda's tattoos flared, brighter than before. Çeda sensed it was coming from the gateway—she could feel something powerful approaching—but she could spare no time for it. The sudden vitality flowing through her tattoos allowed her to throw off Thaash's spell. With a ragged cry, she stood, lunged forward, and with a mighty upward blow blocked Thaash's swing, preventing him from slaying Davud where he lay.

Çeda thought Thaash would turn on her, or swing for Davud again, but he didn't. He stayed his sword, swung his gaze to the gateway and, with one hand raised against the brightness, peered into the light. The other young gods, though still in thrall to Ashael, stared at the gateway as well. Ashael seemed entranced too, but also wary, as if the focus of all his desires since waking was suddenly worthy of mistrust.

To the left of the gateway, a glowing sigil appeared. Another appeared above it, then three more—five in all, fanning in an arc around the gateway's brightness. The light grew less raucous, became bearable, even pleasant, to look upon. Within, a shadow could be discerned. A moment later, Ahya emerged. And this time, she wasn't alone.

Shapes resolved from the light behind her. They were tall and imposing, as Ashael was. One was black as night with eyes like stars. Another had scintillant skin and a crown of crystalline antlers. A third had eight arms which moved in dreamlike ways. Names came to Çeda: Iri, Treü, Raamajit, Annam, and Bellu. Five elders, five sigils.

As the elder gods stepped onto the snow-covered plateau, the mortal men and women around it, suddenly freed from Thaash's spell, stood and backed away. Ahya and the asirim likewise retreated, as did the young gods.

Only Ashael remained in that inner circle with the other elders. He regarded his fellow gods with a mixture of defiance and fear, and the way he bowed over the wound in his chest, the misshapen spike of ebon steel, seemed more profound than before.

The elders spoke in the same drowsy language Ashael had used earlier. How long it went on, Çeda couldn't say, nor could she understand a single word. It became clear, though, that this was a reckoning of some sort. Or a negotiation. Perhaps it was both.

Çeda feared that they'd come all this way and the young gods would still get what they wanted. Would the elder gods consider the world they'd left behind beneath their notice—might they allow the young gods to walk through the gateway, and in doing so lay waste to Sharakhai and the desert beyond?

When the elders stopped speaking, the silence felt interminable. Iri, the god with skin as black as night, stepped forward and placed a hand on Ashael's shoulder. His opposite hand wrapped around the crooked spike of ebon steel. The others gathered around Ashael and supported him.

As Iri drew the spike outward, Ashael tilted his head to the sky and released a great lament of pain. His knees buckled, but the other gods held him steady.

The spike was freed a moment later. Black blood flowed, but when Iri dropped the spike to the snow-covered earth and touched a finger to the open wound, the flow stemmed, then stopped altogether. Over the passage of several breaths, the wound was healed, becoming little more than a pucker, not unlike the small one on Çeda's right thumb.

Ashael stood taller and breathed deeply. Iri kissed him on the brow. Annam did the same, followed by the others. Their strange reunion complete, the gods turned and, with Ashael, walked beneath the arc of sigils, into the light. All but Iri, who stood and faced the young gods.

Tulathan wept. Rhia stood stock still, her glittering eyes distant. Thaash, still holding his golden sword, stared angrily at the departing gods. Bakhi, meanwhile, spoke to Iri with hands clasped, the tenor of his voice pleading. When Iri spoke, Bakhi immediately fell silent. They listened, then nodded when Iri was done. Finally, without a single glance toward the gathered mortals, Iri turned and followed his fellow elders into the gateway.

Leaving only Ahya, who stood before Çeda once more. "Sweet child," she said, and waved to the brightness behind her. "You did all of this, and with no help from me."

"You did help—"

"No," Ahya said immediately. "I wronged you in life. I *used* you." There were tears forming in her eyes. "In the end, though, you did it."

Çeda embraced her and whispered, "*We* did it. You. Me. All of us."

When Ahya released her at last, she began to retreat toward the light. "Farewell, Çedamihn."

"Farewell, memma."

Ahya's form brightened until it was all but indistinguishable from the other shifting sheets of light. The asirim followed, stepping through the gateway one after another, to be met by those on the other side. Hand in hand, they traveled to the land beyond.

Sehid-Alaz, crooked in form, so exhausted he could hardly keep his feet, watched them go.

Çeda went to him, pulled him up, and kissed the crown of his head as the elder gods had done with Ashael, as Sehid-Alaz himself had done with Çeda when they'd first met. "Go," she said to him, and led him toward the light. "Take your final rest."

As he limped by her side, Sehid-Alaz regarded her with jaundiced eyes, squeezed her hand and, when Çeda could follow him no more, smiled. "I'm proud of you, child." He stepped into the light and was met by his wife. As they walked together, their forms shifting to white, Sehid-Alaz seemed to unbend until the two of them walked proudly, unburdened at last, their heads held high.

Then they were gone, and there was peace on the plateau. The light began to dim. The pillar spearing into the sunset sky dwindled, attenuating until it was but a glimmer. Then it winked out altogether. Only then did the sigils begin to soften.

The ghul, Fezek, studied them intently with his cloudy gaze. When they faded from existence, he collapsed, his soul returned to the land beyond. In that same moment, Çeda stumbled backward, as did everyone else on the plateau. The tether drawing her toward the world beyond had been severed. The gate had closed. The world had begun to heal.

No one knew what to say, especially not to the young gods, who stood staring at the lost gateway. With it gone, their dreams had vanished. They would never follow the elders to the world beyond. Çeda thought they would be furious, and perhaps they were, but their conversation with Iri seemed to have sobered them.

To the east the moons had risen, two crescents over the vast expanse of the darkening desert. With hardly a look toward the mortals gathered on the mountain, Tulathan and Rhia held hands, stepped toward the moons, and disappeared in a flicker of moonlight. Bakhi described a line with one hand, and a wavering thread of light appeared. He stepped through it, and the thread winked out of existence with a sound like a rattlewing rousing. Thaash, the lone god remaining, *did* stare at those gathered on the plateau. His baleful gaze rested on Çeda for a long while, then on Ihsan and Husamettín. He looked as though he wanted to use the golden sword in his hand to slay them all, but he didn't. He sent his sword into its sheath with a clack. Then he turned to stone, crumbled to dust, and was gone.

As the warmth of the desert took the place of the unrelenting cold, Çeda stared down at the harbor, where the last demons were fleeing into the night. The sounds of battle faded, and an uneasy calm fell over the city.

Chapter 54

NEAR HIGH SUN the following day, Çeda and Emre were in the *Red Bride*'s main cabin. They'd managed a few hours sleep, but Çeda was wide awake. The city had been saved, but its future now hinged on the meeting about to take place.

They'd eaten a simple breakfast of flatbread and olives. They'd scrubbed themselves clean with sifted sand, clearing away the blood, sweat, and grime from the previous day's battle. Emre wore his scale armor breastplate, a wide leather belt, and thick bracers along his forearms. He carried his bow and a quiver of arrows. Çeda wore the armor of the White Wolf. She'd thought of wearing something less militant, but peace had not yet arrived—until it did, she wanted everyone to know that she was prepared to fight for her city's freedom.

"Ready?" Emre asked.

Çeda strapped River's Daughter to her side and nodded. "Ready."

They found Sümeya and Kameyl on deck sitting on low chairs and talking over cups of steaming kahve. They wore their Maiden's black. Both were wounded. Kameyl had scrapes and cuts over the backs of her hands and a brilliant purple bruise that covered the right side of her face. Sümeya had a bandage over one shoulder, visible through a tear in her fighting dress that had yet to be repaired. On seeing Çeda and Emre, Sümeya set down her cup and rose; Kameyl did not.

"You're not coming?" Çeda asked Kameyl.

The tall Blade Maiden stretched in her chair like a cat. "I'm done with politics."

Sümeya laughed. "As if you were ever *in* politics."

Kameyl ignored the gibe and waved to the harbor's entrance, where a pavilion now stood. "Just tell me how bad it is when it's all over."

The three of them, Çeda, Emre, and Sümeya, headed down the gangplank together.

Their shattered fleet was still arrayed in its defensive arc. Some few ships were sandworthy, but most were not, their struts having been ruined to create the defensive line against the demonic horde. Shortly after the last of the demons had been routed, Husamettín had ordered over a dozen galleons to be towed further into the desert and readied.

"In case Queen Alansal attacks," he'd said.

The rest of the ships remained precisely where they'd been the day before. Long into the night, they had been used chiefly as field hospitals, to tend to the wounded. Only when dawn's golden light had broken over the eastern horizon had the attention shifted to the dead. It had been agreed that each nation would deal with their own as they saw fit, and it had taken hours to separate the mounds of dead—which were intermingled with the bodies of demons—and move them to their assigned locations.

Çeda had proposed that the people of the desert, be they Sharakhani or desert tribespeople, be taken to the blooming fields later that day and buried beneath the dead adichara in honor of the asirim who had helped Davud and his fellow blood magi to prevent the gateway from opening. The other shaikhs had agreed, as had King Ihsan. King Husamettín hadn't so much approved as *not objected*. So it was that, as they headed toward the harbor, they saw dozens of horse-drawn sleighs stacked with the dead headed for the blooming fields.

It had been late into the night before Queen Alansal had finally agreed to discuss terms. The combined might of the royal navy, the Alliance, and Qaimir had been decimated. But so had Queen Alansal's navy. There was no telling which side would win if hostilities resumed, particularly with the Mirean fleet's main defense, the harbor gates, destroyed. The losses would be devastating on both sides, which was surely why Queen Alansal had grudgingly agreed to come and listen. Interestingly, although it was Ihsan who'd tendered the offer to her, it was Davud who'd convinced her. Alansal had apparently been reticent, but after speaking with Davud for nearly two hours, she'd accepted.

Çeda wondered how earnest Alansal was about working toward reconciliation, though. Now that the sun had risen, and it was clear the city was no longer threatened by the horde or the young gods, would she see things differently? Would she still try to hold onto Sharakhai?

Çeda, Emre, and Sümeya were just heading toward the pavilion when they spied King Ihsan standing near the prow of a royal galleon. His gaze was fixed on the pavilion. Or perhaps it was the dunebreakers and Alansal's navy *beyond* the pavilion that had captured his attention. In his arms was his baby daughter, Ransaneh. He held her lovingly against his chest while swaying her back and forth. Nearby, Ransaneh's stout wet nurse and two Blade Maidens stood in attendance.

Çeda, Emre, and Sümeya hiked over the sand toward him. "Have you slept?" Çeda asked when they came near.

"No," Ihsan said, jutting his chin toward the harbor, "and neither have they." Within the harbor, the Mirean navy could be seen making repairs, readying their ships to sail. Or to fight.

"Do you know something we don't?" Emre asked.

"No, but old habits die hard, and it's difficult to trust a woman who less than a day ago was ready to feed us to the horde if it meant she could keep the city." He gave Ransaneh to the waiting wet nurse, smoothed his khalat down, and waved to the pavilion. "Shall we?"

The four of them headed toward the pavilion and met Shaikh Aríz and Frail Lemi at the entrance. Emre and Aríz shook forearms, then hugged one another tightly.

"You're one lucky bastard," Emre said to Aríz, "you know that?"

Aríz had been one of those who'd led the valiant charge into the harbor, making way for more to enter as the horde approached.

"Not luck"—Aríz's puffed his chest out the way Frail Lemi often did while bragging—"but skill!"

Frail Lemi laughed and shoved Aríz hard. "A *bit* of skill." The big man stared at Aríz through a tiny gap between his thumb and forefinger. "A *bit*."

Emre pointed to a ruby brooch on Aríz's chest. "Wasn't that Shal'alara's?"

The saying went that Shal'alara had more lives than a cat, which Shal'alara herself attributed to the very brooch Aríz now wore. She'd displayed it often on the colorful head scarves and turbans she liked to wear.

Aríz, suddenly serious, touched the brooch fondly. "It was, yes. She gave it to me before the battle. She said it would protect me."

Shal'alara had died in a valiant charge to keep the demons from gaining the harbor. Aríz's own charge to gain the harbor had been every bit as brave and foolhardy, and yet he'd survived. Çeda didn't want to attribute either outcome to something so small as a brooch, but at the same time she found herself hoping Shal'alara's final gift granted Aríz a long and fruitful life.

After a moment of silence to honor the dead, all six of them headed into the pavilion, where the floor was covered in a myriad of carpets and two vast rings of pillows had been set out. The inner ring of pillows was meant for the meeting's primary participants, the outer for advisors, viziers, and honored guests. King Hektor and Ramahd were already sitting in their places in the inner ring, across from the entrance.

Çeda bowed her head to King Hektor, then shared a small smile with Ramahd. "Lord Amansir," she said.

"Çedamihn," Ramahd said back. His smile deepened, becoming familiar. Perhaps *too* familiar.

It earned him a glare from Emre, but Ramahd made nothing of it and soon he, Çeda, and Aríz had taken their places in the inner circle of pillows, while Sümeya and Frail Lemi sat behind them. King Ihsan folded himself onto a nearby pillow, somehow managing to look regal while doing so.

As the pavilion filled with shaikhs, viziers, and military commanders, Çeda's eye was caught by the curious young man in the far corner. His name was Willem. Davud had apparently discovered him hiding in the collegia. There was a bright-eyed innocence to him that warred with the general feeling of tension that pervaded the pavilion. He sat at a low table with a book, inkwell, and quill laid out before him, apparently ready to chronicle the council that was about to commence.

With Davud's blessing, Willem had taken up Fezek's journal, where he'd kept notes and formulated the epic poem that catalogued the grand tale of the gateway's making and eventual closing. Çeda wondered whether Willem was up to the task—she wasn't entirely comfortable with how she might be portrayed—but she liked the idea that the entire saga would be recorded. It was a tale that deserved retelling.

Soon, the only people missing from the pavilion were King Husamettín and Queen Alansal. An uncomfortable feeling started to settle in Çeda's gut when someone new entered—perhaps the last person she would have expected. It was Djaga, her old mentor from the pits. Çeda hadn't seen her in years. She looked older, and her black, kinky hair had a lot more gray in it, but she was still fit, her frame a match for any of the muscular statues on display in Thaash's temple.

"What are you doing here?" Çeda said as she stood and embraced her.

"I was asked not to tell," she said in her thick Kundhuni accent. She held Çeda's at arm's length and looked her up and down with clear maternal pride. "You've done me *proud*, girl. It nearly makes me forget all the skis you ruined on my skiffs."

Çeda laughed, remembering what a poor sandswoman she'd been at the time. "I can come wax them if you'd like."

"A woman of honor would do just that!"

"Then I will."

Djaga winked. "I'll brew the tea while you work off your debt."

Çeda wanted to speak further but was interrupted by the arrival of a Malasani man wearing a chiton of orange and blue, who bore a striking resemblance to King Emir of Malasan. Djaga waved to him, and the two sat together.

Next to enter were Juvaan Xin-Lei, Queen Alansal's chief diplomat, and Davud. Juvaan cut a lithe figure. His bone-white skin and straight white hair were a stark contrast to Davud's darker skin and curly brown mop. Juvaan was regal, commanding, and yet Davud, who'd come wearing the robes of a collegia scholar, was every bit his equal. Davud seemed wise beyond his years, and confident as a king.

"We're missing one," Davud said on taking stock of those in attendance. King Husamettín had yet to arrive.

Moments later, Çeda saw him through the pavilion's flaps. He wore his black armor and turban. Night's Kiss hung at his side. He was speaking with several Blade Maidens, including the First Warden. After sharing a few words in parting, he entered the pavilion. He looked much as he had when Çeda first met him: like an intense, strong-willed man of precision. The only thing that had changed about him was the mark of the traitor, the scar that had been carved by Kameyl upon his forehead. His turban was wrapped lower than it had once been, but the mark was still visible between and above his eyebrows.

As he surveyed those in attendance, his grave look turned flinty. "Where is your queen?" he asked Juvaan.

Davud answered. "I'll explain in a moment," he said while waving to the last remaining pillow in the inner circle.

Husamettín remained where he was near the entrance. "You will explain now."

Davud, perfectly composed, bowed his head. "Queen Alansal has been presented with an offer, an offer she seems inclined to accept, if all parties are in agreement." He tipped his head politely to Juvaan. "Which is why Juvaan is here in her place."

"She sends an *ambassador* to speak at a council of Kings?"

"She sent her ambassador," Juvaan said in flawless Sharakhan, "to carry your decision back to her. I am here as an *observer*, King Husamettín, to hear your reply to an offer of mutually beneficial arrangement which she has already nominally accepted. Not only is her presence not required, she felt it might detract from your deliberations. So please"—he motioned to the full gathering—"discuss. Deliberate. When you're ready, I'll take your answer to my queen."

Though it was unconventional, the approach seemed reasonable given the circumstances, though apparently Husamettín didn't agree. As his attention swung to Davud, his look darkened even further and the scar on his forehead turned red. "An arrangement she has already nominally accepted . . ."

"Yes," Davud replied.

"An offer crafted by whom?"

"By me."

It was difficult to read Davud's intentions. He must know that any sign that he, a collegia scholar and a blood mage, might be challenging or manipulating the others in the tent might provoke Husamettín. For one of the original Kings of Sharakhai, it was a given that someone like Davud would be deferential. But the way Davud was standing, tall and proud, and the way he stared unflinchingly into Husamettín's eyes spoke of a man ready to challenge, so much so that Çeda was intrigued by what he might have offered Queen Alansal, and what it would mean for Sharakhai and the desert.

"You were not granted authority to negotiate on our behalf."

"And you were not granted the right to sacrifice an entire people for your benefit, and yet that's precisely what you and your fellow Kings did. The scales were tipped too far on that night, centuries ago. It's time they were righted."

Husamettín gave Davud a good, long look. "And how does a scholar from the collegia propose they be righted?"

"By giving voice to all people of the desert. As a show of good faith, the armies of Mirea, Malasan, Kundhun, and Qaimir will leave the desert in peace. They will respect the borders that were in place before the war began."

"And assuming they do?" asked King Ihsan, his tone making it clear he was *prompting* Davud.

"They will receive better trade rights than they enjoyed in the past," Davud replied. "They will be allowed to trade with one another more freely at certain caravanserais, avoiding the need for travel to Sharakhai. This will create a boom in trade, which will spur industry, which will create even greater trade, thus offsetting the loss in increased taxes that we're proposing."

Davud became more and more animated as he spoke. His eyes lit up as he described his plan in greater detail. It was clear that he not only *understood* every aspect of what he was saying, he *believed* in it.

"That trade will be further enhanced in the years to come by a pact between our universities: we will openly share knowledge on engineering, alchemy, and the red ways, so that all may prosper. We'll set up a program to exchange students, scholars, and masters. We'll share in certain sciences, including architecture, city planning, and ship building, so that we can all capitalize on advances. Within a handful of years of its implementation, this plan will offer vast benefits to each of our five nations."

He waved to King Hektor, Djaga, and the Malasani nobleman, who was surely there to represent King Emir's interests. Djaga, Çeda now understood, had come as an ambassador for Kundhun. She had no doubt already been communicating with the Kundhuni warlords in the city.

"And you propose that we, the Kings, simply *let* you conduct such a program?" Husamettín asked.

"No," Davud said. "I'm proposing that a new *government* sanction and provide initial funding for it."

"A *government?*"

"Yes, a parliamentary system in which everyone, the people of the city *and* the desert tribes have representation. Power will be derived from an overarching covenant, which will be drafted and ratified by an interim parliament made up of—"

"You think to take power from the Kings," Husamettín declared flatly.

"Power has *already* been taken from the Kings," Davud said evenly. "Taken from all of us. At the moment, all we have is by leave of Queen Alansal, who has agreed that the city will not be ceded to her unless we agree to move forward with this plan."

"*Your* plan."

"Mine and others." Davud waved to Willem, who was furiously taking notes. "Willem played a major part in the early drafting. As did others: collegia masters who've specialized in governance, others who've studied economics, caravan masters and experts from the tribes, including the daughter of Shaikh Zaghran, who spends as much time in Sharakhai as she does in the desert. We've spoken to magistrates, to leaders of industry, to the peace-minded political leaders in the Shallows."

"You would do away with the royal houses."

"No. They and the tribal shaikhs would all be given seats in a body known as the House of Stone. Those titles will be passed down by blood, and others may be given by appointment if they so choose. Another body, the House of Sand, will have its appointees elected by various constituencies."

"Constituencies chosen by whom?"

"The dividing lines in Sharakhai would be chosen by the interim government. The desert is *already* divided into thirteen tribes. And so the people of Sharakhai, the desert, the thirteen shaikhs, and the traditional royal houses would all be represented in the new—"

"And the House of Kings would cease to be."

Davud tilted his head in an expression of denial that avoided outright confrontation. "I wouldn't put it that way. The current head of each house would still—"

"And who would rule?" Husamettín's flinty eyes scanned those sitting on around the circle. "You? Çeda?" His gaze paused as he came to Aríz. "A *shaikh?*"

Davud collected himself. He and everyone in the pavilion knew this was where Husamettín had been headed all along. "No *one* person would rule," Davud said carefully, "not completely—"

"You would have a head of state?"

Davud nodded. "A Sultan, yes."

"And who would that be?"

"The Sultan will be chosen by the senators from the House of Sand and the House of Stone." From the table where Willem was sitting, Davud picked up a stack of papers. He walked toward Husamettín and held it out to him. "It's all here, described in detail. It's subject to change. I'd like your opinion."

Husamettín took the stack of papers. A cheerless smile had formed on his lips. "Subject to change."

Davud nodded. "We can make adjustments to make this fair for everyone."

In all her time with Husamettín, Çeda had never seen him laugh. But he did then. His whole body shook from it.

Ihsan stood. "Husamettín, I've read it. You should too."

But Husamettín cut him off. "You think that I would stand by and allow this to happen when it was me—me!—who found a way to win back the city?"

Ihsan waved to Çeda, Aríz, and the other shaikhs. "I seem to recall the tribal alliance playing a rather large part in it."

"You think I would stand by and let another take my throne?"

"Our time is ended, Husamettín. Surely—"

Ihsan never finished. He reeled back, arms raised, as Husamettín threw the papers at him. They scattered over the carpets, over those gathered in a circle to talk of peace.

"Never," he snapped, and marched out.

Those in the pavilion stared at one another. No one was shocked by Husamettín's reaction. Not really. All had known he would be the least accepting of change.

Çeda went after him. "You can't do this," she called as she ducked beneath the pavilion's flaps.

He glanced over his shoulder, but kept on marching, stopping only when Çeda ran ahead to put herself between him and the galleons, his destination.

"Won't you at least read it?"

"No, I won't." He put two fingers to his lips and whistled loudly. Çeda turned to see his galleons, ships of the royal navy, obeying his order and making preparations to sail. Husamettín had clearly sensed something like this was in the offing.

"You knew this day would come," Çeda said. "You knew, even on Beht Ihman, that one day the House of Kings would fall. The only question was whether it would be from within or without." Çeda waved toward the harbor, to the dunebreakers and the palaces on Tauriyat. "As it turns out, it was both. It crumbled from within for centuries, and your enemies took advantage of that. But all is not lost. Sharakhai is wounded, but it can heal. Her greatness can be restored."

"On that count, at least, you're right. It can and it will."

"Not like that." Çeda waved to the royal galleons beyond the arc of wounded ships. "Not with you as the lone King."

"I'll tell you what's going to happen," Husamettín said coolly. Behind Çeda, the sound of winches could be heard, the clatter and clank of rigging being drawn through pulleys, the ruffle of sails catching the wind. "I'm going to board my ship. My fleet is going to sail, and then we're going to take back the city, no matter the cost. Fear not, it won't take long. Alansal was already weakening, and she won't hold a city she knows she cannot keep. Once the city is won, the House of Kings shall rule, as it has for centuries, and we will make those who've betrayed us pay for it in blood. *That* is Sharakhai's future."

He tried to bull past her, but Çeda placed herself in his path again.

"I can't let you do that," she said.

He tried again, and this time grabbed the front of Çeda's armor. He tried to throw her over his hip, but Çeda had been expecting it. She gripped his armor tight and brought him down with her.

He rolled away and came up with Night's Kiss in his hand. The sword thrummed strangely, as if it were laughing.

Çeda held her hands up, still keeping herself between Husamettín and the fleet. Behind her, several Blade Maidens had approached. They stopped when Husamettín raised one hand. Behind Husamettín were Sümeya, Emre, Davud, and the others. All had worried looks on their faces. Willem looked horror-stricken. Kameyl came from the *Red Bride*, looking ready to draw her shamshir and fight alongside Çeda, but she dropped her hand from the pommel of her sword when Çeda motioned for her to stand down.

"It doesn't have to go this way," Çeda said.

"Oh, I think it does."

He took a step forward. When Çeda didn't retreat, he lunged with such blinding speed that his sword cut into her leather breastplate, the ebon steel ringing against the bright steel studs.

He swung again, but in a flash, Çeda drew River's Daughter and blocked it.

"In a way, you're helping me." Husamettín pointed to the assembly behind him. "You, more than any of them, represent the resurgence of the desert tribes. You, more than anyone, represent the fall of the Kings. And when you die by my sword, they'll see it for the fatuous dream it always was."

He charged and they traded blows, the sort of quick strikes one gives an enemy while feeling them out.

As they regained their distance, Çeda became aware of how keenly everyone was watching, not just those on the sand nearby, but the soldiers on the royal galleons, the warriors on the tribal ships, the Mirean soldiers standing on the harbor walls.

He was right, Çeda realized. As much as she hated to admit it, she *was* a symbol. And killing her would send a terrible signal to those in the desert and the city, both.

"You want symbols?" Çeda asked. "Why don't we start with the truth about you?"

She charged, feinting low then striking high. When he blocked and riposted, she was ready. River's Daughter met Night's Kiss halfway along its length. Catching his blade against her crossguard, she powered toward him until she was close enough to reach up and grab his turban. She yanked it free as she danced away, leaving his long, peppery hair to fall about his shoulders.

Revealed was the mark of the traitor on his forehead, which Kameyl had carved into his skin after realizing that everything Çeda had been telling her about the Kings was true: that they'd made a bargain with the desert gods on Beht Ihman, that they'd sacrificed the thirteenth tribe to secure it, that they'd kept them enslaved for centuries while claiming they were the city's holy warriors, sent by the gods to protect it.

Husamettín's face turned red. Many knew about the mark, but such was his force of will, his gravitas, that as long as it had been covered, most ignored it. To those who believed in him, he was a force of nature: unbreakable as granite, vengeful as an ehrekh, permanent as Tauriyat itself.

Exposing the scar that a former Blade Maiden had given him was something else. There was no more shameful a mark in the desert. And it showed in the way Husamettín's eyes scanned the gathering ranks of Blade Maidens and Silver Spears.

"I told you that you would pay for what you've done," Çeda said to him. "To my mother. To the asirim. To the people of the thirteenth tribe and those from the west end. Your crimes are too numerous to count, but I was willing to set it all aside if you would let the city heal. I still am."

It was her final appeal, her thin hope that Husamettín might still see reason.

His answer was a lift of his long, two-handed shamshir, a charge, a swing that was accompanied by a full-throated battle cry.

Çeda dodged the powerful blow. She blocked the next, then parried over and over, giving ground, hoping Husamettín would wear himself out. But he was no normal man. The power he'd been granted by the desert gods was with him still and he pushed her harder and harder. Night's Kiss blurred. Their blades rang against one another, over and over, until Çeda's ears were deafened by it.

She blocked one blow poorly, and her arm went numb.

Husamettín took advantage with a swift upward slash to set up a vicious strike that made him look as if he were trying to fell an acacia with a single blow of an axe.

Çeda managed to block it but lost her grip on River's Daughter in the process.

As it went flying through the air, she backed away. A whistle came from her left, the Maiden's signal for *shield* and *be wary.*

She turned while retreating to see a buckler flying through the air, thrown by Sümeya. Çeda caught it, blocked two swift strikes from Husamettín, then dove away, rolling over one shoulder to retrieve River's Daughter.

She barely parried his next swift cut.

They flew over the sand, trading blow after blow. And all the while Çeda saw the mark of the traitor staring back at her. It made her think of her mother, who'd been caught and hung for her crimes, having been tortured by King Cahil. Like Husamettín, Ahya had had marks cut into her skin. *Whore*, on her hands. *False witness*, on her feet. And on her forehead, a complex design that looked like a fount of water beneath a field of stars, the ancient design of the thirteenth tribe.

As the day before when her mother, Ahya, touched the old wound on her right thumb, Çeda's tattoos came alive like burning flames. Brightest of all was the one on her right hand, given to her by Matron Zaïde to help hem in the adichara's poison. It encircled the skin around the puckered scar and wrapped around the back of her hand. Within its elegant designs were two prophetic phrases: *Bane of the unrighteous* and *The lost are now found.*

Soon, the other tattoos burned just as brightly. The one her left arm had been designed and inked by Sümeya: a peacock, its head bowed low. Above it, written in the old tongue, were words: *Savior of Sharakhai.*

The one between her shoulder blades had been inked against her will by Dardzada. She'd thought the sign had meant *bastard*, but she'd learned later, from Husamettín himself, that it had meant *one of many* and *many in one.*

Around that once-shameful tattoo was one from Leorah that recounted Çeda's role in the Night of Endless Swords, the great battle in King's Harbor. Mount Tauriyat, as viewed from the harbor, hovered over Dardzada's sigil. Around it was a retelling of the battle and its consequences, including Mesut's death at Çeda's hands. It looked like a spread-winged falcon, the tips of the wings wrapping around Çeda's shoulders and the rounded muscles of her upper arms.

Her final tattoo had been given to her by Sehid-Alaz: the acacia tree which spread across her back. Its very design was made up of the names of every member of the thirteenth tribe that had been betrayed by Husamettín and the other Kings.

What had begun as a tale of revenge had blossomed into a fight for the survival of the thirteenth tribe. But it had grown since then. Now Çeda fought for *all* the people of the desert—those who called Sharakhai home and those who came from the desert.

In the past, she'd often gripped her right hand to summon the power of the desert. As she fought one of the Sharakhani Kings, there was no need for it—whatever her mother had done the day before had changed her in some fundamental way. She no longer felt as if *she* were commanding the *desert*; it felt as if the *desert* were commanding *her*.

The hot wind gusted. The sun warmed her skin. She felt the heat of the sand and the shape of the dunes around her. She sensed Husamettín's every blow long before it came. In that moment, she *was* the desert, and Husamettín, once a King of Sharakhai, was inconsequential.

She blocked blow after thunderous blow, moving with the grace of swirling spindrift. Struck with the force of a sudden summer storm. She was the Great Mother itself, and Husamettín had no hope of standing against her.

Husamettín retreated. He blocked River's Daughter with Night's Kiss, but the sword no longer seemed triumphant, it seemed cowed. Then Çeda released a series of blows that came like a landslide, unending, unrelenting.

Husamettín fell—bloodied, wounded, and weakened from a dozen cuts. Holding Night's Kiss across his guard, he stared up at Çeda with a mix of fear and defiance.

Standing over him, Çeda swung River's Daughter with such fury that Night's Kiss was thrown from his hand.

For one long moment, the two of them stared at one another, father and daughter, both sweating in the dry desert heat, their breathing like two jackals after a long, interminable chase. Then Husamettín's look hardened. The sweaty hair plastered to his forehead only partially obscured the mark of the traitor. "Don't tell me you've found compassion now, Çedamihn."

Çeda took in all those around her. The Blade Maidens. The Silver Spears. The desert tribespeople. The ships. Tauriyat and the House of Kings. Even Sharakhai itself.

Then she looked at Husamettín.

Gone was the enmity. Gone the hatred. Gone the regret over what she might have done, what *he* might have done, to reach a different outcome. All that was left in her was acceptance, and the realization that if *she* were a symbol of the new, *he* was a symbol of the old. With it came a cold certainty that sometimes, for one thing to thrive, another must die.

That knowledge in mind, she raised River's Daughter high and brought it down across Husamettín's neck.

Epilogue

ÇEDA STOOD IN Eventide's great hall beside Emre and three hundred others. All were silent, awaiting the arrival of Sharakhai's new Sultan.

Çeda and Emre had been in the city for two weeks in anticipation of the coronation. She'd spent time wandering Roseridge, the bazaar, the spice market, noting the changes that had come over the city in the months since she and Emre had been gone. The bazaar and the spice market were rowdy again. Roseridge was quiet. The traffic along the Trough and the Spear and around the Wheel, the great circle at the center of the city, were as busy as ever. The city had become, dare she say it, normal, which was as deeply satisfying a feeling as she ever remembered having.

In the great hall, Çeda wore an elegant jalabiya of auburn silk. Her thin golden belt matched the beaten coins she'd woven into her plaited hair. Emre's tan thawb and brown khalat complemented her dress, as did the supple leather slippers and his old bracers. He'd let his hair grow back in the six months since the gateway's closing, and it hung past his shoulders. It was unruly enough that Çeda had insisted on a golden circlet.

Emre had objected at first, but when he'd looked in a mirror, he'd smiled.

"I swear to you, Çeda, my mother must have made a deal with the gods to secure so much beauty."

Çeda had rolled her eyes.

At the head of the hall, Shaikh Zaghran of Tribe Tulogal, the desert's eldest statesman, entered from a small side door and stepped onto the dais bearing Yerinde's bright spear and a red pillow, upon which lay a laurel wreath wrought from gold. Both spear and laurel wreath represented many things. Most associated the wreath with the collegia, its students, scholars, and masters, but a laurel wreath had originally symbolized *peace through knowledge*.

The spear had been wielded by Yerinde and was a reminder of the grief and strife that the city and desert had endured because of the gods' scheme. Had it been held by Yerinde only, it would represent only aggression and deceit, but it had also been wielded by Nalamae against her fellow gods, and as such had come to be seen as a righteous instrument of justice.

The twin badges of office were opposite ends of a spectrum: war and peace, the perfect symbols for the office of the Sultan of Sharakhai.

The first two rows of the assemblage had been left empty. In the third row were several officers of state: the High Magistrate, the Lord Commander of the Silver Spears, and the Blade Maiden's High Warden, who was none other than Sümeya. She'd been reinstated only the day before, and seemed to have slipped back into her former role with ease.

Çeda caught her eye and nodded. Sümeya took note of Emre, then gave her a brief, winsome smile.

Notably missing from the hall was King Ihsan. In the weeks after the gate's closing, he'd helped to solidify support for Davud's bold plans, but had later gone into hiding with Ransaneh after a failed assassination attempt. Some said the remains of the Moonless Host wanted him dead. Others said it was his own house, his descendants who thought him a traitor to the old guard. Whatever the truth, he hadn't been seen since.

The doors opened at the back of the hall and Çeda turned to look with the rest of the audience as the procession filed in. The Protectorate Council, thirteen members of the newly elected senate, came first. Then those who'd won seats in the elections that had been held three days earlier. Last to come was their newly elected Sultan, Davud Mahzun'ava, who'd been chosen by the senators themselves.

Davud had grown so much in the past few years, but in his smile Çeda caught a glimpse of the boy who had so impressed a collegia master that he'd sponsored Davud's attendance at the collegia. He beamed at Çeda as he walked along the aisle toward the dais. Soon enough he was past her row and taking the steps up to the dais. Shaikh Zaghran welcomed him to his new role as guardian of the city and desert both. Others gave short speeches, and all too soon Davud was kneeling before Zaghran, who laid the golden wreath across his brow. Davud rose, Zaghran gave him the spear, and the crowd whistled and cheered, some calling out high ululations in the style of the desert tribes.

A celebration followed. Finger food was served: huge, pitted olives stuffed with spicy peppers; lemon crackers topped with sharp cheese and dusted with saffron and dill; roasted skewers of onions, tomatoes, and cubes of lamb that had been marinated in orange, lime, and rosemary, then roasted to perfection. Drinks of all sorts were on offer, including a dozen varieties of fine araq. Near the serving table, Shaikh Zaghran seemed to be having fun with several local senators, who were pitting the araq made in Sharakhai against the famed Tulogal blend. In one corner of the room, a group of men and women were sampling the latest fashion imported from Kundhun: fermented and dried tabbaq leaves, bundled tight and smoked like a pipe.

The room was alive with conversation, and it was joyous. It was *hopeful*. Çeda spoke with many who were there to celebrate Davud's coronation. Djaga was one who'd come representing Kundhun, as she had during the peace talks. Çeda spoke with her for a long while, trading old stories of their fights in the pits and sharing memories of Osman when he was in his prime. Juvaan Xin-Lei had come to offer the congratulations of Queen Alansal and to sign the first official trade agreement, which would apparently be ratified by the senate in the coming days as one of its first official acts. King Emir of Malasan had also sent a dignitary. Qaimir, the last of the four kingdoms surrounding the Great Shangazi, was represented by Ramahd Amansir.

Çeda was standing with Emre, Shaikh Aríz, and Frail Lemi, who was regaling three stunningly beautiful women with how he'd traded blows with

Thaash, the god of war himself, when she spotted Ramahd heading toward their group bearing two glasses of rosé.

Çeda squeezed Emre's arm and broke away. "I thought you'd tired of the desert," she said to Ramahd as they met halfway.

"I did. I still am." He cast his gaze across the room and breathed deeply. "But there's something about it that never leaves you."

Çeda smiled. "I know what you mean."

He held a glass out to Çeda. "From Qaimir. From the winery I bought on my return."

Çeda accepted the glass, noting, as she had several times over the past few weeks, how miraculously free of pain her right hand was. In the days following the gateway's closure, the ever-present ache had lessened more and more until it had simply disappeared. She sipped the wine, enjoying the pear and persimmon that finished with a sweet, cut-grass aftertaste. "So, a winery . . . ?"

Ramahd smiled. "A winery."

"You had no desire to reside in Santrión?" Santrión was the palace in Qaimir's capital, Almadan, the seat of King Hektor's power.

Ramahd laughed. "I may have been wrong about never wanting to visit the Great Shangazi again, but I can honestly say that pulling on the levers of power holds no allure for me."

"Did it ever?"

He sipped his wine and shrugged. "In truth, yes, some. But those days are behind me. I'm content by the sea. I'm content to visit my vineyard and walk along the rows of grapes."

"Content with your new wife?"

When news of Meryam's death reached Qaimir, the royal houses had entered a period of escalating tensions that threatened to boil over into an internecine war. King Hektor had quelled the unrest capably, sometimes ruthlessly, and as part of the negotiations for a lasting peace had arranged for Ramahd's marriage. Ramahd, surprisingly, had willingly agreed to it.

"Lila is a fine woman," he said to Çeda. "We've come to respect one another."

"Not love?"

"Love may come in time." He motioned with his glass to Emre, who was laughing as Frail Lemi gesticulated wildly. "And you? Are you content?"

Çeda and Emre had both taken on the role of shaikh. As had been done in the desert from time to time, they ruled the thirteenth tribe together. It wasn't always easy; they were still trying to find the right balance, but it was coming. And in the meantime, they'd sailed to several fellow tribes, partially to discuss the future of the desert but also to enjoy her wonders. They'd gone to see the famed golden lake in the northern reaches of the Great Shangazi. Then the sprawling field where round geodes could be found and broken open to reveal a galaxy of fine blue crystals. Çeda had taken Emre to the salt flats where Ahya had taken her when she was young. They'd picked up the tiny shrimp and fed the blazing blues together.

"I *am* content," Çeda finally said.

Before Ramahd could say more, Davud himself arrived. "Thank you for coming, Lord Amansir," he said. "Might I steal Çeda away?"

Ramahd bowed. "Of course."

Davud, still wearing his golden wreath, held out his arm. When Çeda took it, he led her up to the empty dais. For a time, the two of them were silent as the sound of lively conversation enveloped them. It wasn't for lack of anything to say—Çeda knew there was something important Davud wished to speak to her about. But he, like Çeda, was letting the moment sink in.

"I have a proposal," he finally said.

"I hope you're not going to ask me to be a senator." Though some of the shaikhs had agreed to do so, Çeda had decided the role wasn't right for her. She'd feel beholden. She'd start to resent the position. She and Emre had nominated the Shieldwife, Jenise, for the position instead.

"No, not a senator. Difficulties have arisen in negotiations with the hardline shaikhs."

Çeda frowned. "*I'm* a shaikh now, Davud."

"I know, but you're also from Sharakhai. I need someone who can help craft policies that benefit the desert *and* the city. Anything we draft would still need revisions, of course, it's just . . ." He paused. "You're from both worlds, Çeda. I trust you. And so do the shaikhs. I see it in them, even the ones who were once aligned with Hamid. I need someone who can champion a union, not just within her own tribe, but all the tribes."

Çeda considered it. "I'll need to talk to Emre."

"Of course."

She was sure Emre would agree. He cared about Sharakhai as much as she did. In fact, this felt like the perfect place for them both. "Then I accept, pending my discussion with my better half."

Davud's smile was as broad as it was infectious. "You'll become a diplomat yet, Çeda."

"You take that back, Davud Mahzun'ava."

He laughed, and they clinked glasses and drank.

"Speaking of diplomats," Çeda said, "has there been any word of Ihsan?"

Davud's stunningly beautiful wife, Esmeray, came to the foot of the dais with a look of impatience. She had a long, straight scar on her left cheek, evidence of the cut she'd received from Thaash's blade during the battle for the gateway. Davud nodded to her and waved, a plea for patience. "No one has seen him in months. For all I know he's dead."

"And his daughter?"

"Gone as well. We're still searching. I'll let you know if we find him, but with his affliction . . ."

His words trailed away, the implication clear. Like Nayyan, Ihsan had been stricken with the black mould after drinking so many of the elixirs they'd made together. The affliction had advanced quickly in Nayyan, and even Dardzada thought Ihsan would have succumbed to it by now.

"Oh, and I have something for you." Davud retrieved a package wrapped in sage-green linen and tied with a blue ribbon from a small table nearby and handed it to Çeda. "It's a present."

It was heavy and rather book-shaped. "From whom?"

"From Willem. He's finished Fezek's work. I must admit, it almost does the whole affair justice." He tapped the package. "The two of them made real magic together."

Çeda unwrapped it to find a leatherbound book. The script was gorgeous. "Willem penned it himself?"

"He did."

"Is he here? I would like to meet him properly."

"He doesn't do well in situations like this"—Davud raised his forefinger to Esmeray, who was staring knives at Davud—"but he sends his fondest wishes."

"Send him mine in return," Çeda said.

"I will," Davud promised, and with that he left.

After the grand affair following Davud's coronation was over, Çeda and Emre stayed overnight in the palace. Çeda spoke to him about Davud's offer, and Emre quickly agreed. In the morning, Davud met with them and begged them to meet with Tribe Rafik, whose shaikh was still frustrated by the territorial lines that had been drawn up as part of Alliance.

They left Eventide late that morning in a carriage and were dropped off at King's Harbor, where they walked along the quays toward the *Red Bride*. Royal galleons dominated the harbor, obscuring the *Bride* until they came near. Their yacht looked like a skiff in comparison to the great ships of war. The harbor's doors, recently rebuilt, stood open, a sign of peaceful times.

As Çeda stared up at Eventide, wondering over all that had happened, Emre gripped her hand tightly. "Did you leave the hatch open?" He sounded worried.

She looked and saw that the hatch leading into the ship was open. "No, I locked it when we left."

"You're certain?"

"Absolutely."

Neither of them wore swords, but both bore knives. They drew them as they neared the ship. Çeda slipped down the ladder carefully, wary of thieves or assassins, and when she reached the forward cabin, she discerned a figure in the shadows. As her vision adjusted to the relative darkness, she saw a handsome man of forty or so summers with tightly cut hair sitting in one of the cabin's two simple wooden chairs. He wore a thawb, its hood currently bunched around his shoulders, and was bouncing a child on one knee, a child who'd grown quite a bit in the months since Çeda had last seen her.

It was Ihsan, the last Sharakhani King, holding his daughter, Ransaneh.

"Hello, Çeda." He leaned to one side and stared into the passageway beyond her. "Emre . . . How was the coronation?"

"What are you *doing* here?" Çeda asked.

"Please." Without taking his eyes from Ransaneh, he waved them into the cabin. "Come and sit."

"How very gracious of you to offer us a seat in our own ship," Emre said.

"I only meant to say that there's nothing to fear. I mean you no harm."

"Everyone thinks you're dead." Çeda sat on their bunk and set Willem's book aside. Emre leaned against the doorway, his forearms folded across his chest while he glared at Ihsan.

"I nearly was." Ihsan's eyes roamed the cabin's ceiling. "Seven times, by last count."

"Assassins?"

"Indeed. Most were sent by my own great-grandson, who's convinced I betrayed him and the entire house by negotiating with Queen Alansal."

"He preferred King Husamettín's way, I take it."

"Not only preferred. *Demanded it.* He wants my head to prove that the old guard is truly gone and a new one can rise to take its place."

"There are ways of dealing with such things," Emre said.

Ihsan laughed. "Kill him first?"

"Well, certainly that's *one* way, but I meant the Silver Spears. They've cracked down hard on those opposing the senate's formation."

"True, but my great-grandson's attempts on my life will naturally be difficult to prove. And my defense would necessarily require my involvement, which would open me up to *more* attempts on my life, from him or other sources."

"Other sources."

He made a show of nearly letting Ransaneh slip off his knee. Her body went tight, then she laughed. "No less than five shaikhs now have a bounty on my head."

"Tell me which," Çeda said. "We can put pressure on them to—"

"It won't matter, Çeda." He regarded her seriously for the first time. "The story of the Kings is nearing its end. *My* story is nearing its end. I cannot escape what we did on Beht Ihman. Not forever. And even if I could—"

He bared his teeth, showing his gums, which had turned dark brown, then stuck out his tongue, which had almost no pink flesh remaining—like his gums, it was mottled brown, and had small lumps on it besides.

"Then why are you here?" Çeda asked.

His eyes returned to his daughter, then he lifted her and set her back down so that her back was to his chest and Ransaneh was facing Çeda and Emre. "While my story is ending, *hers* is just beginning."

A heavy silence fell between them. Ransaneh blinked her mismatched eyes: one brown, one hazel.

"I cannot keep her," Ihsan went on. "If I do, she will die. She'll be killed when I am, and even if she somehow escapes, she'll be a target for the rest of her life. But if *you* took her, she might live. You're respected in the city. You're revered in the desert. Wherever you choose to go, Ransaneh would be safe."

"People would know she's your daughter."

"Only if you tell them," Ihsan said. "She could be a war orphan. There are plenty of them, and that would create sympathy in all who meet her. While your adoption of her would show your generosity, further cementing Ransaneh's safety."

Çeda stared at the child, lost for words. "Have you no family you could leave her with?"

"None that I trust. And even if I did, she would be found. She is an heir to my throne. She'd be dead within months." Ihsan kissed her head, which was thick with dark brown hair. "I don't ask this lightly. I know she will be a burden to you, but I hope she'll bring you joy as well. Ransaneh has been the light of my life."

"Then join us," Çeda said. "Sail with us. We'll find a place for you."

Ihsan shook his head sadly. "The moment she's linked to me, she will become a target. No one can know." Ihsan had seemed aloof and uncaring when they'd entered. Now he seemed desperate. "I'm not asking you to do this for me. I've earned every bit of your scorn. Do it for Nayyan. She sacrificed her life that we might all live. Without it, we would never had stopped Ashael, and you would never have had a chance to speak with your mother."

The gambit was a transparent one. By invoking Çeda's time with her mother, Ihsan was playing on her emotions, forcing her to recognize that those few precious moments with Ahya—a gift Çeda could never have hoped for—had only been made possible with Nayyan's final, brave act.

Emre looked to Çeda. When she said nothing, he turned to Ihsan. "You did much to atone for your betrayal of our people, but to take a child—"

Emre stopped when Çeda put a hand on his arm. "We'll take her."

"Çeda—" Emre started.

But he stopped when Çeda squeezed his arm. "She'll die without us, Emre."

Ihsan's ploy might have been transparent, but it had worked. Everything he'd said was true. Çeda had always felt as if she were not only *unwanted* by her mother, but a necessary evil, a tool to be used in Ahya's far-reaching plans. Seeing Ahya, speaking to her for that last time, had opened a small window into her mother's true feelings. It had allowed Çeda to make peace with her mother's death and given her a sense of contentment—with herself, with her origins, with her place in the world—that she'd never felt before. And it had been made possible, in part, by Nayyan's sacrifice.

And, she admitted, she owed Ihsan. She would not honor him. He'd played no small part in Beht Ihman. He'd betrayed hundreds, thousands, in his centuries as a Sharakhani King. But he'd also scoured the Blue Journals for the truth. He'd worked to uncover and then foil the desert gods' plot. He'd done as much as anyone to save Sharakhai.

Emre looked like he wanted to argue—there was still a part of him that wanted to reject anything related to the old Kings of the city—but he softened the longer he stared at Ransaneh.

Ransaneh burbled and wriggled in Ihsan's grasp. She made a sound, baby-speak, while staring at Emre, who licked his lips and swallowed hard as he met Çeda's gaze. Then he nodded to Ihsan.

The tightness in Ihsan's shoulders eased. "Thank you."

"Something still bothers me," Çeda said, knowing this was probably the last time she'd ever speak to Ihsan. "Ashael. His departure."

Ihsan nodded. "Let me guess. You're wondering why the other elder gods accepted him after going to such great lengths to bind him to this world."

It was clearly something Ihsan had given quite a bit of thought to. "Precisely," she said.

"I can't say for certain, but I have a few thoughts. At the time, Ashael and I were both caught in the spell of the zhenyang. I couldn't understand their words, but as those moments passed, I felt a release from Ashael, a feeling that his punishment had been sufficient, that he'd atoned for his crimes, or *would* in the next world. More interesting to me, though, was the impression I got from the other elders."

"And that was?" Emre asked.

"They they'd *expected* his return."

It took a moment for the implications to sink in. "Are you saying the other elders struck Ashael down *knowing* he would one day reach the farther fields?"

"That's precisely what I'm saying."

Çeda stared at him, confused. "But why?"

Ihsan shrugged. "Perhaps they couldn't kill him. Perhaps they couldn't find it in themselves to destroy one of their own. Perhaps it was some twisted form of penance. The point is I think they laid the groundwork for his return to them from the moment they drove that ebon spike through Ashael's heart and forced him into the earth."

Çeda felt suddenly cold.

It was Emre, echoing Çeda's own thoughts, who spoke, "You're saying they planned it all."

Ihsan's look was the sort a mentor gets on discovering their student has finally mastered a difficult concept. "Is it so hard to believe the elders foresaw the young gods' plan? That Ashael would be swept up into it? Remember the final, crucial verse of their poem." He recited it in a singsong voice: *"When at last the fields do wither, When the stricken fade; The gods shall pass beyond the veil, And land shall be remade."* After a pause to allow the words to sink in, he went on, "I thought, we all thought, those words referred to the young gods, but in the end it was the elder gods who passed beyond the veil." He waved, as if taking in the harbor, Tauriyat, and the city beyond it. "And can anyone doubt that the land has been remade?"

The very thought was dizzying, and in truth, Çeda didn't want to think about it. She'd felt like a pawn so many times over the course of her long and winding journey to start worrying about the machinations of elder gods. "Perhaps you're right, Ihsan."

Ihsan smiled his wry smile. "It's just as likely my mind is performing contortions to make sense of it all. But it's a theory." He turned his daughter around, kissed the top of her head, and hugged her chubby frame as if he were protecting her from a sandstorm. Tears welling in his eyes, he lifted her until her tiny, slippered feet were on his thighs and she was eye to eye with him. "You'll listen to them." His tears fell, trails of diamonds along his cheeks. "You'll be good."

After kissing the crown of her head once more, he stood and handed Ransaneh to Çeda, who shifted Ransaneh onto her right hip.

"So where will you go now?" Çeda asked.

Ihsan shrugged. "There are rumors of a cure for the black mould. It's likely a fool's errand, but I'll chase it all the same."

With her free arm, Çeda hugged him. "Then go well, Ihsan."

"Go well, Çedamihn." He turned to Emre and held out his hand. "And you, Emre."

Emre gripped forearms with him. "May the fates show you kindness."

Ihsan laughed and pulled the hood of his thawb over his head. "The fates will do as they've always done and shower me with cruelties." He tipped his head toward Ransaneh. "But hopefully they'll spare her."

With that he climbed the stairs and left the ship. Çeda and Emre returned to the deck to watch him go. He walked along the quay, weaving through the crowd, and was lost beyond the prow of a nearby galleon.

Soon a team of Silver Spears were pushing the *Red Bride* away from the dock. They were towed beyond the harbor doors by mules, where Çeda and Emre could catch the wind and set sail. When they were underway and heading east, a strong wind came, kicking up dust and sand. Çeda went down to the cabin and picked up a blanket to protect Ransaneh, but stopped when she saw the book Willem had given her.

She opened it to the first page and smiled when she saw the title: *The Song of the Shattered Sands*. It fit, she thought. It was tempting to turn to the first page, to begin reading. But after a moment she closed the cover and set the book on a nearby shelf.

Another day, she thought, and went up to deck with the blanket. There, she wrapped Ransaneh and held her close while Emre steered, the skis hissed, and the *Red Bride* heeled over an easy dune.

ASIRIM'S CURSE

Twelve Kings weep,
In desert deep,
On sand dark bargain met;
The Gods of old,
Hear story told,
Now blood will be their debt.

The Lords of Stone,
Speak low and cold,
Of price, ancestral blood,
Wave kings to field,
Poor faith revealed,
As Rhia shears fragrant bud.

King of stolen eye,
Does speak,
He of golden lake;
Granted he,
Is summer's key,
Now he shall ever wake.

With sleepless eye,
Fair King shall watch,
And rest he'll ever seek;
His weary bones,
His dulcet tones,
One close his doom shall wreak.

One is young,
His honor stung,
By pact is he brought low;
Goes he to field,

For harvest yield,
The reaper for the sown.

Draws young groom
From night's bright bloom,
A chalice dripping red;
Should brier kiss,
In heed remiss,
His life blood withered.

Sharp of eye,
And quick of wit,
The King of Amberlark;
With wave of hand,
On cooling sand,
Slips he into the dark.

King will shift,
'Twixt light and dark,
The gift of onyx sky;
Shadows play,
In dark of day,
Yet not 'neath Rhia's eye.

Winter King,
With emerald ring,
Quick and bright his blade;
His words revealed,
His fate concealed,
In blood his debt is paid.

With rising moon,
Comes Goezhen's boon,
Death, her door assailed;
Should steel lay by,

Embrace denied,
Crown black, his rage unveiled.

From deepened vale,
A King most hale,
Sincere entreaties lost;
Fought he alone,
On plain of stone,
Yet there his fate embossed.

Thaash did see,
In King of three,
A foe made long ago;
Said Thaash to King,
Your words shall ring,
Yet true name brings you low.

This Lord stares down,
On those around,
Memory hidden, and thought;
With crown of stone,
Thy will is shown,
While his cannot be sought.

As winters die,
As summers rise,
Weighty lies his crown;
Yet set aside,
Crown shan't abide,
In dreams this king will drown.

The King of Smiles,
From verdant isles,
The gleam in moonlit eye;
With soft caress,

At death's redress,
His wish lost soul will cry.

Yerinde grants,
A golden band,
With eye of glittering jet;
Should King divide,
From Love's sweet pride,
Dark souls collect their debt.

His reign began,
As taken man,
A King with loosened tongue;
With but a sigh,
Near Bakhi's scythe,
His form is drawn and wrung.

When Gods of sky,
Do close their eyes;
Dread hunger burns and aches;
Though horror grows,
Like budding rose,
By blood his thirst is slaked.

One stood pleased,
By lifeblood seized,
By day lost souls are sought;
With granted gem,
And moonlit stem,
To heel Lost Tribe is brought.

Stained are souls,
By blessed kohl,
From this they cannot run;
If lost is stone,

His fate bemoan,
Blue throne shall be undone.

From golden dunes,
And ancient runes,
The King of glittering stone;
By inverted thorn,
his skin was torn,
And yet his strength has grown.

While far afield,
His love unsealed,
'Til Tulathan does loom;
Then petals' dust,
Like lovers' lust,
Will draw him toward his tomb.

King with eyes of jade,
Did speak,
His hand waved over field;
If King should peer,
Through smoke o'er mere,
Dark trick shall be revealed.

See far his eyes,
Through cloak and guise,
Consumed by sight is he;
Yet as death nears,
Will grow his fears,
Still, blinded shall he be.

From amber groves,
And lowing droves,
A King of slender frame;
All is heard,

Of whispered word,
With eyes of blue aflame.

The whispers speak,
Of all that's bleak,
Inveigle they his mind;
In shadows deep,
Will he find sleep,
And there his reason find.

One King betrayed,
One King unmade,
King of Thirteenth Tribe;
With withered skin,
And fallen kin,
His fate the Gods ascribe.

Rest will he,
'Neath twisted tree,
'Til death by scion's hand.
By Nalamae's tears,
And godly fears,
Shall kindred reach dark land.

When at last the fields do wither,
When the stricken fade;
The Gods shall pass beyond the veil,
And land shall be remade.

Appendix

aba: a loose, sleeveless outer garment woven of camel's or goat's hair

aban: a board game

abaya: long-sleeved robe worn by women, often with a headscarf or veil

açal: rattlewings, poisonous beetles

adichara: thorned trees that only spread their flowers in moonlight; their petals grant heightened awareness and strength

Adzin: a soothsayer, a "mouse of a man"

agal: circlet of black cord used to keep a ghutrah in place

Ahya (full name: Ahyanesh Ishaq'ava or Ahyanesh Allad'ava): Çeda's mother

akhala: rare breed of very large horse, "widely considered the finest in the desert"; "giants of the desert"

Al'afwa Khadar: a/k/a the Moonless Host; men and women from Sharakhai or the desert wastes, sworn to fight the Kings

Alamante: Ramahd's second after Dana'il

Al'Ambra: old set of laws the desert tribes had used for thousands of years; precedes the Kannan

alangual: half of a whole (couple), meant to "hold hands in the farther fields"

Alansal: Queen of Mirea

alchemyst: one who works in the ways of chemicals, agents, and reagents to produce magical elixirs

Aldouan shan Kalamir: king of Qaimir, Ramahd's father-in-law

Alize: one of Okan's riders in the Traverse

Almadan: capital city of Qaimir

Altan: a collegia student collecting the names of the thirteenth tribe, sent to his death by the blood magi, Nebahat

Amal: Çeda's best dirt dog student

Amalos: a master of the collegium

the Amber City, Amber Jewel: where Çeda lives, a/k/a Sharakhai

amberlark: a pretty bird with a lonesome call

amphora/amphorae: narrow-necked bottle/bottles

Anila: a necromancer who gained her powers when Davud used her as the source of a spell that went out of control

Annam: one of the powerful elder gods who imprisoned Ashael

Annam's Crook: a peak in the Shangazi

Annam's Traverse: legendary horse race, held once every three years

araba: a horse-drawn carriage

araq: an intoxicating beverage with a strong smoky flavor

Aríz: shaikh of Tribe Kadri, cousin of Mihir

Armesh: husband of Şelal Ymine'ala al Rafik; "the man who'd done the most to shelter Leorah and Devorah after their parents had been killed"

Ashael: an elder god, abandoned in the world of mortals when the other elders left for the farther fields

ashwagandha: a healing herb

Ashwandi: beautiful, dark-skinned woman, sister of Kesaea

asir: individual asirim

the asirim: the cursed, undying warriors of the Kings of Sharakhai, members of the thirteenth tribe

Athel: carpetmonger, father of Havasham

Austral Sea: a large sea to the south of Qaimir

Avam: a cook with a food stall near the spice market

Bagra: physic of Tribe Rafik

Bakhi: god of harvest and death

Bahri Al'sir: a legendary adventurer, musician, and poet; a common figure in mythic tales of the desert

ballista/ballistae: a large crossbow for firing a spear

Behlosh: a male ehrekh, one of the first made by Goezhen

Beht Ihman: the night the Kings saved Sharakhai from the gathered tribes

Beht Revahl: the night the Kings defeated the last of the wandering tribes

Beht Tahlell: the holy day to commemorate when Nalamae created the River Haddah

Beht Zha'ir: the night of the asirim, a holy night that comes every six weeks. "The night the twin moons, Tulathan and her sister, Rhia, rose together and lit the desert floor."

Bellu: one of the powerful elder gods who imprisoned Ashael

Benan: son of Shaikh Şelal

Bent Man Bridge: the oldest and bulkiest of Sharakhai's bridges; crosses the dry remains of the River Haddah

Beyaz: a former King of Qaimir

Biting Shields: a nickname for the people of Tribe Rafik

Black Lion of Kundhun: Djaga Akoyo

black lotus: an addictive & debilitating narcotic

the Black Veils: of Tribe Salmük

the Black Wings: of Tribe Okan

Blackfire Gate: one of the largest gates into the old city; also the name of one of the wealthiest neighborhoods in the city

Blackthorn: Lord Blackthorn: pseudonym for Rümayesh as an opponent of Çeda's in the pit

Blade Maidens: the Kings' personal bodyguards

blazing blues: migratory birds that travel in great flocks, considered good luck

Blood of the Desert: bright red mites no larger than a speck of dust

Bloody Manes: a nickname for the people of Tribe Narazid

Bloody Passage: a massacre in the desert in which Ramahd Amansir's wife and child were killed

the Blue Heron: Ramahd's family yacht

bone crushers: the large, rangy hyenas of the desert

Brama Junayd'ava: a thief, Osman's "second story man"

breathstone: one of the three types of diaphanous stones; it needs blood. When forced down the throat of the dead, they are brought back to life for a short time.

Brushing Wing: name of Kameyl's sword

Burhan: a caravan master

the Burning Hands: a nickname for the people of Tribe Kadri

burnoose: a hooded mantle or cloak

burqa: loose garment covering the entire body, with a veiled opening for the eyes

caravanserai: a small village or trading post built on caravan routes; provides food, water, and rest for ships and their crews caravel: sailing ship

Cassandra: a collegia student collecting the names of the thirteenth tribe in various records

Çeda (full name: Çedamihn Ahyanesh'ala): daughter of Ahyanesh, a fighter in the pits of Sharakhai, a member of the thirteenth tribe

Coffer Street: See: The Wheel

Corum: one of Ramahd's men

cressetwing: beautiful moth; also known as irindai (See also, gallows moth)

Dana'il: first mate of Ramahd's Blue Heron

Dardzada: Çeda's foster father, an apothecary

Darius: one of the Moonless Host

dasheen: edible roots

Davud Mahzun'ava: one of Tehla's (the baker's) brothers

Dayan: shaikh of Tribe Halarijan

Derya Redknife: female rider for Tribe Rafik; "thrice Devorah's age but also thrice the rider"

Desert's Amber Jewel: a common name for Sharakhai

Devahndi: the fourth day of the week in the desert calendar

Devorah: Leorah's sister

dhow: sailing vessel, generally lateen-rigged on two or three masts

Dilara: a blood mage and member of the Enclave, sister to Esmeray

dirt dog: someone who fights in the pits

Djaga Akoyo: Çeda's mentor in the pits; known as the Lion of Kundhun

doudouk: musical instrument

Duke Hektor I: the brother of King Aldouan, slain by Queen Meryam for treason

Duke Hektor II: the son of Duke Hektor I and the rightful king of Qaimir

Duyal: the shaikh of Tribe Okan

Ebros: one of the tribes; a/k/a the Standing Stones

Ehmel: was to have competed in Annam's Traverse but broke his leg

ehrekh: bestial creations of the god Goezhen

Emir: the king of Malasan, son of Surrahdi the Mad King

Emre Aykan'ava: Çeda's roommate, her closest friend since childhood

Enasia: see: Lady Enasia

Esmeray: a blood mage who lost her ability to use magic when the Enclave's inner circle burned it from her

Esrin: a blood mage and member of the Enclave, brother to Esmeray

falchion: short medieval sword

fekkas: a hard biscuit, can be sweet or savory

fetters: a length of tough, braided leather wrapped tightly around one of each fighter's wrists, keeping them in close proximity

the Five Kingdoms: a name used to indicate Sharakhai and the four kingdoms that surround the desert

The Flame of Iri: a/k/a the Sunset Stone; a giant amethyst

Floret Row: Where Dardzada's apothecary shop is

the Four Arrows: one of the oldest and most famous inns along the Trough

Frail Lemi: a giant of a man; suffered a bad head injury when he was young; is sometimes aggressive, sometimes childlike

Galadan: stone mason Emre sometimes works for

galangal: aromatic, medicinal rhizome of the ginger plant

gallows moth: beautiful moth; sign of imminent death but also, to those who know it as cressetwing or irindai, it is considered a sign of luck

Ganahil: capital city of Kundhun

Gelasira: Savior of Ishmantep; former wearer of Çeda's sword

ghee: clarified liquid butter

Ghiza: elderly neighbor of Çeda & Emre

ghutrah: a veil-like headpiece worn by men; an agal keeps it in place

Goezhen the Wicked: god of chaos and vengeance, creator of the ehrekh and other dark creatures of the desert

golden chalice of Bahri Al'sir: from Tribe Narazid to the winner of Annam's Traverse

Goldenhill: an affluent district of Sharakhai

Gravemaker: the name of King Külaşan's morning star

greaves: plate armor for the leg, set between the knee and the ankle

Guhldrathen: name of the ehrekh Meryam consults

Haddad: a caravan owner from Malasan

Haddah: the river that runs through Sharakhai, dry for most of the year

Hajesh: Melis's oldest sister

hajib: term of respect (not to be confused with hijab)

Halarijan: the tribe of Sim and Verda; a/k/a the White Trees

Halim: Lord of the Burning Hands (of Tribe Kadri); the tribe's shaikh

Hall of Swords: where the Blade Maidens learn and train

Hallowsgate: one of the twelve towers spaced along the city's outer wall; is "due west of Tauriyat and the House of Kings, at the terminus of the street known as the Spear"

Halond: a craftsman, wanders the desert looking for lightning strikes

Haluk Emet'ava: a captain of the Silver Spears, "a tower of a man" a/k/a "the Oak of the Guard"

Hamid Malahin'ava: one of Macide's men and a childhood friend of Çeda & Emre

Hamzakiir: son of Külaşan, the Wandering King

a hand: a unit of five Blade Maidens

hangman's vine: a distillation that can make one lose one's memories

Hasenn: a Blade Maiden

Hathahn: Djaga's final opponent in the fighting pits before she retired

hauberk: chainmail tunic

Havasham: handsome son of Athel the carpetmonger

Hazghad Road: See: The Wheel

Hefaz: a cobbler

Hefhi: carpet maker

Hidi: one twin fathered by the trickster god, Onondu; brother is Makuo. Hidi is "the angry one"

hijab: Islamic headscarf (not to be confused with hajib)

the Hill: where the Kings live; a/k/a Tauriyat

Hoav: driver who takes Ramahd to the inner docks

House of Kings: a collective name for the House of Maidens and the thirteen palaces on Tauriyat, the home of the Kings of Sharakhai

Hundi: the fifth day of the week in the desert calendar

Ibrahim: old storyteller

Ib'Saim: a stall owner from the bazaar

ifin: an eyeless, bat-like creature with two sets of wings, a creation of Goezhen

Irem: a spy for Hamid

Irhüd's Finger: a desert landmark; a tall standing stone

Iri: an elder god, called three times before the sun awoke in the heavens

Iri's Four Sacred Stones: a/k/a the Tears of Tulathan (Result of the breaking of the Sunset Stone)

irindai: beautiful moth; also known as a cressetwing, considered a sign of luck (But see also: gallows moth)

Ishaq Kirhan'ava: Macide's father and Çeda's grandfather, one-time leader of the Moonless Host, Shaikh of the newly formed thirteenth tribe

Ishmantep: a large caravanserai on the eastern route from Sharakhai to Malasan

Iyesa Külaşan'ava al Masal: Külaşan's dead daughter

The Jackal's Tail: smoke house known as a seedy place

jalabiya: a loose-fitting hooded gown or robe

Jalize: a Blade Maiden and one of Sümeya's hand

Jein: Mala's sister

Jenise: a Shieldwife

Jewel of the Desert: Sharakhai

Jherrok: shaikh of Tribe Narazid, a tall man

Juvaan Xin-Lei: albino from Mirea and Mirea's ambassador to Sharakhai

Kadir: works for "a powerful woman," i.e., Rümayesh

Kadri: See "Tribe Kadri"

kaftan: alternate spelling

kahve: a bean, a stimulant when ground and brewed to make a hot drink

Kameyl: a Blade Maiden and one of Sümeya's hand

Kannan: laws written by the Kings and based on the much older Al'Ambra, the laws of the desert tribes

Kavi: a jeweler

keffiyeh: a cotton headdress

kefir: a milk drink

Kenan: one of the tribes

kenshar: a curved knife

Kesaea: a princess of the thousand tribes, sister of Ashwandi

ketch: small sailing ship

khalat: a long-sleeved, Mirean silk outer robe

khet: a copper coin

Khyrn: see "Old Khyrn"

kiai: a percussive sound used when striking an opponent

King Azad: King of Thorns; makes mysterious draughts, never sleeps

King Beşir: King of Shadows, can move between shadows

King Cahil: the Confessor King, the King of Truth; known to be cruel

King Husamettín: the King of Swords and Lord of the Blade Maidens

King Ihsan: the Honey-tongued King, serves as Sharakhai's chief ambassador, known to be plotting and conniving

King Kiral: supreme among the Twelve Kings; "with burning eyes and pock-marked skin"

King Külaşan: the Wandering King, the The Lost King

King Mesut: the Jackal King, Lord of the Asirim

King Onur: once known as the King of Spears, more often referred to as the Feasting King or the King of Sloth

King Sukru: the Reaping King, controls the asirim through use of a magical whip

King Yusam: the Jade-Eyed King; sees visions in a magical mere granted by the gods

King Zeheb: the King of Whispers, rumored he can hear speech from far away, particularly when it relates to the Kings' business

King of Glittering Stone: appears in the poem; a cipher

King's Harbor: where Sharakhai's war ships dock

Kirhan: Macide's grandfather

the Knot: a district in Sharakhai; a "veritable maze of mudbrick"

kufi: a hat

Kundhun: a kingdom west of Sharakhai and the Shangazi Desert, a vast grassland

Kundhunese: a people, a language

Kundhuni: adjectival form

Kydze: (f) one of the best fighters to come out of Kundhun since Çeda's own mentor, Djaga

Lady Enasia: Matron Zohra's companion

Lady Kialiss of Almadan: a dirt dog, one of Djaga's opponents

Lasdi: the sixth day of the week in the desert calendar

lassi: a yogurt drink

lateen: a rig with a triangular sail (lateen sail) bent to a yard hoisted to the head of a low mast

Leorah Mikel'ava al Rafik: Devorah's sister, Ihsaq's mother, Çeda's great-grandmother

Lina: a girl in one of Çeda's childhood memories

Lord Veşdi: King Külaşan's eldest living son; Master of Coin

Macide Ishaq'ava: leader of the Moonless Host

Mae: a qirin warrior in service to Queen Alansal of Mirea

Makuo: one twin fathered by the trickster god, Onondu; brother is Hidi

Malahndi: the second day of the week in the desert calendar

Malasan: a kingdom east of Sharakhai and the Shangazi Desert

Malasani: inhabitant of Malasan

Masal: one of the tribes; a/k/a the Shining Spears

Master Nezahum: a woman on the faculty of the collegium

Matrons: healers and trainers from the House of Maidens

Matron Zohra: an aging woman, owner of an estate in Sharakhai

Mazandir: a large caravanserai on the southern route from Sharakhai to Qaimir

Meiying: a powerful Mirean blood mage, one of the Enclave's inner circle

Melis: a Blade Maiden and one of Sümeya's hand, daughter of King Yusam

Meliz: former dirt dog, Djaga's mentor

Memma: like "mommy"

Meryam: Queen of Qaimir; sister of the murdered Yasmine, aunt of the murdered Rehann; a powerful blood mage

merlon: on a battlement, the solid part between two crenels

Mihir Halim'ava al Kadri: son of the desert shaikh of the Kadri, Halim

mind's flight: one of the three types of diaphanous stones; is said to bestow the gift of mind-reading when swallowed, though the imbiber dies rather quickly

Mirea: a kingdom north of Sharakhai and the Shangazi Desert

Mirean: adjectival form

the Moonless Host: a/k/a Al'afwa Khadar; men and women of the twelve tribes that once ruled the entirety of the Shangazi Desert; sworn to fight the Kings

Mykal: Ramahd's nephew and pageboy

nahcolite: a carbonate mineral, naturally occurring sodium bicarbonate

Nalamae: the goddess who created the River Haddah in the Great Shangazi desert, the youngest of the desert gods

Narazid: a desert tribe; a/k/a the Bloody Manes

Navakahm: captain of the Silver Spears, Lord of the Guard

Nayyan: First Warden before Sümeya, daughter of King Azad, Sümeya's one-time lover

Nebahat: a powerful Malasani blood mage, one of the Enclave's inner circle

Neylana: shaikh of Tribe Kenan

nigella seeds: a spice used in desert cuisine

Night Lily: a sleeping draught

Night's Kiss: the blade the dark god, Goezhen, had granted to Husamettín on Beht Ihman

Nijin: a desert harbor

niqab: veil made of lightweight opaque fabric; leaves only the eyes uncovered

Nirendra: a slumlord lady, rents space in rooms

Old Khyrn Rellana'ala: judge from Tribe Rafik

Old Nur: a shipmate of Emre's

Onondu: the trickster god, "God of the Endless Hills," god of vengeance in Kundhun; father of the godling twins Hidi & Makuo

Ophir's: the oldest standing brewery in Sharakhai

Ornük: Urdman's son

oryx: large antelope

Osman: owner of the pits, a retired pit fighter and a one-time lover of Çeda's

oud: a kind of lute

pauldrons: shoulder guards

Pelam: the master of games, the announcer for the gladiatorial bouts held in the pits

pennon: flag, pennant

Phelia: one of Melis's sisters

physic: a medical doctor

prat: an incompetent or ineffectual person

Prayna: a powerful Sharakhani blood mage, one of the Enclave's inner circle

Qaimir: a kingdom south of Sharakhai and the Shangazi Desert

Qaimiri: adjectival form

qanun: musical instrument, a large zither

Quanlang: a province in Mirea

Queen Alansal: of Mirea

Quezada: one of Ramahd's men

Raamajit: one of the powerful elder gods who imprisoned Ashael

Rafa: Emre's brother

Rafik: one of the tribes; a/k/a the Biting Shields

Rafiro: one of Ramahd's men

rahl: a unit of currency, gold coins stamped with the mark of the Kings

ral shahnad: "summer's fire," the distilled essence of a rare flower found only in the furthest reaches of Kundhun

Ramahd shan Amansir: of House Amansir; one of only 4 survivors of the Bloody Passage

Rasel: Scourge of the Black Veils; former wearer of River's Daughter

rattlewings: see "açal"

The Reaping King: a/k/a King Sukru, one of the twelve; commands the asirim by use of a magical whip rebab: a bowed string musical instrument

Red Crescent: a neighborhood near the quays of the western harbor

Rehann: Ramahd's murdered daughter, Meryam's niece

Rengin: footman on Matron Zohra's estate

Rhia: goddess of dreams and ambition, the sister moon of the goddess Tulathan

River Haddah: created by the goddess Nalamae in the Great Shangazi desert

River's Daughter: the name of Çeda's sword

Roseridge: Çeda's neighborhood

Ruan: half-Sharakhani man who works for Juvaan Xin-Lei

Rümayesh: a female ehrekh, one of the first made by Goezhen

Saadet ibn Sim: killer of Emre's brother, Rafa; a Malasani bravo

Sahra: Seyhan's daughter

Salahndi: the first day of the week in the desert calendar

Saliah Riverborn: a witch of the desert, the goddess Nalamae in disguise

Salmük: one of the tribes; a/k/a the Black Veils

saltstone: one of the three types of diaphanous stones; can be swallowed, but is more
  often sewn beneath the skin of the forehead. It slowly dissolves, bleeding away
  memories until none are left. The victim becomes completely and utterly docile

Samael: an alchemyst

Samaril: capital city of Malasan

Savadi: the seventh day of the week in the desert calendar, the busiest along the Trough

Sayabim: an old crone, a Matron at the House of the Blade Maidens, a sword trainer

scarab: a name for a member of the Moonless Host

schisandra: a woody vine harvested for its berries

the scriptorium: a kind of library

Sehid-Alaz: a King of Sharakhai sacrificed on Beht Ihman, cursed to become an asir

Şelal Ymine'ala al Rafik: shaikh of Tribe Rafik

selhesh: a term for dirt dog

Serpentine: a winding street in Sharakhai

Seyhan: a spice seller in the Roseridge spice market

a shade: a mission to ferry goods or messages from place to place in Sharakhai

shaikh: the leader of a desert tribe

Shal'alara of the Three Blades: one of the elders of the thirteenth tribe, a storied
  swordswoman and adventurer

the Shallows: slums

shamshir: curved saber having one edge on the convex side

the Shangazi: the desert, a/k/a Great Shangazi, Great Desert, Great Mother

Sharakhai: a large desert metropolis, a/k/a the Amber Jewel

Sharakhan: the language spoken in Sharakhai and much of the desert

Sharakhani: adjectival form

shinai: a slatted bamboo practice sword

Shining Spears: a nickname for the people of Tribe Masal

shisha: hookah

Sidehill: a neighborhood in Sharakhai, a nickname for Goldenhill

Silver Spears: the Kings' guard, the city police

Sim: works for Osman

Sirina Jalih'ala al Kenan: Mala's mother, a lover of King Mesut

sirwal trousers: loose trousers that hang to just below the knee

siyaf: term of respect for a master swordsman

song of blades: tahl selheshal; a/k/a sword dance

the Spear: a large street running from the western harbor to the gates of the House of Kings, "one of the busiest streets in Sharakhai"

the Standing Stones: a nickname for the people of Tribe Ebros

Sümeya: First Warden, commander of the Blade Maidens, daughter of King Husamettín

Sun Palace: the lowest of the thirteen palaces on Tauriyat, once belonged to Sehid-Alaz

The Sunset Stone: a/k/a The Flame of Iri; a giant amethyst

Sunshearer: King Kiral's sword

Surrahdi: the dead king of Malasan; a/k/a the Mad King of Malasan

Sweet Anna: a fragrant plant

Sword of the Willow: from Tribe Okan to the winner of Annam's Traverse

Syahla: Mihir's mother, Halim's wife

sylval: unit of currency

tabbaq: a cured leaf, commonly smoked in a shisha

tahl selheshal: song of blades, a/k/a sword dance

tamarisk: a tree

tanbur: a stringed instrument

Tariq Esad'ava: one of Osman's street toughs, grew up with Çeda & Emre

Tauriyat: Mount Tauriyat, home to the House of Kings, Sharakhai's thirteen palaces, and the House of Maidens

Tavahndi: the third day of the week in the desert calendar

the Tears of Tulathan: a/k/a Iri's Four Sacred Stones (result of the breaking of the Sunset Stone)

Tehla: a baker, friend of Çeda; Davud's sister

tessera, tesserae: tiles of a mosaic

Thaash: god of war

Thalagir: Rümayesh's new name, given by Brama

thawb: a common outer garment in the desert, consisting of a length of cloth that is sewn into a long loose skirt or draped around the body and fastened over one shoulder.

Thebi: character in a tale of the god Bakhi

the Thousand Territories of Kundhun: another name for Kundhun, one of the four kingdoms surrounding Sharakhai

Tiller's Row: a street in the Shallows, "one of the few with any businesses to speak of"

thwart: a seat in a rowboat

Tolovan: vizir of King Ihsan

Treü: one of the powerful elder gods who imprisoned Ashael

Tribe Ebros: one of the twelve desert tribes; a/k/a the Standing Stones

Tribe Halarijan: one of the twelve desert tribes; a/k/a the White Trees

Tribe Kadri: one of the twelve desert tribes; a/k/a the Burning Hands

Tribe Kenan: one of the twelve desert tribes; a/k/a the Rushing Waters

Tribe Khiyanat: the name the thirteenth tribe chooses when they form anew; khiyanat means "betrayed" in the old tongue of the desert

Tribe Malakhed: the ancient name for the thirteenth tribe, abandoned when the tribe is reborn

Tribe Masal: one of the twelve desert tribes; a/k/a the Red Wind

Tribe Narazid: one of the twelve desert tribes; a/k/a the Bloody Manes

Tribe Okan: one of the twelve desert tribes; a/k/a the Black Wings

Tribe Rafik: one of the twelve desert tribes; a/k/a the Biting Shields

Tribe Salmük: one of the twelve desert tribes; a/k/a the Black Veils

Tribe Sema: one of the twelve desert tribes; a/k/a the Children of the Crescent Moons

Tribe Tulogal: Devorah and Leorah's childhood tribe; a/k/a the Raining Stars

Tribe Ulmahir: one of the twelve desert tribes; a/k/a the Amber Blades

the Trough: the central and largest thoroughfare in Sharakhai, runs from the northern harbor, through the center of the city, and terminating at the southern harbor

Tsitsian: capital city of Mirea

Tsitsian Village: an immigrant neighborhood in Sharakhai

Tulathan: goddess of law and order, sister moon of the goddess Rhia

Undosu: a powerful Kundhuni blood mage, one of the Enclave's inner circle

Urdman: one of Narazid's riders in the Traverse

Vadram: Osman's predecessor in the shading business

Vandraama Mountains: a mountain range bordering the desert

Verda: works for Osman

Lord Veşdi: Külaşan's eldest living son; Master of Coin

vetiver: the root of a grass that yields fragrant oil used in perfumery and as a medicinal

vizir/vizira: a high official, minister of state

Wadi: Devorah's borrowed stallion

Way of Jewels: location in the city

the Well: a neighborhood near the Shallows; Osman's pits are there

western harbor: the smallest and seediest of the city's four sandy harbors

the Wheel: the massive circle where four thoroughfares meet: the Spear, the Trough, Coffer Street, and Hazghad Road

White Wolf: Çeda's moniker in the fighting pits of Sharakhai

Willem: a brilliant young man with strange magical abilities bound to the blood magi, Nebahat, in Sharakhai's collegia

wyrm: worm

Yael: mother of Devorah and Leorah

Yanca: Çeda and Emre's neighbor in Roseridge

Yasmine: Meryam's murdered sister, Ramahd's wife and mother of Rehann

Yerinde: goddess of love and ambition; once stole Tulathan away "for love"

Yerinde's Kiss: a honey collected from the rare stone bees' nests; used as an aphrodisiac

Yerinde's Snare: the convergence of a twisting, misshapen web of streets & the most populous district in Sharakhai

Yndris: a Blade Maiden with a hot temper, the daughter of King Cahil and an enemy of Çeda

Yosan Mahzun'ava: one of Tehla's brothers

Zaïde: a Matron in service to the Kings; heals and takes Çeda into the House of Maidens

zilij: a board Çeda fashioned from skimwood, used as a conveyance to glide easily over sand

Zohra: i.e., Matron Zohra, resident of an estate in Sharakhai

Acknowledgments

And so, at last, we've reach the end of this epic tale. In many ways, it feels like the journey has passed quickly. I have to remind myself sometimes it's been an endeavor that has taken nearly a decade. The first glimpses of Shara-khai, Çeda, and the series at large came in roughly 2012, while I was still working on my first epic fantasy series, The Lays of Anuskaya. Now, in 2021, after six full books, a shorter triptych of novellas, and many other standalone tales, it really has taken on a life of its own. When viewed from that perspective, the journey feels long indeed.

One major, major source of help in seeing this project reach its full potential has been Paul Genesse. Thank you, Paul, for the many reads, the conversations, your keen insights and your suggestions. All have helped Çeda to reach the end of her grand tale and to find peace at last. A big thank you as well goes out to Femke Giesolf, who gave valuable feedback, including on Ashael and his incarnation, which helped make him feel more fearsome and enigmatic.

My publishers, DAW and Gollancz, provide tireless work and expertise to get these books onto shelves (both physical and virtual). To Betsy Wollheim, you have my undying gratitude for believing in this series and for guiding it along the way. Thank you as well for including me in the cover art process. That's something I particularly enjoy. To Gillian Redfearn, you've not only put in a ton of effort into the series, your guidance has helped me to become a better writer, so thank you for that. To Marylou Capes-Platt, thank you for grounding me and my writing, and paying such close attention to how readers will view the material. It's really helped to put things into perspective for me. And to the DAW and Gollancz production, marketing, sales, and back office support teams, thank you once again for your tireless efforts.

I am indebted to my agent, Russ Galen, not only for this book, but for helping to ensure that the full series ended up seeing the light of day. Many thanks to Danny Baror and Heather Baror-Shapiro as well for your dogged efforts in bringing this series to readers all over the world.

Lastly, I'd like to thank all the Shattered Sands fans for your support and enthusiasm. It has helped me immensely to keep this series going and to put my heart and soul into it. I hope you enjoyed the ride as much as I did.